BEARER OF SECRETS

A CELINE SKYE PSYCHIC MYSTERY

NUPUR TUSTIN

Foiled Plots Press

Bearer of Secrets
A Celine Skye Psychic Mystery
Foiled Plots Press

Published by Foiled Plots Press

ISBN 979-8-9863995-5-3

Typesetting services by bookow.com

Acknowledgments

Many thanks to Mark Winter at Degas Experts for responding to an email question on authenticating Degas. For the elder abuse subplot in this story, I am indebted to the writers and law enforcement agents on Crime Scene Writer as well as the Facebook group Writers' Detective.

I am especially grateful to Pam D. Workman and Susan Horsnell who went above and beyond in providing detailed information. I've made use of several of the facts they provided for Clara's story.

Thanks also to Scott Morales, Mary Morrison, Ken Shoemaker, A.J. Scudiere, Lily Gibson, Emily Nesbitt, K.M. Rockwood, Donnell Ann Bell, Wil, and Cindy Goyette.

To my new Catholic friends, Barbara, Mary, and Julie, thank you for your enthusiasm about my books. Many thanks to the librarians at the Parker Public Library. You ladies rock! And to Betsy Smith, a longtime fan of all my stories. Readers like you keep me going!

Last but not least I'm grateful to my wonderful husband, Matt, who makes this work possible. And my three children, Rena, Gunner, Hunter, who allow me to lead and teach them. God bless you all!

ALSO BY NUPUR TUSTIN

JOSEPH HAYDN MYSTERIES
A Minor Deception
Aria to Death
Prussian Counterpoint
Murder Backstage
Death of a Soprano

CELINE SKYE PSYCHIC MYSTERIES
Visions of Murder: Prequel
Master of Illusion
Forger of Death
Bearer of Secrets

SOPHIE'S ADVENTURES
The Pompadour Necklace
Theft in Sleepy Hollow

ANTHOLOGIES
Murder in Vienna: A **FREE** Joseph Haydn Mystery
Murder in the Sun: A **FREE** Women Sleuths Mystery

FREE Mysteries Available from NTUSTIN.COM

Chapter One

Celine Skye gripped her wine glass and forced herself to look at the thick file on her lap. The room spun around her; her head swam. She stared aghast as the floor surged up to meet her face.

Don't let me fall, she heard a frail voice whisper. *Don't let me fall.*

Celine felt herself choking; heard the sobbing sound that was wrenched painfully out of her throat.

"Celine!"

Blake's voice, warm with concern, filled her ears. Under the gentle pressure of his hand squeezing hers, the disorienting sensations subsided.

"It's okay, Celine. Take it easy."

She smiled gratefully at him. It had been months since she'd perused the FBI file on the Gardner Museum heist. Months before she could bring herself to even touch the thick folder, much less open it.

But Blake—Special Agent Blake Markham of the FBI's elite art crime team —had been remarkably patient with her. She hadn't expected him to understand the sickening sensation of guilt that engulfed her every time she thought about their last venture.

They'd recovered a Rembrandt, but at what cost?

But Blake understood—and sympathized. Not Julia, though.

Celine stole a cautious glance at her friend, retired FBI agent Julia Hood, who sat across the coffee table from them in a comfy plaid-covered armchair —grim and tight-lipped, with no trace of her usual warmth in her weather-beaten features.

"I'm sorry," Celine said in a low voice.

Julia nodded curtly, acknowledging the apology.

Celine swallowed hard, took a sip of her wine—a robust Syrah cultivated and fermented in the vineyard and winery she'd inherited last year—and willed herself to look down again.

Blake's hand was still on hers, dispelling the venomous voice in her head and the accusing pale blue eyes that perpetually haunted her.

The file was open to the page on the Gardner's Dutch Room, from where the most valuable of the thirteen works had been grabbed. Celine had already helped Blake and Julia recover three of them. But Penny Hoskins—the Gardner's Director—was hopeful Celine's psychic insights would help retrieve the remaining Rembrandts and the Flinck as well.

Celine stared at the page. Black-and-white photos taken prior to the notorious heist contrasted starkly with color images of empty gold picture frames, stripped of the canvasses they should've encapsulated.

There was Rembrandt's *Storm on the Sea of Galilee*. Before it had been stolen. The facing page showed the same room with the empty picture frame. Next to that was Francisco de Zubaran's *A Doctor of Law*. And beneath that, a drop leaf table.

The black-and-white image showed a slender beaker with a flaring neck on top of the table. It was missing in the color picture.

"Are you getting anything?" Julia's voice was tight with an emotion Celine couldn't identify. Anger? Frustration? Impatience?

Accusing blue eyes swam into focus. Celine shook her head, trying to dispel the image. Her long red-gold hair fluttered about her face.

"Nothing?" Julia sounded skeptical.

"I just see Belle," Celine said as the black-clad Lady who'd never left her side shimmered into view.

Arms outstretched, she held the gu—the ancient bronze Shang dynasty wine vessel that had disappeared with the rest of the art.

Don't forget the gu, Celine.

"She has the gu," Celine repeated her guardian angel's words.

Belle wants you to know you're missing something, Celine, her guardian angel informed her.

I know, Sister Mary Catherine, Celine thought.

But what was she missing? What was she forgetting?

"Death?" Blake's voice broke in. "Is that what you're sensing, Celine?"

The presence of Belle—the spirit of Isabella Gardner—usually portended death. Violent death. Celine had sensed it for quite some time now. Ever since she'd gone to visit Clara Hibbert in the nursing home in which she was confined in Boston.

But why would anyone want to murder Clara?

She must've spoken out loud because Julia snorted.

"Oh, God! Not that again. No one wants to harm Clara Hibbert, Celine!" Julia's tone was strident with anger. She shot up, a short, sturdy, white-haired figure. "She's just fine. Has been all these months."

Why'd you take my son, Celine? Why'd you do it? Clara's pale blue, tear-filled eyes gazed accusingly at Celine.

Celine flinched, her hold on Blake's hand tightening.

"Let's call it a night, shall we?" Blake glanced up at his former colleague. "It's been a long day."

"I'll say." Julia snorted. She scooped up her wide leather tote bag and slung the strap over her shoulder.

"I'm sorry, Julia," Celine spoke softly. "I'm trying. I really am."

Julia glanced down at her, her features softening. "Yes, I know, kiddo. You just need to . . ." She waved her hand in a vague gesture as though bidding the words to come to her.

You need to let go, Celine, Sister Mary Catherine said. *Just let go.*

It was the only way she'd get any useful insights. Celine knew that.

But all she could see when she did let go were the despair-filled blue eyes of Jonah Hibbert's mother.

Slipping her hand out of Blake's, she rose, walking Julia to the cottage door.

Julia swung her head around, her thick white ponytail brushing against Celine's chin.

"Look, I know it's been hard on you. For me, too. These past few months have been tough. But we can't change what happened."

She exhaled heavily, staring out at the pinpricks of light in the pitch-black sky.

"And brooding over it doesn't help."

Turning around, she reached up to give Celine's shoulder a quick squeeze and then headed briskly out into the night.

❦

Celine watched as Julia's form rounded the corner of the driveway and receded beyond the boxwood hedges that screened her cottage from the rest of the Mechelen Estate—the vineyard and winery she'd inherited from Dirck Thins and his friend and partner, John Mechelen.

They'd been the closest thing to a family Celine had possessed since she'd lost her parents at the age of twelve. Then John had died—an unexpected heart attack. Months later Dirck had been cruelly garroted, leaving Celine with the raw pain of being orphaned yet again.

It was Julia who'd filled the void in Celine's being, drawing her into the case, giving her something to live for. And now she'd managed to botch that relationship, too.

Will things ever be all right between us, she wondered, clinging to the door-jamb.

"She's right, you know." Blake's voice and his warm, strong hand on her bare shoulder hit Celine like a tiny jolt of electricity.

"Julia's right," he repeated, turning her around and gazing earnestly down at her. "Clara's going to be fine."

Left unsaid was the undeniable fact that Clara Hibbert had been just fine on the countless occasions Celine had dropped—abandoned, Andrea Giordano, her winemaker would've said; deserted, Wanda Roberts, her marketing manager might've added—her responsibilities here in Paso Robles to visit Clara's pricey nursing home in Boston.

There'd been no signs of abuse that Celine could detect. Annabelle— Dirck's sister—who was visiting her son, Bryan, and had offered to check in on Clara from time to time hadn't reported seeing anything amiss either.

She stared wide-eyed into Blake's dark eyes. Logically, he was right. But . . .

He gave her a rueful glance. "But you still sense death, don't you?"

She shrugged, glancing out the still-open door. "There's no reason for the General to want her dead, I realize that."

No one connected with the heist could possibly want Clara dead. There was nothing she knew. The poor woman had Alzheimer's, was on the verge of complete dementia. She represented no threat at all.

"But what if she's being abused?" Celine's green eyes returned to Blake's face.

What would she do without him? There'd been a time—not too long ago —when she'd have aired these worries with Julia, seeking and receiving reassurance from the older woman.

"She's not, though," Blake said quietly. "You've checked it out a thousand times.

He closed the door and led her back to the couch.

"Isn't it possible you're wrong? About Clara being the intended victim, I mean?"

She allowed him to pull her down onto the couch. They both knew he was thinking of Sofia. Celine had been so convinced a witness in their previous case was in danger that it had blindsided her to the true target.

Blake had been furious with her at the time, she recalled. He'd deserved to be. A woman had been killed because of her. How could anyone get it so wrong?

It was Julia who'd comforted Celine then.

Who would reassure her if she got it wrong yet again?

Chapter Two

Blake wished he could do something—anything—to erase that forlorn, haunted look from Celine's green eyes. She was hurting; Julia was hurting.

If only he could heal the rift between the two women.

He understood exactly why Celine was traumatized. He'd been there when she'd hurtled out of Clara Hibbert's room—as though chased by a thousand demons—and crashed straight into his arms.

Clara had lost her only son and Celine blamed herself.

But as a law enforcement officer—albeit one who'd never had to pull the trigger on a suspect—Blake was keenly aware of what Julia was going through as well. Celine's reaction—no matter how understandable—would only seem like a betrayal to Julia in her current state.

His former colleague had been given no choice. Not that he'd been there. But Blake figured that was the case.

He suppressed a groan. He had a unique perspective on the situation. Trouble was he had no idea how to handle it. What could he say—what words could he use—to repair their relationship?

Aware of Celine's eyes still on him, he put down his wine glass.

"What exactly did you see?" he asked.

It was how Julia would've approached it. He'd heard her do it more times than he could remember.

Whenever Celine's impressions didn't seem to jive with reality as they knew it, Julia asked her to describe her visions in detail.

Celine's beautiful eyes shifted away from his, gazing dreamily into the distance.

"She was holding the gu."

"Belle?" he asked, although it was obvious who it was.

Celine nodded. *"Don't forget the gu."*

She was repeating Belle Gardner's words, he realized.

"I feel like I'm missing something." She turned to him. "Forgetting something."

He nodded, frowning. What could she be forgetting?

The last time the FBI had checked out a tip on the twelfth century B.C. Shang dynasty vessel, all they'd found was a well-made copy of the item.

That had been nearly eight years ago.

"Problem is we have no probable cause for a second search warrant on Hugh Norton's premises." He was talking to himself.

Struck by a thought, he turned to her.

"If you're sensing death, Celine, isn't it most likely to be you?"

Who else could it be?

But she shook her head, smiling faintly.

"The General doesn't want me dead. Not yet anyway. Not until I lead him to the Dutch works he lost the night of the theft."

The same works Julia wants you to focus on.

The thought entered unbidden into Blake's mind. He squelched it.

There'd been a time when he'd been suspicious of Julia. Absolutely certain she was as corrupt as her co-workers, who'd been discovered working hand in glove with the Irish mob in Boston. Not anymore, though.

Julia was on the up-and-up, he told himself firmly.

❧

The same works Julia wants you to focus on.

The thought inserted itself insidiously into Celine's head. Where had it come from?

The poisonous suspicion was followed immediately by another. Had Julia really been given no choice?

If Jonah were still alive, Celine thought, *we could've questioned him. Figured out what he knew.*

But as it stood, the rookie journalist had taken his secrets to the grave.

Assuming he had any, Celine, she reminded herself.

Impulsively, she leaned forward, resting her palm on Blake's knee. She saw his eyes widen but didn't comprehend the reason for it.

"Would you have done things any differently if . . .?" her voice trailed off.

He seemed to know what she was getting at.

"I wasn't there, Celine," he reminded her gently. "If you were in danger" —he swallowed—"I'd have reacted the same way Julia did."

His dark eyes gazed into hers with an intensity that made her turn away.

"And I'd have no regrets."

"*I had to . . . you know that, don't you?*" Julia's question echoed in Celine's head.

Of course she'd had no choice, Celine upbraided herself. To think otherwise was churlish.

"Julia saved your life, Celine," Blake's voice interrupted her thoughts. "It was a tough call, but you were in danger. She did the only thing anyone could under the circumstances."

He's right, Celine, Sister Mary Catherine said. *Let it go.*

Inexplicably, the dark clouds that seemed to have been hanging over Celine lifted. Relief flooded through her being.

She turned to Blake.

"Thank you for being so patient with me!"

Smiling, she flung her arms around him, drawing him into a close hug.

"You've been a good friend."

❧

Blake groaned. It was the second time she'd thrown herself into his arms. He didn't think he could take it anymore.

He tightened his hold around her. Then before he could stop himself or even think about what he was doing, he'd lifted her chin up, dropped his face down, and claimed her mouth.

To his utter amazement, she was returning his kiss.

"Celine!" he murmured, stroking her face, her hair, his hand sliding down to her breast.

She thrust herself closer into his arms.

Then just as abruptly, she'd pushed him away, her eyes staring at him—wild, confused . . . *betrayed*?

Goddammit!

Clearly, he'd misread her signals.

"I'm sorry," he said. "I shouldn't have. . ."

Words failed him. *Goddammit*, he cursed himself. What had he been thinking?

Heaving himself off the couch, he headed for the door.

❧

"Blake, wait!"

Celine watched, dismayed, as Blake pulled the door open and strode out into the darkness.

Thanks, Sister Mary Catherine, she thought bitterly. *Thanks.*

The kiss had been unexpected but not entirely unwelcome. She'd actually been enjoying it until her guardian angel's bellowed *"What are you doing, Celine?"* had completely ruined the moment.

Startled, she'd pushed Blake away only to see the pain of rejection slamming into his eyes. His face had shuttered down, a frozen blank expression settling upon it.

Then he'd stalked out.

Great, that's another friend I've lost.

Don't be silly, Celine. You haven't lost a friend, Sister Mary Catherine retorted. *But sleeping with him would have been a mistake.*

How would you know? Celine was defiant.

It's always a mistake, the nun said firmly. *Because of the expectations people bring to the situation.*

Trust me, I had no expectations. Good grief, she was an adult, she knew what she was doing!

You need to get to know someone bef —

That's what we were doing, Celine interrupted the nun, *until you nearly shattered my eardrum.*

Good heavens, how else were you expected to get to know someone?

"You've got to test-drive a potential partner," a college boyfriend of hers had once said sagely. The relationship hadn't lasted beyond a few months, but his advice had stayed with her.

She recalled it now, repeating it for her guardian angel's benefit.

Blake's not a car, my dear, the nun responded. Celine could've sworn she was chuckling. *Neither are you.*

Celine rolled her eyes. Was she never to have companionship? She'd lost her family. She was losing what few friends she had. And now it looked like she was going to be denied the consolation of sex as well.

Don't be ridiculous, Sister Mary Catherine admonished her. *Go to confession, Celine. It'll do you good.*

Why? Celine rolled her eyes. *For the sin of almost having sex?*

So that you can take communion again, Celine.

Was that her mother's voice? Celine shook her head. No, it was probably just her imagination.

She'd refused to take communion after her parents had been killed. *What is the point of it all?* she'd cried when Sister Mary Catherine had tried to overcome her objections.

Determined not to give in, Celine had refused to go to confession as well. You couldn't take communion if you didn't confess your sins.

Pushing her memories away, Celine hefted the thick file Julia had left behind onto her lap.

She'd managed to offend both her friends. The least she could do was to make herself useful. It was possible looking at the photos of the crime scene and the stolen art would trigger some impressions.

Gritting her teeth, she turned the pages.

If only she could come up with something useful. Maybe then she'd be able to win them back.

Chapter Three

Celine shivered, huddling closer to the stone pillar that flanked the wooden church door. Why had she come here? She wasn't even dressed for the cold. It was freezing, the series of narrow arches above her affording little protection against the miserable weather.

A gust of wind blew in, spraying her with tiny pinpricks of sleet. Dear God, the weather was awful! Wrapping her arms around her slender body, she turned to face the double wooden doors.

To her amazement one of the panels stood ajar. They'd both been tightly shut just a moment ago. A warm glow of light illuminated the gray mist outside. Heat seeped out, sharpening the unpleasant sensation of the sopping wet socks that clung to her icy feet and the thin cotton shirt that was twisted around her torso thanks to the gust.

She stretched out a frozen hand, gripping the brass door handle, barely able to feel the cold metal against her skin. It took an effort to tug the door open, but she managed it at last, wincing at the grating sound of wood scraping against concrete.

"Celine!" Sister Mary Catherine, standing by a pillar, waved her in. "I'm so glad you could make it."

"You're alive?" Celine stepped forward. She was vaguely aware of the stained glass windows high above her, illuminated in the flickering light of innumerable candles.

"Of course, I'm alive, child." The nun sounded amused. "Why wouldn't I be? Come on in. There's no need to stand out in the cold."

Carefully treading upon the cold floor, Celine approached the nun. Were they back in the private Catholic school she'd attended in Los Angeles? She craned her neck back, taking in the enormous vaulted ceiling.

This place looked different, though. Gold-framed paintings hung on the walls on either side of her. Where were the Stations of the Cross?

But Sister Mary Catherine gave her no time to ask any questions.

"Come, I want you to meet Jesus." The nun dipped her hand in the silver stoup of holy water attached to the pillar beside her and made the sign of the cross on Celine.

"He's here?" Celine said, surprised. "Jesus is here?"

And he wanted to see her? What about?

"Where else would he be?" Sister Mary Catherine was already striding down the nave.

Celine hurried to keep up with her. The walk seemed interminable. Empty pews out stretched on either side of them. Paintings hung on the wall.

It seemed an eternity before they were at the altar. Pushed forward by the nun, Celine glanced up expectantly. There was the crucifix at the center, the Savior hanging from it. It was flanked by a figure of the Sacred Heart of Jesus and another of the Holy Virgin.

Then to Celine's astonishment, the figure of the Sacred Heart came to life and Jesus stepped down, coming closer.

What was that in his hands? A chalice? Celine leaned forward, squinting her eyes to sharpen the hazy image wavering before her eyes.

But the Savior was already directing her attention to his right toward the immaculate heart of Mary.

"I need you to visit my mother, Celine."

Celine swiveled her neck, staring at the lifeless statue of the Virgin Mary in a white garment and a blue cloak.

"Visit your mother?" She heard herself repeating. How was she to do that?

The rosary? But she hadn't prayed it in over a decade.

"Visit my mother before it's too late, Celine. You need to see her—before it's too late."

His voice echoed in her head, taking on a familiar nasal overtone.

Where had she heard that voice before?

"Are you listening, Celine?" Her guardian angel gently pressed her arm.

Before it's too late. Before it's too late.

The words were still reverberating in her brain when Celine's eyes opened. The pale light of dawn streamed in through her curtains.

She twisted her head, squinting at the clock on her nightstand. It was barely six. She'd been dreaming.

Clearly. But what had it meant? Anything?

Celine turned her head back, her gaze fixed on the white ceiling looming over her. She'd been poring over the Gardner Museum file—just as Julia had suggested— before she went to bed.

"Who knows, it might trigger some psychic dreams," the former fed had suggested. It was the only thing they could think of when their usual strategy of inducing a trance had failed miserably—producing only vivid and terrifying images of the shot that had taken Jonah Hibbert's life.

"I can't do this," Celine had gasped. "I can't do it anymore, Julia."

Even the memory of it made her shudder. Tight-lipped, she tore her mind away from the impressions swarming her brain.

So, she'd been looking through the Gardner file last night. What had she focused on?

The gu. Belle had told her there was something about the wine vessel she was forgetting.

Then she'd turned the page to the five Degas sketches taken from the Short Gallery. A large color photo of the Manet the thieves had made off with was mounted on the facing page.

In her mind's eye, Celine had seen a large golden key sitting atop the pages. The image had been so vivid, she'd reached out to touch it, only to feel the glossy paper of the photographs and the thick, rough texture of the paper on which they were mounted.

She'd understood that to mean that the stolen Impressionist works were the key to—what exactly? Some clue or information she was missing about the gu?

Would finding the Degas and the Manet lead to the Shang dynasty wine vessel?

And how did the church fit in? Why had she found herself there anyway?

It wasn't a church in either Los Angeles, where she'd spent her childhood, or Paso Robles, her home for the past eight years.

Boston? The voice she'd heard coming from the figure of the Savior had sounded so familiar. Where had she heard it before?

Why would she be in a church in Boston?

Because of Blake, the thought jolted through her mind.

Oh, good grief! Celine pushed herself up, impatiently shoving a second pillow behind her to support her back.

So that's what the dream had been about. Not a psychic dream at all, just the product of an overheated mind. Her overwhelming need to see Clara Hibbert had intermingled with the incipient guilt her guardian angel had induced over the trifling incident with Blake the night before.

And the result had been—well, predictably stupid.

Don't dismiss it, Celine, she heard Sister Mary Catherine whisper. *Don't dismiss your dream.*

Nice try, Celine told the nun. *You're not getting me back into a church that easily, Sister Mary Catherine. Forget about it!*

Chapter Four

The raucous screeching of his work cell phone jolted Blake out of his state of semi-wakefulness. The intrusion wasn't unwelcome. He'd spent most of the night tossing and turning, the memory of Celine's rejection churning in his brain.

He reached for his phone, hitting the green button on the screen to accept the call.

"Hello?" His voice sounded hoarse and scratchy, just the way his eyes felt. He'd have to remember to use his prescription eye drops.

"Blake? I hope I'm not disturbing you." Ella Rawlins' voice was muffled, as though she had her hand cupped around the receiver of the landline she was using. "Were you asleep?"

Blake glanced at his clock. Barely 6 a.m.

"No, it's fine," he assured his personal assistant. He cleared his throat, pushing himself into an upright position on the bed. "What's up?"

"Listen —" Ella hesitated. "Do you think you can make it back here? Pronto?"

"Sure!" After last night, the prospect of fleeing Paso Robles and the guest cottage he was staying in on Celine's wine estate was as welcome as a strong rope to a drowning man.

It took a second for the urgency in his personal assistant's voice to sink in.

"But why?" He slid his legs out of the bed, feet groping for his slippers on the carpeted bedroom floor. "What's going on?"

His mind raced through a list of possibilities. Other than the Gardner Museum case—which seemed to be at a standstill—they weren't working on anything particularly important. A couple of minor art thefts had been reported in the past few months.

But both works had been successfully recovered and returned to their owners. The thieves—inept and apparently extremely new at the business —had been easily caught when they'd tried to use one of the antiques stores the FBI was monitoring to get rid of the hot items.

"We got a tip," Ella began. "About a Degas."

"One of the Gardner items?" Blake's hopes surged. Recovering even one of the five Degas sketches would be a small—but much-needed—victory.

If they could do it without Celine's psychic insights, so much the better.

He was getting tired of the persistent media insinuations that the FBI— bereft of any investigative ideas—was in bed with a psychic. Of course if any journalist had seen him passionately groping Celine last night, it would've given a whole new meaning to the accusation.

He winced, resolutely pushing the memory out of his mind. *Don't go there, man!*

" . . . Laundrywoman series," Ella's voice drew him back to the present.

"Sorry, what? I missed what you were saying. Bad connection," he lied. He was damned if he was going to let her know why his mind had been wandering. Ella was sharper than a well-honed bayonet, and there was very little she missed.

It wouldn't take her long to figure out what had gone down last night. And he didn't want to hear it—whatever his rabidly feminist personal assistant thought about the way he'd idiotically acted out his attraction to Celine, Blake didn't want to hear it.

Not now at any rate.

"It was reported stolen in 1998," he heard Ella say.

"What was?" he asked, frowning.

The exasperated whoosh of air that filled his ears was enough of a clue that he was severely trying Ella's patience.

"I mean, which Degas was it?"

"I told you, Blake. Weren't you listening? *Woman Ironing.*"

She succinctly repeated the details. A woman had called in the tip to the FBI hotline. That she'd steadfastly refused to leave her name had given Ella pause. Nevertheless, the tip had been too specific to ignore.

But when Ella had researched the painting, she'd discovered that Degas had painted a series of three oils on canvas—with the same title and the same theme. "The Met in New York has one. The second is in the National Gallery of Art in Washington. And the third's in the U.K. in some museum in Liverpool."

"So a bogus tip?"

Where exactly was Ella going with this? Blake was beginning to feel a headache coming on.

"No, there's more to it."

The caller had provided such specific details, Ella had felt obliged to keep digging. She'd called the Connecticut museum where the stolen item in question was currently on loan for an exhibition on the Impressionists.

The Van Hoyt Museum of Art had confirmed the item in question was hanging on the walls in one of their galleries. Although no tests had been conducted, they had no reason to believe it was anything but an authentic Degas.

"Apparently Degas created a little-known fourth work on the same theme. But it was a pastel. Few people—even art historians—know of its existence. The Van Hoyt was actually quite chuffed to have it on loan."

"And the provenance checks out?"

"As far as they can tell," Ella said. "I told them we'd received a complaint from an individual that they were passing off a Degas copy as an original."

Blake stifled a grin. Naturally the museum had been eager to assure Ella the work was genuine.

"But it's still not evidence the work was stolen," he pointed out, walking to the window.

The embarrassment that had afflicted him the entire night was beginning to subside under the thrill of delving into a new case.

"You're right, it's not."

But the anonymous tipster had also helpfully provided the name of the private collector from whom the Degas pastel had been stolen.

"So I called the individual, a Harrison Sullivan. He and his wife are both dead. But Harrison Junior said the work had been stolen in 1998."

"And . . .?" Blake probed, sensing there was more.

"Junior said the theft had been reported to the ALR"—that was the Art Loss Registry; founded in 1990, about eight years prior to the theft—"but get this," Ella paused, the rhythmic tapping of her pencil the only sound audible for a few seconds, before continuing, "the ALR has no record of the theft."

She'd searched the database several times before eventually calling to ask why the database was missing a vital piece of information—only to be told it had never been registered as a stolen work.

"Who was handling the investigation? Local police?"

If that had been the case, Blake could see why standard protocol hadn't been followed.

"Nope. It was the FBI."

Ella had found an old report in the FBI archives. It had been a compelling reason to follow up on the information. "But the work was never recovered and Junior said the family eventually accepted the hefty insurance payout and moved on."

"Interesting!" Had the Sullivans orchestrated the theft themselves, Blake wondered. There were only two possible motives he could think of.

The first and most obvious one: to collect on a generous insurance payout. The second was far more subtle and devious. But the Sullivans wouldn't be the first—or the last—to resort to this desperate measure.

Ella interrupted his musings.

"SAC wants an agent on the ground to look into this," she was saying.

"No problem. Book me on the first flight out of here."

He'd have to let Celine and Julia know he was leaving. He wasn't looking forward to it, but at least the potential awkwardness he'd suffer would be brief.

"And one more thing, Ella," he spoke briskly into the phone, not allowing his mind to dwell on last night's mishap. "Start digging into the Sullivan's finances at the time of the theft."

"Okay?" Her tentative response irritated Blake. "But are you su—"

"Look, it's clear something fishy is going on. We need to get the ball rolling on this."

"Fine." Ella still sounded reluctant but offered no further objections.

"And while you're at it, see if the Sullivans had any kind of agreement to donate their Degas to a museum."

Chapter Five

"Anything happen between you and Blake last night?" Julia's tone was casual.

The question caught Celine off-guard. Her head pivoted sharply to face Julia. But the former fed was occupied in strapping herself into the passenger seat. All that met Celine's suspicious gaze were the thick silver-gray strands of Julia's hair.

Oblique rays of wintry light filtered through the windows and windshield. The Pilot's engine hummed, the heat beginning to flow through the vents gloriously warm against the early morning chill.

Celine frowned. What exactly had Julia heard? Had Blake come running to her to complain about . . . what exactly? How she'd strung him along only to chicken out at the last minute?

Just at that moment, Julia raised her head, her sharp blue eyes the picture of innocence.

"I couldn't help noticing that he didn't leave when I did." The corners of her lips twitched. "And he sure was quick to call it a night."

Julia's lips spread into a mischievous smirk.

Oh, for mercy's sake! Celine pursed her lips, swiveling around to face the front.

"We were looking at the Gardner file," she said tersely. "That's all that happened."

"Oh?" Out of the corner of her eyes, she saw Julia's brows rise. "And?"

"It looks like we're missing something."

Satisfied that both the rear window and the windshield were sufficiently defrosted, Celine shifted the gear to drive and eased the car forward. It would be several hours before the Delft would be open for business, but Celine made it a point to get to the bar early.

It was good for employee morale—and her own, she figured. She'd neglected the business long enough. There was yet another compelling reason to go in early this morning.

Paso Robles Cab-er-Neigh—a local wine touring company with a horse-drawn carriage in the shape of a wine bottle as its logo—was scheduled to drop off a group of tourists at the Delft. Celine had promised to personally oversee the wine tasting at the bar before accompanying the group to the Mechelen for a guided tour of the winery.

"Trust me, there's nothing like having that personal touch," Shirley Douglas, the tour operator, had advised Celine. "The owner of the winery herself there to talk about the history of the vineyard, providing an overview of the wine-making process."

Shirley had used her broad palms to frame an imaginary picture in the window as she spoke.

"They'll love it!" The stocky, white-haired woman had beamed delightedly at Celine. "Your sales will be through the roof, my dear. You'll see."

Julia's voice filtered through Celine's memory, bringing her back to the present.

"I beg your pardon, what?" Celine slowed down as she approached the wrought iron gates of the Estate, waiting for Bob Massie, their handyman-slash-guard, to open them for her.

"What are we missing?" The former fed spoke slowly, as though repeating herself.

Celine sighed. "I wish I knew."

Returning Bob's wave, she pushed down on the accelerator and cruised smoothly through the gates.

"I keep seeing the gu in Belle's hands. She's telling me not to forget it."

It's connected, Celine, Sister Mary Catherine whispered.

What's connected, Sister Mary Catherine? But her guardian angel remained frustratingly silent.

"The only clue we've had about that in all these years"—Julia rolled down her window, letting a whoosh of cold wind into the car—"is the one Laurie Robbes phoned in all those years ago."

And that had been a tenuous tip at best. It had certainly not panned out.

Shivering against the brisk wind, Celine pulled her scarf up. A Boston native, Julia was used to far frostier weather than Celine. For Julia, fifty-nine degrees signaled a pleasant fall, and in January hinted at a beautiful spring.

Celine debated requesting the former fed to roll up her window, then decided to tough it out. They were getting along fairly well this morning. There was no need to rock the boat.

"I still think Hugh Norton is somehow mixed up in this," she said instead.

Six months ago, she'd sensed a powerful male figure at the heart of the Gardner theft. Not the General—who was a vicious mobster—but his well-connected, well-heeled accomplice.

Norton, an art insurer, certainly fit the bill. The man had a rich nexus of connections that insulated him from any investigation.

Last year, the FBI had discovered a mole in its ranks. It had been Norton's recommendation that had enabled the mole to find its way in. When the matter had been brought to his attention, Norton had apologized profusely.

"I'm astounded—and, needless to say, embarrassed," Blake had reported him saying. "I had absolutely no idea. I thought I was doing a friend—a casual business acquaintance, really—a favor. But young people these days . . ."

More suspiciously, it was Norton who'd compelled a well-known sculptor to create copies of the Gardner's stolen Dutch art. But they had nothing more than Celine's insights, bolstered by some witness statements, about this.

The only person who could've provided solid evidence against Norton—Anthony Reynolds, the sculptor in question—was dead.

Murdered.

"And Norton's a huge fan of Impressionist art," Celine pointed out.

Recalling the golden key she'd seen the previous evening, she proceeded to share the details of her psychic vision. It was possible Julia could make something of it.

But the former fed seemed to be as much at a loss as she was.

"I agree it all fits." Julia exhaled heavily. "But it's so circumstantial. What insider connection does Norton have with the Gardner? He's a donor, maybe. But we're looking for someone on the inside, right?"

Celine nodded. "So we are. Someone with a vital connection to the museum, who'd know the ins and outs of every decision made."

She had to admit that didn't sound very much like Hugh Norton.

Could he have purchased the sketches and the Manet from whomever they were looking for?

"It's a possibility," Julia agreed. "But we have no reason to obtain a search warrant against him. And trust me, once our guys know we're onto him, he'll be as dead as a Carolina parakeet." The bird had apparently gone extinct in the early twentieth century.

Penny Hoskins, the Director of the Gardner Museum, had provided that tidbit.

"Overhunted by farmers." Penny had made a rueful face as she'd presented them with a gorgeous print of the yellow-headed birds on bare boughs—a small token of her appreciation for the works Celine and Julia had recovered so far. "We're extremely fortunate to have a visible reminder of them in Audubon's works."

Chapter Six

The Delft Coffee & Wine Bar on 13th Street didn't open until 11 a.m. But the back door would be open. Blake pulled into the tiny parking lot behind the bar, guiding his rental to a stop.

Celine's silver Pilot was in the spot next to his. Blake clenched his lips. Damn, he'd been hoping to avoid her. But that would be beyond rude. Celine had allowed him to stay—at no charge—in one of the guest cottages on the Mechelen.

Bad enough that he'd likely offended her with his unwelcome advances. The least he could do was to leave graciously.

He pushed open the heavy metal back door and walked along the narrow hallway. The kitchen was on the left, already bustling with the hum of staff cooking and baking the wares the Delft offered along with its wines, specialty teas, and coffees.

The door to the stocking room, lined with wooden wine racks, was ajar. He found Julia, Celine, and Wanda Roberts, the Delft's marketing manager, in the room, busy unpacking crates of the Estate's red and white wine.

He cleared his throat and knocked on the door. "Hey!"

Celine, he noticed, barely looked at him—her long lashes fluttering quickly up and then down again. His heart sank. That bad, was it?

Fortunately, his former colleague was more friendly. She glanced up, smiling broadly, as did Wanda.

"What's up?" Julia slid a bottle of a dark red wine into an empty slot in the wooden rack behind her. Her shrewd blue eyes slid knowingly from him to Celine—he wasn't sure why—and her lips twitched.

"I've gotta go," Blake began. He cleared his throat again. "Back to Boston."

His gaze shifted toward Celine. He saw her brow beginning to furrow, and then her eyes widened.

"Blake, you really don't have t—" Celine began much to Blake's consternation.

She'd barely opened her mouth when he caught the look that passed between Wanda and Julia. *Jesus*, she'd actually shared the sordid details with them!

Unwilling to be embarrassed any further, Blake brusquely cut her short.

"We got a tip about a Degas." Damned if he was going to let the women think he was fleeing the scene just because of last night's mishap!

He was pleased to see Julia's eyes swiveling back toward him. His words had wiped the annoying grin off the former fed's face as effectively as a Swiffer power mop.

"One of the Gardner sketches?" She stepped around from behind the table, eager to hear the news.

He was shaking his head when Celine murmured, "It's connected."

"No, it's not." The words were out of his mouth—a terse, abrupt dismissal —before he could even think about it. Dammit! He'd done it again, discounted her psychic insights out of hand.

"It's not related to the Gardner theft," he repeated more gently before turning to his former colleague. "We've got word a Degas pastel stolen in 1998 has resurfaced. It's in a Connecticut museum."

He succinctly shared the few details Ella had provided him.

"You're thinking insurance fraud?" Julia asked.

"Sure looks like it. SAC wants a man on the ground ASAP."

"Of course he does." Julia grinned, familiar with Patrick Walsh's tendency to kowtow anytime a case involved one of the wealthy members of New England's patrician families. And this one involved two. The Sullivans in Boston and the Dodds—Henry Dodd, to be precise—in Connecticut.

The SAC probably felt the need to act the part of peacemaker. Henry Dodd had likely acquired the Degas in good faith. After all the Art Loss Registry had never listed it as a stolen item. Not that their failure to adequately report the theft would prevent the Sullivans from laying claim to their oil pastel.

Blake had said his goodbyes and was headed out the back door when he felt the electric jolt of cool fingers lightly touching his hand.

His head jerked around. It was Celine. He'd been too wrapped up in his thoughts to sense her presence or hear her footsteps following him.

"Listen, about last night—" she began.

"No need to explain," he interjected hastily. "I totally understand."

She wasn't into him. Probably never had been. And when they'd unexpectedly lost a key witness about six months back and Blake had lashed out at Celine, he'd surely destroyed any good feeling she'd ever harbored toward him.

Naturally, she didn't want to be with him. She needed a rock to depend upon, but he was a coward—a chinless wimp who turned around and blamed the first person he could when an operation went south.

Why would anyone want to be with a guy like that?

She opened her mouth—preparing to be nice, he figured, but he cut her off.

"It's okay. It really is."

He pulled his hand out from her grasp and hurried to the safety of his car. The sooner he was outta here, the better.

Chapter Seven

Celine watched, dismayed, as Blake pulled out of the parking lot into the alley, tires squealing. Boy, he sure was in a hurry to leave. He hadn't even let her make amends.

It takes two to mend bridges, Celine, Sister Mary Catherine whispered.

But that's exactly what I was trying to do, Celine protested.

He blames himself, Celine.

For what? The question shrilled in Celine's head. Surely not last night. How had that been Blake's fault?

But her guardian angel wasn't done speaking.

It takes two to mend bridges. And they both need to believe it can be done.

Meaning, what? Celine thought, frustrated. That Blake didn't believe they could restore their relationship?

She turned on her heels, exasperated. It was the most ridiculous thing she'd heard. She was aware of the loud, staccato tapping of her heels on the stone tile of the hallway.

Blake hadn't even allowed her to explain how the stolen Connecticut Degas and the Gardner theft were connected. Although—she stopped a few steps away from the stocking room—how exactly were the two thefts connected?

Don't forget your dream, Sister Mary Catherine whispered.

It's not one I'm likely to forget, Celine responded.

And, frankly, she didn't see how a visit to Church—any church—could furnish her with the answers she needed.

She stepped into the stocking room. Wanda and Julia glanced up, features lit up with smiles as brilliant as a halogen work light.

"You two got something going on we should know about?" Wanda's smile widened. "No need to blush. You guys make a cute couple, don't they, Julia?" She winked broadly at the former fed.

Dear Lord, not this again!

"They certainly do." It was Julia's turn to rib Celine. "Everything okay between you two?" she asked with mock concern. "You guys kiss and make up? It seemed a tad awkward there."

Celine was at the end of her tether.

"Oh, for heaven's sake!" she exploded. "There's nothing between us. Why would there be?"

She glared at Wanda, taking in the woman's tight curls and dark skin, before turning to stare at Julia.

Wanda's smile faded. "Uh, no reason." She cleared her throat, handed one last wine bottle to Julia, and then cleared her throat again. "I guess, I'd better go see how they're doing in the kitchen."

Head stiffly erect, Wanda strode past her and out the door. Celine had barely time to step aside.

Instantly contrite, she reached out to touch the marketing manager on the arm, but Wanda had already gone. Dear Lord, why had she snapped at her friends like that? What was the matter with her?

"I'm sorry." She turned to Julia, voice coming out in a hoarse croak.

"It's okay." Julia came out from behind the table, blue eyes shrouded in concern.

"It's this new case, isn't it? You're sensing something?"

Celine's heart muscles clenched, a sure sign of death, just as she began to lower her head.

"They're connected," she managed to get out. And there was death.

Violent death. Not Clara Hibbert's. But more imminent than that.

Dear God, Clara really was in danger? But why?

Don't forget your dream, Celine. Her guardian angel's admonition echoed in her brain.

Celine reached out, fingers struggling to grasp something—anything. Julia took her hand.

"Come, sit down." The former fed led her to the solitary chair in the room.

"What are you seeing?" She pushed Celine into the chair and knelt on the floor beside her.

"A woman." Celine struggled to make sense of her impressions. A vague misty form of a woman bent over the receiver of a phone formed in her mind. "She's ill. Betrayal. I sense betrayal."

"And she'll die?" Julia queried. "Because she called in this tip?"

Celine shook her head. "No, her illness will take her away. But she shouldn't have stirred the waters. There's resentment brewing—and death. Murder."

And there was more than one person who was ill. More than one person who would die.

"You said it was connected?" Julia probed gently. "Connected to the Gardner theft?"

"The same people. The same players." She raised her eyes. "I can't help but think Hugh Norton is involved."

Julia got to her feet. "I'm calling Ella."

Chapter Eight

"Yes!" Ella Rawlins leaned into the phone receiver.

She'd been pleasantly surprised to receive a call from Julia Hood.

"Yes, the caller was a woman. Did Blake tell you that?"

It wasn't like the man to consult with his former colleague, but if he'd changed his policy about involving Julia and Celine in their other cases, all the better, Ella thought. When it came to art recovery, the two women had an excellent track record.

They'd already recovered three of the Gardner Museum's stolen artworks —and the Gardner theft was a case the FBI had long considered so cold, it might as well have been dead.

"No." Julia sounded surprised. "No, actually, he didn't. So the tipster was a woman, you say?"

"Yes." Ella wondered why Julia was making her repeat the information. Had Celine sensed the truth? Ella's hopes soared. If they could rope Celine into the case—better still, if she voluntarily chose to be involved—they'd have a better than zero chance of getting to the bottom of this affair.

"Look, Celine's been getting something on this," Julia was saying.

"Yes?" Ella leaned forward, pen at the ready.

"She thinks they're connected . . ."

"Connected?"

Ella pressed the receiver closer to her ear, not sure she'd heard correctly.

"You mean this Degas and the Gardner heist?"

It was such a vague tip. Didn't Celine have anything more specific?

Ella tamped down the disappointment she felt. Maybe there was more.

She sure hoped there was something more concrete than that. They weren't very much closer to discovering who was behind the Gardner theft. A mobster who went by the moniker, the General, and an art-loving elite she'd nicknamed the Boston Brahmin.

But who these men were was still a mystery.

"The same players," Julia said, seeming hesitant. "Hugh Norton. Has his name come up at all in reference to this theft?"

Ella frowned. "I'm not sure. I'll have to check. The FBI does have a report —filed in 1998 when the theft took place. But—" She glanced at her computer screen. "Let me call up the report and see what I can find out. I'll call you back, okay?"

"Sure." Julia hung up.

It took no more than a few minutes to locate the report in the FBI archives. Ella downloaded it onto her computer and opened up the file.

A two-page document filled her screen. Eyes narrowed, Ella scanned it. The report contained very little that she didn't already know. The Degas—a little-known pastel—had been reported stolen in 1998 from the home of the Sullivans.

It had been insured. The name looked familiar, and . . . *Oh boy!*

Ella whistled. She jotted down a couple of words on her notepad, then scrolled back up, looking to see who the agent in charge was.

She pursed her lips. Celine was right. There was a connection. A tenuous one—but it wasn't looking good. Was that why the theft had never been reported to the Art Loss Registry?

There was no good reason for the stolen pastel not to be in the ALR files. Of course, they only had Sullivan Jr.'s word that the FBI had promised to take care of the details. There was no reason the Sullivans couldn't have reported the robbery to the ALR themselves.

Although at the time, it had been more common for law enforcement to handle these things. And when the Sullivans had cut their losses and accepted the insurance payout, they'd have washed their hands off the artwork as well.

Technically, it would've been up to the insurance company to apprise the ALR and other dealers that the Degas was stolen.

Ella glanced at her watch. She'd booked Blake on a noon flight out of San Luis Obispo. She still had about ten minutes to get in touch with him before his plane took off.

Chapter Nine

Hands loosely clasped together, long legs stretched out on either side of the single piece of carry-on luggage he'd be taking with him, Blake stared gloomily out the thick plate glass window in the boarding area of San Luis Obispo Airport.

The tarmac was a hub of activity—tiny figures in red and blue scurrying around, matchbox-like vans moving back and forth.

The Boeing 737 that would be carrying him and his fellow passengers to Dallas Fort Worth loomed in his view—a behemoth of a machine. Beyond it, the sky was as cloudy as his disposition. He hadn't handled the situation with Celine very well—in fact, *be honest, man*, he'd completely botched it.

The prospect of a grueling haul back to Boston had further soured Blake's mood, making him grumpier than usual.

The flight was long, always involving a stopover. He'd known his sudden departure meant he'd be flying coach. But he'd hoped Ella would at least have managed to get him an aisle seat.

The prospect of being packed like a sardine between two other passengers had been bad enough. That his only in-flight snack choices were dry pretzels, a seven-dollar snack bag with a granola bar and Greek yogurt, or an eight-dollar pouch of sea salt almonds had been the last straw.

Famished by the time he'd arrived at the airport, Blake hadn't relished the news.

"No, sir, you may not take any food on board," the young attendant at the boarding desk had curtly informed him. "It's strictly against airline policy."

Showing her his FBI badge hadn't had much of an effect either.

She'd brusquely indicated the café behind them. "You can pick up something to eat back there. You have an hour until your flight boards." Blake had automatically glanced over his shoulder to see the thrumming space, crowded with bar stools and tables.

Now sprawled in the uncomfortable leather-and-aluminum tandem sling seat, he stared at the unappetizing remnants of the egg salad sandwich he'd bought himself. Blake liked egg salad—with or without bread. But this was nothing like his mother's egg salad sandwiches.

The bread—thin and dry—had crusty edges. The filling was comprised of some kind of yellow substance—a mixture of mayo and egg yolk with a few bits of egg white thrown in and minuscule fragments of green masquerading as celery.

Jeez, could his day get any worse? Behind him two women nattered away, their voices unconscionably loud. Children raced each other on the hardwood floor, shrieking their lungs out. Nearly every available seat was occupied. It looked like the entire city was headed to Dallas.

He was just about to shove the last bite of his sandwich into his mouth when his phone trilled, the noise cutting through the din surrounding him.

He dropped the crusty bread back into the plastic sandwich case, registering the fact that it was his work phone that was ringing.

"Hello?" He didn't bother to identify himself. It was most likely Ella with the information he'd asked for.

"Special Agent Markham?" The male voice—all too familiar—took him by surprise. "Lawrence O'Rourke here."

"Hey," Blake greeted him weakly. What did the editor of the *Boston Gazette* want?

The tentative alliance forged six months ago between the FBI and the online newspaper—in particular, its prestigious arts section—had remained in place despite journalist Jonah Hibbert's betrayal and ultimate death.

But Blake trusted O'Rourke about as much as he'd trust a rattlesnake in repose to refrain from striking out at the first opportune moment.

"Is it true?" O'Rourke's voice cut through his thoughts.

So O'Rourke knew about the Degas, did he? *Un-f—in'-believable*! How did these media types do it? Blake had received the news just that morning. And here was O'Rourke already prowling around like a shark that had caught the unmistakable scent of blood.

"Is what true?" Blake kept his voice light, trying to buy time.

"That a Degas pastel stolen eight years after the Gardner theft has turned up in Connecticut?"

Blake frowned. Why had O'Rourke brought up the Gardner Museum heist? As far as he could make out there was no connection between the two thefts. A Degas pastel; five Degas sketches. The stolen works had an artist in common, that was all. Other than Celine—

Inhaling sharply, he stopped short. What exactly did O'Rourke know?

Out loud, he said, "Whether it's true or not I can't say. We've received a tip. We're looking into it. It could be something. Could be nothing. Who knows?"

There was a pause. He heard the sound of a pencil slowly tapping, a sign that O'Rourke was carefully ruminating the information—attempting to search out any inconsistencies or contradictions he could pounce upon.

"So there's no truth to the fact that the FBI is investigating a connection between this theft and the Gardner heist?"

Outrage slammed into Blake at the innuendo. "Jesus Christ, O'Rourke! Where exactly are you getting this bullshit?"

Another pause. What did the guy know?

Blake felt his blood pressure rise. He thrust himself up, about to stand up. The plastic sandwich case slid off his lap, hitting the ground. *Damn!* He cursed under his breath.

A dark-haired mother with three young children in tow frowned at him, staring pointedly at the discarded case.

Oh, for f—'s sake! Blake glared back defiantly. He scooped the case off the floor and got to his feet.

"Listen, O'Rourke. I realize you have a newspaper to sell, and most likely it won't unless you publish every salacious bit of gossip you can find. But—"

"We had a call," O'Rourke interjected so softly, Blake had to strain his ears to hear the words. "Last night."

"What about?" Blake paced the floor, weaving a course between a straggling line of backpacks and rolling luggage toward the busy café.

"A Degas pastel that's been sighted in Connecticut. And its possible connection to the stolen Gardner works."

The caller, a woman, had apparently refused to identify herself, claiming only to be an FBI agent close to the investigation. O'Rourke—good man— had hesitated to publish the information on her say-so.

"I told her I'd need to verify the information with you."

"And?" Blake had reached the café.

An eager barista looked up at him, waiting for him to place an order. Reluctant to spend any more money at the overpriced establishment, Blake swiveled around, his phone clutched to his ear.

"She hung up on me."

So the caller had been a woman. Presumably the same person who'd called the FBI.

But she hadn't said anything about the two thefts being connected, had she? Blake couldn't recall Ella mentioning it.

So why make the insinuation to a newspaper, then? And why pretend to be a well-placed source within the FBI?

To stir up trouble? For whom?

"Special Agent Markham?"

"Still here," Blake reassured the man. "Listen, that must've been some kind of hoax. I've no idea why anyone would suggest the two thefts are related. I wasn't lying when I said we just received the tip. We haven't had time to investigate it."

He hesitated.

"All I can tell you is that it was a woman who called in the tip."

Chapter Ten

"Are you thinking it was the same person?"

O'Rourke's question caused Blake a twinge of discomfort. The man had an uncanny ability to put two and two together.

"Could be, couldn't it?" O'Rourke persisted. "But why hint at something like this?"

Hell hath no fury . . . The words entered Blake's mind, coming out of left field.

Could someone have it in for whoever had stolen the Sullivans' Degas? Or was this a desperate ploy to get back at the men behind the Gardner theft?

One man in particular—the Boston Brahmin.

"Listen, there's some—" O'Rourke had just begun speaking when a crisp female voice sounded over the intercom, drowning out the editor's words.

"Your attention please, passengers. American Airlines Flight 1180 to Dallas Forth Worth will begin boarding now. Please have your boarding passes ready."

Blake waited patiently for her to stop speaking, but the woman issued a constant stream of instructions.

"Now boarding Rows 20 through 30."

Blake pulled his crumpled boarding pass out of his tee shirt pocket. Row 22. *Shit!* He'd better get moving.

"Listen, O'Rourke. I'll give you a call when I get into Boston, okay." It wasn't a promise he meant to keep, but it would get the editor off his back. "And I'd hold off on publishing anything at the moment. All we have is a tip. It still needs to be checked out."

Disconnecting the call, Blake shoved the phone back into the holster on his belt. Then pulling out the retractable handle on his carry-on luggage, he wheeled it to the boarding gate.

He'd just settled into his seat—the aisle seat was still clear, thank God! Maybe he wouldn't be hemmed in, after all—when he felt his phone vibrating again. He tugged the device out of its holster and looked down.

Ella. Great! Maybe she had the information he'd requested.

"Hey—!"

Ella ignored his greeting. Her voice, uncharacteristically breathless and anxious, poured into his ears like a torrent of raging waters.

"Blake you'll never believe what I discovered. Celine's right"—

Celine had called Ella? Blake had barely time to consider the implications of that news—

"These two thefts are—well, they're more closely linked than we suspected. Bill McCormick was the agent in charge."

"Okay . . . ?" That didn't exactly come as a surprise. Anything pertaining to art theft in the 1990s would've been investigated by McCormick. A notoriously corrupt agent, he'd miraculously survived the fallout from the unsavory revelation that many of the FBI's finest were in bed with Whitey Bulger and the Irish mob.

Several agents had been axed, their reputations destroyed. A couple had been indicted. Only Julia had survived.

And William J. McCormick.

It was McCormick who'd called the Gardner Museum back in 1997 in a not particularly subtle attempt to discover whether they'd received a tip about their stolen gu being sighted in Hugh Norton's residence.

Having confirmed that it had, McCormick had proceeded to convince the museum there was nothing to the tip. That was before it had even been investigated. Shortly after, the tipster—Laurie Robbes—had mysteriously fallen to her death.

Laurie's demise had been ruled an accident, but Celine, her colleague, had always suspected foul play. Celine's friend, Detective Keith Elliot, had concurred.

"I guess that's why the theft was never reported to the ALR," Blake surmised. Corrupt and lazy—that was McCormick for you.

"Yes, and you know why?" It was a rhetorical question. Ella's voice had taken on a strident tone. Blake could almost see her jabbing the air emphatically with her forefinger.

"The insurance company that insured the work," Ella went on without missing a beat, "and that promptly paid the Sullivans barely eighteen months after the theft—without batting so much as an eyelid—was Morgana Insurance!"

"Morgana?" Blake repeated. It sounded vaguely familiar. Where had he heard that name before?

"That's Hugh Norton's company. Blake."

"Oh!" he said, the penny dropping at last.

Ella's voice had vibrated with barely concealed impatience. Blake chose to ignore it.

His personal assistant had an irritating habit of expecting him to carefully file and retain every mundane piece of evidence into his brain. Blake had never seen any reason to comply. Wasn't that why he had a personal assistant?

"And that's not all, Blake," Ella went on. "When the Sullivans accepted the insurance payment, they not only relinquished all claims to the painting, they—"

"Sir!" A slender, attractive stewardess stared sternly down at him.

Blake held up his hand. "Just a sec. This is important."

Couldn't she see he was on the phone? Customer service just wasn't what it used to be.

"Sir!" The woman's voice rose a notch. Her nostrils flared, pencil-thin eyebrows drawing together into a thin disapproving line.

Blake put his hand over the mouthpiece. "Yeah, what?"

"Sir, we're about to take off. I need you to turn off your phone."

Blake nodded. "Sure. Ella, better make this quick. We're—"

"Sir, please!" To Blake's horror, the stewardess reached for his phone. He twisted his torso, managing to evade her grasp.

"Okay! Okay!" Reluctantly he disconnected, about to put the device away.

Jesus Christ, they hadn't even started taxiing down the runway yet.

But the stewardess wasn't done giving him grief yet.

"I need you to turn off your phone, sir. And please buckle your seat belt."

Chapter Eleven

The phone rang just as Celine brought out the 2019 Rosé. Uncorking the bottle, she glanced up in time to see Julia reaching for the receiver.

Ella, Celine thought. *It's Ella. She has news.*

A surge of nervous excitement jolted through her veins. But aware of the wine-tasting group before her, Celine reluctantly forced her attention back to the party. Whatever it was, Julia would find a way to convey the news to her. The Delft had been open for no more than a half-hour, and already it was busy.

"This is a Mechelen special," she informed her group—a middle-aged couple with their college-age daughter, Melody, and a younger couple who, according to the woman, had only recently begun dating each other.

"A pink wine!" Melody exclaimed, brushing back her thick, glossy hair. "I've never heard of such a thing. I thought red and white were the only options." She was a bubbly, vivacious girl, and Celine had been enjoying answering her questions.

But before Celine could respond, Ethan, the young man, directed his earnest bespectacled features toward the young girl. "It's a New World thing," he told her, his tone precise and pedantic. "You won't find Rosés in Europe."

Celine had found him irritatingly pretentious and wondered how long his relationship with June would last.

Not very long, Sister Mary Catherine laconically whispered.

Stifling a grin, Celine poured the last glass of Rosé and slid the wine glass across the counter.

"That's actually not true, Ethan"—Celine kept her tone light, pasting a pleasant smile on her face to soften the correction—"Rosés are made all over Europe—in Austria, Germany, Portugal, Italy, France. They're especially prized in Languedoc-Roussillon in France. American varieties do tend to be sweeter, however."

Ethan sniffed. His girlfriend, June, glanced anxiously at him, then turned back to Celine, wrinkling her nose. "Are you sure about that, Celine? When it comes to wine, Ethan is quite well-informed. He's a professor, you know."

"Assistant Professor, my dear," Ethan immediately corrected her. "I haven't got tenure yet."

And his degree, according to June, was in history not in oenology. But it didn't look as though Ethan was about to provide any disclaimers about his knowledge of wine—or lack thereof.

Melody gulped down the contents of her glass. "I like this pink wine! What's it called again?"

"It's our 2019 Mechelen Pink." Celine angled the half-empty bottle toward the young girl to show her the label. She'd guzzled it a little too hastily to truly appreciate it, treating it like a can of orangeade. On the other hand, the wine's fruity notes and mild sweetness did make it easy to quaff.

"Made last year?" Melody's father looked quizzically at Celine. "Isn't that a bit odd? I thought wines needed to age."

"Some do," Celine explained with a smile. "But our winemaker prefers bottling our Rosés after just three months of fermentation. That gives the wine its fresh, vibrant character."

"Not bad," Ethan admitted, carefully swirling the contents of his glass and taking another small, careful swallow. "Although I do prefer the more robust reds. When are we getting to those?"

Most pretentious people do, Celine thought, reaching down for the next wines on the menu. Fortunately, there were just two more for the group to sample.

"And they're both red," Celine said, displaying the Grenache and the Syrah she'd pulled out from under the counter.

Fifteen minutes later, the group had left—Melody and her family with several bottles of the Mechelen Pink; Ethan and June, unsurprisingly, with nothing.

❧

"I take it Professor Know-it-All wasn't impressed."

Julia, who'd just finished attending to the last of a long stream of customers, strolled up to Celine.

"I don't think he particularly enjoyed being corrected before his girlfriend," Celine replied. She neatly stacked the hundred-dollar bills Melody's father had used to pay for his purchase and closed the cash register. "Was that Ella calling?"

"Yes." Julia kept her voice low. Her eyes busily scanned the bar, watchful for any customers who might need help. Or anyone who might get close enough to overhear their conversation.

"Our old friend Bill McCormick was in charge of the investigation. No surprise there. I should've realized myself he would be given the timing of the theft."

"And Norton?" Celine pressed. A strong whiff of cologne enveloped her; the strong scent of a powerful male. A familiar image flitted through her mind. Hugh Norton surely was involved in this thing. He had to be? All her senses were screaming at her that he was.

"The Degas was insured by his company." Julia surveilled her surroundings again. "I'm really not sure what to think. Technically, the pastel is his now."

Celine frowned. "Because of the insurance payout? How long did the Sullivans hold out?"

"Not long at all, apparently. It was a pretty large payment—actually larger than you'd expect for a Degas pastel."

"Not particularly well known either." Celine recalled the facts Blake had recounted. A small pang whipped through her at the thought of the special agent. She'd come to think of him as a friend—nothing more than that, she realized. But she'd inadvertently managed to hurt his feelings, and there didn't seem to be any way to repair the situation.

You'd have hurt him even more if you'd gone ahead, my dear, Sister Mary Catherine interjected.

Celine's lips tightened. *I don't think that's true*, she countered, determinedly shutting out her guardian angel's voice.

She turned her attention back to Julia.

"So how long after it was stolen did the Sullivans give up on finding it?"

"Eighteen months, give or take a few," Julia replied. She smiled and waved at a customer on her way out with a couple of wine bags. Celine smiled warmly as well.

Chapter Twelve

The seat on Blake's right remained empty, but it was small comfort. The sweaty, overweight schlub on Blake's left—he'd reached out a moist, pudgy palm and introduced himself as Gavin—was going to make the three-and-a-half-hour flight to Dallas nothing short of intolerable.

He hadn't stopped yakking since the plane had taxied down the runway. Hemmed in by the man's ample form, resenting Gavin's sticky, sweaty wrist plastered next to his own, Blake had attempted to move to the aisle seat only to be stopped by the same flight attendant who'd taken him to task earlier.

"Sir! We're about to take off. You need to sit down. At once!" she'd barked when Blake had tried to protest.

Frustrated and resentful, Blake had reached into the seat pocket in front of him. But the in-flight magazine was missing.

"I didn't get one either," Gavin said, seeing Blake digging into the pocket on the backrest before him. The aisle seat was missing its copy as well.

"But look! Someone left a newspaper," Gavin pointed out helpfully. "Lucky for you, huh?"

Blake didn't bother to reply. He pulled out the crumpled paper from the seat pocket.

The Massachusetts Post. Great! He was on a flight from hell, and all he had to read was this rag.

Gavin leaned in closer, tilting his head until it almost rested on Blake's shoulder. *Jesus F—in' Christ!* Blake shifted in his seat, but there wasn't much room to move.

"Wow! Would you take a look at that?"

"Take a look at what?" Blake growled as his eyes darkly followed Gavin's pudgy finger.

"*Stolen Degas Pastel Surfaces,*" Gavin read the title out loud, finger pointing to each word—as though Blake were illiterate.

So that's where Lawrence O'Rourke had gotten his news. Why hadn't he mentioned that?

Gavin's pudgy finger moved, uncovering the rest of the title. What he saw made Blake's blood pressure spike.

"*Link to Gardner Heist Suspected.*"

Gavin's light tenor rang in Blake's ears long after his own eyes had run over the title.

Holy shit! What god-awful tale had the *Post* spun this time?

Blake could only hope Penny hadn't laid eyes on the headline.

⨎

"I wonder when Dodd bought the Degas." Celine busied herself with the wine glasses.

The counter had a small sink set into it. She rinsed out each glass, gently rubbing a soap-filled sponge on the outside and inside, while Julia stood by with a washcloth.

She didn't want Wanda or any of her other employees thinking she and Julia were slacking off. That would never do.

"If it was after the Sullivans received their insurance payout, then technically the painting was Norton's to sell," Julia said thoughtfully.

"But why not report the find to the FBI and close the file? It's hard to believe that was an omission."

"That was my thought as well." Julia pursed her lips. "And I can't help but think keeping the theft from the Art Loss Registry files was an intentional decision."

An alarm pinged in Celine's brain. Her mind filled with the image of a painting with an enormous red "x" in front of it. Whoever had sold it, it hadn't been a legitimate sale. She shared the insight with Julia.

"I'm inclined to agree. But"—the former fed exhaled heavily—"If Norton's such a Degas enthusiast, would he have sold the work? It's not like he's hurting for money."

It's not want of money that causes one to steal, Sister Mary Catherine whispered.

"Well, yeah, I guess not," Julia conceded when Celine relayed the nun's words to her. Although neither woman was sure if the nun was confirming their suspicion that Norton was behind the theft.

"The question is," Julia continued, "would a Degas fan pass up the opportunity to possess an authentic work by the artist. His laundress series are beautifully executed—the play of light, the texture of the clothing, the raw flesh tones of the women's arms . . ."

Celine ceased to hear Julia's voice. She found herself looking down at a pastel of a thickset woman, her red, beefy arms pressing down an iron on a starched white shirt. A sense of revulsion and loathing filled her. God, how could anyone stand to look at this dumpy broad? Her solid features were devoid of any beauty; her body was like a thick, sturdy column of flesh.

How had Degas managed to look at the woman long enough to capture her?

Nauseated, she averted her eyes from the pastel. But it was currently valued at half a million dollars—sure to appreciate in the future. Not something you'd want to look at. But still a good buy. A sound investment.

"Celine? Celine!" The sound of Julia's voice calling her name barreled closer, growing ever louder.

Celine stared down at her soapy hands and the wine glass clutched between them. Like a bubble that had burst, the image of the Degas had dissolved. The disconcerting sensation of disgust that had washed over her dissipated now.

"I don't think he appreciates women," she said, her voice low and hoarse. "The laundresses are too coarse. The ballet dancers too fleshy. He's only interested in their value, their worth as high-quality investments."

"Who?" Julia was puzzled. "Norton? Or Dodd?"

Celine glanced up, her green eyes wide and staring. "I have no idea."

Out of the corner of her eye, she saw a van pull up to the curb. The tour was here.

Chapter Thirteen

Sitting in her spacious fourth-floor office in the Renzo Piano wing of the Gardner Museum, Director Penny Hoskins stared miserably at the *Massachusetts Post*. Her assistant had handed her the newspaper as soon as Penny had arrived that morning. The paper had been folded back to the article that was the cause of Penny's heartsickness.

A Degas had been recovered. A pastel—not one of the works stolen from the Gardner. Yet Penny's pulse had leapt. How could it not?

The recovery of a stolen work—any work—was a momentous event. The further news that this stolen Degas could provide leads to the Gardner's stolen treasures had caused a dam of hope to burst in Penny's being.

If the FBI could find the unnamed collector mentioned in the *Post*, question him, search his premises, could they—would they—be closer to recovering the Gardner's art?

But as Penny sipped her coffee and perused the article, the hope that had flared within her gradually fizzled out.

Was any of this true? The *Post* was notorious for publishing sensational rumors. Worse still, the rumors were usually based on a kernel of truth, albeit twisted beyond recognition in the newspaper's version of events.

Like the article the *Post* had put out six months ago.

At the time, the *Post* claimed to have uncovered evidence of insider involvement in the Gardner heist. It had hinted that the FBI's psychic consultant, Celine Skye, was the source of its information.

That had been a colossal lie—Celine hadn't divulged any of her psychic insights to the media. But Penny had subsequently discovered that the young girl had indeed sensed an insider connection. Not only that, both Special Agent Blake Markham and retired Agent Julia Hood were seriously considering the lead.

The realization had come as an unpleasant shock.

Neither Blake nor Julia had bothered to call Penny to share the new lead they were pursuing. And true to form, Blake hadn't called about the recovery of the Degas pastel this time either.

Nor that it might lead investigators to the Gardner's treasures.

So typical of the FBI, Penny thought bitterly. *They play their cards so close to the vest, they can't even be bothered to provide an update on the case.*

Well, Blake wasn't going to brush her off that easily, Penny decided. Taking another sip of her coffee, she lifted the receiver off her phone and began tapping out his cell phone number. She was going to demand an answer. She deserved it.

When there was still no reply after the fourth ring, Penny Hoskins pursed her lips and reluctantly set the receiver back in its cradle. Special Agent Blake Markham was clearly unavailable.

Or he was deliberately avoiding her call.

With the FBI, one never really knew.

Was there any point calling his Chelsea office number? She'd get his PA, Ella Rawlins. Maybe Ella could be prevailed upon to divulge some information or at least pass on an urgent message to Blake.

But a persistently busy signal forced Penny to give up on that plan as well.

Chapter Fourteen

"Let's read it, shall we?"

Before Blake could push him away, Gavin reached over, flipping the newssheets— page after loudly crinkling page—to the arts section. The man was a veritable battleship. Shoving him aside would be akin to pushing the Boeing 737 they were on.

Couldn't airline companies have weight requirements for passengers? Thoroughly disgruntled, Blake resigned himself to the inevitable.

Gavin found the article at last. Aware the guy was a civilian, Blake schooled his features into a blank expression of impassivity. He didn't want to risk giving anything away.

Gavin emitted a low whistle. "Wow, they've got an FBI agent commenting on the case. Would you just look at that?"

"*A source close to the FBI investigation* could mean anything," Blake pointed out, tight-lipped. "It could be someone's golfing buddy. A secretary. A janitor, for f—" he cut himself short just in time, preventing the expletive from coming out.

"Oh come now! A janitor? A secretary? Seriously?" Gavin licked his lips as his eyes avidly scanned the article. But he fortunately remained quiet, allowing Blake to digest the news in silence.

The reporter from the *Post* claimed to have spoken with his source on Monday. Hadn't the tipster—a woman—called the FBI hotline on Monday night? It was Wednesday today; it had taken Ella a day to check out the information.

Yet the caller claimed the FBI had already recovered the pastel and was looking into a possible connection to the Gardner theft?

Yeah, right! Even in the best of times, they didn't—couldn't—work at quite that lightning speed.

Blake made a mental note to ask Ella to call the paper to find out when they'd received the call from their so-called source.

Also, was it a woman who'd made the call? They'd need to ascertain that. O'Rourke's mysterious caller had been female, claiming to be an FBI agent. Blake had to hand it to her, the woman had some chutzpah.

He nudged the paper up, scanning the last few paragraphs. An article provided by law enforcement would've included a hotline for readers to call in further tips. But the *Post* reporter had provided nothing of the sort.

Likely because his caller hadn't supplied the information. Yet another fact that should've clued in the inept bozo who'd written the piece that he was being had. But most likely the guy didn't care.

Not as long as he had a sensational headline to blast out the next day.

Blake grunted.

"What?" Gavin glanced up, his dark beady eyes glittering. "Don't tell me, you're still thinking this is some kind of hokey. Looks legit to me."

It would, Blake thought but kept his mouth shut.

Gavin chuckled. "Hard to believe isn't it? Here's this painting, stolen twenty-two years ago, all traces of it gone. Then, poof! It turns up in the Van Hoyt of all places."

Still chuckling, he glanced up, directing a curious gaze at Blake.

"Ever been there? It's in Norwalk."

"No," Blake responded tersely.

The caller had gone into great detail about the Degas pastel and its current location.

But she—assuming his hunch that the woman who'd tipped off the FBI had also tried to get the *Arts Gazette* to run the story was correct —hadn't been quite as clever as she imagined.

Chapter Fifteen

The Cab-er-Neigh tour bus sped past Walmart and the Paso Robles Golf Club, cruising onto Linne Road.

Sitting in the front of the bus, microphone in hand, with Shirley, Celine felt her shoulders relax.

Leaving the confines of downtown Paso Robles for the open vista of beautiful wine country that stretched on either side of them was such a liberating experience. Even in the winter, Paso Robles was gorgeous. Smiling, she peered out the window.

"That's the Brady Vineyard on the right," Shirley pointed out for the benefit of the group. "And we'll soon see the Rasmussen Vineyards on the left." She turned around to face the passengers. "We'll stop by both those on our way back. But for now, we're headed to the Mechelen, Celine's vineyard."

"But it looks so bare and desolate!" one of the passengers cried. "Where are all the grapes?"

Celine glanced around at the speaker, a slim blonde fifty-year-old. What was her name? Beth?

"Summer and fall are the best time to visit if you want to see grapes," she explained to the woman. "The vines are dormant in the winter, conserving energy for a new season."

"You mean there's nothing happening right now?" Beth's neighbor, Mike, heaved an exaggerated sigh of disappointment. He was recently widowed, Shirley had told her, and tended toward pessimism.

"Has a good heart, but he's a bit of a negative Nancy," Shirley had confided.

"Figures, I'd pick the wrong time to visit," Mike grumbled.

"Well, actually," Celine said with a smile, "there's quite a lot that's happening at this time. As we drive by, you'll see workers pruning the vines. That helps with new growth. Do you see the horizontal training wires? Each vine is reduced to two canes. At the Mechelen we favor a divided system."

All twelve passengers dutifully peered out the windows, craning their necks to see row upon row of dormant vines. The driver had slowed down to give them a better view.

"What's that growing on the ground?" Beth wanted to know.

"Different types of grasses. They hold the topsoil down, preventing it from being eroded."

"Are any wines being fermented?" another woman inquired.

Celine shook her head. "Most have been bottled by this time. But you'll still get a tour of the winery. Our winemaker, Andrea Giordano, is from Italy and extremely well-informed about every aspect of winemaking. He's a treat to listen to."

"Excellent work, Celine!" Shirley spoke in a low voice. "Talk the whole thing up as much as you can. I'd hate to have to issue refunds."

Beth glanced at her curiously, blue eyes raking her up and down. "Shirley said you inherited the business. Who started it? Your dad? Your grandfather?"

Celine felt her fists clenching. It wasn't a question she was keen to answer.

"John Mechelen, the man who started the winery, and Dirck Thins, who operated the Delft on 13th Street, were both like foster fathers to me. They'd been art students in Boston when they realized they'd never make it in that profession. So they headed out west sometime in the 1990s."

She forced herself to smile. "That was about the time I was born. Later as an art student in New Hampshire, I came to the same conclusion they had. I enjoyed making art; I just wasn't good enough to make a career of it. Dirck and John were looking for a marketing manager at the time. A mutual friend"—she was referring to Sister Mary Catherine—"brought us together."

"And the rest," Shirley chimed in, "is, as they say, history. Incidentally, Celine here"—she wrapped a plump arm around Celine's shoulders—"is also an art sleuth. You may not know it, but she's the psychic whose insights have helped recover some of the Gardner Museum's lost art. The FBI was at a complete loss until she came along."

Celine felt herself cringe. Lord have mercy! Why had Shirley chosen to bring that up?

"I think I heard about that." Mike studied Celine closely. "Wasn't there some talk about those guys making off with the Gardner art and selling it to finance their business?"

"There was," Celine said, tight-lipped. "And it was just that. Talk and lies."

"Besides"—Shirley gave Celine an anxious glance—"Dirck Thins died trying to return the Gardner's Vermeer. That's what set the ball rolling, in fact."

Celine deliberately averted her head. She was tired of dealing with that old gossip. Tired of the never-ending insinuations.

"So what do you think of the current theory, then?" Beth's voice rang out.

Celine could see her in the rear-view mirror, leaning forward, her intense blue eyes glittering with curiosity.

Reluctantly, she turned around. "What theory?"

"She means the Degas pastel that the FBI recovered in Connecticut," Mike said. "Apparently the guy who had it was behind the Gardner Museum theft. I take it you've had no psychic insights about that?"

"The FBI has recovered a Degas pastel?" Celine repeated.

How did these two know about that? Hadn't it been just that morning that Blake had heard the news?

News travels fast, my dear, Sister Mary Catherine remarked. *You should know that.*

Boy, it sure does, Celine thought. She gaped at Mike. But he stared stonily back at her. Her gaze shifted to Beth, who responded eagerly to her unvoiced question.

"It's in the *Massachusetts Post*. Page three." Beth handed a folded newspaper to the woman in front of her, urging her to pass it up to the front.

Chapter Sixteen

Pressing the buzzer on her desk, Penny Hoskins summoned her assistant in.

"Cynthia, could you tell Clay Reid"—that was the Gardner's security director—"I'd like to see him in my office. Immediately."

Fifteen minutes later, when Clay, a burly forty-five-year-old, pulled out a chair and sat down across from her, she showed him the article.

"I haven't heard a word from the FBI about this, Clay. Have you?"

Clay looked up, his blue eyes sympathetic.

"Listen, Penny, if there was any truth to this—and that's a big if—you'd have heard from Special Agent Markham. Trust me, you would have. You want my opinion, the *Post* is just looking to titillate its readers and gin up interest in a story that frankly isn't exactly the sexiest news item ever."

He jabbed at the grainy photo of the pastel.

"I mean this is a Degas, sure. But few people have heard of it. It's not exactly the scoop of the century. Does the *Arts Gazette* have anything on this?"

"No." Penny shook her head. "In fact, no other newspaper does. And that did give me pause."

She glanced down at the paper as Clay slid it back across the desk to her.

"There you go, then." Clay got to his feet, tucking his thumbs into his belt.

"The way I see it, the only connection between that theft and ours is the artist. It was a Degas in both cases. Big deal."

Maybe, Penny thought after he'd left. *Maybe not.*

She pushed back her chair and stepped toward the window. A gray, foggy Boston morning greeted her. Evans Way Park was barely visible across the street. It was such a desolate scene—tree branches bare, dusted with snow; the ground blanketed with snow; the street wet, sand mixing with snow to create an ugly brownish sludge.

The *Post*'s stories—however exaggerated—were always based on a grain of truth. It might be a solitary fact, but it was there. Could she find a way to discover what it was?

She unfolded the newspaper she'd carried with her to the window and cast her eye over it again.

❧

Forty minutes later, Penny Hoskins had a plan. She pulled the phone toward her and dialed a number, pulse racing.

It took a couple of rings before her call was picked up.

"Van Hoyt Museum," a crisp voice answered. "Sarah Williams' office."

"This is Penny Hoskins, Director of the Gardner Museum. Is Ms. Williams available to talk?"

"Let me put your call through," Sarah's assistant said.

It was possibly a welcome change not to have to field calls from the media, Penny thought, amused at the alacrity with which the assistant had agreed to put her through.

"Penny!" Sarah's alto was warm and grateful. "I'm so glad you called. This has been . . ." her voice trailed off.

"Horrendous," Penny supplied, sympathetic. "I know. Listen, is there any truth to this news?"

Sarah hesitated. Would she confide in her, Penny wondered. They'd met briefly at a conference a few months ago and had chatted over drinks afterward, getting along quite well. But neither woman had made much of an effort to keep in touch.

"We do have a Degas pastel on display," Sarah eventually said. "But as far as we know it was legitimately purchased. In fact, the provenance checks out. There really doesn't seem to be anything suspicious."

Penny frowned. "But your statement to the *Post*?" she asked, puzzled.

"We'd been alerted to the possibility there might be a problem. That was yesterday."

So the FBI had at least warned the Van Hoyt there was a potential issue with the work. That was the tiny nugget of truth the *Post* had based its speculations on.

"But, Penny"—Sarah's voice rose to an indignant wail—"the FBI hasn't even had time to investigate, and already the news is splashed all over the media. I have to say that really annoyed me. I certainly wasn't expecting to hear from the *Post* guy. The only thing that could've made it worse is if I'd been completely in the dark about this situation."

"And the collector in question?" Penny began.

A wealthy individual, no doubt, avariciously collecting—by any means necessary—valuable works to satisfy his ego and his investment portfolio. Could there be something here?

"He has impeccable credentials," Sarah assured her. "That's why this entire thing is so ludicrous. He's an art enthusiast par excellence and a generous donor to several museums. The FBI's sending an agent out today or tomorrow. Blake Markham?"

"I know him. He's on the Gardner case."

"Oh, good! Oh, Penny, I wonder, could you talk some sense into this guy? There's just no way Dodd's involved in any shady goings-on. It's simply impossible!"

"Dodd?" Penny's ears perked up. The name sounded very familiar.

Hadn't there been something in the notes her predecessor had left her about a Dodd? Penny couldn't for the life of her recall the man's first name. Nor could she put a face to the name. But the name was very familiar.

"Yes, Henry Dodd. He was in Boston before he moved to Connecticut. Do you remember him?" Sarah was sounding anxious now. "He's mentioned you—commended the work you're doing. I got the impression he knew you quite well. I was hoping you could vouch for him with this Special Agent Markham."

Penny drummed her fingers on her desk, hardly able to breathe thanks to the tension that coiled tightly within her chest. She'd need to send Cynthia over to the archives. The name Sarah had mentioned had struck a chord within her.

A very unpleasant chord.

"I'll do what I can, Sarah," she promised before quickly hanging up.

Chapter Seventeen

Passed from hand to hand, Beth's rolled-up newspaper made its way to the front of the tour bus. Celine watched it approach with an acute sense of dread. The *Massachusetts Post* was known to be a gossip-ridden tabloid.

Yet if Beth and Mike, the two wine tour passengers at the back of the bus, were to be believed, the tabloid had managed to weave a story around a kernel of truth. Who was responsible for the leak this time?

A feeling of déjà vu enveloped Celine. Last July, the *Post* had, thanks to an unfortunate leak, gained access to and published a piece of information that should never have been released. The leak had nearly cost Celine her life. It had left Clara Hibbert bereft of a son.

Where had the *Post* gleaned its information from this time?

"Celine?" Shirley's rising soprano broke into her thoughts. The older woman gently nudged her in the ribs, prodding Celine to take the newspaper one of the passengers was holding out to her.

Gingerly, Celine stretched out her arm and plucked it from the woman.

"Don't you want to read it?" Shirley urged with another nudge.

Celine unrolled the paper. "It's on page three," Beth called out.

Nodding curtly, Celine turned the pages. The thin sheets rustled loudly against the silent whir of the van's air conditioner and the smooth purr of its engine.

A little-known Degas pastel stolen in 1998 may soon be recovered, a source close to the FBI investigation on the theft said Monday.

What source close to the FBI investigation? Blake had only just heard the news. Ella couldn't have known any later than yesterday, having to confirm the tip before calling Blake. She certainly wouldn't go running to the media.

"Must've been one of the agents investigating the case." Shirley's breath tickled Celine's cheek.

A woman, Celine thought.

But who? The person who'd received the tip?

She bent her head to read the next paragraph:

The surprise find may also yield clues to the still unsolved Gardner Museum heist which occurred in 1990, the source said.

"I never said that," Celine murmured. She'd considered the two thefts to be linked in some way. But she had not supposed that the Degas pastel would —or indeed could—provide clues to the Gardner theft.

On the other hand, if the same players were involved . . . Hugh Norton, Bill McCormick. Celine felt her brow furrowing.

Was it possible that tracking the Degas pastel from its theft all the way to Dodd's collection could yield clues to the Gardner heist?

Why had the *Post*'s source—whoever it was—made such insinuations?

To call attention to her?

Celine had long sensed that the General had no intentions of taking her out. Not just yet anyway. Not until she'd led him to his precious Dutch works—the ones that after leaving the Gardner Museum had inexplicably never reached him.

But if he had the slightest inkling she was closing in on him, he wouldn't hesitate to have her killed.

Was Norton behind this article? But as soon as the thought entered her mind, Celine dismissed it. The FBI—Blake and Julia, at any rate—already had its sights set on Norton. It was unlikely he'd do anything to launch an investigation into his activities.

Sister Mary Catherine confirmed her hunch.

He doesn't want his name dragged through the mud, Celine. He can't afford to be exposed. It will all unravel.

Celine rapidly scanned the article. The nun's last words—*it will all unravel*—reverberated in her brain as her eyes glided disbelievingly over the closely printed news columns.

FBI agents have reason to believe the recently recovered Degas pastel and the stolen items from the Gardner "may have shared storage space for some time until the items were disposed of."

She gripped the paper. She stared at her fingers in dismay. They looked so white, bony, and nerveless. *It will all unravel*, she whispered to herself. Malice, like a hot, burning acid, flowed through her veins, consuming her being. *And it serves him right.*

She'd paid a horrendous price for her part in the whole affair. The cancer had sapped her of her beauty and vitality, making her all but bald.

She'd done it for him. She'd thought he loved her, that he cared.

But all he cares for is himself. Self-centered bastard.

Her long white fingers tapped out the well-remembered number.

"The Manet was supposed to be my insurance policy," Celine heard herself rasp out. "But it's worth absolutely nothing. You knew that, didn't you?"

"Listen, I had no idea. I'm as flabbergasted as you are, sweetheart."

Lies. All lies. To think she'd once loved him, fallen for that phony charm.

"My bills had better be taken care of," she croaked. "There'll be hell to pay if they aren't."

"Of course."

Lies. All lies.

She smiled maliciously. "Don't forget I know where the bodies are buried."

Someone was shaking her shoulder. "What bodies, Celine? What bodies?"

Shirley's voice rang alarmingly close to her ears, jolting Celine out of the trance she'd fallen into.

"What are you talking about, Celine?"

Feeling as though she'd been slapped into wakefulness, Celine blinked and looked around. The dark living room she'd found herself in with its stench of illness and death had dissolved. She was back in the Cab-er-Neigh tour bus with Shirley and twelve other passengers.

At the back of the bus, Beth rose. Holding onto the seats as the van's momentum caused her to sway and bob, she made her way to the front.

"You've had some kind of a vision, right? What was it?"

Rattled and unnerved by what she'd experienced, Celine shook her head.

Beth's eyes were on her, skeptical. Celine would have to offer some kind of explanation for what had happened. But what?

What could she say?

An image of a plant filled her head.

Déjà vu, Celine, her guardian angel whispered. *Déjà vu.*

Swallowing, she met Beth's gaze squarely.

"I was remembering the last time someone planted false tripe like this," she said, her voice hoarse. "It was in July. The lies the *Post* chose to publish impelled a man to kidnap me. I nearly lost my life."

It was mostly true, she thought. Thinking she'd veered close to the truth, threatened by her insights, the General had sought to kill her.

"That's right!" Shirley's plump, heavy arm encircled Celine's shoulders in an affectionate hug. "Poor Celine! That was a horrific experience. This article must be dredging up some terrifying memories."

Not really. The event had been traumatic, but Celine had managed to get over it. And she doubted anyone was after her this time. That wasn't the point of the article.

Nevertheless, encouraged by Sister Mary Catherine—*they're hardly entitled to the truth, my dear*—she bowed her head and dutifully nodded.

A sympathetic murmur filled the van. Someone tugged the newspaper out of her hands. "Here, take that thing away! Get her some water."

But as Celine quietly sipped her water, she found herself deeply troubled by what she'd seen.

Whoever the *Post*'s source was, she had intimate knowledge of the Gardner theft and its perpetrators. Who was she? Whom had she been threatening?

The Manet was supposed to be my insurance policy.

If only Celine could hear the name the woman had whispered.

Chapter Eighteen

Blake's eyes were riveted on the paragraph below the one that had so amused Gavin.

Calling the find an "unexpected stroke of good fortune," our source said: "It would never have been discovered if one of our agents hadn't been looking through a Van Hoyt Museum catalog."

Blake had never set foot in the Van Hoyt and didn't know much about it. But he did know the museum didn't mail out its catalogs to just anyone. You had to be on their mailing list—as either a donor or someone who'd purchased one of their works.

Their tipster was obviously on the Van Hoyt mailing list. It wasn't much, but it was a start. It narrowed down the suspect field considerably. Special Agent-in-Charge Patrick Walsh, Blake's superior at the Boston field office, received a catalog.

Blake doubted Walsh so much as glanced at the publication. Nor that he'd recognize the Degas pastel for what it was—a stolen work of art—based on a photograph in a museum catalog.

And although Walsh enjoyed basking in the dazzling glare of media attention, even he wasn't enough of an attention whore to start calling a rag like the *Massachusetts Post*.

"Wonder who the collector was?" Gavin muttered beside him.

He jabbed at a paragraph toward the end of the piece.

"They should've dug a little more, tried to discover his name. I mean, how hard could it be to figure out which private collector in Norwalk lent a painting to the Van Hoyt? Can't be too many of them, know what I mean?"

Blake grunted a response. It was the only part of the story that had redeemed his belief in humanity. The Van Hoyt's Director had stalwartly refused to divulge the name of the art collector and donor who'd loaned them his Degas pastel.

She'd also stated emphatically that the museum would continue to stand by the individual until a fuller investigation furnished evidence of foul play. Good for her! Sarah Williams had refused to be cowed by the media.

She'd played it remarkably cool, too. He doubted Williams had even heard from the FBI when the *Post* reporter had called. The news must have come as a bombshell.

The fact that Henry Dodd, the collector in question, wasn't so much as mentioned in the article suggested the reporter had no idea he was involved. Clearly, the *Post*'s source hadn't thought to mention the man.

But why? It couldn't be because she was unaware Dodd was openly claiming to be the owner of a work that in all likelihood was the Sullivans' stolen property.

Or Hugh Norton's, to be more precise. After all, the Sullivans had accepted a hefty settlement from Morgana Insurance in place of the painting itself.

But his obese flight companion was right. Despite the Van Hoyt's best efforts, discovering Dodd's name wouldn't be too hard. Was that the point of planting this article?

Was the woman Dodd's ex? A mistress who considered herself betrayed? He'd need to get Ella on that as well. The insinuation that Dodd's pastel and the Gardner's stolen sketches had at one time shared storage space was clearly an attempt to implicate Dodd in both thefts.

"Once they figure out who this mysterious collector is," Gavin's voice intruded unpleasantly upon his thoughts, "they'll know who's behind the Gardner theft. I mean, come on, it can't be a coincidence that five Degas sketches were stolen from the Gardner and then eight years later, this."

Gavin jabbed a thick finger at the grainy color photo of the Degas pastel the *Post* had included with its article.

"Even that psychic the FBI's been consulting agrees. Guess there's something to this whole psychic business after all. Who knew? And now the FBI has corroborating evidence."

Blake had noticed the *Post*'s subtle endorsement of Celine's insights, and it had worried him. Normally, the news media never failed to seize every possible opportunity to dredge up and regurgitate the FBI's suspicions of Celine and her now-dead employers.

Last year, the FBI had gone so far as to raid the winery, expecting to find the stolen Gardner works. The raid had proven to be a bust, but in the media's eyes even that wasn't enough to get Celine off the hook.

Blake allowed the paper to drop from his hands. What exactly was going on here? Who was this woman? And what nasty can of worms had she opened up?

At best, she was implying that Dodd was in possession of stolen property.

At worst, that he was the Boston Brahmin. *Christ!* Feeling sick, Blake leaned back in his seat and closed his eyes.

For close to a year now they—no, he—had focused on Hugh Norton as the most likely associate of the General. Had they been utterly wrong? Norton was a Degas enthusiast and, sure, there were some suspicious connections to the Gardner heist and the people involved.

But not even his worst enemy could accuse Norton of being closely associated with the Gardner. Not to the point that he could reasonably be regarded as an insider.

Was Dodd their man? *Holy shit!*

Chapter Nineteen

Celine cradled the receiver of the Mechelen office landline against her shoulder and sighed. The news that the FBI's latest tip had been leaked to the media was mind-boggling enough. But Julia had taken it in her stride.

The visions Celine had received were another matter.

"You're saying there's a third person involved?" Consternation and dismay underscored Julia's every word.

Celine sighed again. She'd been glad to hand off the twelve tourists on the Cab-er-Neigh bus to her winemaker. Andrea could take care of them. And hopefully her own absence would deter any further questions about the Gardner heist and the unfortunate article the *Massachusetts Post* had seen fit to run—unverified, no doubt.

Unavailable for comment, my foot, she thought. *The reporter never even bothered to call. Of course, even if he had I might not have given him the time of day.*

Out loud she responded to Julia's question: "It seems that way."

In all the time they'd investigated the Gardner theft, the possibility of a third person helping to mastermind the heist had never come up. Like Julia, she'd been perturbed by the insight.

"A woman." Why did the thought trouble her so? "A career woman, independent, beautiful. Or she was once. She's dying of cancer now."

Julia harrumphed thoughtfully. Celine heard the muted tap of fingers. Julia was calling up the article on the iPad they kept under the counter at the Delft.

"You think it could be an FBI agent? It says here"—the former fed began reading from the article—"the *Post* names their source as someone *close to the investigation.*"

Celine hesitated. "I don't know," she hedged.

If anything, she'd sensed the woman was close to the crime.

"A career woman. Independent. It fits," Julia persisted. "I don't like the idea—and really it needs to be checked out—but from everything you've said . . ." her voice trailed off.

Celine stared at the Mechelen grounds through the office window. The afternoon sun was blazing into the room, bathing her in a warm glow. Winters were mild in Paso Robles compared to the Midwest or the East Coast states. But you could still detect the seasons. There was a noticeable nip in the air in January.

"Let's say it is an FBI agent," she conceded. "Not that I sensed anything of the sort. Wouldn't that mean the FBI was involved right from the start?"

Julia was silent for so long, Celine thought they'd been cut off. She plucked the receiver from her ear and shook it, twirling the red cord that attached it to the instrument.

"Julia? You still there?"

Julia exhaled heavily. "There's always been talk about that, Celine. Even within the FBI. In particular, the other offices. It's been thirty years, there's no sign of the stolen works. No lead we've investigated has panned out. That reeks of a cover-up."

"But that's not the only reason you're considering this, is it?"

Julia had spent most of her career in the FBI's Boston office. She'd been there when Boston police had first called about the Gardner theft. She'd been part of the investigation from day one.

It would take more than a few rumors to get Julia suspicious.

The phone crackled in Celine's ear as Julia let out a soft whoosh of uncertainty.

"I've not mentioned it before because I've never been sure how relevant it is. But—"

In her mind's eye, Celine saw Julia grip the receiver hard. Then, mind made up, the former fed briskly filled her in.

The lax security at the Gardner Museum and its vulnerability to theft had been known to thieves for some time. A pair of ruffians had, in fact, tentatively planned a strike. Or so the FBI's Bill McCormick had claimed, taking the tidings at once to the museum's Director and its head of security.

"If it had been six months before the actual heist—instead of nine years prior," Julia finished, "I'd have been suspicious. But . . ."

Celine nodded slowly. "Nine years is a long time to wait to carry out a theft."

"But then you have Bill McCormick. It's hard to believe the guy warned the Gardner out of the goodness of his heart."

The image of corrupt Bill McCormick trying for once to do the right thing brought an amused smile to Celine's lips.

"It is hard to imagine."

Struck by a thought, she frowned. "Do you think there was some other reason for his warning? An attempt to coerce the museum into doing something it was unwilling to do?"

Her senses flared, lighting up in a shower of sparks like a Roman candle. She was on the right track. But where did the track lead to?

Julia didn't seem to know either. "But what—spend more money on security? There was a constant fight about that. Everyone agreed it was necessary, yet the funds were never available. There was never enough money in the budget."

Frustration, Sister Mary Catherine whispered. *It builds up, Celine. It can build up to an explosion in nine years.*

But Julia was skeptical when Celine communicated this to her.

"All right, so someone was trying to make a point. We're definitely looking at an insider if that's the case. But why not return the paintings after that? Why hold on to them? The theft was a momentous wake-up call. Everyone was stunned. The entire city—not just the folks associated in some capacity or other with the museum."

Celine could see Julia shaking her head, strands of silver hair flying.

"Back to your impressions. What else are you getting?"

Celine cast her mind back, firmly ignoring the flashback to her dream Sister Mary Catherine insisted on projecting onto her brain. It wasn't relevant.

What else had there been?

She'd sensed betrayal. And malice. Those were the emotions that had triggered the call—both to the newspaper and the FBI. She conveyed this to Julia.

"She knows everything will unravel as a result," Celine repeated the words she'd heard over and over.

"Unravel? Meaning what? That a thorough investigation into the Degas and its journey from the Sullivans' living room into Dodd's hands should provide some interesting detours?"

"Something like that," Celine confirmed. The metallic sound of the mail slot opening drew her attention.

A thick bundle of envelopes fell through the slot, plopping into the tray she kept for the purpose. Bills, she thought. And wine club memberships and orders. A second thick bundle followed the first. January was a busy time for both the Mechelen and the Delft.

Leaning away from the receiver, Celine cocked her ear toward the door, waiting for the hard raps that announced the arrival of packages. But there was nothing today. She brought the receiver back to her ear.

"She was counting on the Manet," she went on. "It was supposed to be her insurance policy."

"Meaning what? The Manet that was stolen was . . .?"

"A forgery. That may have been the reason it was taken."

Julia inhaled audibly. "The Manet never did fit. In the eighty-one minutes the thieves spent in the museum, there's no sign of them entering the Blue Room. There's no evidence of the motion sensors being doctored, so that's reliable evidence."

"The portrait of his mother was out to a restorer's, wasn't it?"

When Julia confirmed that, Celine went on: "I think I recall Penny saying the *Chez Tortoni* was due for a cleaning as well. I'm guessing whoever replaced the original was afraid the change would be discovered."

The silence stretched out for several minutes as both women pondered the consequences of this possibility. Had the entire theft been orchestrated to conceal the truth about the *Chez Tortoni?*

"Unlikely," Julia eventually said. "I'd bet whoever was responsible was just taking advantage of a heist that was already set to go through. But that again points us to a museum insider. Someone well connected."

Someone like Hugh Norton. The thought, flitting through Celine's mind, prevented her from hearing Julia's next words.

"I'm sorry, what?"

"Any idea who our mystery caller was speaking with?" Julia repeated her question.

Celine shrugged. "Someone she was sexually involved with." It had been an illicit affair, she was almost certain. "Someone who has the wherewithal to pay her hospital bills."

"That could point to either Dodd or Norton."

Julia sounded disappointed but she quickly recovered herself.

"Fortunately, we have reason to investigate Dodd. I'll let Ella know Dodd's finances bear looking into. And any affairs he might have had. Anything else?"

Your dream, Celine, Sister Mary Catherine urged. *Remember your dream.*

But Celine ignored her guardian angel. *It's not relevant.*

"Nope," she said out loud. "That's all I've got."

Chapter Twenty

Julia's mind was spinning like a washer on overdrive.

The Manet, a forgery?

In the nearly thirty years she'd spent working on the Gardner theft, no one had come up with that theory.

Could Celine be right?

For months Julia had waited for Celine to get out of the slump she'd fallen into after Jonah's death—Julia wasn't about to call it murder; the guy had deserved to die—and the subsequent trauma of that event on the reporter's mother, Clara Hibbert.

Now that was a woman Julia did feel sorry for.

No mother should have to outlive her son. Certainly no mother should have to learn what a sorry excuse for a human being her son had been much less have that information broadcast to the entire world.

Not that Clara—poor woman—was aware of much that went on around her.

Her mind brooding over these thoughts, Julia mechanically rang up the bottles of wine and the cup of mocha latte a customer brought up to her. She handed a thick paper bag with the Delft logo on it to the woman and then printed out a receipt for her.

"Hey!" The woman, a shrill thirty-year-old, called so loudly, Julia nearly jumped. All eyes inside the bar, Julia noticed, had turned toward the cash register. *Great!* "You charged me for five bottles of the Grenache. I only bought three. What gives?"

Eyes blazing, dark, finely-drawn brows drawn together, she confronted Julia.

Squelching the urge to sock the woman in the jaw, Julia smiled appeasingly at her. *God, this was the worst undercover job ever!*

"Sorry, my bad! Here"—she reached out for the bag—"let me correct that for you."

She promptly voided the sale, rang up the bottles of wine again, and printed out a new receipt for the woman.

The woman studied the receipt, frowning suspiciously before forking out a wad of cash to pay for her purchase.

"Pay attention, Julia!" Wanda hissed once the woman had left. It was the second time since Celine had called that Julia had dropped the ball. God, what a doozy the young woman had dropped into her lap. Julia had been hoping for insights on the location of the Gardner's stolen Rembrandts and its Flinck.

Instead, she was faced with breaking the awful news to Penny Hoskins that the Gardner's *Chez Tortoni* might've been taken even before the 1990 theft.

"Enjoy the wine!" Julia smiled as she handed a customer her bag.

"Wine?" The woman gaped back at her. "But I bought tea. Five boxes." She peered into the bag as if to reassure herself that those were the only items in it.

"Yup! That's what I meant. Same difference." Julia's gaze shifted to the next person in line.

But Wanda was at her side before the person—a nerdy-looking college kid —could step up to the counter.

"Time to take a break," she hissed through clenched teeth. "And just stay there until you can gather your wits together. You're driving away customers."

Julia's eyes swept over the crowded bar. It didn't look like her absentmindedness was having much of an adverse effect on business, but one look at Wanda's stormy features told her this was no time to argue with the younger woman.

Or to point out that she wasn't one of the Delft's staff members. Just a friend of the owner's who helped out from time to time.

"Sur—" Julia was about to agree when her phone trilled loudly for the third time that morning.

"Oh for Christ's sake!" Wanda rolled her eyes dramatically. "Just go, okay!"

❧

You should have mentioned your dream to Julia, Sister Mary Catherine murmured as Celine scooped the mail off the tray and carried it to the vast desk John Mechelen—and later Dirck Thins—had used.

Celine tried to ignore her guardian angel. But as she sifted through the envelopes, the nun's muted voice buzzed persistently in her ear. There was something about the cancer-ridden woman she'd perceived that bothered Celine.

What was it? She glanced down at an envelope. It was yet another wine order. She set it aside; Andrea could deal with that. The next one in the stack looked like an invoice.

She used the slender letter opener to slit it open. Just as she'd thought, an invoice. Feeling lethargic, Celine forced herself to process it, her mind still running over her vision.

She'd sensed a wild mixture of fury and desperation in the woman. Why? Because the Manet she'd pinned her hopes on was a dud? There was no doubt in Celine's mind that it was the Gardner's *Chez Tortoni* the mystery woman had been thinking about.

We're so close to solving this thing, she thought. *So close to recovering the paintings.*

But it felt as though an enormous wall barred her way.

It's your own mind closed to the possibilities, Sister Mary Catherine pronounced in a low but firm voice. *It's your own mind.*

The answers are in the church.

Was that Sister Mary Catherine or her own mind? Whoever it was, the suggestion was so ludicrous, Celine pushed it away.

She called up the vision she'd received of the mystery woman. She'd been sitting in a darkened living room. Angry because of what she'd sacrificed.

A horrendous price, the woman had called it. She couldn't have meant the cancer, could she?

You can eat and drink judgment upon yourself, Celine. Sister Mary Catherine told her bluntly.

Celine rolled her eyes. *I don't even know what that means*, she responded sharply.

As she opened another envelope, Celine's mind returned to the woman. Had she sacrificed her marriage? Jeopardized her job? Put her reputation on the line?

But who'd know of her involvement in the Gardner theft? *And given the lax morality of our times*, Celine thought, *fewer still would care even if they did know.*

As for the woman's sense of betrayal, it was not the pain of a woman who has loved deeply. More a stunning realization of how tenuous her hold was on the man she'd assumed was enamored of her. What a shock that must have been!

Despite herself, Celine felt a sharp stab of sympathy for the woman.

Not that she deserved it. Celine hadn't got the impression the woman had borne her paramour much love either. Instead, she'd relished the power she exerted—or thought she did—over him; the seductive power of her sexuality.

The relationship had long ended—with few regrets on either side, as far as Celine could tell.

Nevertheless, there was deep-seated regret, anger, and fear—

Fear? The word gave Celine pause. Was she right about that? She closed her eyes, calling up the vision again.

Yes. It was definitely fear. Raw fear. Over something the woman thought she'd irrevocably lost.

If we only knew what it was, Celine said to herself. She opened her eyes and picked up another envelope. The Boston stamp caught her eye. Her glance pivoted to the return address printed in neat green letters on the left.

Clara Hibbert's nursing home. Instantly alert, Celine sliced open the envelope.

Dear God, is everything all right with Clara?

She pulled out a thick wad of folded pages from within.

It was an invoice. Just an invoice.

She cast her eye over it, reaching for her checkbook.

But a nagging sense of doom continued to plague her. *Why am I feeling this way?*

Remember your dream, Sister Mary Catherine's voice startled her.

This time Celine didn't resist, seeing in her mind's eye the church she'd found herself in and the altar she'd stood before.

I need you to visit my mother, Celine.

The words echoed over and over in Celine's mind, the annoying nasal tone filling her ears.

It was so familiar. So annoying. She could hear the voice so clearly in her head. If only she had a face to go with it.

She turned back from the Virgin Mary to—

Jonah Hibbert?

Celine's eyes widened in shock. What was Jonah—a confirmed atheist— doing in a church? It had been months since she'd thought of the reporter.

She glanced down at the invoice, spread out on the desk before her.

I need you to visit my mother, Celine.

It was Jonah's voice calling out to her. Clara was in trouble. There was no doubt about it.

Trembling, Celine reached for the phone. Clara was in trouble.

Don't let her die, Celine. Jonah's voice was anguished. *You can't let her die.*

Chapter Twenty-One

The phone had stopped ringing by the time Julia got to the kitchen. She glanced at the screen. Penny Hoskins. She must've read the *Massachusetts Post* article.

Calling Penny back would be the polite thing to do. But would it be wise?

Trays of freshly baked ham-and-spinach quiche bites, savory cheese tarts, and brownies lined the enormous steel kitchen tables. Smiling at the kitchen staff who bustled about her, Julia filled a paper plate for herself.

She was still debating the merits of responding to Penny's call when the decision was taken out of her hands. Her phone shrilled again.

Stuffing a quiche bite into her mouth, Julia answered the phone. "Hi, Penny."

"I haven't caught you at a bad time, have I?" the Director of the Gardner Museum asked anxiously. As always she sounded slightly breathless, her voice trembled a little making her sound like a young girl anxious to please her superiors.

"Nope." Julia pulled out a chair and plopped down. "I just got on break."

But it was time to take the bull by the horns.

"I take it this is about the *Post* article."

"You've read it?" Penny's voice rose, instantly indignant.

"A customer alerted us to it," Julia replied wryly. Was there any point sharing Celine's insights? They only confirmed their initial hypothesis that an insider was closely involved in orchestrating the theft or in helping to organize it.

A theory Penny had never taken kindly to.

"I've been trying desperately to get in touch with Blake, but I can't get through to him, Julia."

Not sure whether to laugh or cry, Julia contented herself with rolling her eyes as she popped a cheese tart into her mouth. Her younger colleague had a veritable gift for rubbing most people the wrong way. Penny was one of them.

"That might be because he's on a plane, Penny," she explained gently. "On his way to Connecticut to check out the details. The first he heard about it was this morning when Ella called him."

"Oh! I see." Penny seemed mollified, but it was the proverbial calm before a storm. "But why release the news to the media, then? Wasn't that a rather precipitate move? It's most annoying, as I'm sure you can imagine. And I can tell you Sarah Williams is incensed—quite rightly, in my opinion—about this situation. There are reputations to preserve—although—"

Julia wondered why she'd cut herself off so abruptly. It was completely out of character. What was Penny holding back?

"Look, if there's anything you know, any detail that could help the investigation, you should get in touch with Blake—or Ella, since Blake's not available."

The sound of troubled breathing filled Julia's ears. Unable to help herself, she clenched her fists. *Come on, Penny. Spit it out, for heaven's sake!*

"Has Celine read the article?" Penny hedged. "Any fresh insights from her?"

Julia hesitated. Divulging the only relevant detail to Penny would be like waving a red rag before a raging bull.

"Nothing that contradicts what she's said earlier," the former fed replied cautiously. But she might as well have thrown caution to the winds.

"So Celine still thinks a well-connected insider was behind the theft?"

Julia sighed. "Listen, when you think of the Degas sketches—"

"I am thinking of the Degas sketches," Penny said quickly. They'd been displayed in the Short Gallery, a small hallway on the second floor. "And I think Celine's right."

Julia clutched the phone to her ear, ignoring the heat emanating from the device. Had she heard aright?

"You think Celine's right?" she repeated.

There was no reason not to, of course. Situated between the Raphael Room and the Little Salon, the Short Gallery was largely ignored by visitors. The tall cabinets within it, designed to hold the drawings and prints Isabella Gardner had avidly collected, didn't merit much attention either.

Few people would consider the drawings worth their attention. Almost no one would think them valuable enough to steal. If any thief had so much as given the cabinets a second glance, they'd be more likely to have pilfered Michelangelo's drawings than the hastily drawn Degas sketches.

In other words, only someone intimately familiar with the Gardner's layout, its holdings, and where each work was displayed would've known where to look for the Degas sketches. They were certainly not items likely to be pulled out on the spur of the moment.

Yet Penny had until now been resistant to their rationale. What had changed?

"Listen, this man—" Her voice low and broken, Penny seemed to be having a hard time articulating her thoughts. "This anonymous collector—"

"Yes," Julia urged her, unconsciously leaning forward. Her plate was still piled high, but she'd lost all interest in the food.

"Sarah tells me it's a man called Henry Dodd."

It seemed like a statement, but Penny's voice had risen as though she were seeking confirmation of the fact.

"Yes, Henry Dodd. He's an art collector, I believe."

"Julia, Dodd served as a member of our board! He left six months before the museum was hit. If there was anyone who knew the museum inside out, it was him. And he had an especial fondness for the Impressionists."

"That could just be a coincidence."

Penny sounded so distraught, Julia felt obliged to calm her down. But her own mind was reeling as well. Had Dodd stolen the Manet? For his mistress?

All the more reason to have Ella look into his finances. See if he was paying regular amounts to a hospital.

"That's not all, Julia." Penny swallowed audibly. "Remember the warning the FBI gave the Gardner in 1981? About a man called Royce? He'd cased the museum, as they say, and was planning a hit?"

Julia pursed her lips. "Only too well."

Louis Royce had stolen artworks before and was intelligent enough to recognize what each was worth. Royce had been in prison at the time the Gardner Museum was hit. But he'd admitted his motive in stealing the Gardner art was pure profit.

He'd hoped to interest a wealthy collector in the stolen works.

The details of Royce's plan had also been remarkably similar to the theft as it had actually gone down. They'd intended to make their move at night —dressed as cops.

When Penny mentioned this, Julia nodded. "Yup," she said. "If Royce hadn't been in prison, he'd have been our prime suspect."

"Well, Dodd was one of the two board members present during the briefing. The notes in our archives indicate the FBI had strongly recommended beefing up security, especially at night. But Dodd was dead set against that.

"Would you believe it, Julia? We're being warned about a potential strike and all Dodd could recommend is that we insure the paintings?"

Julia's ears perked up. The Degas Pastel technically belonged to Norton's insurance company now. Had Norton sold it to Dodd? Did he and Dodd know each other?

"Did Dodd have an insurance company in mind?" she asked.

"If he did, our notes don't reveal that," Penny replied. "It was a ludicrous suggestion, though."

She sniffed.

"As though insurance would be of any use in the event of a theft. And it's not that the premiums would be very much lower than what we'd spend hiring more guards and installing a more sophisticated security system."

But Julia was only half-listening to this tirade.

Was it possible they'd been barking up the wrong tree? Was Dodd the Boston Brahmin, not Norton?

"Listen, Penny, can you check up on something for me?"

"Absolutely. What do you need?"

"Was Hugh Norton ever on the board? Or was he a frequent visitor to the Gardner?"

"Hugh Norton?" Penny seemed taken aback. "He's a well-known donor. I know he's been very generous to us. But I really doubt . . . Oh, well, it can't hurt to look. I'll see what I can find out.

"But Julia, please don't ignore Dodd. Tell Blake to look into him, will you?"

Chapter Twenty-Two

The tourists were back. The phone call to Julia would have to wait. Bidding them a hurried goodbye, Celine prepared to return to the office.

"Aren't you driving back with us?" Beth leaned against the heavy wood-and-glass door of the Tasting Room to keep it from closing.

"No, I have work to do." Afraid she sounded overly curt, Celine forced a smile on her features.

"But your car—?" Shirley began.

"Don't worry," Celine assured her hastily. "Andrea can give me a ride back. Enjoy the rest of your day, folks."

Waving expansively, Celine whirled around and sped back to her office.

"We need to get to Boston," she began urgently when Julia answered her phone. "Clara's in trouble."

Succinctly she shared the details of the previous night's dream.

A disconcerting silence greeted her. "Are you sure?" Julia finally said, her voice low.

Judging by the hum of voices and clang of metal in the background, the former fed was in the kitchen. Was Wanda with her? The clamor grew distant.

"Listen," Julia's voice was still hushed. "It's been a busy afternoon, and without Annabelle here to help, Wanda's been rushed off her feet."

That meant her marketing manager was getting snippy. An image popped into Celine's mind—Wanda snapping at Julia. It was replaced by her dream and Jonah's desperate voice.

You need to see my mother. You can't let her die.

No, Celine couldn't let anything happen to Clara.

"Wanda will just have to deal with it." Her voice was uncharacteristically sharp. "There's a life hanging in the balance—"

Julia blew out a stream of exasperated air. "Are you sure about this? We've been through this before. Why would—?"

"I don't know," Celine interjected, frustrated. Was there no way to convince the former fed? "I don't know why anyone would want to harm her. I just—"

All she had was a strange dream—and an invoice. No hard evidence. Just a nagging sense of danger. *My God, why couldn't the signs be any clearer?*

"This whole church thing," Julia began delicately, "couldn't it just be a reaction to . . . er, you know. . ." Her voice trailed off uncomfortably.

She was referring to Blake.

"That was my first thought, too," Celine cut in. "That's why I haven't mentioned it. But it *was* Jonah. I heard his voice. I'm still hearing it."

Where was her guardian angel when Celine needed her? Celine could hear her whisper something, but the sounds were too murky to be discerned

"Couldn't Annabelle. . .?" Julia began, but Celine was only half-listening. She strained her ears trying to detect Sister Mary Catherine's words.

An image of an open notebook with a pen lying across the page filled her mind. It reminded her of Jonah and the tiny reporter's notebook he always carried in his pocket.

Report . . . reporter . . . He was a reporter. What do reporters do, Celine?
Follow their instincts—and their insatiable curiosity.

The response floated into her mind, unbidden. Celine inhaled sharply.

The sound must've startled Julia for the drone of her voice immediately subsided.

"What is it, Celine?"

"Jonah fancied himself something of an investigative reporter, didn't he?" Celine asked.

Julia's only response was a derisive snort.

"Fancied is the operative word there."

"Yes, but what if he was digging around and found something? Something important, germane to the case, maybe."

"Okay," Julia sighed. "I'll bite. So how does Clara fit in?"

Twisting silken strands of her long red-gold hair, Celine considered her dream again. Jonah had been bearing something in his arms. A symbol for the secret he'd discovered and was harboring?

Holy Mary, Mother of God, Sister Mary Catherine recited. *The Ark of the New Covenant.*

"What if Clara"—Celine picked her words with care—"or to be more precise, her room, is the repository for whatever it was Jonah discovered?"

Julia sighed again. "You're thinking—?"

"Yes," Celine eagerly interrupted. "Whatever Jonah found, a piece of the puzzle, some type of evidence—it's in Clara's hands. Think about it, Julia.

What could be a better hiding place? Who'd think to search for something like that among the belongings of a woman who's completely out of it?"

"Judging by your dream, someone already has," Julia pointed out wryly.

"Maybe they've searched his apartment, his workplace, come up with nothing."

"I . . . Okay, fine. But I still think we should let Annabelle look into this before we head out for Boston. I'm telling you you're going to have a mutiny on your hands if you insist on abandoning ship yet again."

Celine winced. Abandoning ship, was that what she was doing?

"Fine. We'll do it your way. I'll call Annabelle. Maybe she can head back before we fly out."

They'd have to leave for Boston soon, Celine was certain. But would Annabelle agree to cut short her vacation if—and when—it came to that?

Celine fervently hoped so.

Chapter Twenty-Three

"Hard to believe it's only half past four, isn't it?"

The burly middle-aged man sitting at the bar counter slid his wine glass over to Celine for a refill.

"That it is." Celine smiled. Glancing out the window, she reached under the counter to pull out the bottle of Mourvedre her patron had been quaffing. It was getting dark, although the sun had yet to set.

Trees, buildings, and people cast long shadows on the narrow street and sidewalk outside.

Annabelle still hadn't called. The thought intensified Celine's uneasiness for Clara.

She filled the wine glass, held it delicately by the stem, and set it before her waiting customer. He sipped at it appreciatively but was mercifully silent.

Celine was in no mood for small talk.

Too late. Too late. Jonah's warning rang incessantly in her ears.

What had Jonah discovered? What did Clara know?

"Anything to do with Dodd?" Julia had asked when Celine returned to the bar. "Looks like he could be our insider connection."

The former fed had given her a quick summary of the details Penny had uncovered.

They were damning. But . . .

Something just doesn't add up, Celine murmured to herself.

A blast of cold air hit her, forcing her to look up. The door had been yanked open, and a woman stood framed in the doorway. Celine's eyes narrowed as she took in the slender blonde with a backpack slung over her hunched shoulders.

Was that Beth? From the Cab-er-Neigh tour? What was she doing here?

Celine hadn't taken her for a wine aficionado. More the Diet Coke or Pepsi type.

Beth slowly scanned the room until her eyes met Celine. With a wave, she strode over to the bar.

"I think I left my spectacle case and change purse here," she said, shrugging off her backpack. She let it drop to the floor. "Mind if I look around for it?"

"Not at all."

"Buy you a glass of wine?" the man at the bar—he was sitting at the exact spot Grayson Pike had occupied last year—offered. Dirck had still been alive then, Celine thought with a pang.

Beth turned toward him, lips stretching into a slow smile. "Sure. Whatever you're having."

Then she swiveled her neck, taking in the crowded room, the groups of wine and coffee drinkers surrounding the tables that scattered the floor. The bar thrummed with the comfortable noise of cheerful conversation.

Celine watched her as she carefully poured out a measure of Mourvedre. Beth didn't seem in any particular hurry to locate the items she'd supposedly lost. Why had she returned?

"Feel free to walk around," Celine suggested. She reached across the counter to hand Beth her wine glass.

Smiling, Beth lifted her glass to her lips and took a small sip.

"I just might," she said. She nodded her thanks at the burly guy, then proceeded to ignore him.

Extending her wine glass, she pointed over Celine's shoulder. "I like the paintings you have there. Mind if I take a look?"

Before Celine could stop her, Beth was behind the counter, examining the brilliant seascapes and wine country scenes that lined the wall. The Delft had a long tradition of carrying works on consignment. Artists at heart, Dirck and John had done everything in their power to bolster local talent.

"They're all by local artists," Celine informed Beth, although she doubted the other woman gave a hoot.

"Cost a pretty penny, don't they?" Beth tried to lift the lower edge of the frame of one of the works. Celine frowned. What the heck was she looking for?

"Please don't do that, Beth," she called sharply. "You might damage the works."

Beth turned to face her.

"That valuable, are they? Or do you guys tack on a hefty upcharge as part of your commission?"

"The prices are set by the artists themselves," Celine informed her, struggling to keep her tone even. There was a latent hostility in the woman that was unnerving. Celine could sense it simmering and swirling in the older woman like the eddies of a whirlpool.

What had brought it on?

Beth returned to the other side of the counter and hoisted herself up onto a bar stool.

"You know I'm a little surprised you don't have any famous paintings here?" she said. "Especially after what you said earlier this afternoon about the Manet being your insurance policy."

Celine felt her cheeks flaming. Her vision that afternoon had been triggered by the *Post* article. It had come upon her without warning. As always, in that state, she had no control over the words she uttered, whether she spoke them out loud or not.

The burly guy with a shock of busy hair was the only other person at the counter, but Celine could tell he was avidly following their conversation, his mouth agape.

"You have a Manet?" he asked.

"No, I don't," Celine replied. She watched Beth closely. What had brought Beth back to the bar? Why was she asking about the Manet?

She's thinking about the Chez Tortoni, Celine thought. *But why does she think I have it?*

An image of Clara sitting up in her nursing home bed, resting against a bank of soft pillows, floated into Celine's mind.

Did Beth know Clara? Had Clara Hibbert said something to her? Was Beth a friend of Jonah's? A colleague? She was too old to have been his girlfriend.

Celine was about to ask when Beth lobbed another grenade at her.

"I kinda got the impression you liked the Dutch artists. I mean your bar and winery both have Dutch names. But you don't have any Dutch works on the walls here."

Dutch works? Celine gaped at Beth, at a loss for words.

Tell her it's not a Rembrandt, it's a Flinck, Sister Mary Catherine murmured into Celine's ears.

The words were accompanied by an image of a stormy landscape. Dark clouds loomed in the top third of the work. Trees with gnarled, twisted barks rose out of the ground. In the middle of the canvas, an obelisk reached toward the sky.

Celine faced Beth, her fists clenched by her side.

"It's really commendable that you want to help the Gardner recover its lost art, Beth. Even if it's only for the reward money." She spoke firmly. "But you're not going to find the paintings here.

"And a word of advice: you might want to start off with a little research on the paintings themselves. *Landscape With an Obelisk* isn't by Rembrandt. It's by an artist who was a student of his, Govert Flinck."

Beth's eyes blazed, but she didn't say a word. Draining her glass of wine, she got off the bar stool.

Celine hoped she was leaving, but her hopes were dashed when the phone rang. It was the black landline phone under the counter. And much to her dismay, Beth made no move to leave.

Excusing herself, Celine reached for the receiver. She recognized the voice on the other end instantly.

Annabelle!

"Hey! What's the word on. . ." She let her voice trail off, aware she had listeners. Beth slid onto a barstool.

Celine wanted to ask if she could return Annabelle's call, but the older woman was in a hurry.

"I'll make this quick. I need to cook dinner and start packing."

"You're heading back?" Celine's voice rose.

"I'll have to, won't I, if you and Julia are planning to come out?"

Celine bent her head close to the receiver.

"You think we need to?" she kept her voice low.

"Oh, absolutely. Clara keeps asking for you, Celine. Physically, she's about as healthy as you could expect. Mentally, I don't know. She's petrified of something. It comes over her features off and on—this look of pure terror. Whether it's warranted or not, I can't tell. But I'm convinced you and Julia need to be here."

Celine felt her brow pucker. Was Clara being abused? Or was something else going on? Whatever it was, it didn't sound good.

"Could you get anything out of her? Has she said anything that seems strange or out of the ordinary?"

"Well, she still thinks Jonah is alive. Says he's asking after you. *Why doesn't Celine come to see us anymore?* The slightest sound startles her. And she keeps mumbling something about church."

"Church?" Celine was startled.

Could this have something to do with her dream?

"Clara mentioned church?"

She wished she hadn't spoken out loud when she saw Beth's gaze fastened upon her. She turned to face the wall.

"She may just be on her way out, Celine. That's my take on it. And she needs familiar people around her. I've spoken with her nurses. They agree."

Celine's spirits sank. Was Clara's obsession with church and her dead son simply a symptom of her stage in life?

A woman close to death, and reluctant to go without receiving the last rites?

Chapter Twenty-Four

Hutchinson House, Clara's nursing home, was located in Jamaica Plain, almost directly across from Jamaica Pond and the serene gardens Frederick Olmstead had designed for Boston.

"I hope this isn't another wasted trip," Julia muttered as she navigated a bend in the road. The former fed was talking to herself, but Celine heard the remark nevertheless.

It stung, reminding Celine of the countless prior visits they'd made to the nursing home. Based solely on her intuition—faulty as it happened—that Clara was in danger. Although this time, when Wanda had objected to their departure—"For God's sake, Celine, you can't keep doing this!"—Julia had supported Celine.

"She's an old, frail woman, Wanda. Close to death and probably terrified at the thought of it. She needs familiar faces around her. And"—here, Julia had thrown Celine a quick glance—"maybe, just maybe, Jonah left behind some clues with her that we can work with."

That had been two days ago. But it was clear now Julia didn't set much store by Celine's psychic impressions. "Or my interpretation of them," she said to herself.

Clenching her fists to her side, Celine stared out her window. *The only way this trip won't be a waste is if Clara's not in danger. Are we really hoping her life's in jeopardy?* The words flashed through her mind, but she forced herself not to speak them out loud.

Bare trees, branches laden with snow, lined the gently curving road. The dark, rough tree trunks cruising past filled her vision. It had been a long flight, but they'd opted to check in on Clara before going to their hotel. They'd rented a car at the airport. The thirty-minute drive from Boston-Logan had been spent mostly in silence.

As Julia maneuvered the car onto Jamaicaway Court, an image slid into Celine's mind. Jonah sitting on a bench by the pond. A vista of trees stretched behind him. From time to time, he looked over his shoulder, craning his neck to see. Watching. Waiting. Impatient.

"He spent a lot of time here," she said out loud.

"Who?" A puzzled frown wrinkled Julia's brow.

"Jonah."

"Oh, yeah?" Julia was looking straight ahead, but Celine caught the muted sarcasm in her voice. Her lips tightened.

"I meant by the pond." She pointed her thumb at the rear window. "Waiting for someone."

"Who?" Julia seemed a little more intrigued now.

Celine shook her head.

"I don't know. I can see it was in the summer. The trees are green, the grass lush."

"About the time we were here last?" Julia's voice rose. They'd been investigating sculptor Tony Reynold's murder. Jonah had insisted upon accompanying them.

Celine nodded. "All those times he wasn't with us, he was here."

"Not visiting his mother?" Julia's shrewd blue eyes bore into Celine's face before turning forward to the road.

"Not all of the time, no."

"Must have been meeting his handler, then," Julia surmised.

They had turned onto Beaufort Road and were approaching a snow-covered island with a bare tree rising from it. The road circled around it, leading to the parking lot of the nursing home.

"I guess," Celine said. But that wasn't what it felt like. She closed her eyes, tapping into the image of Jonah and the sensations she'd felt coursing through him.

He had the impatience of a predator waiting for his prey. Impatient—and nervous—as though his prey could, if carelessly handled, tear him to pieces.

He had a story, Sister Mary Catherine told her. *He was like a dog with a juicy bone.*

A scoop! That's how he'd thought of it, Celine realized. It was a wonder she hadn't sensed this before.

You were too distraught, Celine, her guardian angel pointed out. *Your senses are jammed at a time like that.*

"I wonder if he mentioned it to Clara," she said, not realizing she'd spoken out loud.

"About meeting his handler?" Julia queried, sliding smoothly into one of the narrow parking spaces outside the two-story brick building. "I seriously doubt it."

But Jonah must have said something. Or someone thought he had. Why else was Clara in danger? A sudden painful spasm in her heart muscles confirmed Celine's interpretation of her impressions.

Clara was about to die. The only question was: could they prevent it?

You'll need to act fast, Celine, Sister Mary Catherine warned. *The storm clouds are gathering. No time to dilly-dally.*

Chapter Twenty-Five

"Special Agent Markham!" Sarah Williams, Director of the Van Hoyt Museum, stood up, reaching across her desk, arm outstretched, to greet Blake. "What a . . . a"—she wrinkled her nose, searching for a suitable adjective, then gave up—"a surprise to see you."

A surprise. Not a pleasant surprise, Blake noted, registering the sour expression on Sarah Williams' attractive features. She was a slim brunette with shoulder-length hair that curled at the ends.

"I was told you were expecting me," he said, eyebrows raised.

Williams seemed flustered. "Well, yes, of course we were." She gestured at the seat across her desk and sat back down. "But a heads-up would've been nice."

"I guess it would." Blake crossed his leg, black boot touching his left jeans-clad knee. He'd considered calling and then decided against it. Best to catch the Director off-guard—and preferably alone.

"I could've asked Mr. Dodd to be present—with the papers that establish his ownership of the work." Sarah Williams sounded annoyed now. "As it stands, I'm not sure when he'll be able to see you."

Blake smiled. He'd suspected she might call Dodd. That's why he hadn't alerted her to his arrival. "I'm sure we'll figure something out," he said lightly.

After what he'd learned about Dodd, he'd decided it would be best to interview him separately.

"I do have to say I haven't appreciated the considerable media attention this incident has garnered." Sarah's finely shaped eyebrows gathered into a displeased frown.

"Neither have I, Ms. Williams." Her eyebrows shot up, but Blake didn't give her an opportunity to respond. Leaning back, he folded his arms. "Tell me about the Degas."

"There really isn't much to say. It's a pastel—a little-known work in a series of similar executions on the same theme. Mr. Dodd was kind enough to loan it to us for our exhibition on the Impressionists. We have a small collection, but it is fairly impressive—if I do say so myself."

"And you know it's a Degas because . . .?" Blake let the question hang in the air.

"Because it's quite obvious to any but the most obtuse idiot that it is." Sarah Williams got to her feet. "Would you like to see it?"

"Absolutely. That's why I'm here."

The Impressionists the Van Hoyt had collected for the exhibition were displayed in the Avery Gallery on the first floor. The Degas was in a shaded corner, away from the window.

Blake wondered about that decision.

"Pastel is an extremely fragile medium, Special Agent," Sarah Williams explained as she led him to the framed thirty-by-nineteen-inch work. "Prone to falling off the support. And many of the pigments Degas used are fugitive, tending to fade in strong light."

"We're fortunate to have three of Degas's pastels." The Director of the Van Hoyt indicated the two works hanging on adjoining walls on either side of Dodd's pastel. "You can see the marked similarities in technique."

She waited quietly while Blake examined the works. He wasn't an expert on art, but he did know how to use his eyes. And damned if Williams wasn't right.

Despite the differences in subject and finish—Dodd's Degas and the work on loan from the Met had a more finished quality than the hastily drawn sketch on his right—they did look as though they'd come from the same hand.

"Degas has a tendency to suggest features," Sarah Williams said, pointing to the Met's *Woman Having Her Hair Combed.* "The black outlines are more evident in the sketch"—it was called *Repasseuse* and showed a woman ironing—"but you can see it also in the sleeves of the woman doing the combing in the Met's pastel. And in the arms of the woman in Mr. Dodd's pastel."

Blake peered closely at the works, head pivoting from one to the other. The original green of the paper supports had faded to a warm gray in all three. The flesh tones were warm—an odd mixture, when one looked closely, of greens, pinks, and yellows.

"That's typical Degas," Sarah Williams said when he commented on the fact. "Notice how even in the sketch, there's a luminescent quality?"

Blake nodded.

"It's because of the opaque white highlights Degas uses. I could have our conservator use raking lights on all three, and we'd notice even more similarities. The corrections in the charcoal underdrawings, the layers of pigment Degas carefully built up."

"Couldn't a good forger replicate those techniques? Tom Keating did." Blake dropped the name casually, aware that, whether she wanted to or not, Williams could hardly deny the notorious British forger had succeeded in fooling countless experts like herself.

He turned to face her. "If this is an authentic Degas, that puts your friend Dodd in the very precarious position of being in possession of stolen property.

Williams' nostrils were pinched and her lips pursed as she regarded him, evidently torn between the Scylla of acknowledging the pastel was a forgery and the Charybdis of admitting the possibility that Dodd was a reprehensible art thief.

It was a hard choice, and Blake felt for her. But those were her only two choices.

"Did you know Dodd was on the board of the Gardner Museum—resigning just six months prior to the infamous theft?" he asked gently.

"Of course, I did." Her brown eyes flashed angrily at him. "What does that have to do with anything?"

Unfortunately, everything, he thought but didn't dare utter the words.

He faced the pastel. It was a remarkable piece of work—the woman's stance, arms pressing down on her iron, was so vivid, it was evident Degas had long observed—and absorbed—the particular motions of laundresses in their various attitudes of work. There was a boldness to the line work that no mere copyist could have achieved.

"You were satisfied with the provenance?" He turned to face her. "Whatever Dodd told you about how he acquired the work?"

"Of course." Williams gently lifted the pastel off the wall and carefully turned it over. "The labels on the back tell us everything we need to know. It was sold by the artist himself to Paul Durand-Ruel. He was Degas's dealer, you might be aware, Special Agent. Henri Dupuis, a French collector, acquired it from him."

Dupuis's descendants had sold it to an American collector, who in turn had donated it to the Lowell Museum in Boston.

"The Lowell Museum?" Blake stared at the tea-stained museum sticker affixed to the frame. Sarah had tapped it a couple of times as she spoke.

"Rest assured, the museum exists, Special Agent," Williams informed him dryly.

"I'm well aware of it," Blake replied. It was the museum the Sullivans had decided to donate the work to after their deaths. But when it was stolen, the Sullivans' acceptance of the insurance payout instead of the Degas had voided the agreement.

The Lowell had never owned the work. The theft had robbed them of the opportunity to do so.

"And Dodd bought it from the Lowell?" Blake turned troubled gray eyes to Williams.

"It's a small museum, Special Agent. When they sent the Degas to a restorer, they found themselves unable to pay the hefty bill. It happens more often than you think. The museum agreed to let the restorer take possession of the work."

A faded red stamp on top of the Lowell Museum sticker indicated the restorer's acquisition of the work. But Blake could barely make out the letters.

"The restorer, as you can well imagine, Special Agent, had no real use for the pastel."

He'd sold it to Dodd at a price well below its market value, albeit at a tidy profit, thus recuperating his expenses.

"It was a good buy for Mr. Dodd," Williams said earnestly. "A real steal when you consider its current valuation—about three million dollars."

"I'm sure it was," Blake replied. "I'm sure it was. When exactly did he buy it?"

"It would've been in the year 2000."

Two years after the theft, the same year the Sullivans had accepted their insurance payout.

"Do you happen to know the month and the date?" he asked.

She specified the date. It was precisely three months before the Sullivans had accepted their payment.

Something fishy was going on.

The only thing Blake wasn't certain of was whether the Sullivans had been innocent victims in this entire affair. Or had they been in on it right from the start?

Chapter Twenty-Six

No time to dilly-dally.

Sister Mary Catherine's warning echoed in Celine's brain as she swiftly crossed the length of the portico to the front door of Hutchinson House.

In life, her guardian angel had frequently directed those words to her charges.

Today is all we have, the nun would say. *Make the most of it.*

With her hand on the brass door handle, Celine waited for Julia to catch up. The sidelights and nine-paned window of the white door afforded a view of the nursing home's sunny lobby with its soothing beige walls, richly carpeted floors, and tastefully done watercolors.

It was a sight long familiar to Celine. But the attractive brunette manning the reception desk was a stranger. A new appointee, Celine thought as she pushed open the door and walked in with Julia.

Dressed in a maroon tee sporting the nursing home's gold logo, the receptionist glanced up as they approached. She tilted her head to the side as an expectant smile lit up her pretty features.

"Yes?" Her eyebrows lifted slightly to match the lilt in her voice.

Her eyes, a vivid blue, took in Julia's stocky figure, then roved back to settle upon Celine's face.

"We're here to see Clara Hibbert," Celine said.

"Ms. Hibbert?" The smile remained pasted upon her face, but Celine sensed a caginess in her. The woman's eyes drifted fleetingly toward Julia and then returned to Celine.

"I'm actually not sure how receptive she'll be to visitors."

Celine gaped at the receptionist, unsure what to make of her response. It was unusual for staff at a facility like this to discourage visitors. After all, visits from loved ones brought the residents—elderly and frequently verging on senility—out of their shells. So why was this woman warding them off?

She's protecting Clara. The answer drifted unbidden into her mind. But more questions followed.

Protecting Clara from what? Whom?

From the certainty of death. Sister Mary Catherine's voice was low.

Celine's heart muscles clenched painfully. Was it from her own death or the knowledge of Jonah's that Sandy was trying to protect Clara?

But sensing Julia growing restive beside her, she quickly spoke up: "You're new here, aren't you?"

Leaning forward, she tried to read the name printed on the tag dangling at the end of the woman's lanyard. But it was hanging too low for Celine to make out her name.

She raised her eyes. "I don't think we've seen you on our previous visits. Have we, Julia?"

Julia shook her head wryly. "No, we have not." Her gaze bore into the young woman's.

The receptionist's eyes faltered. Her smile slipped. Celine sighed. Julia was clearly making the poor woman nervous, treating her like a hostile witness.

"What is your name?" Celine asked.

"I'm Sandy Brooks, ma'am." The woman turned to her, visibly relieved to break eye contact with Julia. "Part-time nurse and receptionist. I've been here about a month."

Well, Sandy Brooks"—Julia placed her hands on her hips— "you might want to let us in. We're the closest thing to family Clara has."

"Oh!" Sandy's eyebrows rose. She looked closely at Celine. "Oh," she said again. The smile returned to her face. "You must be Celine Skye!"

The wariness had gone. "I'm so glad you could make it!"

And just in time, too. Just in time.

Celine heard the words as clearly as though Sandy had uttered them out loud. Her eyes swiveled toward Julia, but of course Julia hadn't heard a thing.

Sandy was pulling the visitor register toward herself when Celine glanced back at her. Intent upon filling out the columns, she seemed oblivious to Celine's questioning gaze.

Just in time for what? To save Clara?

Was there any way to find out what precisely Sandy had meant?

"How is Clara?" she probed.

Sandy gave her a quick look from under her long lashes.

"Oh, well enough, all things considered. I'm sure she'll be pleased to see you. She has been asking after you."

"Does Clara get a lot of visitors?" With the instincts of a former cop, Julia had homed in on Sandy's odd behavior. When Sandy's head jerked up in surprise, she clarified: "You seemed quite protective of her a little while back—before you realized who we were."

"Well . . ." Sandy nervously scanned the empty lobby, her large blue eyes finally alighting on the huge plate glass windows that gave onto the snow-covered grounds at the back of the property. A yoga class was in session under an enormous canopy. Most of the residents and staff seemed to be in attendance.

"A bit brisk, isn't it, for an outdoor yoga session?" Julia commented. "Is that where Clara is?"

Sandy bit her lip, then seeming to come to a decision, reached under the counter for a BE BACK sign that she placed on the reception.

She jabbed her thumb at the door behind her.

"There's an office back there. Why don't you come in for a bit, and we can chat?"

❧

The office was the size of a large closet, equipped with a small desk and three folding metal chairs.

"It was you who suggested to Annabelle Curtis that we come, isn't it?" Celine said at the same time that Julia demanded: "What exactly is going on here?"

Sandy's eyes ping-ponged from Julia to Celine.

"Yes, yes I may have mentioned it. It was just a thought." She twisted her hands. "Ms. Hibbert has been asking for you. And to be honest, she's been acting very strangely."

"In what way?"

"She's very reluctant to leave her room. She should be out in the garden with the other residents," Sandy went on. "But she refuses to budge."

"That's nothing new," Celine said. "Clara was never especially sociable. But ever since she lost Jonah, she's lost all interest in even the few activities she did enjoy. I imagine that's natural. No mother expects to outlive her child."

"Yes, of course. But nothing will persuade her to leave her room. Some fresh air would do her a world of good. And frankly, the room needs to be aired as well. We do have staff going in to clean, but it's much easier when the residents are out of the room."

"I imagine it would be," Julia said dryly.

It would also be easier to search her room. But Celine kept the thought to herself. Was it possible, Clara was sufficiently in control of her faculties to realize someone was after whatever evidence Jonah had spirited in with her belongings?

"Has she ever given a reason for not wanting to move?" she asked.

"She insists her son"—Sandy looked uncomfortable—"I gather he's no more?"

"You gather right," Julia said tersely. "Anyway, you were saying?"

"She claims to see him. He's in her room, and Ms. Hibbert says she needs to be with him while she can. *It'll be time for him to leave soon. I need to be here*, she says. She even speaks with him, although when she's aware of having listeners, she immediately stops."

"It's cuckoo, I'll grant you that," Julia said. "But it's nothing new. Seems to have gotten worse, though. I don't recall her wanting to be cooped up in her room all day."

"What about visitors?" Celine asked, recalling that Julia's question had gone unanswered.

"I've found it's best to restrict visits to those who come often enough that they're familiar to her. Anything strange or unexpected terrifies her. She starts shrieking. One of our visitors—it was on the day we host our tours—accidentally wandered into her room. Boy, did that set her off! She was screaming like a banshee."

Celine saw Julia frown. "Wonder what she's afraid of?" she murmured to herself. She turned to Sandy. "I'm surprised neither the Executive Director nor the Resident Care Director has brought this to our attention. Why is that?"

Sandy looked down, twisting her hands together. "That I couldn't say." She looked up. "I just thought you might be able to talk some sense into Ms. Hibbert. She doesn't even eat well. I have a friend on the kitchen staff. She says Ms. Hibbert's tray comes down practically untouched."

Sandy's expression was grave.

"We give all our residents a full hour to take their meals. Many of them, you see, are slow eaters. But most manage to finish at least half their tray in that time."

"That doesn't sound good," Celine admitted, exchanging a worried glance with Julia.

"No, it doesn't." It was the first they'd heard of this "Anything else?" Julia turned back to Sandy.

"She's been asking to see you, Ms. Skye. Not that she says it in so many words. What she does say is that Jonah, her son, wants to know why you don't visit anymore."

"And she's been talking about church," Celine added, recalling Annabelle's report.

To her surprise, Sandy shook her head. "That I've not heard. In fact, based on what I know of the family, I took her to be a non-believer. But if she's talking about church, that would certainly fit. She may feel she's—" She spread her hands wide.

Close to death, that's what she's trying to say, Celine thought.

Sandy looked apologetically from Celine to Julia and back again.

"I realize it's not always convenient to visit, but under the circumstances, I felt—"

"It's fine," Celine assured her, comprehending at last what was going on. Overly solicitous, Sandy had—on her own authority—decided to reach out to them. Taking the matter to the Executive Director or the Resident Care Director would land the young woman in trouble.

"Just because Clara is in a nursing home doesn't mean her friends and family bear no responsibility for her."

Sandy smiled gratefully. "I'm glad you see it that way. I have my fingers crossed that with your help we'll get Ms. Hibbert back on track. Now"—she stood up—"if you'll both just sign the visitor register, I can take you up to her room."

Chapter Twenty-Seven

Back in the car he'd rented at Bridgeport Airport Blake pulled his prescription eye drops out of his pocket. Peering at himself in the rearview mirror, he squeezed a couple of drops into each eye.

It had been a two-hour flight from Boston, then another thirty-minute drive to the Van Hoyt in Norwalk. His eyes felt dry and scratchy.

He dropped the bottle back into his pocket and gazed at the imposing brick structure on the left of him. What exactly had he accomplished? Technically, the Degas—assuming it wasn't a forgery—had still belonged to the Sullivans when Dodd had acquired it.

To the naked eye, it looked genuine enough, but Blake had extracted a reluctant promise from Sarah Williams to conduct further tests on it.

"I don't see why, Special Agent Markham," she'd protested when he made the request.

He reversed smoothly out of the parking lot, tires scrunching on hardened snow, as he recalled his response.

"It's not that I don't trust you, Ms. Williams. But I'd feel better about this if we verified our impressions. If it turns out we're mistaken about its authenticity, you and I are both going to look like utter asses for dragging Dodd's name through the mud over a mere copy."

Her expression had soured but she'd conceded his point. Blake had advised her to verify that the pigments used in Dodd's pastel matched the ones used in the other two pastels and had been made by Roche, the company Degas favored. An inspection under a raking light would also help, highlighting similarities—or differences—in technique among the three works.

"You're fortunate in having two other works whose authenticity isn't in question. It's a heaven-sent opportunity to compare the three works, maybe even enlighten your colleagues further about Degas's technique."

"I can tell you right now no forger in his right mind would buy Roche pastels. Each half stick can cost upward of fifteen dollars. A set of ten half sticks would set you back over a hundred dollars. That's before you factor in shipping from France and VAT."

"Just humor me, okay?" he'd insisted.

He was out of the parking lot now, cruising slowly north on East Avenue toward the three-star hotel Ella had booked him into: The Norwalk River Inn. A break in the trees and buildings afforded a glimpse of the river in question. Then it was gone.

Getting Sarah Williams to part with the names and mailing addresses of the five thousand-odd people to whom the Van Hoyt regularly mailed catalogs had been far harder.

"Is this absolutely necessary, Special Agent Markham?" Sarah Williams had snapped. "It's an unwarranted intrusion into their lives, wouldn't you agree?"

Blake's gray eyes had held her gaze.

"Remember the media coverage you weren't happy about? Turns out the person who called the *Post*—the same person, by the way, who called the FBI—saw a photo of Dodd's Degas in one of your catalogs."

"You're saying one of our members—or donors—saw the photo of the Degas and then concocted a story about it being related to the Gardner theft?" Williams had stared back at him, one eyebrow quizzically raised. "Why?"

Blake had shrugged. "To prod the FBI into looking for a connection, maybe."

He'd paused before adding softly, "Or as a veiled threat to someone involved in both thefts."

"Meaning Dodd?" Her questions were like baseball bats bludgeoning his head. He wasn't prepared to provide a definitive guilty verdict on Dodd yet. But things weren't looking good.

"Isn't it obvious?" he'd countered with a question of his own. "Someone knows the history of the work, is familiar with its provenance, and knows for a fact it ended up in Dodd's hands."

Someone familiar with Dodd. A beautiful woman, a former mistress. Ella had shared Celine's insights with Blake when he'd checked in at the office yesterday.

Someone with a motive to bring Dodd crashing down.

A large white sign set amidst a wide lush lawn told him he'd arrived at the Norwalk River Inn. It was a brick building—just like the Van Hoyt. He swung left, slowing down as he drove into the enormous parking lot.

❧

"I think she's hiding something." Julia threw Sandy Brooks a quick glance as she turned the knob on the double doors that opened onto a large patio. "Or at least knows more than she's telling."

A line of visitors had been waiting to check in when they'd emerged from the tiny office behind the reception desk. "I'll take you up in just a minute," Sandy had promised them. "Is that okay?"

Reassuring her that it was, Celine and Julia had taken the opportunity to get a breath of fresh air. After a while, the welcome warmth of the overheated lobby had given way to a suffocating stuffiness.

"What's your take on this?" Opening the patio door, Julia looked over her shoulder at Celine as she stepped onto the large gray concrete paver outside.

A blast of cold air greeted Celine as she followed Julia out. The door clicked shut behind her. She adjusted the thick scarf around her neck, swiveling around to cast an appraising glance at Sandy as she did so.

"She's worried about Clara, that's for sure," Celine said slowly.

"If I didn't know any better"—Julia moved away from the door, beginning a leisurely walk—"I'd say Sandy strongly suspects abuse and is covering up for it."

Celine considered this. "There might be an element of that."

Feeling suddenly dizzy, she stretched her hand out to steady herself. It was the same lightheadedness that had overcome her when she'd been looking through the Gardner file in Paso Robles the other evening.

"You okay?" Julia's firm hand clasped her shoulder, directing her toward one of the pillars supporting the patio.

"I'm fine." Celine reached for the stone pillar, gripping it hard. The pergola where the residents' yoga class was in session was up ahead. "Just a little unsteady on my feet. It's been happening of late whenever Clara comes to mind."

Were these sensations afflicting Clara as well?

"I keep feeling someone's pushing me, deliberating shoving me to the ground."

"Meaning you're in Clara's shoes," Julia guessed. "That's unusual, isn't it?"

Celine nodded. It would be the first time she'd perceived a situation from the victim's perspective rather than the perpetrator's.

"Before you ask, I can't see who it is pushing me. Whoever it is, the person's behind me." Strong hands shoved her shoulder blades. A man's hands? Celine couldn't tell. The pressure from Julia's hand on her shoulder felt equally strong.

She absorbed the scene before her. It looked like something out of a Christmas card. The hedges and trees draped in snow; the paving stones on the path below, slick with moisture; an ice-covered pond; puffy white clouds that floated in a sapphire-blue sky.

It was hard to believe any menace lurked beneath the serene, placid land-scape that stretched out before her.

"Abuse—plain, simple abuse for the sake of it," Julia said thoughtfully, "doesn't fit with one thing Sandy mentioned. Clara's reluctance to leave her room. You'd think she'd feel safer with the other residents than alone in her room."

She knows Clara isn't long for this world, Celine. Her mind harked back to her guardian angel's assertion.

Turning to face Julia, Celine shared the insight.

"I have no idea how Sandy knows that. Or even what she knows. But she's as convinced as I am that Clara is in danger."

"Because of the abuse?" Julia looked steadily at her. "Or something else?"

Celine studied the gray pebbles that filled the joints between the concrete pavers. Dark clouds loomed over Clara; the storm was about to break.

"Back when we were in the car, cruising past Jamaica Pond, I saw Jonah."

"Yes, I remember. You mentioned it."

"He was waiting for someone—someone he had incriminating informa-tion on."

A shaft of icy air stung Celine's cheeks. She pulled her woolen jacket closer together. It hung loose on her frame, unable to combat the cold. Her hands, encased in thick gloves, felt frozen and numb.

"Meaning he'd discovered something?" Julia pulled her gloves back on and thrust her hands into the pockets of her thick insulated teal jacket.

Celine nodded, making a mental note to buy herself an insulated jacket like Julia's.

"I'm guessing the key to what it is and where he secreted it must be in Clara's room."

"And she's aware of this?" Julia's voice rose in skepticism. "That's why she's afraid to leave her room?"

Clara's following her son's instructions, Sister Mary Catherine whispered. *She trusts him.*

"She's just doing what Jonah's telling her to." Celine had long been con-vinced Clara was in touch with her son. How else could Clara have known Jonah was dead? That it was Celine's fault, he'd been killed?

Relentlessly, she drove the images of the bullet that had spattered his brains out of her mind. *There's no point dwelling on that now*, she told herself. *No point at all.*

Aloud she continued: "I think Jonah's behind this sudden yearning to see us. He probably figures if we can get this piece of evidence—whatever it is —out of her hands, she'll finally be safe."

Julia snorted. "Great. Sounds just like Jonah. Gets himself into a mess and then expects everyone else to clean up after him."

Celine turned to her. "So what do you think we should do?"

The patio door opened before Julia could respond. Sandy thrust her head out.

"Ready to go upstairs?"

"Yes." Julia moved briskly forward. "Sandy, did you say Clara's room needs a thorough cleaning?"

Sandy glanced over her shoulder as they followed her into the warm lobby.

"Yes. If you could persuade her to step out for a while—"

"We'll do you one better than that," Julia offered heartily. She pulled off her jacket and rolled up the sleeves of the white turtleneck she was wearing under it. "We'll clean the room ourselves."

Sandy hesitated, startled. "Oh, no, that's not nece—"

"Oh, it is!" Julia held out her palm. "It's the least we can do after what you guys have endured."

Chapter Twenty-Eight

Bushed from the long flight, Celine found herself struggling to match Sandy's brisk pace as she strode down the carpeted hallway to Clara's second-floor studio apartment.

Judging by her labored breathing, Julia was having trouble keeping up as well.

Ahead of them, Sandy stopped before a door at the far end of the hallway.

"Here we are!" The receptionist looked over her shoulder, her smile patient and encouraging.

Like a parent urging her toddler to hurry up.

Celine smiled as she caught the irate thought that flashed through Julia's mind.

"Just one more thing"—Sandy leaned closer as they approached, panting from their exertions; she'd issued a constant stream of instructions as they rode up the elevator—"don't mention anything about her son being dead. She refuses to believe he's gone, and you'll only get her upset."

"I'll bet," Celine murmured.

She had no intention of bringing up the painful event. Clara had not only found it hard to accept Jonah's death, she'd blamed Celine for it. It was a blessing in disguise if Clara had come to believe Jonah was still alive.

"So pretend he's still with the living?" Julia asked laconically.

"Just follow my lead." Sandy smiled confidently. Turning to the door, she rapped sharply on it, then bent down to put her mouth to the keyhole.

"Ms. Hibbert? It's Sandy Brooks from the reception desk. I have a lovely surprise for you. A couple of friends all the way from California to see you."

Sandy unclipped a key ring hanging from her belt, selected a key, and inserted it into the keyhole.

"Hold on a minute!" Julia was aghast. "You're not just going to let—"

"We're coming in, okay?" Sandy called, talking over Julia's protestations.

A minute later, the click of the latch releasing sounded and Sandy opened the door.

Clara—a gray-haired, plump figure in a maroon jumpsuit—was sitting on her bed, facing the window. A chair was drawn up close to the bed. Clara seemed to be deep in conversation with an invisible figure within it, quietly nodding her head and murmuring.

"See what I mean?" Sandy whispered. Raising her voice, she called out: "Are you having a nice visit with your son? How's Jonah doing today, Ms. Hibbert?"

Clara's head jerked toward them. At the sight of Sandy, an irritated frown wrinkled her forehead.

"He's dead. How do you think he's doing?" she snapped.

Sandy reacted as though she'd been slapped. Her breath caught in an audible gasp; her cheeks turned a vivid red. Celine held her breath as well, bracing herself for the onslaught of fury that was sure to come her way.

But Clara ignored her. Frown deepening, her eyes swept toward Julia.

"Who are you? Why are you here?"

Julia seemed unfazed by Clara's brusque tone.

"I'm Celine's friend." She indicated Celine with her thumb. "You remember Celine Skye, don't you?"

The question elicited another horrified gasp from Sandy. *"You absolutely do not want to ask her if she remembers something. It's a trigger question."*

Clara's gaze shifted to Celine's. It was only when Clara smiled at her that Celine realized she'd been holding her breath, waiting for an outburst.

"Jonah said you were coming. We've been waiting for you."

Was Jonah's spirit visible to Clara? Celine found her eyes drawn toward the empty armchair. If Jonah was present in the room, why couldn't she— the psychic—see him?

Clara must've noticed Celine gazing at the empty chair.

"Oh, he's just stepped out for a minute."

Clara pushed herself up to a standing position. "I think I'd like to go out as well." She reached for and gripped the window sill by her bed. "I've been cooped up here long enough."

Celine exchanged a glance with Julia. That had been far easier than they'd expected.

She turned in time to see Clara's head slowly pivoting toward her. "Would you take me for a walk, Celine?" She peered closely at Celine. "You are Celine, aren't you? Jonah said you'd be coming."

When Celine nodded, Clara continued: "Give me a minute to change. I'll be out in a jiffy."

Seeing her lurch toward the bathroom, Sandy wrenched herself out of the stupor she'd fallen into.

"Careful, Ms. Hibbert, you can't go to the bathroom by yourself."

"Thought you couldn't tell them what to do or not do," Julia muttered. Celine stifled a grin. Sandy had forgotten her own rule.

"Sure I can. I can do anything I please." Clara tipped her head back defiantly. The movement made her totter. Celine bit her lip, itching to rush to Clara's aid but prevented from doing so by Sister Catherine's urgent:

Don't do it, Celine. You'll shatter the delicate trust she's built toward you. Just let it go. She'll be fine.

But she could fall, Celine remonstrated.

"Doesn't she have a walker?" she whispered, leaning in toward Sandy. The receptionist nodded.

Pulling the walker out from behind the couch, Sandy wheeled it to Clara.

"It might be a good idea to use this. Dr. Roth asked that you do." To Celine's relief, Clara accepted the walker without any resistance, allowing Sandy to help her into the bathroom.

Once Clara was safely in, Julia repeated her offer to clean the room.

"I'm not sure that's such a good idea, Ms. Hood." Sandy looked profoundly uncomfortable.

"Julia," The former fed insisted. "Call me Julia. And I disagree. It's an excellent idea."

Sandy continued to protest. There were strict protocols against such a thing. What would the Executive Director and the Resident Care Director say when they heard?

But Celine could see she was reaching for excuses. And Julia remained undeterred.

Rolling up her sleeves, the former fed did a slow spin about the room.

"Just show me the supply closet."

"Very well." Heaving a sigh, Sandy walked over to the narrow broom closet that separated the kitchenette from the entrance, concealing it from anyone standing at the front door.

She'd barely touched the closet handle when a shrill shriek startled them, sending a jolt of nervous electricity up Celine's spine.

"No! No! Stay away from there!" Clara screamed making Sandy jump. "No! No! Get away from here, robber. Thief!"

Flustered by the commotion, Sandy hastily dropped her hand.

"Well, it's all in there, brooms and other stuff," she began, but Clara's screeches cut into her remark.

"No, no! Get away! Now! Go, go!" Clara flung her arms in the direction of the door.

"I guess I'll leave you to it." White-faced and embarrassed, Sandy fled.

Clara's shrieking stopped as suddenly as it had started. She smiled sweetly at Celine, the receptionist and her terrible faux pas forgotten.

"Well, are you ready to go out?"

Celine hesitated. Was it worth mentioning that Julia intended to tidy the room?

She has Alzheimer's, Celine, Sister Mary Catherine said. *You need to be especially careful about not treading on her toes.*

Gripping the edge of the small breakfast table, Celine tipped her head in Julia's direction. "I asked Julia to help me spruce up your apartment. Is that okay?"

Clara's brow wrinkled. "I'm not sure what Jonah would say to that."

Dear Lord, what am I to say to that? Celine tapped her foot, seeking inspiration.

"Actually, it was Jonah who asked us to help out," Julia chimed in.

Clara turned to her, puzzled. "Who are you?"

"Julia." The former fed pointed to Celine. "Celine's friend, remember?"

Clara turned to Celine, her lips stretching into a happy smile. "Jonah said you'd come. Can we go for a walk now?"

Chapter Twenty-Nine

It was only one o'clock, but Ella had assured Blake he could check in earlier than the usual 3 p.m. check-in time. Blake thanked his lucky stars for that.

He parked his car, retrieved his laptop case and luggage from the trunk, and headed for the elegant black front door. With its enormous verandah and façade of white siding, the Norwalk River Inn resembled a mansion from a bygone era.

Inside, the place was just as opulent with a broad staircase sweeping up to the upper floors at the back of a large lobby. Chairs surrounded a massive marble fireplace on the left. The check-in desk manned by a pimply-faced youth was on the right.

"Are you planning on cooking, sir?" the young man asked as he swiped Blake's credit card.

"I beg your pardon?" What kind of hotel had Ella checked him into?

The desk clerk looked up. "Every suite is equipped with a kitchenette sir, and the one in the Hoyt Suite is especially fine. If you wanted to cook—"

"I don't," Blake interrupted the teenager. But his question reminded Blake he hadn't eaten since his meager breakfast that morning. "Isn't there a dining room in this place?"

"Afraid not." The boy—his name was Job—looked suitably apologetic. "But there is a Mexican Food Truck over at the park half a mile away."

Blake made a face. He was in no mood to walk or drive anywhere. And he didn't trust New England Mexican to be anywhere near as flavorful as the authentic Mexican he'd sampled in California.

"Anything else?"

"J.B.'s Deli & Pizza on Tierney Street delivers," Job told him.

"That'll do." Taking his key and asking Job to have a large Buffalo chicken pizza delivered to his room, Blake prepared to mount the staircase. The place had no elevators, apparently.

"We've tried to stay true to the 1750s look of the original farmhouse," Job had said earnestly. The farmhouse had been converted into an inn in the 1790s.

"Great! Does that mean I have to use an outhouse?"

That elicited a chuckle from the boy. "Oh no, sir. Each suite has an attached bath with modern plumbing and hot and cold water."

Fifteen minutes later with the pizza on the leather ottoman that served as a coffee table, Blake settled himself into one of the two bamboo occasional chairs in the living room and scoured the Internet for any information he could find on the Lowell Museum.

He took a large bite out of his pizza, savoring the spiciness of the Buffalo sauce that coated the chicken, and stared at the pictures of the three-story brick building on Pinckney Street. It had once been the home of art dealer Philip Pendleton.

Pendleton had converted his home into an art museum in the 1920s when the Great Depression was raging and many of his clients had been forced to sell their art. Rather than turn around and sell the works he'd acquired, Pendleton had hung each painting on his walls, allowing members of the public free access to his art collection.

It wasn't a sustainable operation and before long Pendleton had needed an infusion of money to keep it going. The necessary funds had come from Elizabeth Lowell Putnam who in return had requested that the museum be renamed for her grandfather, John Lowell.

The exterior of the museum had a quaint appearance that no one had thought to correct. Pinckney Street angled up, and the steps leading up to each front door slanted up at a noticeable angle from the brick-paved sidewalk as well.

But the interior had been thoroughly modernized and was suitably climate-controlled to house its sizeable collection.

Pendleton had left behind a vast collection of art—much of it financed by Elizabeth Lowell Putnam. The Lowell had acquired the rest as a result of bequests from wealthy art collectors who presumably had no one to leave their collection to.

It was a small museum, not particularly well known. But Blake wasn't buying the story that the Lowell was so lacking in funds, they'd had to let go of the Degas to pay for the restoration they'd commissioned on it. Even in the nineties, the Degas had been worth several hundred thousand dollars.

Why give it to the restorer? Why not sell it and use some of the funds to pay the guy?

Nope, something wasn't adding up. Finishing his pizza, he tapped out the Lowell's number on his phone and waited for his call to be picked up.

✵

Celine gently cradled Clara's elbow as they stepped out of the elevator and steered a course across the lobby toward the patio door. Sandy was checking in visitors but still managed to notice them.

Much to Celine's relief, the encounter went off smoothly.

"Nice to see you, Ms. Hibbert!" Sandy called cheerfully. Whatever discomfiture she may have felt had clearly long evaporated. "Enjoy your walk."

Clara, too, had forgotten her earlier anger at the receptionist and returned Sandy's sunny greeting with a wave and a smile.

"I feel bad not recalling her name," she confided to Celine. "She always makes it a point to say hello when she's visiting her father."

In Clara-speak that meant Sandy spent time with her, Celine guessed. She'd learned not to take everything Clara said at face value, but to look instead for the kernel of truth underlying her words.

"Her name's Sandy and she does seem very friendly," she said out loud.

Few people—professionally trained or not—would've recovered their composure as well as Sandy had after a rough encounter with a patient.

But Sandy was ready to forgive—and forget.

The best attitude to adopt with an Alzheimer's patient, Celine had learned.

"And she doesn't keep telling me Jonah is dead," Clara said as Celine helped her onto the patio. She turned to Celine. "Because he isn't, you know."

Celine pressed her lips tightly together. There was no point setting Clara off. But how could she confirm an outright lie?

It's not exactly a lie, my dear, her guardian angel pointed out. *His soul is alive.*

Yes, but his body is not, she responded impatiently.

She turned to find Clara's blue eyes and pleasant features gazing expectantly up at her. Unwilling to substantiate an utter lie, Celine hedged.

"What do you and Jonah do when he visits?"

The question served its purpose. Eyes brightening, Clara smiled.

"We sit there and chat." She pointed to the pergola.

Celine's gaze followed her pointing finger.

The metal garden chairs and tables that had been cleared for the yoga session were now back in place—artfully scattered around the pergola. Potted poinsettias, set under the pillars, added a touch of bright color to the stark white landscape surrounding it.

Clara's head pivoted back to Celine. "Can we go there now? It's been a while since I've enjoyed the fresh air."

I'm not surprised, Celine thought. *Jonah's been dead these six months.*

Be careful not to dismiss her impressions, Celine, Sister Mary Catherine warned. *She really does see him.*

"Too cold for Jonah to bring you out?" Celine asked, making an effort to humor Clara's need to discuss her son.

Gripping Clara's elbow, she guided her small, round form to the edge of the patio.

"Oh, I don't mind the cold," Clara assured her. "Neither does Jonah. But it's not safe. Jonah says it isn't safe to leave the room."

It was advice Celine could agree with—assuming Jonah had provided it. With Clara's balance issues, it wouldn't be safe to leave the room by herself.

But was there more to the advice?

After all, there were any number of nurses on hand to accompany residents on a walk. And from what Sandy had said, they'd made every effort to encourage Clara to stroll the grounds. To no avail.

Something was different today.

Questions churning through her mind, Celine regarded Clara. Her plump form was bent forward as she gingerly lowered a foot onto the stone steps that descended to the ground.

Was it possible, Jonah had set his mother on guard to protect the evidence he'd concealed in her apartment? Her banshee-like shrieks were loud enough to bring every staff member running to her apartment.

And as a living person—albeit elderly and frail—she had a better chance at keeping intruders out of the room than her dead son.

"O-oo-h!"

Feeling Clara stumble on the icy step, Celine tightened her hold on the older woman's elbow. "Are you okay?" she asked anxiously.

Clara nodded but there was a grimace on her face. She rolled up her sleeve, vigorously rubbing her elbow where an angry red bruise had formed.

Celine's eyes widened. Had that been her doing? "I'm sorry," she began, but Clara waved the apology aside.

"It's not your fault. I have thin skin. It bruises easily."

She shrugged her shoulder out of her thick, blue paisley-patterned jacket to reveal red splotches in various stages of healing on her upper arm. "See?"

Celine's breath caught in her throat. "How did you get those, Clara?"

Clara looked puzzled. "I don't remember. It must've . . . "

Her voice faded out. To her horror, Celine found her own fingers digging deep into Clara's soft shoulders as she shook the woman hard.

Where is it, you stupid cow? Where did your son tell you he kept it?

Clara's plump jowls shuddered, her blue eyes were round with alarm.

"Celine? Are you listening? Celine?"

The images that had filled Celine's head faded. Still rubbing her elbow, Clara stared up at her, nonplussed.

"What is it? You look like you've seen a ghost."

"I feel like I've seen a ghost." Celine attempted a smile.

The vision had left her shaken. Clara was being physically abused—had been abused at least once—for something her son may have entrusted to her.

For heaven's sake, Jonah, how could you do this to her?

Was it a visitor? A doctor? Or one of the staff?

How were they ever going to find out?

Chapter Thirty

Remember the clock's ticking!

Her undercover mentor's advice replayed in Julia's mind. She draped her jacket on the back of the white chair at the tiny breakfast table and eyed the supply closet Sandy had pointed out.

Was that a good place to start her search?

Tall and narrow, it flanked the faux granite countertop, bookending the kitchenette.

It wasn't the most secure hiding place. On the other hand, Clara's reaction had been quite telling—assuming it wasn't simply the result of her condition.

Identify the most likely place and begin there, Julia. Her mentor's voice rang in her ears.

Jesus, what was the most likely place in this excruciatingly tiny apartment? So small, only the seven dwarves would've considered it spacious. What the heck was—?

The bed. She swiveled around to regard the white comforter with its printed blue floral pattern. Two plump pillows rested against the white headboard.

No, too obvious—even for someone as lacking in common sense as Jonah.

Under the mattress?

Maybe. She strode over to the bed, straightening out the comforter, fluffing up the pillows, and then with a quick glance at the front door, she slid a hand under the mattress.

Nada.

But the need to be thorough—drilled into her at Quantico—made her pull the mattress up. It was only a full, but it was heavy. Grunting from the effort, she managed to heft it to an upright position.

Okay, nothing. Where now?

Time is against you in a covert search, Julia. Consider your target's intelligence—or lack thereof.

The bathroom? There were a couple of potential spots that would make excellent hiding places. But was Jonah smart enough to have thought of them?

Likely not.

There was a tiny walk-in closet that led to the bathroom. Another possible location. But Julia's mind—and eyes— kept returning to the supply closet.

Clara had burst into a full-blown hissy fit at the mere sight of Sandy reaching for the closet door. She'd abruptly stopped screeching the minute Sandy had skedaddled out the front door.

Yup, right there, Julia decided.

It was just the kind of idiotic place a cocksure jackass like Jonah would choose. Probably figuring no one was clever enough to discover it.

She swiftly crossed the room, grabbed the handle, and yanked open the closet door.

A heavy, musty smell assailed her. Covering her nostrils, Julia surveyed the contents. A green-handled broom with a white dustpan attached to the handle. Near it, a bucket with a sponge or two inside it. Spray bottles of window cleaner and all-purpose cleaner.

Nothing out of the ordinary really. Other than an open box of blue nitrile gloves. The kind that nursing staff wore. That caught Julia's eye.

She plucked it off the shelf, shook it, and shoved her hand through the slit, groping inside it. There didn't seem to be anything other than the gloves. Still, it was a curious find.

Left behind during a routine medical visit? Or had someone, interrupted in their search, hurriedly stuffed the box back here?

Julia took a picture of it and pulled out a pair of gloves for herself before replacing it.

Never leave any traces of your search, Julia, her mentor had impressed upon her.

Everything needed to be returned to its place. But she also wanted to be sure not to leave fingerprints. Just in case anything she discovered became material evidence in a case.

Fingers encased in the gloves now, she began shifting items around inside the closet. *Okay, Jonah, where is it?* The dead man had clearly possessed more ingenuity than she'd given him credit for.

It was at the back of the closet that she found something unusual.

It stood out just as the disposable nursing gloves had.

❧

Julia studied the heavily rusted, rickety stepladder she'd discovered.

Who had brought it here? Jonah? Or a member of Hutchinson House's staff who'd been intent on searching Clara's studio?

The gloves she'd found ruled out a visitor, although, at this juncture, it would be premature to close off that possibility entirely.

She dragged the stepladder out.

It clattered open easily—too easily, perhaps. It closed just as easily. One leg seemed a tad shorter than the other.

Unsteady. Not the kind of thing you'd expect a frail, elderly woman—especially one with balance issues—to use.

Julia opened it and closed it several times, even lifting it up to look at the metal tubes that made up the side rails.

The rubber anti-slip foot on one of them had come off, making it shorter than the other. But the metal tube wasn't hollow, making it impossible to hide anything there.

Thwack!

The sound startled her, making the hairs on the nape of her neck rise up. Had someone entered the room—undetected?

She spun around, adrenaline pumping through her veins.

The room was empty, the front door still closed. But her teal jacket now lay in a sprawling heap on the floor.

Julia chuckled. It was the soft slap of her jacket hitting the floor that she'd heard.

Crossing the room, she retrieved the jacket and slung it over the backrest. It slid off almost immediately. Julia frowned, plucking it off the floor a second time.

It fell yet again. What the hell was going on here?

The curtain rustled. An apple rolled out of the white ceramic bowl on the breakfast table, coming precariously close to knocking the slender vase and the rose it held off the table.

She stood still. Her skin crawled with the creepy sensation of being closely watched.

"Jonah?" Her voice came out in a croak.

She'd killed him. Was he here to take revenge?

The thought spooked her. But she had no intention of letting him see he'd rattled her.

Don't feed the fear.

Another warning from her instructors.

Whatever you do, Julia, don't let them see you're afraid, her mentor had emphasized when she started working undercover.

"Listen, Jonah! I'm sorry about what happened. But I'm here to help now. I'm on your side. Clara's in danger. Celine's been sensing it for a long time."

The apple wavered, rocking slightly from side to side, before coming to a standstill.

"If you're really here"—God, she felt so stupid doing this—"why don't you make yourself useful? Tell me what you've hidden. Tell me where it is."

The blue floral-patterned curtains hanging from the cornice above the window streamed into the room, floating on a barely perceptible current of air.

Intrigued, Julia walked over. She'd slid the window open earlier, but there was barely a rustle of wind outside. The linen curtains were made of heavy fabric, too thick to be moved by a gentle breeze.

Grabbing the curtains, Julia felt along the length of the fabric. There was nothing under the lining. She ran her hand along the broad hem. Nothing there either.

She stifled a grunt of impatience. Couldn't Jonah be a little more direct?

"All right," she said aloud, "so it's near her bed. Her nightstand?"

Lowering herself onto the bed, Julia pulled out one drawer after another. Dental floss, breath mints, throat lozenges, and a change purse jostled for space in the top drawer.

Tucked under them was a hardcover Bible, the roses pictured on it faded and worn.

Julia pulled it out. *The Woman's Daily Bible*, she read the title.

If it was Clara's, she'd read it avidly at one time only to give up on the good book. The first few chapters were thickly highlighted. But somewhere in the middle, the highlighting had stopped.

"You didn't get your atheism from your mother, did you, Jonah?" Julia murmured.

The middle drawer contained several used bottles of nail polish in vivid shades of red and pink. Remnants from Clara's days as a working mother. She'd been a receptionist, Julia recalled.

Was it at an insurance company or a corporate law firm that investigated insurance fraud?

Julia wasn't sure, but it was something to do with insurance.

An unremarkable maroon leather case—the kind more likely to be owned by a man—occupied the left side of the drawer. Julia unzipped it.

She found a pair of nail scissors, nail clippers, and a small file for fingernails and a larger one for toenails. A clear plastic pocket held an old, faded color photograph of Clara on her wedding day, folded in half so you couldn't see the groom.

Curious, Julia extracted the photo.

The bride—slender and vivacious—stood on the steps of a church, smiling happily at the camera. Julia turned it over to see the other side. Clara's husband, tall and nondescript, stood unsmiling beside his bride. Obviously the marriage hadn't stood the test of time.

Replacing the photo, Julia returned the leather case to the drawer.

The bottom drawer contained more odds and ends. An old desk calendar, a roll of string, some cheap jewelry. Under them all was an eight-by-eight sheet of thick photo paper.

Julia pulled it out and turned it over. She stared at the black-and-white group portrait taken in front of what appeared to be an office building.

Clara, plump but still pretty, was recognizable in the center front row.

A tall, handsome man with a patrician air stood beside her, one arm thrown casually around her shoulders, the other draped in a friendly fashion around the shoulders of a male employee.

An untidy inscription was scrawled in black at the bottom of the picture. Julia held it up to the light, struggling to read the words.

It took about thirty seconds to decipher Clara's writing.

With my boss, Henry Dodd.

Dodd? Clara had known Henry Dodd?

Julia's fingers tightened around the edge of the photo. Her mind buzzed with questions.

As his receptionist, how much had Clara known about Dodd's involvement with the Gardner? Was it Dodd—not Norton—who along with the General had masterminded the theft?

If so, was this photograph the clue Jonah had discovered and hidden? The gloves she'd found and the stepladder clearly indicated an illicit search. Had Clara's room been ransacked for this?

Photograph your finds. Don't take anything, her mentor had warned. *Ill-gotten evidence is the fruit of the poisonous tree.*

But Julia was reluctant to let the picture go. Yes, it would be best to put it back; to let a routine search of the room—sanctioned by a warrant—yield it up.

But then, what grounds did they have for a warrant? Someone was after Clara—and the secrets she held.

It was only a matter of time before the photograph was found and made to disappear.

No, Julia wasn't willing to take that risk. Clara would never know it was gone. And by the time the case went to trial, they'd figure out a way to make the evidence stick.

Mind made up, Julia closed the drawer and walked over to her jacket. Unzipping an inner pocket, she slipped the photo into it.

The curtain rustled again. Clearly, Jonah approved.

Chapter Thirty-One

"We've been awaiting your call, Special Agent Markham," Arthur Bentley, Senior Curator and Acting Director of the Lowell, wheezed into Blake's ear the moment he identified himself. "It's been a full two days since the news came out."

So, he'd read the *Post* article.

Blake wondered where the Director was only to be told that "Dietmar," a German hire, had been caught replacing originals with fakes to finance his lavish lifestyle.

"Fortunately, he hadn't been able to sell more than three before we discovered the truth. And we've been able to recover all three," Bentley said in his high-pitched voice.

"Was Dietmar around in the 1990s?" Blake asked.

There was a pause. "Well, I suppose he must have been."

What the heck did that mean? Blake was about to ask when Bentley clarified:

"I mean he's in his thirties, so he was born sometime in that era."

Blake stifled his impatience. "Were you with the Lowell at the time? In 1998," he specified, "when the Degas was stolen."

"Oh, yes, I'd been with the Lowell about eight years by that time. I was a relatively young man. Only forty-three. Just promoted to Senior Curator. I'm sixty-five now."

"So you would know," Blake persisted, "if the Degas belonged to the Lowell at the time or not, wouldn't you?"

There was another pause.

"Well, yes and no," Bentley hedged.

Blake couldn't restrain himself any longer. "What the heck is that supposed to mean?" His voice rose, frustrated. "Either it did or it didn't. Which is it?"

He heard an audible whoosh of breath.

"Well, it's a complicated story."

"Try me," Blake said.

"The Sullivans didn't know the first thing about pastels. That was quite evident when they first reached out to us in 1995 for advice on restoring the work. It had been hanging in strong light, the glass on the frame the original glass Degas had chosen. No UV protection at all. The colors were fading.

"We made some suggestions for restoration and maintenance, but the Sullivans had begun to realize owning a pastel entailed more than they—or Junior, their heir—could handle. They made it over to us with the stipulation that they would retain possession of it until their deaths. At which time, of course, the Lowell would take ownership."

"So, technically, the Degas was yours when it was stolen?"

"Technically, yes. Although the Sullivans would keep paying the premiums to have it insured against both damage and theft. Upon their deaths, the Lowell would add the work to our insurance policy."

"Were any papers drawn up to that effect?" Blake wanted to know. This situation was getting more complicated by the minute.

"No, Special Agent. It was an agreement between gentlemen, settled by a handshake."

"But you affixed a label to the back of the work so there'd be no doubt to whom the Degas really belonged?"

"Yes, and the Sullivans changed their will to reflect that transfer of ownership."

"It was a simple transfer?" Blake leaned forward, staring intently at the screen. Had that furnished the motive for the theft? "No money changed hands?"

"That's correct, Special Agent. I'm assuming you've seen the work. Is it genuine? Will the current owner be willing to return it to us?"

Blake tackled the easier question first. "It looks genuine enough." He shared Sarah Williams' insights and explained the further tests the work would be subject to.

"Excellent! Excellent!" Bentley said approvingly, then returned to the more pressing question. "When can we expect the work back, Special Agent? In a month, perhaps?"

Blake cradled his aching forehead in his hands, digging his fingers deep into his brows.

"Did the Sullivans tell you they accepted the insurance payout for the work when it was stolen?"

"Oh, yes. We were told the insurance company had paid up. The Sullivans had no idea whether—or even when—the work would ever be recovered.

There was no question of indefinitely paying premiums on a work they didn't even possess."

So the Sullivans had chickened out of explaining the full implications of their decision. God, how had he managed to get himself into the miserable situation of having to be the one to break the bad news?

Blake took a deep breath, and then blew it out.

"You're not going to like this, but when the Sullivans agreed to accept the insurance payout, they also agreed that the Degas—if and when it was recovered—would now belong to the insurer."

"B-but," Bentley stammered. "But that's not fair, Special Agent. We had an agreement."

"Rendered null and void by Sullivan's decision to accept payment," Blake said. "You're sure there was no paperwork drawn up to back up what you've just told me?"

"Well, I can look, but no, I'm quite certain there was not."

"There's just one other thing," Blake added, recalling the faded red stamp on the Lowell Museum sticker on the back of the pastel. "Which restoration company did you use when the Lowells first contacted you?"

"It was no company, Special Agent. The work was done in-house by our conservators. We pride ourselves on that."

"And if the Sullivans had needed any further restoration after what you initially did—?" Blake probed.

"They'd have reached out to us, of course."

Chapter Thirty-Two

Sunlight slanted into the pergola bathing them in a pleasant glow. Clara had been quiet since they'd settled into their chairs. Celine was itching to discover what she knew but had no idea how to direct the conversation where she wanted it.

Keep her talking about Jonah, Celine, Sister Mary Catherine advised. *She likes talking about him.*

"Is Jonah working on anything interesting for his newspaper?" Celine finally asked.

Clara shook her head. "He doesn't talk to me about his work."

"No?" She was about to ask what he did like talking about when Clara volunteered the information herself.

"He likes discussing the old days."

"The old days?" Celine repeated in what she hoped was an encouraging tone.

Clara nodded. "Yes, when I used to work for Dodd."

"Dodd?" Celine's back stiffened. "You don't mean Henry Dodd, do you?"

"That's the one. He sold life insurance. Started the company himself. *Dodd's Life Insurance.* But despite all that, he was a most unassuming person. He helped us quite a bit when Fred—that's Jonah's father—ran off with a much younger woman."

Not wanting Clara to veer off onto a monologue on her ex, Celine steered the conversation back to Dodd. "What else did Dodd do?"

Clara frowned. "Well, he was on the board of that museum—you know the one?" She turned to Celine, brow furrowed. "The one that got its art stolen?"

"The Gardner?"

"Yes. Jonah liked talking about that museum. We did get to visit a few times. Henry Dodd would send a car for us. I still remember the first time. Oh, how excited Jonah was! He was only eleven."

"Did he have a favorite painting?" Celine meant Jonah, but Clara must have been thinking about Dodd when she replied. A whiff of expensive cologne assailed Celine's nostrils—one of Clara's pervasive memories of the man she'd worked for.

"You know the one of a man in a black suit and a top hat?"

Clara gesticulated, struggling to capture in words the portrait she was seeing in her mind's eye. But Celine caught a glimpse of the image in her mind.

Dear God, it was the Manet. Clara was describing Chez Tortoni.

"Henry really liked that one, you know."

"Yes, I do," Celine quietly responded, noting that Clara had switched to using his first name.

She studied the woman sitting across from her. It couldn't possibly have been Clara who'd called the *Post* and the FBI hotline, could it?

But Clara had been close to Dodd.

Close enough, apparently, to be on first-name terms with the man. Close enough to know whether or not he was behind the biggest art heist of the previous century?

"They should've insured the art," Clara reminisced. "Henry always said that. It annoyed him so much when they stubbornly refused his advice."

"What did Jonah say when you told him that?"

Clara shrugged, her eyes taking in the snow-blanketed grounds. "Oh, he jotted a few notes in his little leather notebook. You know how he was."

"Yes, I do." So Jonah had been interested in these details, and Clara had been only too happy to reminisce about the old days.

Seeing her opportunity, Celine made a show of surveying the grounds. "By the way, where is Jonah now? Chasing a story?"

"Oh, no, my dear. Jonah's dead." Clara gazed steadily into Celine's eyes. "There's no chasing stories where he is now. You know that, don't you?"

Celine cringed, waiting for the long wail, the weeping, and the screamed accusations.

It's your fault he's dead. Your fault.

But Clara's smile remained stretched into a beatific smile.

"You must tell your friend to look harder. Jonah says she needs to do a better job looking."

Celine looked around her, but if Jonah was lingering near them, she couldn't sense his presence.

"He's still with your friend. She needs to do a better job looking."

❧

"Ms. Hibbert! It's time for your lunch."

The voice, flat and harsh, barely concealing its impatience, jolted Celine out of her calm. In the peace of her mind, a murder of crows burst abruptly into flight, filling her senses with darkness.

Eyes wide, she spun around at the same moment as Clara, wide-eyed and alarmed, twisted her head to face the intruder.

"Beth?" It was her nemesis from the wine tour.

Celine took in the slender blonde's maroon shirt and the brass name tag pinned to it. *Nurse Hogan.*

"You work here?"

Beth hadn't mentioned she was a nurse or that she worked at the Hutchinson House. Not that Celine was entitled to her life story, but it was odd considering how much Beth had gleaned about her life from the media.

"Yes." Beth's lips curled. "What are you doing here?"

She was carrying a wooden tray, Celine noticed, with a full plate—mashed potatoes, steamed carrots, peas, beans, and some type of meat encased in a dark sauce. It wasn't gourmet food, but it was substantial.

"She's here to see me," Clara said, her chin jutting out defiantly. "She's my son Jonah's friend."

"Oh, yeah?" Beth muttered. Her blue eyes were venomous. *Some friend. Let's face it, you're here to mine her memories.*

The words were audible to Celine even though Beth's lips hadn't uttered them. Her throat constricted at the undercurrent of menace that swirled like a dark fog around the nurse's presence.

"Visiting hours are over, by the way." She thrust the tray out at Clara. "Ms. Hibbert needs to eat her lunch, take her meds, and take a nap. Doctor's orders."

Clara shook her head adamantly, but Celine felt the fear radiating from her.

"I'm not eating that." She looked at Celine. "I don't want to eat that."

"She needs to have her meds," Beth repeated flatly. "And they need to be taken with food."

"Maybe we can find something in the dining room," Celine suggested. "Would you like to do that, Clara?"

"Suit yourself, but you're not going to find anything different there." Beth jerked the tray forward. "This is what's on the menu. Take it or leave it."

Celine had heard enough.

"Are you always this brusque with your patients?" She stared squarely into Beth's eyes. "I don't think the Executive Director will be too pleased to hear that. And it doesn't take a psychic to know that being fired three weeks into a new job won't exactly make you a dream candidate for any future employment opportunities."

"Look." Beth heaved a weary sigh, pressing the tray close to her midriff. "I'm just trying to do my job. If she doesn't eat, doesn't take her meds, guess whose job is on the line? Yours truly."

Celine held out her hand. "Give me whatever medication Clara needs. I'll make sure she takes them."

Beth's lips thinned into a grimace. "Fine. But what am I supposed to do with this tray?" She lowered her gaze; an expression of disgust flickered over her features as though she were looking at a plate full of vomit.

"Can't it be a given to another resident?"

Of course not, Celine. It's doctored. Sister Mary Catherine's voice erupted out of nowhere.

Startled, Celine reached out to take the tray from Beth's hands, but the nurse jerked it out of her reach.

"Never mind that. There's a five mg dose of Aricept in my pocket. And a dose of Metamine. See that she takes both—either before or after she eats."

Minutes later, as they made their way to the dining room, Clara leaned closer to Celine and whispered: "You have to watch out for her. She's a bad one."

Celine studied Beth's slim figure as it disappeared through the doorway.

She recalled the way the woman had questioned her about the Gardner art back in Paso Robles. Her presence here was a troubling coincidence.

She's not the real threat here, Celine, Sister Mary Catherine whispered into her ear. *She's but a pawn in the hands of others.*

Chapter Thirty-Three

The distinctive click of the door latch releasing caught Julia's ear. Her left hand—busily replacing the fruit that Jonah had tumbled out of its bowl yet again—stilled for a fraction of a second.

Then with a rapidity born of long practice she whipped around, bringing her right hand to her hip—only to recall she'd left her weapon in the car. Damn!

Julia's hand was still resting on her hip when the door opened and Sandy poked her head in.

"Hey, Julia! How's it going? Everything okay? I w—"

"You've really got to stop doing that."

Heart still thundering from the unexpected intrusion, Julia glared at the young receptionist.

"I realize Clara isn't in her right mind—probably a bit of a pain in the tush. But she's entitled to her privacy. You can't—"

Before Julia could finish, a firm thrust pushed the door farther back. A stately black woman with a mass of curly hair strode into the room, leaving the receptionist clinging to the door, her blue eyes wide.

"Sandy was acting under my orders," Stately explained crisply. Built along the lines of an aircraft carrier, she loomed over Julia and Sandy. "Every member of our staff is authorized to enter a resident's room when the resident in question either doesn't respond to our calls and knocks or when we hear unusual sounds."

Her brown eyes regarded Julia steadily before shifting pointedly to Julia's left hand still resting upon the fruit on the tiny breakfast table.

Damn! Julia silently cursed Jonah under her breath. He was more trouble dead than alive.

Stately's gaze returned to Julia.

"We value our residents' privacy. But their safety and well-being, as I'm sure you'll understand, is even more important. Especially with a patient as non-compliant as Ms. Hibbert seems to be."

"Yup." Julia nodded. "Sure." She forced a sheepish smile onto her lips. "I'm just having a tough time keeping the fruit in its bowl. There seems to be an art to stacking it that I haven't yet acquired."

For some reason, Jonah had been reluctant to allow her to return to the supply closet and resume her task.

"I'm supposed to be cleaning, dammit!" she'd hissed. It was also the only way she could search Clara's apartment for any further evidence.

But from the time she'd pocketed the photo with Clara and Henry Dodd, Jonah had been playing tricks on her. Was he against her taking the photograph?

Too bad! Julia was determined not to leave without it.

"Let me help," Sandy offered, undraping herself from the door she'd been clinging to. She scurried over to the table and busied herself.

Stately held out her hand. "Sheila Cooke, Resident Care Director for Hutchinson House. And you are?"

Julia allowed her hand to be gripped, trying not to wince as Cooke squeezed it hard enough to crush the bones.

"Julia Hood. Former FBI." Out of force of habit, she withdrew her badge from the clip holder attached to the belt loop on her jeans.

"FBI!" Cooke's eyebrows lifted. Her gaze traveled over the tiny studio. "Were you expecting to find anything here?"

"I beg your pardon?" Julia deadpanned. How the heck had Cooke cottoned onto what she was up to?

"It looks like you were searching Ms. Hibbert's room, Special Agent Hood. Does this have anything to do with her son's death?" Cooke's eyes were like shiny brown beads of suspicion.

"It looks like nothing of the sort," Julia countered firmly. "And it's Ms. Hood—or Julia, if you like. Not Special Agent Hood. I'm retired."

She tipped her head at Sandy, who was still dealing with the fruit. "Sandy here told me Clara was giving the staff a hard time about having her room cleaned. So I offered to do it."

"And, in case you're wondering," she added, "I'm a close friend of the woman who's currently footing Clara's bills."

Cooke's lips were still pursed, but she accepted the explanation without comment.

"For safety reasons, we don't allow visitors to clean or tidy residents' apartments." Cooke cast another glance around the room. "If something were to disappear, Hutchinson House would be held accountable. An untenable position, as I'm sure you'll understand, and one that could open us up to a lawsuit."

"Clara may not like a stranger handling her things," Julia said mildly. Sheila Cooke was far more perceptive than she'd given her credit for.

A worthy opponent. Albeit, a rather annoying one.

Cooke's lips stretched for the first time into a small smile.

"Well, in that case, let me send one of our orderlies up to oversee the proceedings."

"Fine," Julia said. *If that's how you'd like to play it, fine.*

"While you're at it, could you replace that rickety old stepladder in the supply closet? It's falling to pieces, and if something were to happen to Clara while using it, I can promise you, there'd be no escaping the lawsuit that would ensue. Ms. Skye is a wealthy woman."

Cooke's nostrils flared, but she stiffly tipped her chin down in acquiescence.

"Take care of it, Sandy, would you?"

Obediently, Sandy rushed to the supply closet. But she vehemently shook her head as soon as she opened it.

"Oh, that's not ours. Ms. Hibbert's son brought that in. It's her stepladder from where they lived."

"In that case," Cooke declared triumphantly, "you'll need her permission to replace it. We encourage residents to bring their belongings."

Sandy threw Julia an apologetic smile "It gives the place a more intimate, homey feel."

"I'll take it up with Clara," Julia grimly promised.

What had Jonah been thinking, bringing that damned stepladder here? If she didn't know any better, Julia would've surmised he was desperately hoping to get his mother out of the way.

But whatever else you could say about the reporter, you couldn't fault his devotion to his mother. He'd been insufferable. A whining, bellyaching pain-in-the-neck. But he'd genuinely cared for Clara.

Still, why hadn't the staff or Cooke herself—so obsessed with patient safety discouraged Jonah from leaving what was practically a death trap in his mother's apartment?

&

"A search warrant?"

Special Agent-in-Charge Walsh didn't sound too happy at the prospect of convincing a judge to authorize a search of Henry Dodd's properties—his home in Norwalk, the offices of his life insurance company in Boston, and any warehouses or storage units he owned.

"Are you sure we have enough evidence to justify such a request, Markham?"

Blake sighed. This was typical Walsh. The SAC tended to be over-cautious whenever there was the slightest prospect of inconveniencing anyone with pretensions to being one of New England's elite.

"Sir," he prepared to repeat the information he'd already provided. "Dodd bought the painting exactly three months before the Sullivans received their insurance payout, at a time when the work still belonged to the Lowell Museum."

"You're assuming Dodd knew the work was stolen, Markham." Walsh's tone was unusually brusque. There was nothing the man liked less than being forced to hold the powerful accountable for their misdeeds. "What evidence do we have of that? Zero. Nothing."

Blake gritted his teeth, resenting the reminder of how little he had in the way of solid evidence. But they had enough for probable cause. And a thorough search might yield something useful.

He was about to point this out, but the SAC wasn't done speaking. His voice rose as he hammered home his points.

"What we do know, Markham, is that it was never on any relevant database as a stolen item. The ALR had no idea of its existence, for God's sake, let alone that it was gone. There's really nothing to suggest Dodd didn't purchase the work in good faith."

Nothing? Seriously? Nothing? Jesus F—in' Christ! Was the SAC deliberately acting dense?

Clutching the phone to his ear, Blake put his legs up on the leather ottoman, on either side of the large pizza box that contained the remnants of his lunch.

"It would've been a simple matter to check out the provenance, sir. The Lowell Museum attached a sticker on the back of the pastel. I've seen it. It strikes me as highly suspicious that Dodd never sought to check out the story he was fed: that an inability to pay its restoration fees compelled the museum to yield the work up to the restorer. Even in the 1990s, it was worth several times more than the ostensible restoration fees they owed."

Blake jabbed his finger into the air before him—a gesture lost on the SAC, who couldn't see him, of course.

"A simple phone call to the Lowell would have sufficed to ascertain the truth. The man's an art collector, native to Boston. There's no reason not to recognize the museum." Heck, even he had recognized it.

Even the SAC—a philistine if ever there was one—knew of the Lowell.

"Not to mention, the Lowell has an in-house restoration program." Surely someone like Dodd would've known that.

There was pin-drop silence, but Blake could sense the SAC's meager defenses crumbling. He thrust home his advantage.

"Who knows whether he commissioned the theft himself or knowingly bought a hot item? But the fact is Dodd's clearly in possession of a stolen item. He's a Degas aficionado. Isn't it possible he might have the Gardner's Degas sketches as well? Or the Manet?"

Blake heard the rustling of paper.

"Does this have anything to do with the story in the *Post*, Markham?" There was a brief pause, then: "The FBI can't pursue every half-cocked theory the media comes up with, you know."

Yet the FBI had conducted a raid on the Mechelen—based on those self-same half-cocked insinuations in the media. Blake's mouth twisted into a bitter smile at the memory.

"We have reason to believe the woman who called in the tip to the FBI hotline also alerted the media—providing far more details than she disclosed to us."

Walsh either hadn't been informed of that fact or couldn't remember being briefed. Blake could hear his finger tapping impatiently on the phone receiver.

"Why would she—why would anyone—do something like that?" the SAC finally asked.

"We're not going to know until we pursue the inquiry to its logical conclusion," Blake said.

"Talk to Dodd. If he doesn't have a satisfactory explanation for his actions, I'll get you that warrant. But not until you've given the man a fair opportunity to explain, *capiche*?"

Blake muttered his assent.

"Is the Lowell insisting on claiming ownership of the pastel?" Walsh abruptly changed the subject. The SAC was no doubt wondering if the museum could be browbeaten into accepting the inevitable.

That this was a matter for the heavyweights to duke it out among themselves.

"I imagine so." Blake brought his legs down from the ottoman. "The museum had no idea it had lost ownership because of the Sullivans' decision. Is Hugh Norton"—he resisted the urge to call him, *your pal, Norton*—"pressing claims as well—now that he technically owns the Degas?"

"I wouldn't know." Walsh's tone was icy. "He hasn't called."

"I wonder why. The news is plastered all over the media." The other papers had picked up on it as well, and even Lawrence O'Rourke's *Arts Gazette* had a subdued piece on the possible recovery of a Degas pastel.

"You can ask him yourself, Markham." There was a certain relish in the SAC's voice as he made the suggestion. "And while you're at, update him about the case, would you? He is a relevant party and as the current owner of the Degas in question has a right to the information."

Chapter Thirty-Four

"Ready to go?"

Julia whispered the words, her breath making the long strands of Celine's vivid red hair rustle.

"I'm not sure." Celine's voice was equally low.

They looked at Clara, peacefully tucked in bed, her eyes closed. The walk and the heavy meal in the dining room—the same meal Beth had tried to serve her—had exhausted her. "I think I'll take a nap," she'd said when they returned to the apartment.

The thought of leaving Clara here, unattended and unprotected, didn't sit right with Celine. She recounted the troubling vision she'd had of the older woman being manhandled.

"I can't tell whether it's a man or a woman, though."

That's because there's more than one person involved, Celine, her guardian angel informed her.

She relayed the insight to Julia.

"I can well believe it." Julia pointed to the supply closet. "I found a box of nitrile gloves in there. The kind the nurses wear. I'm guessing one of them was searching her room, was interrupted, and hastily shoved it back there."

"That would be Beth Hogan, if I'm not mistaken." Celine swiveled around to gaze at the closet, troubled. After a while, she turned back to face Julia. "That, by the way, is the Beth who was at the winery a few days back."

Julia's eyebrows lifted. "The one grilling you at the bar? Fifty-ish, blonde?"

"The same." She shared her suspicions about the nurse drugging Clara's food. "Clara refused to touch it. And Beth was very reluctant to serve it to any other resident. She wouldn't even let me have it."

"That is suspicious," Julia agreed.

"Listen, I'm convinced Clara won't leave her room because Jonah has her guarding something here. Some piece of evidence he uncovered about the theft."

Had he caught someone searching the studio? He must have. Why else had he convinced Clara it wasn't safe to leave?

"Makes sense." Julia nodded when Celine laid out her thoughts. "And so since she can't be persuaded to leave, the next option is to drug her food. That way she's lights out when they're trying to scour her room for whatever it is Jonah has here."

"And her refusal to play ball on either front has them frustrated." Celine glanced around the room. "Did you find anything? Whatever Jonah discovered, it's something to do with Dodd, I'm pretty sure."

She turned back to see Julia gaping at her.

"How did you know about Dodd? Another vision?"

Celine shook her head. "Clara mentioned working for him. Apparently Jonah insisted on walking her through her memories of Dodd, his association with the Gardner, and their visits to the museum. He even took notes."

Julia scrounged around in her voluminous black leather tote—it was sitting on the breakfast table. A few minutes later, she fished out a photo. "This was in her nightstand drawer. It could be the evidence Dodd is after."

Celine's brow wrinkled. "But why? It's no secret she worked for him. There's probably plenty of evidence to that effect even without the photo. And I'm sure it can all be easily discovered."

"Yes, but it's not a question anyone would think to ask. From what you've said her long-term memories are still intact. Without the photo, anything she says about Dodd could be taken as the ramblings of a woman suffering from dementia. With the photo, you've got valid memories."

"You think that's why Sandy's been asked to discourage visitors."

"Especially law enforcement, I'm guessing." Julia recounted her run-in with Sheila Cooke, the Resident Care Director. "The hostility in the room was so palpable, you could've cut it with a knife."

"She actually accused you of searching the room?" Celine was aghast.

Julia grinned. "Pretty telling, isn't it? I'm guessing she's the head honcho in this operation."

"It must've been Beth who alerted her to your presence here."

In the dining room, Clara had let slip that Julia was in her studio. "I hope your friend finds what she's looking for," she'd said. Beth, who'd been nearby, had immediately pounced upon the remark. Celine's explanation that Julia was tidying the studio clearly hadn't satisfied Beth.

She'd stared at Celine, her blue eyes as cold and hard and glassy as a lizard's. The memory sent a chill up Celine's spine.

"With the rates they're charging you, we really need to get solid evidence of abuse and confront them with it," Julia advised her.

"Oh, I already have evidence." Celine looked grimly at her friend. "Clara has bruises on her body where there should be none." Succinctly, she relayed what she'd seen to Julia. "There's no good reason to grab her by the shoulders or upper arms."

She reached out for Julia's hand. "I'd feel better having an FBI agent—even a retired FBI agent—by my side when I see Sheila Cooke."

Julia squeezed her hand. "In this instance, kiddo, you're better off without me. My badge had no effect on the indomitable Ms. Cooke. She's already inclined to be hostile toward me, and that resentment will be extended to you —and Clara"—Julia's gaze shifted to the bed where Clara lay lightly snoring —"if I'm there. Trust me, you don't want that."

Celine sighed. "No, I guess, I don't."

❧

Sheila Cooke's office was on the floor above Clara's. Celine was glad of that. She hadn't wanted to run into Sandy. The receptionist seemed to genuinely care for Clara, but telling Sandy why she wanted to meet the Resident Care Director was out of the question.

It was just so much gossip until she'd established that Clara's bruises were exactly what she thought they were—a sign of rough handling and negligence.

The office door was ajar, giving Celine a glimpse of a comfortable, spacious interior painted in the palest shades of peach. A red rug provided a touch of vivid color. Potted plants and vases overflowing with tendrils of green were artfully scattered about the room and decorated the edge of the L-shaped desk behind which Sheila loomed.

She glanced up just as Celine was about to knock.

"Ms. Skye! Please come in." Sheila rolled her chair back and gestured to a chair with one hand while pushing aside a thin stack of papers with the other. "I'm glad you came up."

"I'm a little worried about Clara." Celine pulled back a chair and lowered herself into it.

Sheila nodded sagely. "Her appetite, yes, I've heard. Ms. Hibbert refuses to eat."

Celine allowed herself a frown.

"Actually, no, judging by what I saw today, her appetite seems excellent."

She stared at Sheila, defying the Resident Care Director to contradict her.

Framed degrees hung on either side of the wall behind Sheila. An LPN from MassBay, an RN from Boston College, and an online degree in healthcare management from a program Celine hadn't heard of.

Sheila's lips stretched into the smallest of smiles.

"I expect she has good days and bad. I'm going by what the staff tell me." She shrugged her shoulders. "They have no reason to lie."

Celine chose to ignore the remark. Cataloging all the evidence that pointed to someone having infiltrated Hutchinson House would only raise the older woman's hackles.

"Is she being administered sleeping medicines, do you know?"

It was Sheila's turn to frown. "Not that I'm aware of." She turned to her computer, staring at the screen while tapping decisively on the keys. "I can check for you."

She pursed her lips as her eyes ran down the screen.

"No, it doesn't look like she is."

Swiveling back to Celine, she continued: "Why? Do you think she needs them?"

"Not at all. But I have noticed Clara seems afraid to touch anything the nurses bring her. She claims she's being drugged."

"She has Alzheimer's, Ms. Skye," Sheila said with an amused smile. "I'm afraid patients frequently develop a certain degree of paranoia. I recall it wasn't too long ago that she was blaming you for her son's death. She seems to have gotten over that."

Celine flushed at the reminder. *Touché.* Julia had been right about Sheila Cooke. The RCD was a hard nut to crack.

Gripping the edge of her seat, Celine forced herself to continue: "Clara seems especially suspicious of Nurse Hogan. I don't recall having seen her before. A new hire?"

"Yes, and we're very fortunate to have her. She comes highly recommended."

"Does she have any experience working with seniors and people who have Alzheimer's."

"Of course." Sheila seemed somewhat offended by the question. Celine wasn't sure why. "She's worked at some of the best facilities in Alzheimer's care in Boston." The RCD rattled off a few names that even Celine recognized.

"She seems to be having a hard time building rapport with Clara," Celine mused more to herself than to the RCD. Could Beth have faked her work experience?

"With all due respect, Ms. Skye, of late, pretty much everyone's been having a hard time getting along with Ms. Hibbert. Give it some time. Nurse Hogan hasn't even been here that long."

"Neither has Sandy."

Sheila's eyes narrowed. "Your point being?"

"That you seem to have several new hires in the past month." The words dropped out of Celine's mouth before she had time to consider them. She'd wanted to point out that Sandy hadn't experienced any trouble getting close to Clara.

Instead, she found herself being snarky. "Is that because staff attrition levels are higher than expected?"

"Of course not." Sheila's nostrils flared. "Not that it's any of your business, Ms. Skye, but Hutchinson House was most fortunate to receive a substantial grant. The donor specified that it be used to hire new staff and was kind enough to suggest a few extremely qualified individuals that we might be interested in. Nurse Hogan was one of them."

A strong whiff of cologne had assailed Celine's nostrils as Sheila was speaking. Sheila's fingers, she noticed, were stroking the sharp blade of an ivory-handled letter-opener. The woman was clearly nervous. But why?

"Clara has balance issues," Celine abruptly changed the subject. "I noticed when I was helping her climb down the patio stairs. She stumbled."

"Yes, that's a recent development. We do have guidelines on how to support our residents." Sheila pulled out a drawer and reached in for a laminated sheet with black-and-white drawings. "You might find this helpful." She extended it across her desk.

Celine studied the diagrams. An arm around the waist or the shoulders or a hand cradling the elbow sufficed to support patients while walking or standing. To bring a resident to an upright position, you clasped her hands or her wrists.

"She bruises easily, too," Celine murmured softly.

"Yes," Sheila said curtly. "That's why you might notice red splotches in certain areas. The elbow. The wrist. The sides." She stretched out her hand and tapped the laminated sheet with a long, rounded glossy fingernail.

"The problem is"—Celine looked up—"I've noticed bruises on her upper arms and on her shoulders as though someone had grabbed her."

"That's impossible!" Sheila's pupils were dilated. Anger—and fear—radiated from them. "There must be some mistake. Every member of our staff is a professional, well-trained and with impeccable qualifications."

She rose, signaling the interview was at an end.

"If such a thing had happened—and that's a big if—someone would have brought it to my attention."

"My guess is that someone here lacks self-restraint, and everyone else is covering for her—or him," Celine said. She thrust her chair back as well.

"Is that your famous intuition speaking, Ms. Skye?" Sheila sneered. "Is this why you brought a retired FBI agent to our facility, to search out an excuse to serve us with a lawsuit?"

So, they were back to that again, were they? Julia's supposed search of Clara's room?

It's all about money, Celine, her guardian angel whispered into her ears.

Money . . .? An image slid into Celine's mind. A well-manicured hand, the hands curled over a plain white envelope stuffed with bills.

Money has changed hands. Was that Sister Mary Catherine's voice? *There's more where it comes from.*

The implication couldn't be clearer. The Resident Care Director had been bribed.

❧

"Well?" Julia turned to Celine the moment the elevator doors closed. "How'd it go?"

Celine lips tightened. "I don't think we can expect much in the way of help from Sheila Cooke."

"No?" Julia clutched Clara's old stepladder more firmly under her arm.

Clara hadn't objected to their taking it. "Jonah brought it over." But she'd been puzzled when Celine had asked why. "Well, he's not very tall," she'd finally said as though the answer should've been obvious.

The memory ran through Celine's brain on a parallel track as she recounted her interview with Sheila for Julia's benefit.

"She's unwilling to concede that anything's going on or to even consider the possibility of it. Clara's mood fluctuates, and our visit merely coincided with an up. I get the feeling she's hiding something."

"Anything to back that up?" Julia asked, her blue eyes regarding Celine speculatively. "She was pretty cagey and defensive when she barged in on me earlier."

"Yes, about that, she actually accused me of bringing you here to gin up an excuse to file a lawsuit against them."

Julia whistled. "Sounds like she's hiring people who may not be qualified to work here."

"Well, someone paid a lot of money to make sure Beth got hired." Celine related her vision to Julia. "A few other people were specifically recommended. They might be decoys, though."

"Hmmm. . . so Sheila Cooke takes the money, hires whomever she's told to, looking the other way when it comes to qualifications and experience. That could be the basis of a lawsuit if it turns out patients are being abused. The question is: are they? Or is it just Clara who's being targeted?"

The elevator doors opened, and the two women stepped out into the lobby, still mulling over the situation. Sandy caught sight of them and immediately commented on the stepladder.

"Is Ms. Hibbert okay with your taking that?" Sandy peered anxiously at them. "We don't want to upset her."

"Absolutely!" Celine gave her a bright smile but kept walking toward the exit.

Julia snorted. "You'd think Clara's safety would be more important than her supposed attachment to this unwieldy old thing."

As they emerged into the sunny Boston afternoon—there was a chill in the air, but it was overlaid by the welcome heat radiating down from a cloudless sky—Celine turned to Julia.

"Do you think Dodd's behind this—the so-called donation, the new hires, the attempts on Clara?"

Julia shrugged, squinting out into the afternoon glare. "Who else could it be? He's the only one with skin in the game at this point."

But what was so incriminating about that photograph of Clara and Dodd that it had to be spirited away?

"I'd like to take another look at that photo," Celine said as they headed to their rental car.

Julia shifted the stepladder from under her right arm to her left and threw a quick glance over her shoulder. "Better do it in the car. I don't want Sandy or anyone else nosing around us."

Once the stepladder had been deposited in the trunk and Julia had settled herself behind the wheel, she plucked the photo out of her voluminous tote.

"Here you go?" Julia put the car in reverse and carefully backed out of their spot.

"See anything?" she asked, following the curving driveway out of the nursing home grounds.

"I don't know," Celine sighed. It was an ordinary photograph. Dodd seemed like a personable, well-liked individual. His employees—male and female—wore happy smiles for the camera. There were a few attractive women.

Had Dodd been having an affair with one of them? She recalled the woman whose rasping voice she'd heard a few days ago. The woman who'd called in the tip about Dodd's Degas. Implicating him—tightening the noose around him—without ever naming him.

"Do you think Clara knew whom he gave the Gardner's Manet to?"

"What?" Julia's head swiveled toward her, a stunned expression on her features.

"She was his receptionist. A trusted employee, from the looks of it. She would know, don't you think? Especially if it was a fellow employee." Celine tapped the picture. "One of these women."

"You're right," Julia conceded slowly. She took a deep breath, turning the wheel to navigate a bend in the road. "Dear God! No wonder Jonah was leading her down memory lane."

Celine nodded. And no wonder, Dodd wanted Clara dead.

But where did the church fit in?

"I found a Bible in her nightstand," Julia said when Celine voiced her question out loud. "Could be, Dodd met his lady pal in a church. The same one Clara attended?"

That was a possibility. Celine made a mental note to ask Clara about that the next time they visited.

Chapter Thirty-Five

Blake stared at the number SAC Patrick Walsh had given him. It was Hugh Norton's cell phone number. Blake had jotted it down on the napkin that accompanied his pizza delivery.

Six months ago Blake had been looking for an opportunity to butt heads with the powerful art insurer and collector. Now he wasn't so sure he wanted to tangle with the man. Tension coiled within his stomach, wrenching his gut.

His fingers crushed the napkin. This was his one chance to catch Norton in a lie, trip him up somehow. He couldn't afford to drop the ball.

But what if he did?

Norton was tangled up in this somehow. Had to be, Blake thought.

How was it that a painting Norton's company had insured, whose theft the corrupt Bill McCormick had investigated and failed to report to the Art Loss Registry, had ended up in the hands of Henry Dodd, a man who'd served on the board of the Gardner until six months before the infamous theft?

Was Dodd the inside connection Celine had sensed? He'd been against beefing up security. Suspiciously so. Blake would have to find out why.

And he'd wanted the Gardner to purchase insurance coverage for their collection. Had Dodd hoped the Gardner would turn to Morgana Insurance for its needs?

Hadn't Celine felt that the FBI warning about Louis Royce's scheme to raid the Gardner had been about forcing the museum to take some action the board wasn't entirely comfortable with?

Gripping his knee with his left hand, he leaned forward, punching Norton's number into his keypad.

"Hugh Norton." A fruity, well-modulated bass answered the phone. Norton could've been an opera singer, if he'd so chosen.

He sounded like an educated man. A likable, affable man. *Damn!*

Blake introduced himself and the reason for his call.

"Were you aware the Degas—your Degas now, I suppose—had been sighted in a Connecticut museum?"

"Well, of course, I'd read the story. Who hasn't, Special Agent? It was quite a sensational piece of news."

"And you weren't the least bit curious as to its truth?" Blake pressed. "For a pastel, that Degas is worth a sizable chunk of change now. I'm told you haven't put in a call to the FBI so far to inquire about its discovery."

"The news was in the *Post*, Special Agent," Norton snapped. Blake smiled; he'd managed to poke the guy a little. "I don't take everything the *Post* writes as Gospel truth. I figured if there was anything to it, SAC Walsh would do me the courtesy of calling. Why hasn't he, by the way?

Blake shrugged, a little more comfortable now.

"I couldn't say, sir. He asked me—as the agent assigned to the case—to call you and provide you with an update. It's not my place to question his orders."

He paused. A deliberate tactic to catch Norton on the wrong foot. Silence made most people uneasy.

"Well?" Norton sounded impatient. "I take it you've seen the work. Is it the Degas the Sullivans lost all those years ago?"

"It looks like it. Will you be laying a claim to it? I haven't had a chance to speak with Mr. Dodd. I have no idea how willing he'll be now to give up a painting he acquired twenty-odd years ago. And it has, as I mentioned, appreciated in value substantially."

"I'm not planning to dispute ownership of it, Special Agent," Norton said immediately, "if that's what you're worried about. I understand Dodd bought it in good faith. It hadn't even been reported to the Art Loss Registry as stolen, for heavens' sake."

The words snagged Blake's attention. How had Norton picked up that tidbit? That Dodd could not have known he was buying a stolen piece. It hadn't been reported in the *Post*. Ella had discovered the fact—quite by chance, as it happened.

Blake held his breath, forcing himself not to react.

"Actually, it's a little more complicated than that, sir," he said. "You see Mr. Dodd purchased the painting three months before Morgana processed the Sullivans' claim for its theft."

A thick silence filled the air.

"Are the Sullivans—Sullivan Jr. to be more precise—insisting the work belongs to them? They can't do that, Special Agent. They've already accepted the payout. I have the paperwork to prove it."

Blake took a moment before responding.

"It's not the Sullivans, sir. At the time, Mr. Dodd acquired the painting, the Lowell Museum was the legal owner of the Degas. There's even a sticker on the back of the pastel and an accession number to prove the Lowell's claim."

Norton's tense breath, clearly audible over the phone, was the only sign he was still on the line.

"Did the Sullivans ever apprise Morgana of that fact?" Blake pressed on. "That even though they were paying to insure the work, the Lowell was its rightful owner?"

I can't be expected to recall every detail of every painting we've insured, Special Agent.

Norton's terse reply and the abrupt click of the phone as he'd hung up reverberated in Blake's mind. He inserted the flash drive Sarah Williams had given him into the USB port on his laptop, downloaded the PDF file of names saved on it, and emailed a copy to Ella.

That done, he called his personal assistant to alert her to the list he was sending her. Ella had her work cut out for her, he reflected ruefully. There were over five thousand names on the list.

God alone knew how she'd react to the news.

"Just concentrate on the single or widowed women in Boston," he advised her before she could utter a word of complaint.

"I might be able to narrow it down even more," she informed him calmly.

"Oh yeah?" His tone was cautious. He adjusted the phone to his ear. "How?"

He listened intently as she explained, and then let out a whistle of astonishment.

"Clara worked for Dodd? You sure about this?"

"Celine and Julia are," Ella responded as though that was all that mattered.

Why hadn't Celine called him herself? Why hadn't Julia for that matter? He pushed the questions out of his brain.

"And this photo Julia found"—Blake was struggling to wrap his mind around what he'd heard—"that could point us to our mystery woman?"

And possibly to the Gardner's Manet as well. Maybe even the elusive criminals—the Boston Brahmin and the General—who'd masterminded the heist all those years ago.

"Why else would anyone want it?" Ella's brisk voice interrupted his thoughts. It took him a moment to recall they'd been discussing the photo in Clara Hibbert's room. "Clara's memories of the past are intact. Who knows how much Dodd told her about his time on the Gardner?"

"And the photo could trigger some especially awkward memories," Blake said softly. Quite possibly it already had, if Jonah had been delving into them.

Clara had recalled that Dodd was especially taken with the Gardner's Manet. Of course, if Celine's visions were accurate he hadn't retained it for himself, giving it to his mistress instead.

"She called the *Post* after she phoned in the tip to us," Ella told him. "Fortunately for us, the intern at the General Desk had the good sense to log in the time of her call."

"Uhmmm." Blake stared pensively at his laptop. The same questions circled his brain like vultures around carrion. Why had the woman provided the *Post* with more information than she had the FBI? Why, for that matter, pretend to be with the FBI?

"She probably figured the stories swirling the media would pose a more immediate threat to . . ." Ella's voice trailed off. "To Dodd, I guess. The *Post* guy swallowed her story hook, line, and sinker. She didn't really need to give him much in the way of proof."

That was true enough. "But don't rule Norton out just yet," Blake warned her.

He relayed Norton's puzzling words about the Sullivans' Degas.

"Blake, there's no way he could've known Bill McCormick failed to report the theft to the ALR," Ella immediately said.

"Unless it was at his request," Blake said. "Whether at the Sullivans' urging or not is hard to say."

"You're thinking Norton facilitated the sale?" Ella ventured.

"He must have." There was no doubt in Blake's mind about this. Why else had Norton been so careful not to dispute Dodd's ownership of the Degas? "The real question is: who commissioned the theft: Norton or Dodd?"

His money was on Norton. But the evidence favored Dodd. An uneasy tension flared through his being. His mind wasn't entirely satisfied with the evidence. Something told him they were being led astray.

They'd missed something. He drove his fingers through his dark hair in desperation.

Well, there might be one way to get closer to the truth.

"Can Celine use that photo to take Clara down memory lane?" he asked.

Chapter Thirty-Six

"Take Clara down memory lane?" Celine repeated the words Julia had mouthed to her before lowering her chin down to the phone receiver. Ella had called shortly after they'd checked in to the Hilton Garden Inn to convey Blake's instructions to them.

All the evidence pointed to Dodd being in possession of a stolen Degas.

"I'm a little hesitant to take that photograph back," Julia said, as she ended the call and gently set the receiver in its cradle. "But it's the best shot we have of narrowing down who our mystery tipster is. And if we can do that . . ."

Her voice trailed off, overwhelmed by the implications of that possibility.

"I know." Celine regarded the snapshot they'd retrieved from Clara's room. "We'll be able to recover a Manet and get hold of evidence that leads directly to the men behind the heist."

That would be no small accomplishment. But Celine wasn't sure the picture held any clues worth their consideration. She lifted a cup of lukewarm coffee to her lips. It had been served with their lunch—grilled chicken sandwiches on toasted rye.

"And it'll help us keep Clara safe, don't forget that," Julia pointed out. Getting the men who'd masterminded the Gardner theft and their honchos off the street, she and Blake had surmised, would serve to take the target off Clara's back.

Celine fingered the photograph, recalling the cancer-ridden woman with the raspy voice she'd seen in her vision. Was she pictured in this image? Had a long-ago camera captured her features? Would Clara remember her?

She's not here, Celine. Her guardian angel's soft voice was full of regret. *The woman you're looking for isn't here.*

But Julia shrugged when Celine relayed Sister Mary Catherine's insight to her.

"Broaching the subject with Clara might still trigger some memories. Dodd was an attractive man. Still is, come to think of it." She jabbed a finger at the photo. "I'd be surprised if there weren't at least a few of his female employees who had the hots for him."

Glancing down at the photo, Celine took another sip of her coffee. It was too tepid for her taste. Her eyelids felt heavy and drowsy. Her chin lolled onto her chest.

A heavy fog wound itself around her, veiling the sunlit scene before her eyes. She could barely make out the park bench, a few yards from the edge of the pond. But the figure sitting on the bench looked familiar.

Who was it?

Straining her eyes, she peered into the wisps of fog that floated around her. Was that Jonah? An older, bespectacled man sat next to him. Eager to see what was going on, she moved closer, seeming to float on air.

A thick envelope changed hands.

"Here's the money from your donor?"

"My donor?" The short bark of amusement that erupted out of Jonah's mouth caused his companion's gaze to swivel sharply toward him. "Is that what he's calling himself these days?"

He opened the envelope and took a quick peek. Celine made out a thick wad of bills before Jonah quickly pulled the flap down.

"You have the report?" The older man's voice was curt. He leaned forward, hands on his knees, staring straight ahead at the pond.

"Yup." Jonah slid a manila envelope across the bench. Celine didn't have to see inside the envelope to know what it contained. Jonah had been conveying her visions to the Boston Brahmin. Every word she uttered, every vision, every insight. It was all there.

A pang of betrayal stung her. She knew why he'd done it, but it hurt all the same.

She floated closer. If either one of them had turned his head, she'd have been spotted. But Jonah and his companion were oblivious to her presence.

"You grow up here?" Jonah finally broke the silence that enveloped them.

The older man nodded, sunlight glinting on his spectacles.

"Me too," Jonah said, his gaze riveted on the dappled light filtering through the leaf-laden trees in the distance. A bird swooped down to the water.

"You were around when the Gardner heist happened, right?"

Jonah's voice was so soft, Celine could barely hear him. But his companion's head jerked toward him.

"What are you getting at?" he growled.

"Nothing." Jonah shrugged. But Celine saw the smirk that pulled at the corners of his mouth. She sensed the power that seemed to swell within the reporter's being. He possessed an edge over his companion—information that, if acted upon, could yank the man to his knees.

Be careful, Jonah, she whispered. *You're playing with fire. Be careful.*

Before she knew it, Celine's eyes were wide open. She was staring up at the ceiling. A strange white ceiling. Her eyes pivoted around the room, seeing the enormous queen-sized bed with its blue floral-patterned coverlet, the dusky pink wingback chairs around the coffee table, the sturdy form ensconced in one of the armchairs.

She was in Boston. In a hotel. She'd barely come to that realization when Julia's booming voice startled her.

"That was a short nap! Or was that . . . something else?"

Celine glanced down at the soft blanket that Julia had thrown over. Tugging it off herself, she pulled herself up into a sitting position.

"It was something else." She stared at Julia. "It isn't this photograph that's put Clara in danger, Julia. It was something Jonah discovered about his handler." She recounted her vision.

"I have no idea what Jonah unearthed. I'm guessing it's something that inextricably links his handler to the Gardner theft. It may have been evidence of insider involvement in the heist. Whatever it was, he chose to hold it over the other guy."

"Blackmail?" Julia whistled. "Jonah was planning to blackmail him?"

When Celine nodded, Julia whistled again. "I can see why that would put a target on Clara's back. Jonah had no idea what he was getting into, did he?"

Celine shook her head. No, he hadn't. Impulsive to the last, Jonah had been confident he was the only one calling the shots.

"Whatever it was he knew—or thought he knew—it must've been deeply incriminating," she mused.

Julia turned to her. "Did you get a good look at the other guy? Was it Dodd or Norton? Do you know?"

Celine shook her head. She'd just seen a profile. Thick dark hair streaked with silver. Gold-rimmed spectacles. A trim, athletic figure. He had a suave, urbane manner.

"He was a member of the upper crust. Or at least, Jonah thought he was."

Tell your friend to keep looking. Clara's advice reverberated in her memory.

She turned urgently toward her friend. "We'll need to search Clara's room again, Julia. Whatever it is, the Brahmin's looking for, we haven't found it. It's not the photograph. It's something else."

❧

Blake gripped the wheel hard, looking first to the right, then to the left before making his turn onto East Avenue. His nerves were on edge. He hadn't been expecting to meet Henry Dodd so soon. Hadn't made plans to do so until he'd had a chance to absorb the information he'd gathered.

Blake certainly hadn't intended to call Dodd until he was good and ready to confront the man.

But when Dodd had called fifteen minutes earlier, Blake's hand had been forced.

"Special Agent Markham?" The unfamiliar masculine voice, deep and well-modulated, had made the hairs on the back of Blake's neck stand up.

No one other than Ella, SAC Walsh, and his colleagues knew he was in Norwalk. He'd given the number of the inn to Sarah Williams, in case she needed to reach him but had decided against sharing his cell number.

Williams, Blake had a feeling, would be as much or more of a pain in the behind than the Gardner's Penny Hoskins. He could do without the constant nagging and prodding.

But the call had come on his cell phone.

Blake had barely time to wonder who it was—or why—when the voice had continued:

"This is Henry Dodd. I understand you have questions about my Degas."

Blake's brains had instantly scrambled. He was used to hostile witnesses. He was familiar with resistance. But this was unusual. Dodd seemed to be willing—eager even—to talk.

Who had put Dodd up to this? The man had inexplicably decided to take the proverbial bull by the horns. Why?

"Yes, I do, sir," Blake had conceded. "When can we meet?"

It had been a vain attempt to wrest control of the situation, but Dodd had bested him.

"I'm at the Shorehaven Golf Club, Special Agent. It's about two miles from where you are. Would twenty to thirty minutes from now be a good time?"

Now as Blake drove past the rolling, snow-covered cemetery, with its neat rows of white headstones, onto Gregory Boulevard, he wondered what exactly Dodd had up his sleeve. There had to be something for Dodd to call.

Was Blake walking into a trap by agreeing to meet him?

"It's a club," he reminded himself. "A private club, but a public place." There would be people, waiters, staff.

Nevertheless, the weight of his Glock against his hip was comforting.

It was late afternoon. The sun had not yet set, but the winter light was fast fading, and despite the heat radiating within the car, Blake could feel the icy chill caused by the sharp drop in ambient temperature.

The gray structure of the Shorehaven Golf Club was set amidst an undulating, sprawling bank of white-dusted green. The snow had been relentlessly pushed to the sides. As he drove down the driveway, Blake caught a glimpse of the dark blue waters of the Long Island Sound.

Dodd was waiting for him at one of the tables on the largely deserted front patio. A well-built, good-looking man with a thatch of white hair, he was in fine shape for someone over seventy.

In defiance of the cold, Dodd wore a blue polo, short-sleeved shirt and khaki trousers. His grip, when he shook Blake's hand, was surprisingly strong. The heat exuded by his palm made Blake acutely aware of the luke-warm temperature of his own gloveless hands.

"Patio okay with you?" Dodd asked. "Or would you prefer to go inside?"

"This is fine."

Blake would have preferred the warmth of the clubhouse, but he wasn't about to admit it.

Chapter Thirty-Seven

Blake looked at the brown manila envelope Dodd slid across the table toward him.

"It's a certificate of authenticity," Dodd explained when Blake made no move to touch it. "Issued at the time I bought the Degas."

Blake nodded, placing two fingers on the envelope to draw it closer to himself. "It's not the work's authenticity that's in dispute." He raised his eyes, gazing squarely into Dodd's blue eyes. "It's the work's ownership."

Dodd drummed his fingers on the glass surface of the table. "It was stolen."

He glanced down at the folded newspaper in front of him.

So he'd read the *Post* story. But was Dodd asking a question or repeating a fact? Had he known all along he was sitting on stolen property? Or had he just discovered the shocking truth? Blake couldn't tell.

He decided to give Dodd the benefit of the doubt.

"Yes. From a Mr. Harrison Sullivan in Boston in 1998. Two years later, the Sullivans accepted an insurance payout in lieu of the work."

Dodd's eyes narrowed. "They accepted a payout for a work that didn't belong to them?" His fingers curled around the whiskey glass before him. Lifting the glass, he took a healthy swallow. "The Lowell Museum acquired that Degas in 1996, Special Agent Markham."

Dodd was right about the year. But how had he known it was 1996? Blake regarded the older man speculatively.

"I called the Lowell to verify the year," Dodd said firmly, as though Blake had questioned the veracity of his account. "The Sullivans sold the Degas to the Lowell Museum. There's no question about that."

"Transferred ownership," Blake corrected him automatically, his mind elsewhere. Why hadn't Arthur Bentley, the Senior Curator of the Lowell, shared this tidbit with him? "There was no money exchanged."

"What the hell difference does that make?" Dodd jabbed the newspaper. "The Degas belonged to the Lowell in 1996. How could it have been stolen two years later from the Sullivans' home?"

"They had an arrangement with the Lowell," Blake explained. Succinctly, he gave Dodd the details.

"That may be, but from where I'm standing it still looks like a case of insurance fraud. Shouldn't you be investigating the Sullivans, not hounding me?

"The Sullivans were covering the cost of insurance."

Dodd digested that in silence. He took another swig of his whiskey.

"I'm guessing they think they're entitled to the Degas as a consequence." He stared into the amber-colored drink in his glass. "Can't say I blame them. It's appreciated considerably over the years. And whatever piddly amount they received as a payout, it won't compare to the current value of the piece."

"The Sullivans are both dead"—Blake took a sip of his whiskey, his first; it helped to keep the chill at bay—"and their son isn't questioning the arrangement they had with their insurance company. The trouble is at the time you bought the Degas, the Sullivans had yet to accept the insurance payout."

"Meaning what?" Dodd regarded him over the rim of his glass.

"Meaning the Lowell owned the work at the time you bought it."

Dodd leaned forward. "That's not true, Special Agent Markham. The restorer—"

"There was no restorer. No restoration company."

"The pastel was restored. There were clear signs of it." Dodd indicated the manila envelope he'd passed over earlier. "It's all there. In the report."

Blake inhaled, then blew his breath out. He needed another swallow of that whiskey. But he couldn't afford to have his senses—or his judgment—clouded.

"Whatever work the pastel needed, it was done in-house, by restorers employed by the Lowell Museum."

"That's impossible." Dodd straightened up, rigid with outrage.

"It's the truth. You should've followed up with the Lowell, verified the story with them when you called. Why didn't you?"

Dodd was looking shell-shocked.

"I was told the museum was in straitened circumstances."

He leaned back. "It was an embarrassing situation. I didn't want to prod any further."

The explanation made sense. Had Dodd been conned? Was he just another victim here? Or was Blake the one being hoodwinked?

Blake gazed upon the golf course stretching beyond the patio. The sky had turned a vivid orange, contrasting sharply with the midnight blue swathe that stretched above it. He was about to lift his whiskey glass to his lips, needing the drink, when Dodd broke the silence.

"Is the Sullivans' insurance company making a claim as well? They're the current owners aren't they?"

"Morgana Insurance," Blake said.

"Morgana?" Dodd frowned. His fingers clenched around his glass, knuckles gleaming white against his tanned skin.

"Hugh Norton's company," Blake elaborated.

"And he wants the Degas back? After all these years?"

"Actually, he's been magnanimous enough to concede you purchased the work in good faith." Blake saw the muscles in Dodd's face contorting, but the older man continued to listen quietly. "Someone—hard to say who—failed to report the theft to the Art Loss Register. It wouldn't have shown up on any lists as stolen at the time. It still won't, as a matter of fact."

He'd barely finished when Dodd turned to him, his gaze spearing Blake like twin spikes of blue steel.

"I didn't buy a stolen Degas, Special Agent Markham. It was a legitimate sale and I can prove it. I have all the paperwork."

"That'll be a huge help," Blake assured him. But he still had questions about Dodd's time at the Gardner.

❧

She was back in the church. It was heated; Celine could tell because of the warm blast of air that hit her face. But there was no dispelling the deathly cold that insidiously invaded the space.

Someone had left the door open.

It feels like death in here, she complained, wishing she could close the door. But a strange force held her back, preventing her from turning around.

You can't stop the cold coming in, Celine. She could hear Sister Mary Catherine's voice, but the nun was nowhere to be seen. *You can't stop it. You just have to accept it.*

Standing by the font of holy water, Celine shivered and gazed around the interior of the church. The Stations of the Cross were still missing. Gold-framed paintings hung in their stead on the walls on either side.

What was she even doing here? If only she could leave. But there was no closing the door. No turning away.

A soft palm grasped her elbow, propelling her down the nave toward the altar.

Sister Mary Catherine? Celine turned toward the nun. *When did you get here? I didn't see you come in.*

The nun ignored her questions.

The answers you seek are here, Celine, she whispered instead, drawing her relentlessly toward the altar. *You must believe that, my dear.*

As they approached the altar, Celine's gaze caught on a gold cylindrical container topped with a dome. It was the tabernacle, she recalled, where the consecrated hosts were stored. The door to it was wide open.

Isn't that unusual? she asked. The tabernacle was always kept locked. Even she knew that.

Sister Mary Catherine nodded, her face grave.

What happened here was irregular, she conceded sadly. *It shouldn't have happened. But it did. The important thing, however, is to set it right.*

Before Celine could ask any more questions, Jonah shimmered into view. He stood behind the altar, his skinny form clothed in a gray robe.

He shouldn't be there, Celine thought. She turned to Sister Mary Catherine. But having led her to the altar, her guardian angel had disappeared.

You need to visit my mother, Celine, Jonah intoned in his characteristic nasal tone. *You need to visit her before any more people die.*

He turned to his right. Celine followed his gaze, seeing a blanket-wrapped figure wheeling itself toward her. That would be Clara, of course. It looked taller than Clara, though.

The ghastly rattle of the wheels echoed within the church, bouncing off the stone walls, rising to the arched ceiling above them. The figure, hooded, covered in a gray blanket, carried a vessel, but Celine could barely make it out.

Then it shrugged the hood off its head, turning toward Celine.

"Laurie!" Celine gasped. To her surprise, she'd spoken out loud. What was Laurie doing here? She hadn't seen the intern since she'd fallen to her death nearly eight years ago.

"There's another one dead, Celine." Laurie looked pityingly at her. "You didn't see that coming, did you?"

⁊

Celine's eyes flew open. Her heart was pounding. Clara, she thought. Oh, my God, Clara!

Swinging her legs out of the bed, she ran to the hallway-slash-kitchenette that separated her room from Julia's. Pounding her fist on the door, she called for Julia. She could hear her voice, frantic, panicked, screaming.

"Celine?" The door opened. Julia, enfolded in a bathrobe, hair spilling out of her hairband, gathered her into her arms. "What is it, Celine? Come on in."

"There's been a death," Celine rasped out breathlessly. "Clara! You've got to call . . ." Overcome, she paused to take a deep breath.

She saw her friend direct a covert glance at the clock. It was three o'clock. "Are you sure?" Julia's voice was tentative.

She helped Celine into one of the wingback armchairs placed near the back wall of her room.

Celine nodded. "Someone's died." Wearily, she rubbed her hand over her face. "I could see Laurie taunting me."

Dear God, it had been eight years since she'd seen the intern, her colleague at Montague Museum. How far away those days seemed?

"Laurie? Laurie Robbes?" Julia asked softly.

But she didn't know Dodd, did she?

Celine heard Julia's objection as clearly as though she'd uttered the words out loud.

She stared squarely into Julia's skeptical eyes.

"*Visit my mother before any more people die.* That's what Jonah told me, Julia. You've got to call."

Julia glanced at the clock again and then slowly nodded.

"Okay. Here goes nothing," Celine heard her mutter under her breath.

Chapter Thirty-Eight

Mulling over his conversation with Dodd, Blake followed Canfield Avenue as it curved left and turned into Marvin Street. The sky had been ablaze, dusk darkening the golf course, when Dodd had invited him into the clubhouse for dinner.

It was a satisfying meal—a medium-rare steak served with crisp fries and a mound of steamed carrots and peas drenched in butter. Blake hadn't been sure of the wisdom of drinking red wine immediately following their whiskey, but Dodd had insisted on ordering a bottle.

But although supper had left Blake replete with a sense of well-being, Dodd's last words as they stood up had been disturbing.

"Do you know what's worse than being betrayed, Special Agent Markham?"

With his palms pressed down upon the white tablecloth for support, Dodd regarded Blake with a questioning smile.

When Blake shook his head, Dodd supplied the answer to his question. "It's being betrayed by a friend."

The older man had pumped his hand and left before Blake could ask him what he'd meant.

Now as he coasted past Emerson Street, around Roger Ludlow Park, and onto East Avenue, heading towards Sweet Ashley's—an ice cream parlor Dodd had recommended he try—Blake raked through his memory with a fine-tooth comb.

Dodd knew far more about the entire affair than he'd let on. Blake was convinced of that. It was impossible to interview a suspect without revealing some details of an investigation. And what little he'd disclosed seemed to have suggested a name to Dodd.

Someone who'd set him up. Either all those years ago when Dodd had acquired the Degas. Or more recently when it had come out that the Degas was stolen.

If only Blake could ferret out the information.

A blue-and-pink awning came into view. It was the ice cream parlor. Blake drove past it and turned into the parking structure.

Sweet Ashley's boasted handcrafted ice cream. Blake scanned the menu on the blackboard behind the counter and pored over the large tubs in the ice cream cabinet.

"I'll have the Espresso Chip," he said finally. "In a cup."

God knew, he needed the caffeine to clear his brain.

He took his cup out onto the patio where the tables were vacant. He'd barely dipped his pink plastic spoon into the delectable chocolate-brown mound when his cell phone rang.

Clara is all right, Celine, Sister Mary Catherine reassured her.

Celine glanced at Julia, but it was too late. Her friend was already on the phone with Sheila Cooke.

"Yes." The former fed angled the receiver up to her mouth and slowly repeated her request. "Ms. Skye and I would like you to check on Ms. Hibbert. Now would be a good time."

She cocked her head—silver-gray hairs escaping from her untidy ponytail to spill over her forehead and ears—and listened intently.

Then Julia gave an exaggerated eye-roll. A smile tugged at the corners of Celine's lips at the gesture. Julia was a good friend. Not many law enforcement agents would've been willing to "put their ass on the line"—as Blake would've phrased it—to set someone's mind at rest.

Certainly not on the basis of a tenuous psychic dream.

Julia had even managed to concoct a plausible story. She repeated it now for Sheila Cooke's benefit.

"As I've already mentioned, Ms. Skye and I received an unusual call a short while back. It sounded like Clara. She seemed to be in trouble. But the call ended very abruptly. As you can imagine, that's most concerning."

Julia didn't have to explain why it was an anxiety-inducing situation. Clara, like most of the other residents in the nursing home, didn't have a phone in her apartment. Making a call to a family member or friend entailed going out into the hallway and walking halfway down its length, where a communal phone was placed within a walk-in recess in the wall.

With Clara's balance issues, walking without help was an action fraught with danger. That the call had ostensibly ended abruptly was yet another plausible cause for worry.

Julia turned to her, hand clasped over the receiver. "She wasn't happy to do it, but Ms. High-and-Mighty is off now to do her job and check on Clara."

Celine nodded, biting her lip. Should she divulge the fact that there'd been no reason for Julia to place a call? Clara was fine. But Julia had turned away.

"I'm beginning to think that it's not Clara," she began, her voice tentative.

Julia glanced up, eyebrows raised. "What's not Clara?"

Celine took a deep breath, recalling the details of her dream. "Laurie was taunting me"—why had she even seen Laurie? The question ate at her—"I hadn't foreseen this, she said. She was gloating over me. And then Jonah said I needed to visit Clara before—"

Julia's swiveled sharply away. She brought the receiver up to her mouth. Clearly Sheila Cooke was back on the line.

❧

"Well?" Ella's voice rang in Blake's ear. He'd texted her before driving out of the clubhouse, promising to call. But clearly his personal assistant had been in no mood to wait. "How'd it go? Did you find out who Dodd's mistress is?"

Blake spooned the ice cream into his mouth, savoring the chilled coffee flavor before responding. He recalled the fury that had flashed in Dodd's blue eyes. It was the first—and only—time that evening that Dodd had expressed any kind of strong emotion.

"I've never been unfaithful to my wife, Special Agent Markham."

"He was outraged when I asked about it," Blake told Ella. "Said he'd never once been unfaithful."

"And you believe him?"

"His wife died of cancer a few months ago." Dodd's emotion had been genuine. "He's still mourning her."

"Oh!" Ella's tone was subdued.

But Blake knew what she was thinking. Dodd could've been lying. He'd pressed the issue, pointing to the copy of the *Post* that lay between them on the table. "Are you sure there isn't anyone—maybe years in the past—looking to get payback?"

He'd divulged a few of the relevant details: the caller had been a woman, likely not from the FBI.

"I know," Dodd had said much to his surprise. "I called the *Post*. The idiots never even bothered to verify the woman's story. Or get her name. Such shoddy journalism!"

"So there isn't anyone—any woman—who . . . ehmm. . . might've felt scorned?" Blake had urged.

He recalled how Dodd had hesitated before copping to the fact that years ago an employee had come onto him. Happily married at the time, Dodd had firmly rebuffed her overtures.

"But I seriously doubt she had anything against me. After all these years? Besides, she swiftly moved on to greener pastures."

"Could he recall her name?" Ella asked when Blake had relayed this information to her.

"Something with an R, he thought. He couldn't remember."

"Fine, I'll keep digging. Anything to the church connection Celine and Julia suggested?"

Dodd had been nonplussed by the question, Blake remembered.

"I'm an atheist," he'd said, and then defiantly, "but I'm a good man. Church-goers aren't immune from sin, you know. My employee, the man-devouring woman I mentioned, was a card-carrying Catholic! Would you believe it?"

"Wonder if she and Clara went to the same church," Ella said when he'd passed this on.

"Have Celine find out," Blake suggested. "I know Penny's convinced Dodd was behind the Gardner theft. But we talked about that. There was nothing suspicious about his time there."

Chapter Thirty-Nine

"What about Dodd's supposed reluctance to beef up security?" Ella demanded.

Blake had made the mistake of telling her about Dodd's invitation to dinner. She probably figured the meal had allayed his suspicions of the man.

"It made sense." Blake swirled his spoon into his melting dessert.

Dodd had shared with him the appalling conditions that existed at the museum. The lack of climate control; the extreme heat and cold the paintings were subject to; ceilings that dripped; pipes that were prone to bursting.

"We were in danger of having no art worth stealing. I wasn't the only board member concerned about that. With limited funds, spending the money on security made no sense when it was urgently needed for repairs on the building itself and restoration."

Apparently, Dodd and the few board members had even joked that Isabella Gardner would've preferred that her treasures be stolen than that they disintegrate in the museum she'd created for them.

Blake spooned a large heap of ice cream into his mouth. "They figured that if they were ever robbed, the insurance payout would serve to improve the conditions in which the art was being kept," he said.

"You think some of his colleagues seriously considered orchestrating a theft? Maybe as a wake-up call," Ella ventured.

Blake considered this idea as he swallowed another mouthful of ice cream. "Sure seems that way," he conceded. "Wonder if it's the same person who set Dodd up?"

"Set Dodd up?" Ella's voice pierced his eardrum.

"I don't think he realized it until we spoke, but he believes someone set him up." Blake shared Dodd's parting words with Ella.

"It was a third party that handled the sale of that pastel, and apparently Dodd's name was mentioned to them by one of his fellow board members. Someone who knew he'd be on board with rescuing a major artwork from an inept museum."

According to Dodd, from what he'd heard of the Lowell, the conditions there were no better than those at the Gardner.

It was only several minutes later when he'd returned to the Norwalk River Inn that Blake remembered what had bothered him about his conversation with Dodd.

The man hadn't reacted in any way to Norton's name or to the possibility of his claim of ownership. What had stunned Dodd was the timing of the claim.

He wants it back after all these years?

Had Norton been the friend Dodd suspected of betraying him? The person who'd referred him to the art dealer Dodd had bought the pastel from?

Had Norton cleverly played his hand, turning the FBI's suspicions onto Dodd?

Whatever the Resident Director was saying didn't sit right with Julia. Her lips tightened and her stubby fingers closed tightly over the receiver.

"I see," she said finally. "Well, thanks for taking the time."

She banged down the phone and headed to the vacant armchair next to Celine's.

"Turns out Clara was just fine. Fast asleep. But the noise of their entry awoke the poor woman, and as a result all the other residents on the floor are awake as well."

Julia sank heavily into the armchair and raised her legs onto the small ottoman the hotel had placed in front of it.

Celine frowned. "How many people did Sheila take with her?"

Julia leaned back in her chair and closed her eyes. "It seems Nurse Hogan and an orderly were already in Clara's apartment, checking on her. When Ms. High-and-Mighty stormed in through the door, Hogan was so startled, she yelped. That woke Clara up, and well, you can imagine the rest."

Celine's frown deepened. "Nurse Hogan? That would be Beth Hogan, right? Why was she in Clara's room?"

"Sheila seems to think they were doing their nightly rounds, checking on all the residents."

They don't have nightly rounds, Celine, Sister Mary Catherine whispered into her ear.

"I think they were searching her room," Celine announced. "And Sheila intercepted them—or was covering for them."

Julia's eyes sprang open. "You're sure about this?"

Celine nodded, repeating her guardian angel's words for Julia's benefit.

Julia sat up. "So you potentially saved Clara's life. I mean Beth Hogan and this orderly—"

Celine shook her head vehemently. "I didn't save anyone's life, Julia. Someone died tonight. Someone whose death I hadn't foreseen. Laurie was taunting me. I don't even know why she was in my dream."

Why, for that matter, had the church walls been covered in paintings? That was so unusual.

Remember where the answers you seek are, her guardian angel whispered.

Yes, I know, in a church. But which church?

How were they going to find out?

Chapter Forty

The stairwell that led to the hotel parking lot was dark and cold. Celine stood by the door for a few moments, letting her eyes adjust to the gloom. It had been half past three in the morning when, realizing there was nothing more that could be done, she and Julia had finally returned to bed.

Now as Celine made her way slowly down the gloomy concrete stairway, she wondered yet again who had died. That she should've sensed it at all suggested it was a violent death.

Murder.

"It's not Clara, that's all that matters," Julia had said firmly.

And it's no one you've met, Celine, Sister Mary Catherine suddenly whispered into her ears. *That's why you weren't given a warning.*

Not that it would've mattered even if she had. In all the years she'd received her awful visions of death, Celine had never once been able to prevent one from happening.

But it was someone connected to the case. She was certain of that. Why else had Laurie taunted her about it?

A wisp of understanding stirred in her brain, but it was too faint for her tired brain to grasp. Gripping the hard, icy stair rail, she continued down to the first level. Celine had offered to begin the process of defrosting the car while Julia researched spy cams.

The former fed may not have been overly concerned about the death that had occurred—*during the night, as she lay dreaming*, Celine realized with a start—but she was convinced Clara's life was in jeopardy.

The more they'd considered it, the less likely Sheila Cooke's story had seemed. Even if Nurse Hogan had been on her rounds, checking on patients, there was no reason for her to take an orderly with her.

"If Clara's being abused—and it seems likely—we need unarguable evidence that it's happening," Julia had said. "The bruises you saw on her shoulders won't cut it."

Besides, if the video footage they obtained were to confirm their suspicions of Beth Hogan, the evidence—and the threat of a protracted FBI investigation—might force Sheila Cooke's hand, compelling her to reveal the name of her donor.

"It could be Dodd or it could be Norton," Julia had continued, staring at her laptop. "But at this point, my money's on Dodd. Clara's known him since before the heist. If Jonah discovered anything incriminating, it's more likely to have been about Dodd. And if Jonah was blackmailing him . . ." She'd shrugged, the implications of the scenario clear. With Jonah dead, Clara remained the last loose end that needed to be dealt with.

"And catching them rifling through her room might give us some clue as to what they're looking for," Celine had added.

It's definitely not the photograph, she thought, reaching the parking lot.

The pale light of dawn filtered in through the street entrance. Recessed cans in the ceiling provided a weak glow.

There was just enough visibility for her to navigate a course through the stacked rows of parked cars to find the rental they'd driven the day before. Even before she reached the car, Celine knew the windshield wouldn't need to be defrosted. Despite the bone-chilling cold, the parking lot did afford some protection against the elements.

That was a blessing. They had a long day ahead of them. Julia wanted to replace the stepladder they'd taken out of Clara's apartment.

"It'll give us the pretext we need to return today to install our spy cam," she'd confided with a grin. They wouldn't look so out of place carrying a teddy bear or faux plant or whatever item they devised to conceal the camera if they also came with a new stepladder.

Stepladder, Celine thought. Jonah had brought it, hadn't he? But why?

Because he isn't tall, Clara's words returned to her.

Was it up high, whatever Jonah had hidden?

Her pulse racing, she approached the car, intending to start the car to get the heater going. That was when she noticed it—the plain manila envelope tucked under the windshield wiper.

Why Do You Want Her Dead, Celine?

The words inscribed in bold red letters tormented her. Was she seeing things?

Tentatively, she reached out. Her fingers made contact with the thick brown paper of the envelope. Grasping it, she tugged it out from under the wiper.

Her head pivoted around the vast rectangular space.

Who had left this here?

She fumbled with the metal clasp on the envelope, struggling to open it. But her gloved fingers were stiff and difficult to manipulate. Frustrated, she yanked the right glove off and pulled the tabs of the clasp up.

Lifting the flap, she tipped the envelope. A single article cut out from the front page of the *Boston Globe*—dated a few months back—slipped out, falling onto the cold black hood of the rental.

YOU CAN PREVENT THE NEXT DEATH.

The title was highlighted in yellow, and it struck her mind with the stinging force of a hard slap. The "you" was underlined in orange. The initial paragraphs and the black-and-white photos that accompanied the report made it clear it was about elder abuse in nursing homes.

A Massachusetts Commission had uncovered several egregious examples of abuse in nursing homes throughout Boston, including some of the more prestigious ones.

Celine scanned the paragraphs with growing horror. Rough handling; mouth burns due to scalding-hot food; starvation; being left for days in soiled garments. It was horrendous.

The worst part of it was that the Commission had opted to hold family members rather than nursing homes and their staff responsible for what was happening.

It was thanks to the behavior of overly intrusive and discourteous family members that seniors bore the brunt of the pent-up rage of frustrated nursing home staff.

"It's not professional behavior," the Commission Chair admitted, "but it is very human and understandable. And it's certainly preventable. Our choices matter. The way we treat our fellow humans matters. And it all has consequences."

The woman's words had been highlighted as well, Celine noticed.

They were threatening Clara. Dear God, it was a direct threat to Clara. And the message couldn't be clearer. It had been brought about by their nosing around her apartment the previous day.

The black-and-white photograph pictured a nurse taking the vitals of a senior at an assisted living facility in the city. The nurse's slender figure and blonde curls reminded Celine of Beth. But it couldn't possibly be her, could it?

Her eyes drifted to the paragraph adjacent to it.

In the most egregious case, a nurse at the prestigious Adelaide House deliberately falsified a patient's medical records, resulting in the woman being administered medication she was allergic to. The act caused her death in a routine medical procedure.

Apparently, the procedure had been unnecessary as well, recommended only so that the doctors could harvest the patient's organs.

Celine stared at the words printed on the thin newssheet. Was that how they planned to take out Clara? Through an unnecessary procedure and by administering a drug that could cause a massive failure of her organs?

Adelaide House? The name rang a bell. Wasn't that the place where Sheila Cooke had said Beth Hogan had worked before coming to Hutchinson House?

Her gaze slid back to the photo. It looked remarkably like Beth.

Chapter Forty-One

"Ma'am!"

The sharp rebuke uttered in a husky tenor took Celine by surprise. Startled, she dropped the envelope and the article onto the hood of the rental.

A dark-complected, skinny man in navy work pants and a matching jacket had materialized at her elbow.

An employee. Just a hotel employee, Celine told herself, willing her pulse to stop racing. *No one to be scared of.*

As if to reassure her of the fact, he continued sternly: "Ma'am, hotel guests aren't allowed here."

He held out his hand. "If you gimme your key, I can bring your car out to the front fer you."

"My goodness, you gave me a start!" Celine stared speculatively at the man.

The Hilton's parking valet sat in a booth at the entrance to the lot. It would be impossible for anyone to enter or leave without being noticed by the guy.

She indicated the envelope. "I found this on my car, tucked under the windshield wipers. Did you leave it there?"

The valet—Benny Costa, according to the black name tag pinned to his shirt—gave the envelope a cursory glance and shrugged. "No, ma'am. I don't know nothin' about that."

He was telling the truth, but Celine decided to question him further.

"When did your shift start? Did you let anyone into the parking lot since you've been here?"

He regarded her steadily. "You think I wanna lose my job?

"Any cars come in here?" she pressed him.

He rolled his eyes. "No ma'am. It's too early for check-in."

Celine's gaze swept the parking lot from the entrance to the back wall.

Even walls have eyes, Celine, Sister Mary Catherine whispered.

It took Celine a moment to comprehend. Ah! The cameras. Could the men who'd done this have been caught on camera? There'd been more than one, she sensed

"There's one by the entrance," Benny Costa sulkily informed her when she put the question to him. "Dunno why they need one there. I know who comes in and goes out of here."

"What about by the hotel side doors?" There were doors on each level that gave onto the stairwell leading down to the parking lot.

Benny shrugged. "No cameras there. We don't need 'em. If anyone tries to steal a car, they won't get away with it. Not with the camera and a valet sittin' right there."

But the men responsible for leaving this envelope hadn't wanted to steal a car.

Had they entered the parking lot from within the hotel? It would've been easy enough to walk into the lobby, past the reception desk and the bank of elevators to the double steel doors leading to the lot.

She glanced at the entrance again. A brighter swathe of sunlight washed in, lightening the dark gray concrete of the lot. A car swerved in from the street.

"Who's that?" Celine pointed.

Benny glanced over his shoulder. "Who's what?"

"The—" Celine stopped herself. The car had disappeared. She'd been seeing things.

They came in a car, Celine, Sister Mary Catherine told her.

"Would the valet on the night shift have let someone in?" Celine asked Benny. A bribe could've provided sufficient incentive to flout hotel policy.

"Nope!" He shook his head. "Not a chance. No one's allowed to drive in. That's the rule. Trust me, management checks the footage every night. It'd be our job on the line if we didn't follow orders."

Then how had they come in?

❧

"The hotel's security footage should give us a clue," Julia said when Celine had filled her in. They were standing in a secluded corner of the hotel lobby, shielded by the vast fronds of an indoor potted palm.

Too shaken to return upstairs, Celine had requested that the front desk staff put in a call to Julia. "Please tell her it's urgent." The former fed had come down within seconds.

Concern and alarm had flickered in her blue eyes at the reality of the threat to Clara, but had been instantly replaced with her habitual calm.

Now she eyed the envelope in Celine's hands. "I wish you'd remembered not to handle it."

"Fingerprints?" Celine looked ruefully down at the envelope. She'd been too much in shock to remember standard crime scene protocol.

"Don't sweat it. We might still get something useful off of it." Julia's head pivoted around, her sharp eyes scanning the lobby. "I wish I had some latex gloves on me. A plastic bag. Anything."

She sidled up to the reception desk, leaning over the curved black granite surface.

"You don't happen to have latex or nitrile gloves, do you?"

The girl behind the desk shook her head.

"I need something to protect this envelope," Julia said, tipping her head to indicate the envelope in Celine's hands.

"A large Ziploc bag?" the girl suggested. "I could have the kitchen send one over."

"Sure, that'll do." Julia smiled. "And while you're at it, we'd like a word with the head of security."

The girl's eyes widened. Her hand, about to lift the phone receiver up to her ear, froze, hanging limply in mid-air.

"Is there a problem, ma'am?" She gulped. "Anything you've lost? Or . . ." Her eyes slid to the bank of safes on the wall behind her.

Julia smiled reassuringly at her. "Trust me, it's nothing you can help us with."

The receptionist nodded and swallowed, but her eyes veered nervously toward the rows of safes mounted behind her.

"And we don't need to report anything stolen either," Celine added. It was clearly the prospect of theft that was causing the girl to have palpitations.

The Ziploc bag arrived a few minutes later.

"And Ms. Amanda Madden, our security manager, can see you now," the receptionist informed them. She indicated a door set into the wall. Potted palms set a few feet in front of it screened it from curious eyes.

Chapter Forty-Two

A tall, slim, middle-aged blonde with shoulder-length hair, Amanda Madden, rose to greet them as soon as Celine and Julia stepped into her office.

"We'd like to take a look at your security footage—whatever you have," Julia informed her. Once they'd seated themselves, she proceeded to recount the facts.

Celine was glad to let Julia take charge. Between the disturbing dream last night and finding the threatening note this morning, she'd had about as much as she could take.

I need to stay calm, she told herself, gripping the edge of the desk. *Or I'll be no good to Julia or Clara.*

"Oh, my!" Amanda's voice broke into her thoughts. The security manager peered down at the bold red letters on the envelope, white-faced. "Why would anyone do this?"

She raised her eyes, looking from Julia to Celine.

Then, reaching for the Ziploc bag and the envelope it contained, she went on, "May I?"

"It would be best that you didn't," Julia replied. "Fingerprints."

"Oh, yes, of course."

"I can give you the gist of it," Julia offered, proceeding to do so.

Amanda gazed down at the envelope again, her blue eyes wide with horror.

"But this is terrible. And you say it's a friend of yours?" She looked at Celine.

"An elderly Alzheimer's patient who's lost her son recently."

"There was some scandal about organ harvesting in nursing homes," Amanda said softly. "Older people being forced to change their wills in favor of nursing home staff. *The Boston Globe* broke the news. It's hard to believe they're at it again." She raised her eyes. "And going about it so brazenly."

"It's not her they're after," Celine said. "It's me."

Although it was Clara who posed the real threat to the criminals they were pitted against. The risk of Clara inadvertently blurting out what she knew was too great to chance.

But Amanda didn't need to know that. Wouldn't be able to stomach it, Celine guessed.

"Celine's helping the FBI. A mob-related case," Julia explained.

It was as much of the truth as they could reveal.

She glanced pointedly at the clock on the wall behind Amanda. The security manager was quick to take the hint.

"The monitors are in the basement," she said, thrusting her chair back and getting to her feet. "I can take you there. The problem is, I don't know how helpful it'll be. We're not as well covered as I'd like."

A bank of twelve curved monitors lined one wall of the vast basement space that housed the Hilton's surveillance system. An enormous keyboard sat on the desk below it along with another desktop monitor.

"We don't have great coverage, as you can see." Amanda stopped about a foot away from the desk and gestured toward the bank of screens. The uniformed guard monitoring the system was on his feet in an instant, pushing away his swivel chair and standing stiffly at attention to one side.

But Amanda ignored him, looking over her shoulder instead as Celine and Julia came up to stand beside her.

"You've got the lobby covered, I see," Julia remarked, peering at the screens. "And the hotel entrance."

Amanda nodded. She pointed again.

"There are a couple of cameras on each level at either end of every hallway. You can see people exiting the elevators onto the corridors. And you'll be able to see anyone who uses the door at the other end of the hallway. The one that gives onto the staircase leading down to the parking structure."

"But there's no way of knowing which of those people are headed for the parking lot and which ones are simply taking the stairs down to the street," the security guard—Adam, according to the brass name tag pinned to his shirt—interjected.

"Well, the person we're looking for drove into the parking lot in a car," Julia said. "Sometime between last evening—let's say seven o'clock—and early this morning. So as long as the entrance to the parking structure is covered, we're good."

"Can you rewind the tapes, Adam?" Amanda turned to the man, acknowledging his presence for the first time.

Adam cleared his throat. "With all due respect, ma'am, no one can drive into the parking lot. It's against hotel policy. We have valets to deal with parking."

Celine regarded the man—tall, broad-shouldered, with a chip on his shoulder. *He resents Amanda,* she thought. *Resents the fact that she has the job he thinks should be his.*

"I'm just not sure there's much point," he went on.

"Then the only other explanation," she said softly, "is that our perp. is in cahoots with one of your parking valets."

His dark eyes cut toward her. "That's impossible." But he lowered himself into his chair, nevertheless, and pulled himself closer to the desk. "I can rewind the tapes, but I doubt we'll see anything useful."

"What about when your valet is driving someone's car in?" Julia asked as Adam tapped sharply on the keyboard.

"We always have two people in the booth," he informed her tersely. He rewound the tapes to the moment when Julia and Celine returned the previous evening. The camera had captured them stepping out of the car and handing their key over to the parking valet.

"We don't have cameras inside the garage," Amanda said apologetically. "Although it looks like we should think about getting some."

"There wouldn't be much point," Adam gruffly contended. "We've already got the entrance."

The tape rolled forward showing nothing unusual for several hours. The parking valet had little to do after 10 p.m. But at one o'clock in the morning, a white sedan with a blue stripe down the entire length of it rolled up to the booth.

"Boston PD," Celine read the words printed on the side of the sedan. The driver rolled his window down, showed his badge to the valet inside the booth. Seconds later, the barricade lifted up and the car cruised forward.

"Interesting," Julia commented dryly.

Chapter Forty-Three

"That's the only situation in which someone other than our valets would be permitted to drive into the parking lot," Adam explained stiffly. "It's an understandable exception to the rule."

"But why were the police even here?" Amanda exclaimed. "Did we have an incident? I don't recall seeing anything in the night valet's report."

"That's because he didn't report anything," Adam growled through clenched teeth. "He better have a good reason for that." Letting the security footage run, he leaned back in his chair, picked up the phone by the keyboard, and dialed.

The minutes ticked by, the visual staying the same.

Then, approximately eight minutes later, the police vehicle came into view again, this time leaving the parking garage.

Celine stared at the car. There was something off about it.

"But I can't tell what." She shared her tenuous impression with the others.

"You're right, there is something odd about it," Amanda agreed. She paused the video. "I wonder what, though."

"It's not a police car." Julia's voice was unnaturally loud in the quiet basement.

❧

Blake was consuming what passed for a Continental breakfast at the Norwalk River Inn—a dry Danish and over-roasted coffee—when the phone rang. Assuming it was Dodd, he answered without looking at his screen.

"Blake Markham," he spoke crisply into the phone, hastily brushing crumbs off his mouth and chin with a paper towel.

"Any word on the Van Hoyt's Degas," a familiar voice breathed into his ear. It was Penny.

Letting out a long-suffering sigh, he pushed his chair back from the tiny Gingham-covered table in the Inn's dining room and made his way out onto the back porch.

"On the face of it, it seems to be authentic. I'll know more when Ms. Williams finishes conducting the tests I've requested."

Blake was reluctant to go much farther than that. The truth was that the Degas hanging in the Van Hoyt was stolen property—the very piece taken all those years ago from the Sullivans' home.

"And Dodd?" Penny pressed. "Did Ella convey my suspicions about him to you?"

"She did." He gazed at the snow-covered trees that fringed the backyard. Gray clouds hung low in the blue sky, threatening the outbreak of a storm.

Blake didn't want to say much about Dodd either. The two men had been supposed to meet that morning at Dodd's home. Dodd had promised to give Blake a call. But the call had yet to materialize.

He spun around, looking through the glass door at the clock in the Norwalk River Inn's dining room. It was nine o'clock. They'd arranged to meet at eleven—"at the latest," Dodd had said. There was still time, but somehow Blake was uneasy.

Last night, Dodd had seemed like a man on a mission, determined to prove his innocence. Why hadn't he called?

"Blake?" Penny was waiting for an answer.

"I think Dodd was duped," he said. "The provenance based on the stickers on the back was pretty convincing. He even called the Lowell to confirm they'd acquired the pastel from the Sullivans in 1996."

"And?"

"I'm guessing since that part of the story checked out, he figured the rest was true as well. That there'd been no money for a much-needed restoration and that consequently the restorer had claimed the work and was selling it to recoup his expenses."

"The Lowell has its own restoration team, Blake. Everyone knows that."

Apparently, Dodd hadn't. Blake glanced at the clock again. Why hadn't Dodd called? Had Blake himself been duped?

Had Dodd simply up and left? But where could he go? Canada? They were too far from Mexico for that to be a feasible destination.

Do you know what's worse than being betrayed, Special Agent? Norton's words and the sad expression in his eyes assaulted Blake's memory. *It's being betrayed by a friend.*

Dodd had adamantly denied having a mistress—or of being involved with anyone who might after all these years still have it in for him. Was it possible, he was caught in a mess not of his own making?

Had he confronted the man who'd betrayed him?

The uneasiness in the pit of his stomach grew, the acid from the coffee he'd consumed seeming to eat at his insides.

"You've got to interrogate Dodd," Penny urged. "Give him the third degree. He's involved in this thing. If he has one stolen Degas, what's to say he doesn't have the Gardner's five sketches as well?"

Nothing. But there was a way to figure out for sure whether he was or not.

"Penny, do you guys still have the security tape from the day prior to the theft?" The FBI had taken the tape and the logs from the Gardner only to return them. The investigators had determined nothing on the tape was material to the case.

"Of course. We were told we could record over it, but we never did. The Security Director at the time felt it should be retained as potential evidence just in case the FBI needed to comb through it for clues."

"Do you remember why we took it? There was an unauthorized entry into the museum the evening before as well, wasn't there?"

"Yes, it was a museum employee or someone on the board? You're thinking—"

"That it might have been Dodd?" Blake finished for her. "Yes. Look, there was no reason to suspect an insider at the time. And if it were Dodd on the tape, no one would've thought anything of it."

"You're right!" Excitement infused Penny's voice. "I'll get Clay on it right away and get back to you."

"Yup," he said, glad to end the call.

❧

Not a police car? Celine stared at the screen and then turned sharply toward Julia.

"How do you figure that?" Adam swiveled around to face her as well.

He lowered the end of the receiver, cupping the mouthpiece with a large palm. The person he was trying to reach had evidently not responded yet.

"For one thing, it's not a Ford Crown Vic," Julia calmly responded. "And take a look at the hood. It should be blue. The stripe down the side is narrower than it should be with the lettering below it rather than on it."

"But," she conceded, "it would take a pretty sharp eye to notice all of that in a split second."

Adam must've gotten hold of the person he was trying to call. He raised the mouthpiece to his lips and spoke rapidly into it.

Julia met Celine's eyes. "I think we know who's behind this."

Celine nodded. The General along with—Dodd? Who else could it be?

She could see Adam listening intently to the person on the other end of the line. Amanda stood anxiously beside him.

Decades earlier, the General and his partner had used the same MO to gain access to an area that should've been beyond limits. At the time, Reissfelder and DiMuzio had pulled up to the Gardner Museum, pretending to be Boston PD cops.

Now two other men—the driver had looked remarkably familiar—had used the same strategy.

"From what our night valet was told"—Adam's voice broke into her musings—"Boston PD received a 911 call from one of our guests about an incident in the garage. Rickie was shown a badge and told the men needed to do a drive-through to investigate."

The security guard's gaze panned toward Amanda.

"Rickie didn't think to report it because they told him as they drove off that it was a false alarm."

"Can you rewind the footage?" Celine asked. "I want to get another look at the man driving the vehicle."

"Sure." Adam tapped a few keys. The images on the screen reversed motion, speeding to the right until the police car was seen again stopping by the parking valet's booth. The security guard hit a button, freezing the screen.

"Recognize him?" Celine asked, watching Julia carefully.

"Yup." Julia's features were grim. "Mike from the wine tour."

He'd been sitting beside Beth on the bus, Celine recalled. His presence on the tape couldn't possibly be a coincidence.

"We'll need to report this to the police," Amanda said anxiously as Celine and Julia prepared to leave. She'd found out Julia was a retired FBI agent and was no doubt wondering whether it would be kosher to bring local police in on a case involving the FBI.

"Sure, go ahead," Julia replied with a quick thumbs-up.

Chapter Forty-Four

"Sounds like you've rattled some cages," Ella's voice crackled as it came over the speakerphone. "You must be getting closer."

Celine sighed. "That's what Julia says." She twisted her head around to give her friend a wry look.

They were seated on a bench overlooking Jamaica Pond, although from where she sat it looked more like a river. A frozen white river, narrow enough for the other shore to be visible but wide enough that any but the most seasoned swimmer would balk at crossing it.

The sun filtered through the trees, glittering off the icy surface of the water, but it was a cold day.

"The question is what are we getting closer to?"

"Beats me," Ella replied. "But they must think you've got something. What did you guys do with the tracker?"

They'd found it attached to the underside of the rental. Julia, certain their nighttime visitors had a more nefarious purpose in mind than delivering a threat, had conducted a thorough search of the vehicle.

"You're not anywhere near it, are you?"

Julia bent closer to the phone to respond. "We're nowhere near the car, just in case they bugged it. And, as for the tracker"—she gave Celine a broad smile—"it's in a trash can outside of Hutchinson House. They can track that for a while."

Ella chuckled appreciatively. "It might still be a good idea to give the car a thorough sweep. I could send—"

"Don't worry about it," Julia interrupted her. "We're going to see my old colleague Rod O'Neill. You remember him, don't you?"

"Sure. Wasn't he a tech specialist on the surveillance team?"

"Yup. He's got his own hardware store now that he's retired. But behind the shop itself, he's set up to provide his old pals some of the same gizmos he got together for our surveillance operations."

Julia had suggested buying a stepladder from Rod as well as a small security camera cleverly disguised as a household item.

"It could be a picture frame or some type of knickknack. Anything that won't look out of place."

If Clara was in danger, they'd need hard evidence of it to get law enforcement involved.

Celine surveyed her surroundings, the voices of the other two women receding into the background.

Her gaze fell on Hincman's Bench a few yards to the right. It was an odd-shaped bench, curving up on either side in a way that made it impossible to sit on. It was here that Jonah had met up with his handler.

She recalled the way the man had stiffened when Jonah had questioned his use of the word "donor." It hadn't been the reaction of a man dealing with a hireling. Instead, he'd seemed outraged as though expecting Jonah to be grateful for the funds he was receiving.

And, as for his shock at hearing about the Gardner theft, Celine had sensed shame rather than deviousness. Had it been Dodd or a friend of Dodd's? Whoever it was, he'd taken care to pay Jonah in cash.

Blake and Ella had examined Jonah's finances months ago. The regular cash deposits into his account had been a huge red flag, but they'd revealed nothing about the source of the money.

"Did Blake have a chance to question Dodd?" she asked Ella when there was a lull in the conversation.

"Yes." Ella hesitated before continuing. It was an elaborate story, but Celine had to agree with Blake's assessment, Dodd seemed on the up-and-up.

"Mistresses?" Julia asked.

"He lost his wife a few months ago. Cancer. He's still mourning her, and the question outraged him," Ella told them. "But there was someone in his office who hit on him."

"And?" Celine wanted to know.

"He rebuffed her advances."

"You're thinking"—Julia turned to face her—"that this woman could have had it in for Dodd? After all these years?"

"Couldn't have been her," Ella butted in before Celine could say a word. "Dodd specifically said she'd moved onto greener pastures. Shortly after he rejected her."

"Then, it's Norton," Celine murmured. "It's been Norton, all along. Dodd was just collateral damage."

Had Norton killed his mistress? If she'd opened a can of worms with her calls to the FBI and the media, he certainly had a motive. Was she the person whose death Celine hadn't sensed?

No, Celine, Sister Mary Catherine whispered. *She's a keeper of too many secrets to be killed.*

"Clara might know her," Ella was saying. "Sounds like they were co-workers for a time. Maybe they even went to the same church. Dodd claims never to have seen the inside of a church. He's an atheist."

The answers are in the church, Celine, Sister Mary Catherine whispered.

Henry Dodd lived on Scott Street—a narrow tree-lined avenue of wealthy mansions. Dodd's Colonial-style home with its gray shake siding was set farther back from the street than its neighbors. Blake circled around the wide driveway, parking the car a yard short of the portico constructed over the white garage doors.

Not wanting to wait any longer on Dodd's call, Blake had set out for his home shortly after finishing his call with Penny. If Dodd had indeed given him the slip, Blake preferred to find out sooner rather than later.

The garage door was closed. Presumably Dodd's car was in it. Snow dusted the grounds, the tree in the center of the yard, and the flagstone pavers under the portico. He tried the garage door. Locked.

Would Dodd have troubled to lock it if he'd left? Likely not.

His shoes scrunching on the snow underfoot, Blake walked toward the covered front porch, carefully climbing the wide brick steps leading up to the blue-gray front door. A wreath hung upon the frosted pane of the transom window.

Blake peered through it but could only make out a blur of grays and off-whites. Midnight blue drapes covered the widow on the side, concealing the interior from view. Stepping back, he rang the bell and proceeded to wait. A minute later, he jabbed the buzzer again, keeping his finger firmly pressed against it.

His ears were still ringing from the shrill tone of the doorbell when its incessant trill subsided. He put his ear to the door, straining every nerve to detect the slightest trace of sound from within. But all was eerily silent.

"Dodd!" He hammered his fist on the door. "It's Special Agent Blake Markham. Open up!"

Still nothing.

He glanced up. The single bulb dangling from the old-fashioned pendant with its pleated shade was still on. Strange given the hour.

He craned his neck farther back. The security camera placed discreetly above the door clearly wasn't on. The telltale glowing red light was conspicuous by its absence.

It was a sinister combination: a porch light that was still glowing, its light weak against the glare of the sun, and a security camera light that wasn't.

Blake surveyed the grounds. Did the circumstances justify breaking the door open? Did he have reasonable cause to suspect Dodd might be in danger, in dire need of help?

He was still debating the issue when the low purr of a Toyota engine broke the stillness, and a dull green Tercel drove up the driveway.

Chapter Forty-Five

The footage from the old VHS security tape was grainy, black-and-white, and monotonously uneventful. But Penny kept her eyes glued to her computer screen. Somewhere on that tape was the moment that had captured the FBI's attention years ago.

Had it been Dodd on the tape? Barely able to breathe, Penny watched. The office was quiet, the only sound that of Clay's quiet breathing behind her.

When the security director had shown up at her office a half-hour earlier with the tape and a video camera slung over his shoulder, Penny had initially been dismayed. She'd known better than to expect a thumb drive, mentally preparing herself to see a DVD. But a VHS tape!

"Found it!" Clay had triumphantly brandished the security tape, oblivious to the fact that the precious footage was recorded on obsolete technology.

"It's a VHS tape, Clay," Penny had objected. "How are we to watch that?"

But Clay, clever man, had devised a brilliant solution. He held up a slim, white rectangular object.

"It's an adaptor," he'd explained. "The audio video cables connect to a VCR or any analog source." He shrugged the strap of his video camera off his shoulder, setting it on her desk as he continued to speak. "The USB at the other end hooks up to a computer or iPad. Nifty, huh?"

Penny had to agree it was. But all that effort seemed to have been for naught. Nothing much seemed to have occurred the night before the theft at the Gardner Museum. Cars cruised by. A few parked. But no one gave the Gardner more than a passing glance.

Then at midnight, a hatchback pulled up. Penny strained her eyes. There was no way of detecting the color of the vehicle. On the black-and-white video playing on her computer screen, it was a light gray. It may well have been gray or some other lighter color.

A trim figure emerged from the passenger side of the hatchback. It was a man. Medium height. Bespectacled. In what looked like a polo shirt and slacks.

"That's not Dodd!" Penny shook her head. She watched the man approach the Gardner, rap sharply on the window, say something to the guards within, who promptly opened the door for him.

A soft whoosh of frustration escaped her lips. She'd been so sure the video would show Dodd, vindicating her suspicions of the man.

Clay reached over her shoulder to pause the video. "I can see why the FBI returned the tape to us. There's nothing here."

"No, there's not." Just one of the board members—an upstanding guy, a stickler for the rules, Penny recalled. He'd probably forgotten something during the day and returned at night to retrieve it. She hit play just to confirm her impressions.

Sure enough, the man emerged from the museum empty-handed and proceeded to make his way back to the hatchback.

"Wonder why he was even here," Clay remarked, closing the software on the laptop he'd brought with him and tugging the USB end of the adaptor out of the USB port.

"Because he forgot to file a paper or return a folder or book to its proper location." Penny sniffed. "Whatever it was, I'm sure he wrote it in the visitor log. That's the kind of man he was."

Meticulous. That was how her predecessor had described him—rather disparagingly. The kind of man who'd say grace over a snack.

Chapter Forty-Six

"You lookin' for Meester Dodd?" A plump woman, her face wreathed in a welcoming smile, stepped out of the old Tercel.

"Yup," Blake said, wondering who she was. He watched as she dropped her car keys into a voluminous tote and ambled up to the porch.

Drawing a large key from her coat pocket, she inserted it into the lock.

"He probably still sleeping," she guessed. An affectionate smile accompanied this observation. "He expecting guest last night."

The woman—Dodd's housekeeper, Juana Alonzo—recalled setting out a cheese and cracker tray along with some wine glasses.

"You were here when he returned from the golf club last night?" Blake asked her.

"*Si*," she said, thrusting open the door.

Blake followed her into an opulent living room. The blue drapes he'd seen from outside the house were drawn. A tray with a plate of cheese and crackers was on the coffee table. Dodd's gray-brown hair was visible above the armchair facing the fireplace.

"See!" Juana turned, beaming, toward him. "What I say? He sound asleep!"

That explained the porch light being left on. But something was off.

"Mr. Dodd!" he called loudly, moving around to face the man. Juana circled around the other side of the armchair, intent on clearing the tray. Bending down to lift the tray, she half-turned and froze.

Blake saw it the moment she did. Foam frothing from the corner of Dodd's mouth, his head lolling back, his eyes wide open, staring at the ceiling, clouded over and glazed.

"Ahhh—ahhhhh!" Juana's wail of dismay nearly gave him a heart attack. "Meester Dodd!"

She dropped the tray, heading toward Dodd, but Blake caught hold of her arm.

"No. He's dead. There's nothing we can do for him now, Juana. Stay calm." He grasped her firmly around the waist, preventing her from crumpling to the floor.

As the housekeeper cried hysterically against him, he examined the scene. Dodd had died sometime in the early hours of the morning. Rigor mortis had set in and was in full blow now. Dried bits of vomit stained the front of his polo shirt and had dribbled onto the armchair near his neck.

Gingerly he sniffed the air. Underlying the sour smell of the regurgitated contents of Dodd's stomach was the unmistakable odor of bitter almonds. Cyanide, he thought.

The same poison that had taken Laurie Robbes' life—the intern who'd made the mistake of attempting to blackmail Norton all those years ago. A cleaner way to kill someone than garroting—especially for a man like Norton who liked to keep his hands clean.

Was this Norton's handiwork?

"Juana, do you know whom Mr. Dodd was expecting last night?" Her sobs had subsided.

She shook her head, sniffling. "No, no," she hiccupped out. "But we have security camera," she added hopefully. "In basement." She pointed to the staircase located opposite the front entrance.

"I'll take a look," Blake said, not hoping for much. The camera had been disabled—most likely before Dodd's guest had even arrived.

"You stay here," he ordered. "Don't touch anything, okay? Just look around. See if anything seems out of place."

She nodded to indicate she understood. He loosened his grasp on her, reiterating his instructions not to touch anything, and headed for the staircase.

"Whatever Jonah found, it's up high," Celine said, turning away from the half-open window. Even in the icy Boston cold, Julia insisted on rolling the windows down. A chill wind rushed in, curling itself around Celine's neck.

Julia's gaze drifted momentarily away from the road to acknowledge Celine's words.

"The stepladder," the former fed said softly, turning back to the narrow, tree-lined road.

The radio was turned on so their voices would be muffled if, in fact, the intruders had planted a listening device in their car.

Was Dodd really on the up-and-up as Blake seemed to think? Or was he trying to kill Clara, a longtime employee who would know where his skeletons were buried?

Skeletons that he shared with Norton perhaps.

What about the murder last night? Someone had been killed? But who? Nothing had been reported as of yet. Was Dodd behind the murder? Or was it Norton?

And the man who'd been meeting with Jonah, just a short distance from the facility that housed Clara? Who had that been?

Jamaicaway curved into Pond Street. Julia took the curve, traveling onto Arborway. They circled around, turning onto Eliot Street, a narrow, residential area. Bare trees, boughs heavy with snow, lined either side of the street. Moms and nannies bundled up in thick jackets walked toddlers and pushed strollers.

It was peaceful. So very peaceful. Celine's eyelids felt heavy.

She blinked, forcing them open. To her surprise, the snow had disappeared. The trees were covered in bright green foliage. A familiar skinny figure strode rapidly down the sidewalk.

Jonah!

She leaned out the window. What was he doing here? He was looking straight ahead, his eyes intent on something or someone ahead of him.

"What's who doing here?" Julia's brusque inquiry dispelled the vision.

"Jonah!" Celine twisted around to face the former fed. "He was here. Following someone."

"Who?"

Celine thought for a moment. She hadn't seen who it was, but she could take a guess.

"His handler, I'll bet."

But why had Jonah been following the man? Because the guy had been associated in some way with the Gardener Museum.

"I wonder if Norton had an insider in the Gardner," she murmured.

"You mean Dodd?" Julia took her eyes off the street again.

"No." Celine shook her head. "Someone else. Someone he might have had some clout over. Someone he could manipulate."

Someone in a church.

Where had that thought come from?

The houses on either side were large—nearly every one a two-story structure, the siding freshly painted. Christmas lights hung from the eaves and were draped around tree branches and porch pillars.

Did Jonah's handler live here?

It was a home away from home, Celine, Sister Mary Catherine whispered. *A safe haven.*

And Jonah had found it?

The last structure on the street—an imposing building of gray stone with a spire—was not a house.

"A church!" Celine gasped. She turned to Julia. "He was here. Jonah was here."

"Divine Mercy Church," Julia read the words inscribed on the large stone slab erected by the gate. Her eyes met Celine's. "This is the church, isn't it?"

Celine nodded. Across the street was a bank with an ATM machine outside it. She pointed to it.

"Rockland Trust Bank. I think that's where his handler withdrew cash—I'm guessing from his personal account—to give to Jonah."

Julia gave her a wry smile. "Trust me, that doesn't narrow it down as much as you think. But I guess it's a start."

The answers are in the church, Celine, Sister Mary Catherine reminded her.

"If Jonah came here," she said to Julia, "I'll bet he went in—asking questions. Someone's bound to remember him."

Chapter Forty-Seven

Blake bounded down the stairs—two at a time—to the basement. Nearing the bottom step, he slowed to scan the area.

On the left was an open closet door. Next to it a vast laundry room with a storage space behind it. Up ahead, a lounge with leather couches, a large coffee table, and an enormous flat-screen TV.

Where was the security system Juana had mentioned?

He strode into the lounge, hand on his holster. It was force of habit. Dodd's killer was long gone.

Swiveling around, he saw an open door. From where he stood, he made out the corner of an office desk and a sleek white DVR. Okay, that was it.

Blake walked in. As he'd suspected, the device had been turned off. The power indicator light wasn't glowing. The single monitor above it was frozen to a nighttime image of the entrance porch. A small section of the curving driveway was visible. It was empty.

The porch light cast an eerie glow in the area around the porch, washing the trunk of the bare tree in the yard in a dimly glowing band.

Judging by the single monitor, the security camera only covered the mansion's entrance. Dodd clearly wasn't concerned about covering the rear entrance, the garage, or even the interior of the house. From the little Blake had seen, there was no need.

The paintings on the walls were largely prints. The only original canvasses having been created no earlier than the past decade or two—abstract works that might reasonably be expected to appreciate, but which most likely had been purchased more to boost the artist's career than as a long-term investment.

It was the kind of thing collectors did, Blake thought, as he studied the DVR, trying to understand how it worked. He didn't want to make any foolish moves and risk deleting any footage it had managed to capture.

Minutes later, certain he'd figured it out, he turned on the device and held down the rewind button, stopping when he caught sight of Dodd's car slowly cruising up the driveway toward the garage. It disappeared from view.

Five minutes later, Dodd emerged onto the screen. He was approaching the entrance porch, cell phone glued to his ear, engaged in animated conversation.

With his killer? Blake sure hoped it was the last person to see Dodd alive.

This was great! The cell phone records would yield their first clue.

He hunched over the table, gripping its edge as he stared avidly at the screen.

Cradling the cell phone between his shoulder and ear, Dodd reached for the door lock and let himself in.

The DVR had recorded a view of the empty porch and yard for about seven more minutes before being turned off. In his haste, Dodd must've forgotten to turn off the monitor as well.

Blake hit the pause button. Okay. Okay, they had something to work with.

Agitated after his conversation with Blake, Dodd had returned home. Had he made the call? Or received it? Assuming he'd made it, it could only be to the person who'd set him up to purchase a stolen Degas.

Blake glanced pensively at the monitor. Whoever it was, he'd agreed to a meeting but had insisted the security cameras be turned off. Someone familiar with Dodd and the house, then.

And Dodd had agreed. *Damn!*

But the cell phone—even if it was a burner—gave them a tenuous thread to follow. Blake pulled out his phone, opened the notes app, and tapped a reminder to himself: *Get Norwalk PD to look into cell phone records.*

And if it turned out to be Hugh Norton—the last man to see Henry Dodd alive . . . Blake's pulse quickened at the thought.

☙

His ringing cell phone jolted him out of his musings.

"Ella?" He found himself irritated by the interruption. What did she want? An update on Dodd? Because Penny had been pestering her to get one?

"Blake!" His personal assistant sounded more disturbed than he ever recalled hearing her. "Something's happened."

He listened intently, his irritation rapidly giving way to an unsettling feeling in the pit of his stomach. A note threatening Clara. It had been found on the windshield of Celine and Julia's rental. Julia had found a bug as well.

"You think it's Dodd?" Ella ventured, her voice tentative.

"Dodd's dead."

"What!"

Blake brought her up to speed. She emitted a low whistle as he concluded his observations. But she agreed it couldn't have been Dodd issuing threats to Clara and Celine.

Dodd's last hours had been focused on proving his own innocence in the theft of the Sullivans' stolen Degas.

"The cell phone records, Blake," she said immediately. "You'll need to get Norwalk PD on the cell phone records."

"Yes, I know." He rolled his eyes. Ella tended to treat him like a rookie agent at best, an especially obtuse personal assistant at worst.

But the cell phone records were only a piece of the larger puzzle. Dodd must have had some evidence—documentation—to prove his innocence.

Finishing his call with Ella, he tapped out another reminder on the note app. He wanted every scrap of paper Dodd had in his house, his office, and anywhere else he frequented. And he wanted every digital record as well.

Anything that could lead them to the individual who'd sold the unwitting Dodd a stolen Degas.

Chapter Forty-Eight

Celine grasped the heavy church door and tugged it open only to hear the opening strains of a hymn. *Damn*, she softly cursed under her breath. Had Mass begun? Or was it ending?

She peered around the thick plank that formed the door. A small group of altar servers and lectors, with the priest bringing up the rear, processed slowly down the aisle toward the altar.

Clearly, the service had just commenced. They'd have to return at a later time.

Celine was about to close the door and hastily back away from the entrance. But Julia was right behind her.

"What's going on?" the former fed hissed. Several inches shorter than Celine, she couldn't see the interior.

At the same time, a shawl-clad, middle-aged woman standing out of sight by a table—a greeter, probably—stepped toward the door, smiled warmly at Celine, and beckoned her in.

"Come in, come in. There's plenty of room for you." The woman's face was wreathed in smiles. "How nice of you to join us this morning!"

Great, Celine thought, managing to return the woman's smile. *Just great.*

She'd vowed never to attend a Mass, but here she was. With Julia behind her, she tiptoed in, slipping into an empty pew just as the entrance hymn closed and the priest turned to greet the congregation.

Going through the motions mechanically, Celine allowed her eyes and mind to wander. The church looked nothing like the one in her dream, except in one respect. The wall reliefs depicting the fourteen Stations of the Cross each had a gold-painted frame around it. From a distance, they looked like paintings hanging on the wall.

As she stared at the one of Christ stumbling under the weight of an enormous cross, the relief faded, replaced by the Gardner's *Chez Tortoni*. Celine blinked but couldn't get rid of the Manet her mind's eye was seeing on the wall.

She glanced away, but the next Station had been replaced by a Degas sketch—a jockey on horseback. The images assailed her eyes, refusing to be dispelled. Why was she seeing them? Why here, why now?

Were the works concealed here—somewhere within this church? Was that what Jonah had discovered? That the Gardner's stolen artworks had been stashed here all those years ago?

They aren't here anymore, Celine, Sister Mary Catherine whispered.

But they had been at one time, Celine realized. Barely listening to the homily, Celine discreetly shifted in her seat, taking in her surroundings. A wooden confessional was placed to the right of the entrance.

"What are you looking at?" Julia hissed. "No point looking at the door. There's no getting out of here anytime soon."

Celine turned to face her friend. "The night of the theft when Simon and Earl drove the Dutch works to the warehouse, I think Grayson came here with the Manet. He left it in the confessional."

How he'd managed to get it out of the Blue Room without tripping the alarm was anybody's guess, but Celine was quite certain the Manet had ended up here.

Julia frowned. "And then it went to—?"

"Jezebel." The name tumbled out of Celine's mouth. "That's not her name," she explained. "It's her character." That was how people close to the mysterious FBI tipster had regarded her.

"You're thinking Jonah found out about this?"

"I don't know." Celine's gaze was riveted on the confessional. How easy it would've been for someone to come in during the early hours of the morning to retrieve the stolen works. It would have to be someone who was accustomed to coming in early—a parish secretary, perhaps. Whoever it was who laid out the lectionary and the book containing the prayers of the faithful.

Had the Degas sketches made their way here as well?

In her mind's eye, she saw an innocuous manila envelope. A thick hand tucked it into a container and then pushed the container back into its cubby.

Here, but not here, Sister Mary Catherine whispered cryptically.

The Liturgy of the Word was over.

"Be prepared for the endless kneeling and standing that follows," Celine whispered to her friend as they pulled down the kneeler.

"Oh, boy!" Julia groaned, her knees loudly creaking as she obediently folded them under her.

After a few more bouts of kneeling and standing, the assembly began to file out into the center aisle. Celine and Julia remained in their pew, but the woman who'd urged them in approached them again.

"Don't be afraid to go up for the blessing," she said. "If you fold your arms like this"—she crossed her arms across her chest, placing each hand on the other shoulder—"the priest will know you're not ready to receive communion. But he's more than happy to grant you a blessing."

Not wanting to argue, Celine joined the line of people in the center aisle. Julia followed close behind her, arms crossed as the greeter had demonstrated.

A short while later the priest had dismissed the congregation with another prayer and a blessing. Celine and Julia were about to slip away only to be accosted by the priest—a short, plump, bespectacled individual.

"How good of you to join us!" he greeted them, extending his hand. "Annette here"—he gestured toward the greeter—"says you're newcomers."

"From Paso Robles," Julia said.

"And how did you hear about us?" His curious gaze veered toward Celine and then drifted back to Julia.

"From a friend," Celine said immediately. "Jonah. Do you recall him? He was about my height, thin, dark hair and eyes."

"*Was*?" The priest had uncannily picked up on her use of the past tense. "Is he no longer with us?"

"Unfortunately not," Julia replied, her tone warning off any further questions. But the priest remained undaunted.

"Do you wish to have a Mass said for the repose of his soul?"

"He wasn't Catholic," Celine told him. "He was a journalist. We believe he came here to research a story."

The priest's nose wrinkled in confusion, and he looked toward Annette.

"He might've gone to the parish office," she offered. "It opens in an hour. If anyone knows what your friend was looking into, it'll be Marisa."

Celine nodded, desperately searching her mind for further questions to ask. But the priest's attention had been claimed by another parishioner and Annette had started handing out bulletins.

"Do take one," she said to them as they walked by. "It lists Mass timings and other events of interest."

Chapter Forty-Nine

Back upstairs, Blake found Juana standing, head tilted to one side, before the wall-mounted mail and key holder by the door. The mail slot carried a small potted plant—clearly faux since it was embedded in a layer of pebbles. The animal-head key hooks held only a set of car keys.

"Is anything missing?" He was careful to keep his voice gentle. The housekeeper obviously held her employer in deep regard. His sudden demise had come as a shock.

"Meester Dodd's house keys." She turned to him, bewildered. "He always hang them here."

Blake glanced over at Dodd's corpse. Had Dodd, in his haste, forgotten to hang his keys up as usual? Or had his killer made off with them?

A chill entered Blake's bones. If that were the case, the killer meant to return later to search for and gather any piece of evidence—any papers—that could tie him to Dodd and the stolen Degas.

He turned back to Juana. "Were they here yesterday?" he asked. "Do you remember?"

She frowned, thinking back to the previous evening when she'd last seen her employer alive.

"I theenk so," she finally said. Then she shook her head ruefully. "But I no remember."

"That's okay," he assured her. The medical examiner could search Dodd's pockets. (He'd have done it himself if Juana hadn't been around.) But they'd need to operate on the assumption that the keys had been stolen. That meant removing every scrap of evidence and keeping a tight lock on the house until that had been done.

He swiveled around, regarding the living room. There was something off about it. He'd thought so from the moment they'd come in.

Suddenly it hit him. The wine.

"Juana?" He looked at her. "Did you pick out a wine for Mr. Dodd and his guest yesterday?"

She shook her head. "He say his guest bring."

Blake was willing to bet his last dollar the wine had already been poisoned. The killer had taken care to remove it from the scene. Where could the bottle be now that the deadly deed was done?

"But you did set out wine glasses, right?"

She nodded deeply. "*Si*" Then as her gaze followed his, her brow furrowed again. "He wash them already?"

Or his killer had. To remove all traces of the cyanide he'd poisoned Dodd with. Not that Blake mentioned this to her.

Search neighborhood for wine bottle. He filed the note away in his mind, then brought his iPhone out to add it to the memo he'd already created. He wanted to take a few photos of the crime scene as well before Norwalk PD got here. He'd made the 911 call on his way up, identifying himself as an FBI agent.

But Dodd was dead. This wasn't an emergency. It would be a while before the police got here.

"Where's the kitchen?" he asked when he'd taken as many photos as he needed. With any luck, the wine glasses had been left in the kitchen.

"Over there." Juana pointed in the direction of the staircase.

Blake had noticed a doorway on his way down to the basement. Now he followed the housekeeper through it into a spacious kitchen, beyond which was an enormous family room.

"Ah, wine glasses still here." Juana's sense of relief was oddly comical. She must've realized it herself for her features crumpled and tears filled her eyes. "Meesez Dodd pick those out. Long time ago. Before she die, you know."

She walked toward the countertop where the rinsed glasses had been left to dry. Neither one had been washed too thoroughly. Blake could make out wine stains and droplets of wine.

He grinned. It was good evidence. The killer had obviously been in too much of a hurry or just too sloppy to do it right.

Before he could warn her not to, Juana picked up one of the glasses to inspect the inside.

"Huh! Still dirty." She snorted derisively.

"Juana, I wouldn't . . ." Blake cautioned, but he was too late. She'd already slid a finger into the droplets of wine-stained water that had miraculously remained at the bottom of the glass and was sniffing at it.

"O-o-oh!" she groaned, the effects of the cyanide hitting her. She set the glass down, her face a bilious green, and clutched at her stomach.

"Let's wash your hands," Blake said briskly. He clasped her around the stomach, positioned her over the sink, turned on the faucet, and plunged her hands under the cold stream. Pouring a generous quantity of dish soap on her palms, he rubbed them together until a thick lather formed and then ran them under the water again.

"All right, let's go out. You need fresh air."

He settled her on the porch step and called 911 again.

"I need an emergency vehicle here, stat," he ordered, explaining the situation and giving the dispatcher Dodd's address.

Call completed, he peered down at Juana. She still looked sick, but she'd survive. There likely hadn't been much hydrogen cyanide trapped inside the wine glass. Thank heavens for that.

Had the killer worn gloves to wash the wine glasses? Or was it possible he'd been careless enough to leave a fingerprint or two?

Keeping his fingers crossed, Blake joined Juana on the step.

"Hang in there," he said. "There'll be doctors here soon. You'll be fine. Just hang in there for me, okay?"

She nodded weakly.

❧

"Julia Hood!" A tall man in a flannel shirt tucked into blue jeans came forward, arms outstretched, to greet them when they entered O'Neill's Hardware. "I hear you're finally making headway in that Gardner case."

He enfolded Julia in a bear hug. "About time!"

Julia returned the hug and then stepped back. "It's thanks to this young woman, Rod." She indicated Celine. "Meet Celine Skye—"

Celine winced, dreading Julia's next words and Rod's reaction. But she needn't have worried. Julia had thought of the perfect designation for her: "Psychic art sleuth."

It sounded less kooky than "psychic."

"Oh!" Rod's eyebrows rose. He seemed surprised, but at least he wasn't rolling his eyes or regarding her with skeptical suspicion. "I've heard of psychics and I've heard of art sleuths. Never met anybody who combined the two skills."

He shook Celine's hand. "Nice to meet you."

When she'd returned his greeting, Rod shifted his attention back to Julia. Tucking her arm under his elbow, he drew her toward an office at the back of the store.

"What brings you to O'Neill's?"

Celine followed them into the tiny office, the church bulletin still tucked under her arm. She'd brought it along with her to read, figuring she was unlikely to be much involved in the conversation. Rod and Julia would be

182

talking shop, discussing surveillance technology—a topic about which Celine knew precious little.

"We should do a thorough sweep of your car," Rod advised when Julia had brought him up to speed.

"That's why we're here," Julia said with a grin. "And for a few other items."

She leaned over the desk and handed him the short list she'd made in their hotel room.

Rod took a quick look.

"A discreet little nanny cam, eh?" He glanced up. "I think I can find you something useful." He got to his feet, going toward the door.

Julia followed suit. "You okay to stay here?" she asked Celine, pushing her chair in.

"Absolutely." Celine smiled. Ever since they'd left the church, she'd felt an inner sense pushing her to take a look at the church bulletin. Now was her opportunity.

She waited until Rod and Julia had left and then pulled the church bulletin out from under her arm. It listed Mass timings and a schedule for catechism classes. Inside, were the daily Mass readings as well as the homily from the previous Sunday. Whatever she was hoping for, it wasn't that.

Sighing, she ran her eye down a list of names—associate pastor, deacon, music minister, cantors, faith formation—printed inside a blue box on the third page. Other than the parish secretary—Marisa Gomez—none of the names looked familiar.

A box at the bottom of the page—entitled Parish News—caught her eye. But it wasn't as promising as it looked. There were only two items, both requests for prayers of healing for two of the church's parishioners. A picture accompanied the short write-up about each individual.

Deacon Rafferty was struggling with lung cancer. He'd been a parish member for fifty years, heading the RCIA program and offering Bible and Catechism classes for forty of them. Celine's gaze moved toward the accompanying photograph provided by the Deacon's son.

It showed a bald man with shrunken cheeks and eyes that seemed clouded over.

He's not long for this world, Celine thought, startled.

No, he's not. Sister Mary Catherine confirmed her impression. *He needs prayers.*

Celine blew out a slow, frustrated breath. It was unlikely the man was connected with the Gardner Museum or the theft that had robbed it of its artworks over thirty years ago.

He needs prayers, the nun repeated more urgently. *He desperately needs prayers.*

Not something she could provide, Celine thought, turning to the other article in the box.

The second parishioner in need of prayer was also in the late stages of some type of cancer. What exactly it was, the article didn't mention. She was in her late sixties and had long served as a Eucharistic Minister. The color photo, however, was from several years back, portraying a stunningly attractive woman in her forties. She had vivid blue eyes and dark, wavy hair.

Celine ran her finger over the snapshot. There was something hard about the woman—in her eyes and the set of her jawline. This wasn't a person who brooked any opposition to her desires or who tended to put others before herself.

Self-centered, she thought. *Vain, too.* It was an inference she'd made based on the fact that the woman's request for prayer didn't include a recent photograph.

According to the article, she'd lost copious amounts of her hair because of the chemotherapy used to treat her cancer. As a once-attractive woman who took pride in her appearance, she'd understandably objected to being seen in her current state.

Celine glanced at the name printed beneath the photo. Maureen Rita. In every respect, she reminded Celine of the mysterious caller whose mind she'd briefly occupied in Paso Robles.

Was this the FBI's anonymous tipster? A beautiful career woman who now had cancer?

Clara knows, Sister Mary Catherine murmured. *You must remember to ask.*

Chapter Fifty

"He's dead?" Julia's voice rose sharply.

Celine resisted the urge to look at her friend. It would mean taking her eyes off the road, not something she was willing to risk under the circumstances.

But she couldn't help wondering who was dead.

Ella had called just as they were leaving Rod's hardware store. Eager to take the call, Julia had asked Celine to drive. Celine had reluctantly agreed. Despite her undergraduate years in Durham, New Hampshire, she'd never gotten used to driving in snowy conditions.

"Dodd is dead?" Julia sounded like a robot, mechanically repeating what she'd heard.

Celine's heart muscles clenched up—the spasm of pain a delayed reaction to the news. She clutched the steering wheel hard, her gaze riveted on the snow-dusted street in front of her. They were headed to Hutchinson House. She'd need to turn left on Pond Street.

Dodd's dead? she muttered in disbelief as she took the turn. Murdered, obviously. Why else was Ella calling? Why else had she felt the agonizing spasm that heralded every violent death?

So that was the death she'd overlooked. Dear God!

Why hadn't she seen it? Because he was only peripherally connected to the case? Because there was nothing she could've done to prevent it?

"It was cyanide poisoning?" Julia queried. "Blake's sure of that?"

Out of the corner of her eye, Celine saw Julia plug her left ear and hunch in the direction of the phone gripped to her right ear.

She listened quietly to the conversation, keeping her eyes peeled for her next turn: Jamaicaway. She'd need to make a right onto the street. Dodd had been found late that morning by his housekeeper and Blake. He'd been killed presumably in the early hours of the morning.

The wine he'd consumed had most likely been laced with cyanide. Was that why Celine had seen Laurie in her dream? It was cyanide that had killed Laurie, even though the intern's death had officially been ruled an accident.

The attempt on Celine's life last year had involved the use of cyanide as well.

It's cleaner than a garroting, Celine, Sister Mary Catherine spoke softly into her ear. *Clean and impersonal.*

And deadly, Celine thought. Luckily, she hadn't gotten around to tasting the poisoned chocolate sent to her last year. It was Dirck's sister, Annabelle, who'd borne the brunt of the attack. And it was a miracle she'd survived the attempt.

Celine thought of Clara. Dodd couldn't have been behind the threats they'd received that morning. Dodd was collateral damage for . . . ? Celine didn't know who. That's what they needed to find out.

"I just wanted to let you know Dodd couldn't be the person threatening Clara," Ella's voice rang out, startling Celine. She hadn't realized Julia had put Ella on speakerphone.

"No, he couldn't have been," Celine murmured, although it was doubtful Ella heard her.

"Whoever it is," Ella continued, "the guy's still out there. Still watching you. Possibly tailing you."

Celine shuddered. Thank heavens, they'd made the decision to visit Clara first, choosing to question the parish secretary after they'd made sure to install the security equipment Rod had provided them.

The stepladder had a hidden camera that transmitted to the same software as the faux orchid. The orchid's purple bloom concealed the camera lenses, while buried deep within the fake soil was the SD recording card the camera used.

The bodies are falling, Celine, Laurie's voice cackled out. *They'll continue to fall. You need to wake up.*

Celine gripped the steering wheel harder, the taunt acting like a whiplash on her nerves.

You are so close, Celine, Sister Mary Catherine encouraged her. *Don't give up, my dear. You're closer than you think.*

"Dodd's in the clear, then," Julia said softly. "Seems to be, at least."

"Oh, definitely," Ella agreed. "Oh, shoot! I forgot to mention it to Blake."

Apparently, Penny Hoskins had called with the news that Dodd hadn't been on the security camera tape from the evening prior to the theft.

Who was, then? Celine wondered. But Ella had ended the call before she could ask the question.

"It was a museum employee," Julia told her when she asked. "Or someone on the board, I don't recall which. But he was on the up-and-up. That's why we returned the tape."

Celine frowned, biting her lip as she carefully navigated her turn.

"But why was he even there?" she wanted to know. "And why was he allowed in, against the security protocols the Gardner had in place?"

"He had a legitimate reason. I don't remember what it was now. But it was a routine matter, nothing out of the ordinary. We followed up with the man. From what I recall, he was on the up-and-up, as straight an arrow as you could find. A stickler for the rules—annoyingly so, I might add."

The tape is important, Celine, her guardian angel said. *Don't forget that.*

But Julia didn't seem to think so.

She shook her head. "Nope, there was nothing on that tape. It was a promising lead, but it fizzled out almost as soon as we looked into it."

Julia stared straight ahead at the bright, cold morning.

"Looks like it's Norton," she muttered. "Just as we've always suspected. The question is, has he made any mistakes this time? Or will he be too slick for us, as always?"

❧

Blake looked down at his insistently trilling phone. It was Penny Hoskins. With more news about Henry Dodd, he guessed.

With a quick glance at Juana, still looking shell-shocked as she sat on the porch step beside him, Blake stood up and answered the call.

"Listen, before you say anything"— he moved out of earshot—"Dodd's dead. Whatever he knew—"

"What!" Penny's gasp cut him off.

"Dodd's dead. Murder. There's no doubt about it. Someone got to him."

"Oh!" For once, the Gardner's Director seemed to be at a loss for words.

"I guess you saw him on that security tape we returned to you," Blake ventured.

"No, actually, we didn't," Penny said. "That's why I was calling. It was another board member, Dean Rafferty. Like Dodd, he was at the meeting when Agent McCormick warned us a couple of thugs were planning a hit on the Gardner. He was actually even more insistent than Dodd that the Gardner insure its holdings."

"Okay." Where was Penny going with this?

Blake stood near the bare tree in the yard, eyes peeled on the road outside. When would the first responders be arriving? Juana didn't seem much the worse for wear; the effects of the hydrogen cyanide appeared to have subsided.

But—he glanced around at the housekeeper, sitting wan and disconsolate on the porch step—he'd feel much better once she'd had paramedics examine her.

"When the FBI initially asked us about Dean's unexpected arrival at the Gardner the evening before the theft, we didn't really have any cause for concern. Dean had a legitimate reason for being there. He was in charge of taking Manet's portrait of his mother off the Blue Room and getting it ready to be sent out for restoration."

"I see." Blake was thoughtful, processing this information. He'd always known the Gardner's second Manet had been sent out for restoration. But that it had still been in the museum the night before the theft was a new revelation.

The information opened up a host of new possibilities.

"So, he went to the museum, had the guards let him in, and went into the Blue Room to lift the portrait off the wall?"

"Yes," Penny confirmed. "And he must have packaged it and kept it in the downstairs closet ready to be sent out. He should've done it earlier that morning, but he'd forgotten to do so. And it was going to be sent out the next morning—that would've been the day of the theft."

Blake nodded. Technically, it would've been the day before, the theft having taken place in the pre-dawn hours of March 18. But he knew what Penny meant.

"Would anyone have noticed the portrait was missing from its usual place in the Blue Room?" he asked.

"Well, no. We usually put a little notice saying the work in question is out for restoration. I have no doubt Dean made sure to do so. He was always a stickler for the rules."

Blake's mind whirred. The theft of Manet's *Chez Tortoni* had always been inexplicable. The thieves had never made it into the Blue Room. They'd always assumed one of the night guards had taken it off during their rounds—suggesting the guards had been in cahoots with the thieves. But that theory had never been satisfactorily proven.

Why charge the guards with taking down one particular painting? It wouldn't have shaved off more than a few minutes from the duration of the theft.

"Would anyone have noticed if one of the other works in the Blue Room had a similar notice placed in its stead as well?"

There was a pause as Penny absorbed the implications of his question.

"You're thinking . . .?"

"Yes," Blake said succinctly. Pieces of the puzzle were falling into place.

"That Dean took both the *Chez Tortoni* and *Madame Auguste Manet* off the walls, saying they were to be sent out for Restoration?" Penny sounded incredulous. "But we'd have noticed. On the day of the theft, someone would've noticed. You have crime scene photos. . ."

"The guards could've taken the second notice down during their rounds at night or sometime during the day." The galleries hadn't been monitored during the day. With visitors milling around the place, it made little sense to have motion sensors on when the museum was open.

Heck, this Dean guy could've done it himself, and no one would've noticed.

"I—*oh dear!*"

"What's the matter?" Blake demanded, finding himself irritated by the way Penny had abruptly cut herself off. If she'd remembered something, he wanted her to spit it out, ASAP.

"You think Dean helped to orchestrate the theft?" she asked breathlessly. "He was on the board. And he was adamant the Gardner have every piece of art insured. He even suggested an insurance company we could work with."

"Oh, yeah?"

"Yes, Morgana Insurance. I don't know if you've heard of it. It's—"

"I know." Blake clenched his fists. "Hugh Norton's company."

"Celine and Julia have been asking . . ." Penny wittered on, but Blake had ceased to listen. The blood rushed into his head, filling his ears with a thunderous, crashing sound like a gigantic cascade.

He'd get the guy. Goddammit, he'd get the man.

The shrill screech of sirens pierced the air. The paramedics had finally arrived.

"I've gotta go, Penny. Fill Ella in, if you haven't already done so."

Grimly, he hung up and strode down to the gate.

Chapter Fifty-One

"Ah, you're back!" Sandy greeted Celine and Julia with a smile as they walked into the lobby of Hutchinson House. "And with a stepladder?"

"To replace the one we had to take from Clara's room," Celine explained. She held up the orchid. "And we brought a little something to brighten up the area."

"She'll like that." Sandy nodded, coming around from behind the reception desk. She led the way down the hallway to the elevators. "I'll take you up. I'm sure she'll be glad to see you. She's doing much better."

"That's good to know," Julia panted. The former fed had insisted on carrying the sturdy metal and carbon-fiber tool in herself.

"It's heavier than it looks," Rod had cautioned them when he'd hefted it into the trunk of their car. He'd warned them against dragging it or bumping it against anything for fear of scratching the camera lenses or damaging the sensitive equipment it contained.

Clara made no effort to get out of bed when Sandy—after a brief knock —unlocked the door to let them in. Sitting up with her hands neatly folded on top of the colorful comforter on her bed, she gazed serenely at them.

She seemed mellow, Celine thought as she greeted the older woman. Almost too mellow. Had she been sedated? She put the orchid on the window sill, taking care to position the purple blooms so they faced the apartment door and Clara's bed.

"Well, I'll leave you to it." Sandy pulled the door behind her as she left, but failed to close it all the way. A simple oversight or a result of the orders the receptionist had been given? Celine didn't know.

She and Julia had debated taking the woman into their confidence but eventually decided against it. Sandy's loyalty to her superiors would likely override any natural concern she felt for Clara.

"Best not to trust anyone in a situation like this," Julia had said.

"I like the orchid," Clara broke into Celine's thoughts. "But why did you bring the stepladder back? I don't need it."

Celine exchanged a glance with Julia. "We thought Jonah might," she offered. "To reach things up high."

To her surprise, Clara agreed. "Yes, he might, although"—her voice was hushed—"I think he wants it out of sight for now."

Celine surveyed the room. There wasn't much that was out of reach other than a shelf or two in the kitchenette.

Her gaze fell on the supply closet by the door.

According to Julia, there were some high shelves within that she'd been unable to explore. The former fed must have remembered that, for she'd opened the closet door and was setting up the ladder before it.

"It's too big to fit inside here," she said, climbing up the rungs. "But I can set it up just by the closet." She turned around. "And while we're here, I might as well dust those shelves I never got to yesterday."

"I'm too tired for a walk today," Clara announced as Celine lowered herself into the wicker armchair beside the bed. She set the church bulletin on Clara's nightstand.

"I'm so glad you went," Clara said, noticing it. "Jonah said you had. He was pleased." She reclined her head against the pillows behind her and closed her eyes. "He really was pleased. You'll find whatever you need there. And then Jonah will be free to go."

Free to go where? Celine wondered. Before she could ask, the soft tinkling of piano keys—playing the swan theme from Tchaikovsky's *Swan Lake* —filled the room.

"My music box!" Clara's eyes flew open. "So that's where it's been all this while. I was wondering—"

"What are you doing?" Nurse Beth Hogan stood at the door, arms folded tightly across her chest. Celine wondered how long she'd been standing outside the room.

Beth's stern glare took in the former fed on the stepladder and the music box with its twirling ballerina in her hands. "Please put that away. All the residents on the floor are trying to rest."

She reached for the box about to snatch it out of Julia's hands when Clara let out a bloodcurdling shriek.

"No—ooo—ooh! Stop thief! Keep your hands off my property!"

Beth's eyes widened as Clara continued to scream. Her arms hastily dropped to her side and she backed out of the room.

"Just keep it down," she snarled.

Clara subsided, unfazed by the commotion she'd caused.

"That was a Christmas gift from Jonah. With his first paycheck. I don't want anyone to steal it." She grasped Celine's hands. "Promise me, you won't let them take it. Jonah doesn't want them to have it."

"I won't," Celine assured her, covering Clara's soft, wrinkled hand with her own. She eyed the music box. Had Jonah concealed whatever he'd discovered at the church in Clara's music box?

"We can take it with us, keep it safe," she suggested.

"No." Clara shook her head. "I want it here. You can put it back where it was," she said to Julia. "But don't let it fall into their hands, okay?"

"You got it!" Julia smiled brightly at her, but Celine could see the former fed wasn't happy about returning the music box to the closet.

"I'm tired." Clara's head sank back onto her pillows. She squeezed Celine's hand. "You have everything you need, don't you? You went to the church?"

"Yes, we did."

"Then Jonah can be at peace."

At peace? Celine wasn't sure what to make of Clara's words.

He's a suffering soul, Celine, Sister Mary Catherine said. *Surely you remember who those are and how to help them?*

"Would he like a Mass said for him?" Celine asked. If her guardian angel was right, that was the only way to ease Jonah's suffering.

"No, dear." Clara's eyes remained closed. "I don't think it would do much good. Jonah needs to help you. When you have everything you need, he'll be set free."

Her hold on Celine's hand relaxed and her breathing deepened.

Celine got to her feet and caught Julia's eye, who nodded. There wasn't much point staying if Clara was going to doze off. She'd wanted to ask about Maureen Rita, the woman in the church bulletin. But that would have to wait until another day.

You might want to ask her your question before it's too late, Sister Mary Catherine reminded her.

It'll wait, Celine responded firmly. *I'm not going to drag her out of the depths of sleep just to answer a question about a woman she may not even remember.*

Chapter Fifty-Two

One leaf of the double wrought iron gate leading into the Divine Mercy Church grounds was open. Parking on the street outside, Celine and Julia walked through the gate into the cobblestone yard.

A small wooden sign with an arrow inscribed on it informed them the parish office was off to the side, behind the spacious parking lot. They were headed that way when the low rumble of a car engine and the squeal of tires assailed Celine's ears.

Her head yanked around, eyes widening at what she saw behind them. The afternoon sky had darkened. A gray hatchback careened in through the gates, swerving dangerously around the driveway, cutting so close to them, Celine could feel the heat and smoke from the exhaust as she quickly sprang to the side.

"Watch out!" she warned, pulling Julia back with her.

"What the heck?" Julia's loudly expelled oath dispelled the vision.

The winter sky was blue again, and the car had disappeared.

Breathless and disoriented, Celine scanned the parking lot. There was no car. She'd imagined it. Julia's gaze followed hers.

"*Jesus Christ, you gave me a start!*" the former fed said. "What was that all about?"

Taking a deep breath, Celine pulled her senses together, trying to make sense of what she'd seen. A gray hatchback. Exactly like the one parked outside the Gardner Museum all those years ago.

The sky darkened again as she stared at the cobblestones paving the church parking lot. The hatchback was back, parked in the middle. One of the doors was thrown open, and Lenny DiMuzio climbed out of the car.

"They were here." Celine turned to Julia. "DiMuzio and Reissfelder."

"What!" Julia regarded her in disbelief. "Are you sure?"

"Positive." Celine nodded. She faced her friend. "I think the Degas sketches and the gu were brought here as well, Julia." It was the first glimmering Celine had received into the initial whereabouts of these items.

She'd known Reissfelder and DiMuzio had driven off with them and that Grayson had taken the Manet. But where they'd gone with the stolen goods had, until now, remained a mystery.

"Are the works still here?" Julia looked urgently up at her. "Is that what Jonah found out? That the Gardner's lost art is concealed somewhere on the premises of this church?"

Celine shook her head. "They were here at one time. Not anymore."

"They have a key," she added softly, watching as DiMuzio pulled out a key from his pocket and inserted it into the lock of the parish office door. "DiMuzio and Reissfelder have a key."

"Given to them by Norton? Or the General?" Julia wanted to know.

Celine felt her brow wrinkling as she pondered the question.

"I don't know," she finally said. "It might even have been Jezebel," she added softly, only to realize she'd left the church bulletin in Clara's room. She clenched her fists to her side. She should've remembered to bring it with her.

"Jezebel?" Julia stared up at her, blue eyes shrouded in confusion.

"The woman I saw in my visions," Celine clarified. "The one who called in the tip about Dodd's Degas."

It was the woman in the church bulletin, Celine was quite sure. If only Clara had been able to take a look, she might've recognized the woman as the one who'd relentlessly pursued Dodd before moving onto—what had Dodd told Blake?—"greener pastures?"

"We can get another bulletin from in there." Julia indicated the office door with a quick jab of her forefinger. "Better yet, someone might have an address for her."

"And a phone number, although most likely she used a burner phone or a burner app."

⋄

Julia tried the parish office door. It was locked. But there was a small brass buzzer on the wall next to it. It emitted a musical trill when Celine lightly pressed her forefinger into it.

The woman who responded to the summons was middle-aged and pleasant-featured.

"Yes?" she queried, regarding them both with a quizzical smile as she held open the door.

"We'd like to see Marisa Gomez, the parish secretary," Julia responded. "Is she in?"

The woman's smile broadened. "She is. I am Marisa." She pronounced her name with a long e and elongated her i's, her accent giving her words a musical lilt.

She stepped back to let them into a spacious room. Drawers and shelves lined the walls. A set of light blue fabric drawers was pushed neatly into stacks of cubbies. All but one drawer was labeled with initials—presumably of the parish staff.

Celine found her gaze drawn to the only one marked with a "Deac."

For Deacon, she thought, as the room simultaneously darkened. The meager glow from a flashlight illuminated the area, spotlighting the masculine hand that stretched out from the darkness to roughly tug the drawer open.

Reissfelder and DiMuzio had been in here. In the darkness that engulfed the room, Celine heard the softly muttered curses of the two men. The drawer wasn't big enough for—

Her eyes widened, seeing the gu. It really had been here.

Her head pivoted, seeing a cabinet door with a label on it marked, *RCIA*.

"You want to sign up for RCIA?" Marisa's softly accented voice dispelled the vision.

"What?" Confused, Celine turned to face the parish secretary. Her right arm, she realized, was raised, pointing straight at the cabinet. She lowered it to her side.

"RCIA," Marisa repeated patiently. "You want to sign up?"

"What's RCIA?" Julia demanded. Her puzzled glance oscillated from Celine to Marisa and back again.

"Rite of Christian Initiation of Adults," Celine murmured.

"No." She directed her remarks at Marisa. "Not at this time. We're here for a church bulletin."

She glanced around the room, disoriented. Had Jonah expressed an interest in the program?

He'd do anything to follow a story, my dear, Sister Mary Catherine reminded her.

Still regarding them quizzically, Marisa went up to a small table with a stack of bulletins piled high on it. She plucked the topmost one off the heap and returned with it.

"Here you go? Is there anything else?"

"A friend of ours was here sometime last year," Julia began. "He was working on a story."

"Yes." Marisa's smile encouraged her to continue.

"Unfortunately, he passed away without leaving behind any clue as to what he was researching. We're wondering if you might know anything. He talked about coming here."

Marisa cocked her head to the side. "His name?" she asked.

"Jonah Hibbert," Julia said.

Marisa shook her head. The name hadn't rung a bell.

"He was about my height, skinny," Celine added. "Wore skinny jeans. Dark, curly hair. Spectacles."

Marisa looked amused. "That sounds like a lot of young people these days."

That was true enough, Celine conceded, chagrined.

"You have a picture? A photograph?" Marisa asked.

Celine exchanged a glance with Julia.

"Damn, I wish we'd thought of that," Julia swore under her breath.

"You and me both." What were they going to do now? Without a photo of Jonah, their investigation was effectively stalled.

Don't be silly, Celine. You don't need a photograph, her guardian angel said in a low voice. *All you need is a pencil.*

A pencil? Celine was about to roll her eyes when the subtitle of a book on one of the shelves caught her gaze. *A Spiritual Portrait.*

The frustration eased. It had been a while, but she was still handy with a pencil. She turned decisively toward the parish secretary.

"Do you have a pencil and a sheet of paper?"

"Sure." Marisa walked over to the printer, pulled out the paper drawer, and picked up a couple of sheets from inside. From a plastic jar on top of the printer, she withdrew a sharpened pencil.

"What do you think you're doing?" Julia hissed, watching Marisa at work.

"Giving her the next best thing to a photo," Celine replied. She took the pencil and paper and drew a quick sketch.

"There!" She held it out. "That's what our friend Jonah Hibbert looked like."

"Ah! Him, I remember," Marisa said. "He wanted to join the church."

"So he was interested in this RCIA thing?" Julia sounded skeptical. "That doesn't sound like the Jonah we knew and loved."

He was interested in the person conducting the class, Sister Mary Catherine said.

Marisa nodded when Celine repeated the information.

"Your friend wanted to give our Deacon a gift. To thank Deacon for teaching him about the faith. He came here to ask what Deacon likes, his interests, that kind of thing."

But Jonah had told Marisa he didn't have time to sign up for the classes which had been scheduled to begin in September. He was going away, he'd said.

"So I guess this person—your Deacon—would have an idea what Jonah was working on," Julia concluded. "How do we get in touch with him?"

"I'm sorry." Marisa shook her head.

Celine's heart sank. Was it too late already?

Marisa pointed to the bulletin Celine was clutching to her chest. "He has cancer. Late-stage. No hope for recovery, the doctor says."

Marisa looked at their disappointed faces, and added: "But you can speak with Deacon's son. Maybe he can help?"

"Sure," Julia said, taking out a notepad and pen from her tote bag, although Celine could see the former fed wasn't holding out much hope the son would have any information.

She opened the bulletin, about to read the feature on the Deacon again when her phone rang.

"Ella?" Celine walked out of the parish office to take the call.

"Celine, when you go to that church you mentioned—"

"We are at the church," Celine told her.

"Great. Find out if they have a Dean Rafferty in the parish."

Chapter Fifty-Three

"They do." Celine stared at the bulletin. That was the Deacon's name. "Why do you ask?"

"I think he's the inside guy you've been sensing. The Boston Brahmin."

Celine listened carefully as Ella filled her in.

"Blake thinks he took the Manet?" she frowned, considering this. "The night before the actual theft?"

"It fits," Ella said. "It all fits. And when you consider the security footage. . ."

And that Jonah had been pursuing the man.

"Can you get an address for him?" Ella's voice broke into her musings. "I'm guessing he's the guy behind the threats to Clara and the one to you this morning."

"No, he's not. He's in no position to be doing anything of the sort. He's in the ICU, dying of cancer. But he was Jonah's handler."

Had Jonah threatened him?

Not in person, Sister Mary Catherine informed her. *Not directly.*

Celine was about to ask what that meant when an image filled her mind. She saw Jonah huddled in a corner, his phone clutched to his ear. Jonah must have thought the person issuing instructions to him on the phone and the man meeting him in the park were one and the same: the Boston Brahmin.

He'd threatened to reveal the information—unless he was given more money.

"If you've got Rafferty on video, you have reason to look into him, don't you?" she asked Ella.

"Sure," Ella replied. "What are you getting at?"

"Look into Rafferty's finances," Celine advised.

She recalled the ATM right across the church where she'd seen Rafferty in her mind's eye, withdrawing cash. Jonah must've followed Rafferty to the church from their rendezvous point near Hincman's Bench.

"Look for deposits into his account and cash withdrawals that match the dates and amounts of the cash deposits Jonah was making into his bank account."

"You're thinking—"

"That it'll lead you right back to Norton," Celine finished for Ella. "Yeah."

She was about to end the call when Sister Mary Catherine whispered a name into her ear. Jezebel.

"Wait, Ella, just one more thing."

"Yes?"

"That list you have from the Van Hoyt," Celine began. "Could you pull it up and search for a Maureen Rita?"

"Member of the church as well?" Ella asked. Tapping sounds accompanied the question.

"I'm thinking she must be the woman who called in that tip about Dodd's Degas. She's in the parish bulletin. Has cancer." She'd sensed that, Celine recalled. In Paso Robles.

"I wonder if this Maureen woman was involved with Rafferty," she murmured to herself. Somehow it didn't seem likely. From what she'd heard of him, Rafferty didn't seem the kind to openly flout rules that were clearly wrong.

"Well," Ella said finally. "There is a Maureen Rita on the list. But she can't be the woman we're looking for. This one's in Norwalk. We're looking for someone in Boston." The tip had come on a Boston number. "I still think Clara might be our best bet in identifying our tipster."

"I'll have to remember to ask her," Celine said, discouraged.

Would they manage to get a straight answer out of Clara? She'd been so lethargic that morning, Celine was sure she'd been heavily sedated.

Would Clara be sufficiently alert to chat with them next time?

❧

"Sister Mary Catherine was right!" Julia shook her head disbelievingly as they stood on the sidewalk outside the church, waiting to cross Centre Street. "The answers were in a church. All this time. I should've trusted your instincts."

"And I should have trusted my guardian angel," Celine admitted ruefully. Why had she allowed her biases to disregard the nun's message?

Their rental was parked on the other side of the street, in front of the enormous gray granite pavilion known as Soldier's Monument. It had been erected in honor of the soldiers from West Roxbury who'd lost their lives in the Civil War.

"I wish Jonah had come to us with what he knew," Celine continued when a familiar spasm coiled her heart muscles. She gasped, the pain nearly unbearable, and then blinked.

Standing at the foot of the granite structure across the street was Belle Gardner—dressed as always in the figure-hugging black gown in which John Singer Sargent had captured her for eternity.

"What is it, Celine?" Julia's eyes, watchful and anxious, turned sharply toward her.

But Celine could only grasp at a nearby lamppost for support. "Death," she gasped out. "I see more death."

Be careful, Celine, Sister Mary Catherine's voice was like a cannon blast. *You're getting too close. Be careful.*

The pedestrian light—a walking figure—glowed whitely in the distance, signaling it was time to cross. Celine stepped off the curb. A dark blur filled the periphery of her vision, and Julia's screamed "Celine!" simultaneously pierced her ear.

Someone—Julia, most likely—grabbed her elbow, lifting her off her feet and back onto the sidewalk. A fraction of a second later, the dark sedan that had swerved around the corner, zigzagged away from the curb, missing her by inches.

"Oh, my God!" Celine breathed out. She'd come so close to being killed! She'd come so close to . . .

Facing judgment, my dear, Sister Mary Catherine said. *And you weren't ready for it, were you?*

No, no, she wasn't. Tears of relief filled Celine's eyes as she turned to Julia. "Th-that was close," she stammered. "Thanks for . . . "

"No thanks necessary, kiddo," Julia said gruffly, pulling Celine into a close hug. "I'm just glad you're safe." She looked past Celine's shoulder at the car that had disappeared in the distance. "I'm guessing you didn't get a license plate number?"

Celine shook her head, managing a watery grin.

"Yup, me neither," Julia said.

"I won't ask what that was about," the former fed added when they'd settled into their car and Julia had merged into traffic. "I'm guessing we're getting too close to the truth for comfort."

"I still can't believe Jonah kept this information to himself," Celine said. "Why would he do that?"

In the rearview mirror, she saw Belle still standing by the Soldier's Monument. But this time she was joined by a figure in a wheelchair. A figure that Celine felt she should recognize.

She peeled her eyes away from the scene.

"Jonah was either looking for an exclusive," Julia answered her question. "Or he was holding out for more money. I'm inclined to think it was the latter."

Celine nodded. Accommodations at Hutchinson House didn't come cheap. It had cost Jonah far more than he could afford to keep his mother in the facility. But his silence had put Clara in danger.

He's aware of that now, Sister Mary Catherine informed her. *He's trying to make up for it—as best he can, of course.*

"Marisa back there told me Rafferty's cancer took a fatal turn for the worse around about July," Julia said. She kept her eyes on the road. "I'm guessing it was around about that time Jonah confronted him."

"He confronted his caller." Celine shared the insights she'd received during Ella's call. "The anonymous individual who gave him instructions, telling him when to meet Rafferty. He must have thought it was Rafferty— trying to be slick."

Jonah had followed Rafferty to the church and then gone into the parish office fishing for information, in the guise of a friend looking to give the deacon a small token of his appreciation.

"Marisa told him Rafferty was interested in art, especially the Impression- ists," Julia remarked. "And then when she mentioned, quite by chance, that Rafferty was on the board of the Gardner, Jonah must've immediately put two and two together. . ."

"And in typical journalistic fashion come up with five," Celine finished with a grimace.

Julia briefly took her eyes off the road.

"You think Rafferty has the Manet?"

"It's possible," Celine conceded. "We know for a fact Jezebel doesn't."

"That would be Maureen Rita, right?"

"So I thought. But Ella negated that theory. The tipster was calling from a Boston number. Maureen Rita is in Norwalk."

Even the parish secretary had admitted that Maureen Rita was no longer a member of the parish. It was her daughter who'd asked that her mother be featured.

She glanced up at the rearview mirror again. Belle Gardner and the figure in the wheelchair were still visible. Celine was wondering who it was when an image from her dream slid into place.

Laurie Robbes! She was seeing the intern from the Montague Museum. Dear Lord!

Why was she seeing them? Why Laurie?

"Could it be because Dodd was killed by cyanide poisoning—just like Laurie?" Julia asked when Celine mentioned it to her.

"Or because it was the same person doing the killing," Celine said. Laurie had died because she'd posed a threat to Hugh Norton.

Had Dodd been killed for the same reason? Celine was almost positive Clara was being threatened by Norton.

Most likely because there was a clear, undeniable connection between Dodd and Norton—an incriminating paper trail that the FBI could use to finally reel Norton in.

"I'm famished," Julia broke the silence after a while. "What say we stop somewhere for a bite?"

"I'm game."

"Japanese okay?" Julia asked as they cruised past a seafood café with outdoor seating.

"Sure."

They'd placed their orders—a plate of sushi for Julia and Teriyaki salmon with rice for Celine—when a memory filtered through the myriad images in Celine's brain, percolating into her consciousness.

"Laurie Robbes was a threat to Norton, but he didn't do his own dirty work."

"No, he wouldn't," Julia agreed, watching her carefully.

"I'm almost positive the last couple to see Laurie that day was responsible for her murder. We could never prove it—"

"We never had an opportunity to talk with them," Julia said. "The Montague, remember, had no security cameras or visitor logs. Nothing that could give us a ghost of a clue as to who it was."

"Yes, but—" Celine paused, took a deep breath, and then faced her friend. "I saw them. And I can still see them in my mind's eye as clearly as though they were right in front of me."

"That doesn't really—*Oh!*" Julia's eyes widened. "You're saying you could provide a sketch?"

"Absolutely!" Celine nodded her head emphatically. "I don't know why I haven't thought of it before."

It's because you've allowed yourself to develop an aversion to art, my dear, Sister Mary Catherine said kindly.

"But there's no reason why I shouldn't be able to make a good likeness."

"No, there's not." Julia took a healthy swig of the coke a waiter had placed before them minutes ago. "You think the parish secretary would recognize the couple?"

"It's worth a try, don't you think?" Celine replied. "We've already discovered at least one—if not two—parishioners closely connected to the Gardner and its theft. And when you consider that Rafferty was pushing for Morgana to be the Gardner's art insurer"—Ella had revealed this tidbit during their phone conversation; Celine shrugged—"well, I'd be surprised if we didn't get something."

Chapter Fifty-Four

Ella surveyed the Post-it notes spread out on her desk. They contained her scribbled notes on the recent developments in both the Dodd-Degas case and the Gardner theft. It was time to make sense of the information and collate it into a coherent report.

Celine and Julia were too focused on the threat to Clara. Blake was driven by a single-minded obsession with bringing Hugh Norton to justice. It was up to her to deal objectively with their findings.

Tapping her chin, Ella stared at her note on Dean Rafferty. If Celine's visions were accurate, Rafferty had been Jonah's handler, acting as a go-between for the Boston Brahmin.

Ella deliberately refrained from casting Norton as the Brahmin. She was reasonably sure Norton was their guy, but she wanted to follow the evidence. "Go where it leads," she muttered to herself. "Wherever it leads."

Assuming Celine was right, Rafferty had also taken charge of the Gardner's stolen gu, the Degas sketches, and the Manet. They'd all been delivered to the church where Rafferty served as a deacon.

There was more evidence pointing to Rafferty's involvement in the Gardner theft. As a board member, he had inside knowledge of its holdings and where each work was kept. Someone had supplied Reissfelder and DiMuzio with that information. It could well have been Rafferty.

Moreover Rafferty had freely admitted being in the Blue Room the night before the theft to take down the portrait of Manet's mother. He could easily have removed the *Chez Tortoni*.

The motion sensors confirmed his story: showing movement shortly after he arrived that night. But recording nothing the following night when Reissfelder and DiMuzio broke in.

Rafferty was looking good for the theft of the Manet. Ella's glance shifted to the mysterious tipster—the Boston Brahmin's mistress. They'd assumed the Brahmin was Henry Dodd—a Gardner board member like Rafferty, but possessed of the considerable wealth they'd surmised the Brahmin—as a collector—must have.

It was a plausible assumption. Dodd was a huge fan of the Impressionists with an especial fondness for the Gardner's stolen Manet.

He'd also been Clara Hibbert's employer. With Clara's life in danger, it had seemed very likely Dodd was behind the threat.

Even more compelling, Dodd had a stolen Degas pastel—the very pastel the mistress had called in about.

But then Dodd had died. He claimed never to have cheated on his wife. Although he had fended off the advances of an employee. A Catholic, from what Dodd recalled.

Ella's eyes moved to a note on the left. It had the name Maureen Rita written on it with a question mark beside the name. She had at one time belonged to the same church as Rafferty. Her name was on the Van Hoyt's mailing list—making her a viable candidate for their mysterious caller.

"And she has cancer—just like the woman in Celine's visions," Ella murmured. Just a coincidence? Or was there more to it?

Of course, the woman, whoever it was, had counted on receiving the *Chez Tortoni* but had been left with a dud instead. That meant—Ella's eyes turned back to Rafferty—that it was the deacon who had the Manet.

Her hand hovered above the landline on her desk. They might not have enough for a search warrant, but surely a few questions were in order.

Mind made up, Ella proceeded to look up Rafferty's home number. It didn't take long to find. Trying to stop her fingers from shaking, she dialed the number.

Chapter Fifty-Five

"He's a veritable bear of a man." Julia leaned over the armrest of her armchair to peer at the figure Celine had sketched on her pad.

They'd returned to the Hilton Garden Inn, stopping at an art supply store on the way to purchase a drawing pad and a set of pencils.

"This is what he looks like now," Celine replied, tongue pressed to the corner of her mouth as she concentrated on her work. "He wasn't quite so obese back then."

But even at the time, the man she'd seen with Laurie on the day she'd died had cut an imposing figure. He'd been over six feet tall, the muscle in his frame already turning to flab.

Celine turned her attention to the woman she'd seen with him—a tall, leggy brunette. Aging but still beautiful.

"When I saw her, I got the feeling she was just arm candy," Celine confided. "He barely paid her any mind. He was flirting with Laurie the whole time. But I was sure she was his wife, not a girlfriend."

Julia snorted. "Considers himself something of a lady's man, does he?"

"Something like that. He comes across as charming, urbane, suave. He's anything but." Celine closed her eyes to focus her impressions.

"He's a ruthless killer," she whispered, eyes still closed. "Someone who'll stop at nothing to get even a brother out of the way."

He has managed to rid himself of a brother, Sister Mary Catherine said.

It sounded like a reminder, but of what? Celine had no idea. Brushing the remark away, she opened her eyes to resume work on her sketch.

Several minutes later, she handed the finished work to Julia.

"That's the best I can do."

Julia whistled. "It's pretty darned good, I have to say."

"I get the impression the woman has green eyes, although I never did get close enough to see."

"We can make a note of that." *Eyes, possibly green*, Julia scribbled near the woman's head.

The former fed looked up.

"I'd like to fax a copy of this to Ella. Keep it for the Gardner theft file. It's—what?—seven, eight years now. I doubt any witnesses will remember these people. But if they were regular visitors to the Montague"—it was the museum where Laurie had interned under Celine—"we might be able to get a name."

Celine nodded. "But our best bet might still be the Divine Mercy Church parish office, right?"

"Sure sounds like it." Julia got to her feet and stretched out her arms. "So many of our players are associated with that church."

☙

But back at the parish office, no one could identify the couple.

Marisa Gomez, when she saw the sketch, frowned and scratched her chin.

"I don't think I've ever seen these people. They're not parishioners." She looked up. "Are you sure this is what your reporter friend said? That he meet them here?"

Uncomfortable with drawing the lie out any farther, Celine looked to Julia for direction.

"We're not one hundred percent sure," the former fed said, "but we think Jonah met this couple either here or somewhere in the neighborhood of the church."

Marisa shrugged. "Must've been somewhere in the neighborhood."

Two other women who'd stood around, quietly listening in, nodded vigorously, in silent agreement with Marisa.

"Could they be Mr. Rafferty's friends?" Celine asked.

"Could be," Marisa agreed doubtfully, "but I don't think so."

Back in the car, Julia sighed, resting her hands on the steering wheel.

"So much for that. Now what?"

Celine pondered the question.

Remember your dream, Celine, her guardian angel whispered. *Remember your dream.*

I am remembering, Sister Mary Catherine, Celine cried out in dismay. *I'm just not getting anything.*

What had she seen? Laurie Robbes in a wheelchair. Laurie had held something in her arms. Something like a chalice, long and slender. Laurie, whose tendency to blackmail the Montague's patrons—for possessing works of art with a questionable provenance—had led to her untimely death.

Why did Laurie die, Celine? Sister Mary Catherine asked. *What set her murder into motion?*

207

Laurie had offered to go to Hugh Norton's home to inspect the works he was planning to loan to the Montague. There she'd spied . . .

Celine's eyes widened. *Of course, the gu!*

She spun around.

"Do you remember going to Norton's home all those years ago?"

Julia's eyes opened.

"Sure. What are you getting at?"

"The gu was—"

"Yup, a copy."

"And who do we know who fabricated an imitation Shang Dynasty gu around about the same time?"

Julia sat up.

"Anthony Reynolds. You mean—?"

Celine nodded emphatically. "What if the gu Tony made for Sofia's uncle was a replica meant for Norton?"

Julia gazed down at the sketch on the center console.

"You think Sofia and her folks might have some idea of who these people are?"

"It's worth a shot, isn't it? After all, her uncle knew exactly who Peter Standish was."

Standish had been a shady tax accountant who'd counted Hugh Norton as one of his many clients. The FBI had hoped to bring him in for questioning, but the man had been killed before they could do so. As for the financial records they'd subpoenaed, thus far they'd found nothing incriminating on Norton.

"It most definitely is," Julia agreed with a grin. "Call her. See if she can see us today."

Hardly daring to breathe, Celine tapped out Sofia's number.

Chapter Fifty-Six

"Rafferty residence," a no-nonsense male voice answered Ella's call.

"Mr. Rafferty," Ella began. "Mr. Dean Rafferty?"

"No, this is Shawn Rafferty, his son."

"Mr. Rafferty, this is Ella Rawlins from the Boston FBI office. I'd like to speak with your father."

"About?" Shawn asked without missing a beat.

"We've uncovered some new information about the Gardner Museum theft, and we'd like to speak with your father to see if he can shed some light on what we've found out."

"I'm afraid that's impossible."

Shawn didn't seem inclined to say much more. But Ella waited—a tactic she'd learned from Blake. "It forces them to give you more information than they'd intended to," he'd told her.

To Ella's delight, it worked.

"He's in the hospital, for heaven's sake," Shawn said irritably. "In the ICU, fighting cancer. He's in no position to speak with anyone."

"In that case," Ella replied, "I'd like to request your permission to go through his financial records. We have reason to believe a suspect in the theft was using your father to funnel money to a second suspect." It was pretty close to the truth, without necessarily suggesting they were looking upon Rafferty as a suspect as well.

But Rafferty Jr. wasn't about to bite.

"Absolutely not," he snapped. "Get a search warrant."

"Actually, it's a subpoen—"

A decisive bang cut through her words, ending the call.

Ella stared at the receiver, shaking her head in disbelief. Had the guy just hung up on her?

She reviewed the facts of the case. They had Rafferty on the Gardner security footage the night before the theft and the motion sensor outputs from the same time. He'd been the most insistent of the board members that the

Gardner insure its art, using any payout in the event of a theft to upgrade security.

And he'd been vocal about the lack of appropriate security, giving him a motive to orchestrate a theft.

As for the payments to Jonah, if he'd withdrawn cash from the ATM across from the church, all Ella had to do was request the security footage for the days preceding and following Jonah's deposits into his account to build a solid foundation for probable cause.

They could use the same reasons to obtain a search warrant to search Rafferty's premises and any safes or storage facilities he rented.

Ella's mind turned to the mysterious caller. Was it possible she was a Morgana Insurance employee? The Sullivans' stolen Degas had been insured by Morgana Insurance. Had they been aware of what accepting the payout would mean? Had their tipster been instrumental in arranging the payout?

It was time to find out. Ella reached for her receiver again, but before she could lift it off its cradle, it buzzed.

"FBI—"

"Ella, it's Blake," he said brusquely. "Remember, Mary?"

"Mary?" Was Blake losing it, Ella wondered.

"The intern, the—"

"Oh, her! Yeah, sure." It was the woman who'd taken the tip about the Gardner's stolen Vermeer last year. She'd turned out to be a plant, interested only in getting close to the investigation. By the time they'd cottoned onto the fact, Mary had hightailed it.

"I saw her as I was leaving Dodd's." The paramedics had arrived to take care of the housekeeper, Blake told Ella, and Norwalk PD had sent over detectives. He'd been driving down Dodd's street, on his way back to his hotel, when he'd caught sight of a familiar figure in the front yard of one of the neighboring houses.

"Look up the address for me, will you?" He rattled off an address in Norwalk. Ella jotted it down: 72 Grumman Avenue. "It's a stone's throw from Dodd's house," Blake told her.

"It sounds familiar," Ella said. She called up the Van Hoyt's mailing list on her computer, accessed the search feature on the PDF file, and typed in the address.

"Damn," she softly swore, looking at the name on the file. "Damn."

"What's the matter?" Blake demanded.

"The house is listed in the Van Hoyt mailing list as the address of Maureen Rita Flynn, Blake. She attended the same church as Dean Rafferty. Celine wanted me to check her out." She filled him in.

Blake whistled. "It sounds like she could be our caller."
"Could Mary be her daughter?" Ella asked. "By the Boston Brahmin?"
Blake whistled again. "It's possible." There was a slight pause. Then, "I'm going back. Get me a search warrant ASAP. And find out anything you can about her, will you?"

Chapter Fifty-Seven

The setting sun bathed the walls of their hotel sitting room in an orange-red glow. It was incredibly beautiful, but Celine found little to appreciate in it. She stared pensively at the sketch she'd drawn, oblivious to Julia's softly uttered: "It's getting dark. Want me to turn on the lights?"

When Celine didn't respond, Julia pushed herself out of her armchair.

"You've got to give it a rest, kiddo. We'll get our answers soon enough."

Celine considered the advice. It was possible, she guessed. On the other hand. . .

They'd called Sofia Wozniak—the woman who'd once been Anthony Reynolds' fiancée. They'd broken up eight years ago under tragic circumstances, right around the time Laurie had courted death by attempting to blackmail Hugh Norton.

"I'm not sure just how much help I'll be, Celine," Sofia had said. "I'm certainly willing to take a look at what you've got. But it's just not going to be possible today. Can you two come by the store tomorrow?"

They'd agreed to meet Sofia at Rose Antiques, the business she'd inherited from her mother. But Celine wasn't holding out much hope anymore. What if Sofia didn't recognize the couple? No one at the parish office had.

What were the chances that Norton would allow his criminal associates into his social circle?

And, yet it seemed as though they were so close to a breakthrough.

The clouds are gathering, Celine, Sister Mary Catherine encouraged her. *Rain is imminent.*

"Rain is imminent? What the heck is that supposed to mean?" Julia demanded, plonking herself back into the plush armchair after turning on the lights in the sitting room that adjoined their two bedrooms.

"That we're close to the answers," Celine replied, her eyes riveted on the sketch. "Very close."

There was a moment's silence. Then Julia cleared her throat.

"Does it really matter whether or not we find this guy? It was nearly eight years ago. It's going to be hard to prove he had anything to do with Laurie's death. Unless, of course, he also had a hand in Dodd's murder. In which case, there might be justice of a sort."

Had the man—obese now—but with the same cold, expressionless eyes killed Dodd?

A strong whiff of cologne assailed her nostrils and she shuddered. In her mind's eye, she saw the crime scene photos Ella had shared with them. A strong, masculine hand, well-manicured and white, clasped a bottle of wine.

"It wasn't him." Celine tapped the photo. "The Brahmin did his own dirty work this time, but. . ." She frowned.

It was Norton. It had to be Norton. Unless . . . The frown deepened.

She turned to Julia. "What if Norton was holding on to the gu for someone else? Just like Pete Standish?"

The whiff of cologne intensified.

He hasn't been able to enjoy any of his treasures, Sister Mary Catherine whispered. *It's the only justice in the entire affair. His treasures are scattered.*

Was the nun talking about Norton? Or someone else?

"The Manet, the Degas, and the gu," she said to Julia. "They're scattered. With different people."

"People who are involved or in the know, I imagine," Julia replied. "Like Rafferty."

"Rafferty might have the Manet," Celine agreed. It was a possibility—the only one that made sense given that Jezebel had ended up with a fake.

What about the other two items? Who were they with?

Don't forget what you saw in the church, Celine, Sister Mary Catherine counseled. *Don't forget Laurie.*

Laurie had been holding a tall, slender beaker with a flared neck. It was the Gardner's gu, but Laurie had only seen it once. She'd never gotten to hold it. She hadn't taken it out of Norton's house. She'd never had the opportunity. She'd been killed.

Celine's eyes drifted toward her sketch.

Could the Shang dynasty wine vessel be in her killer's possession now? Who in the FBI would think to look for it there?

She was about to share her insight with Julia when her friend's phone rang.

"Julia? Celine?" Penny's voice sounded breathless and agitated over the speakerphone.

Julia bent over the phone she'd set on the coffee table.

"We're both here, Penny. Go ahead."

"You've been asking about Hugh Norton," Penny began. "Whether he was closely connected with the Gardner Museum?"

"Yes. And?" Julia leaned farther forward. Celine slid forward in her armchair as well. What was Penny about to reveal?

"It turns out he was." The Director of the Gardner Museum sounded tearful now. "Moreover, he had a compelling motive to strike out at the Gardner."

Blake retraced his path back to 72 Grumman Avenue. His request for a search warrant had been denied. *Flimsy grounds*, the judge had told Ella. But he was still free to knock on the door and ask a few questions. And he fully intended to.

Earlier, he'd noticed a narrow paved path between 64 Grumman and 70. He decided to pull in and park there, sitting quietly in the fading light. Maureen Rita Flynn's house was clearly visible through the bare trees.

But no one from the house would likely notice the nondescript sedan parked amidst the trees in this narrow path. Sitting in his car, Blake regarded the house.

There was no sign of Mary. The vast white lawn in front of the house was empty. But if Maureen had cancer, then most likely Mary had simply returned to the house.

It was large, Blake noticed. Nothing like Dodd's mansion, but comfortably sized. There was a simple elegance about it, with its white siding, gray door, blue shutters, and covered porch.

He got out of the car, walking a few paces. An SUV was parked all the way in the back next to a small square building that could only be the garage. He guessed the SUV belonged to Mary and that Maureen's vehicle was housed in the garage.

Ella hadn't had time to pull up very much on Maureen. They were still going by their surmises based on the few insights Celine had provided. A twinge of wistfulness laced through his interior as he considered Celine. He wished they'd parted on better terms. He'd been churlish and rude. Way to go, Markham, he told himself bitterly as he approached the curving driveway of Maureen Rita's home.

He strode down the path. The snow-covered hedges, the white window boxes, and the hanging planters in the porch—pretty albeit bare—made hardly any impact on him. Jumping up the steps to the covered porch, he rapped sharply on the door.

Would it be Maureen who answered? Or Mary, the intern?

The door opened and a head surrounded by wavy dark hair peeked out. "Yes?"

"Mary?" Blake smiled, extending his arm. "I wasn't expecting to see you here. It's been a while."

"It's Special Agent Blake Markham," he continued as Mary gaped at him, her jaw slack. "You hightailed it out of our office so fast and so abruptly, I can't tell if you remember me."

"How did you find me?" she demanded, finding her voice at last. She hesitated, swallowing nervously. "Am I under arrest?"

Blake considered the question. "It depends," he said finally.

"On what?" Her slender figure stood rigid and erect before him.

Chapter Fifty-Eight

"On whether you cooperate."

Blake stepped forward, forcing Mary to move back and open the door wider.

"Come in, why don't you?" she grumbled, but she didn't try to make him leave, closing the door behind him instead.

"Why'd you do it?" He turned to face her. A spacious crimson couch separated the living room from the dining area. The fireplace was a tall, white affair. He noticed the Van Hoyt catalog on the coffee table. That came as no surprise. Maureen was on the museum's mailing list after all.

"Why'd you try to bring down an ongoing investigation? Passing on information about one of our consultants"—he was thinking of Celine—"nearly getting them killed? What was that all about?"

"It was about survival, Special Agent Markham," Mary sneered. "Ever heard of that?"

"Survival?" Uninvited, Blake dragged out one of the dining room chairs and seated himself. With a magnanimous wave, he indicated that Mary join him as well.

"I needed the money." Glaring at him, she pulled out a chair and sat down.

"Money that Maureen Rita Flynn couldn't give you?" Blake allowed his gaze to travel over the comfortably furnished space. There were paintings on the wall—prints as far as he could tell. "Who is she to you, by the way?"

"My mom. And she has cancer. The bills"—Mary's eyes filled with tears. Genuine tears, Blake noted with surprise—"the bills have been overwhelming."

She'd received a call shortly after joining the FBI, instructing her to pass on any information about the investigation and any tips that got called in to a phone number she'd been given. Her mother's hospital bills would be taken care of.

And if Mary didn't comply, well, her mother was not exactly indispensable.

"There's no point asking me what the number was. Once I'd told them about your *psychic sleuth*"—Mary made it sound like an insult—"I was never able to get through to it. It was like a ghost number—like it had never existed."

A burner phone, Blake thought.

"And so you ran?"

"What else could I do? Take the rap for somebody else? I don't think so."

"You didn't call yourself Mary Flynn, though," Blake pointed out. And every piece of information she'd provided about herself on her application had been a lie.

"A precaution to ensure I got the job," Mary said. It had been at her mother's suggestion. Her drug arrests and her inability to pass the initial FBI screening process were, according to her mother, insurmountable hurdles to getting even a job manning a tip line.

So Maureen—or her connections—had arranged for Mary's internship. Mary had alluded to her mother's connections but hadn't said much more.

Blake looked around the house again.

"I'm finding it hard to believe you have money worries. This is a large home, the mortgage and the property taxes alone must be a fortune."

"The property was deeded to my mother by the company she worked for, Special Agent. The company owned it outright by the time they gave it to her. And they still take care of the property taxes."

"That's unusual," Blake commented drily. "Highly unusual."

"Maybe so." Mary remained unfazed. "But Mom gave her all to her work. She deserved every penny of what she got."

"What do you know about the Degas?" Blake abruptly shifted gears.

"What Degas?"

But Mary had stiffened. She sat frozen and expressionless in her seat, her blue eyes veiled.

⤲

Norton had a motive for hitting the Gardner? Celine's eyes widened. What had Penny found out?

Before she could react, Julia had plucked the phone off the coffee table, demanding: "How so?"

The former fed's puzzled gaze met Celine's, silently inquiring if Celine had received any psychic insights to that effect. Dazed, Celine shook her head.

She'd sensed insider involvement—and with the gardeners, the guards, and now, Dean Rafferty, there'd been plenty of that. The Brahmin had an insider connection. She'd sensed that as well.

But that he had a reason to hit the Gardner? The revelation left her feeling stunned.

"Norton's father, Jackson Norton, was a prominent member of the board. When he retired, Hugh Norton wanted to take his place. But we didn't have a vacancy, and the only person supporting his candidacy was his friend, Dean Rafferty."

"The deacon at Divine Mercy Parish," Celine whispered.

"Yes, that's right. I take it you've heard Rafferty may have been the one to take our *Chez Tortoni*?"

"Ella did mention it," Celine told her.

"Any idea why the other board members were against Norton joining the board?" Julia asked. "Was it simply because there was no vacancy?"

"Oh, no. You see Jackson Norton had been a person of integrity, extremely interested in Isabella Stewart Gardner's legacy and our role in stewarding her works."

"His son, not so much, I take it," Julia surmised. Her eyebrows rose slightly. She ran her fingers through the ends of her thick white ponytail.

"No," Penny said quietly. "For Hugh Norton, the art represented an investment, valuable only in terms of its monetary value. He was well-informed about it, as he'd have to be, given his profession. And he had—still has, I imagine—an appreciation for the Impressionists—"

"The Degas sketches," Celine breathed out.

"Yes, he had an especial fondness for the jockeys, the horses, the quick, deft way Degas captures movement. He thought those sketches should be displayed more prominently in the Blue Room."

"But that's not what the lady would've wanted." Celine smiled as Belle Gardner, garbed in her black gown, shimmered into view. The museum's quirky foundress was a familiar figure. Celine had beheld her since she was two. Belle held the museum's missing gu in her outstretched hands.

She wants it back, Celine, her guardian angel said. *Bring it back.*

I'm trying. Celine conveyed the message urgently through her thoughts. *Trust me, I really am.*

"Not at all." Penny's denial was swift and crisp. "Mrs. Gardner's will states that any change to her collection—even the slightest change in the way the works are arranged—would result in the entire collection going to Harvard. Yet Hugh Norton insisted the Degas sketches would be better placed in the Blue Room."

"But Rafferty, you say, was on his side?" Julia attempted to bring Penny back on track.

"Yes. Even to the point of insisting we use Norton's company, Morgana Insurance, to insure our works. That's the other reason the board hesitated to bring him in. They feared—rightly, in my opinion—that Norton would misuse his position to make changes to the collection and to insist the Gardner purchase a policy from him to protect our works."

"And when the Gardner didn't bite—" Julia began only to be interrupted.

"I'm convinced he used his mob connections to orchestrate a credible threat of theft. It was shortly after the board had emphatically denied his requests that the FBI contacted us about a possible theft."

"Yet the theft itself took place several years later," Julia softly pointed out.

"We were robbed four short months after Jackson Norton passed away," Penny told her.

Chapter Fifty-Nine

"I doubt Hugh would've dared make his move while his father was still alive."

Celine listened intently while Penny spoke.

"He'd have been swiftly removed from his father's will if he had," the Gardner Director went on.

"But he nursed his grudges," Celine said. "And his anger grew."

She was passing on the impressions her guardian angel was conveying to her. She saw the swirling red clouds, the grasping manicured hand. It was lovingly stroking a frame. The word *Forgery* floated in large letters through her mind.

"Had he managed to gain a foothold within the board, he'd have used his position to change out the collection for forged works."

"Oh, my God!" Penny's gasp crackled over the line.

The manicured finger gleefully traced circles on a gilded frame.

When the enemy applies sufficient pressure, we tend to waver, falling back, Sister Mary Catherine said. *It's what the enemy hopes for—that we won't stand strong.*

"I think he was hoping the board wouldn't stand their ground," Celine said. "That the theft would force their hand to go so far as to consider flouting the stipulations of Belle's will."

Julia nodded shrewdly, her blue eyes sharp. "A fact that he'd expose, thus resulting in the Gardner's treasure being taken over by Harvard."

"What a diabolical plan!" Penny gasped. "How truly evil! Julia, he's got to be arrested."

Julia pursed her lips, shaking her head ruefully at Celine.

"We've got a credible motive for Norton being our culprit. We have a solid reason to keep investigating him. But unfortunately all this is still in the realm of speculation. It's hearsay. It isn't enough to charge him. It certainly wouldn't hold up in court."

"Oh, for heavens' sake!" The frustrated stream of air Penny blew out was clearly audible over the phone line. "Well, at least you've got something to work with, right?" she asked hopefully.

"We do," Julia assured her.

When Penny had ended the call, Julia absently fingered the sketch Celine had drawn.

"If we can get to Norton's mob associate—assuming that's who our portly friend is—we might be able to get him to crack and dish out some dirt on Norton. That's our only hope."

She raised her head, her blue eyes steely.

"We've got to find them, Celine."

She knows something, Blake thought. *Mary had information about the Sullivan-Dodd case.* He tamped down his exultation. He needed to proceed carefully.

"The stolen Degas pastel your mother called the FBI about—let's see, when was it?" He paused to regard Mary. "Oh, yeah, Monday."

Mary looked crestfallen, but oddly relieved as well. Blake noted her reaction, although he couldn't make sense of it.

"She should never have done that," she muttered irritably. "But she never listens to reason at the best of times. And she'd been drinking like a fish that day."

"Turns out she was right." Blake deliberately adopted a reassuring tone—trying to put Mary at ease.

When he gauged he'd succeeded, he dropped his bombshell.

"Obviously, we're wondering how, given that it was never reported stolen."

Mary's eyes gaped. She recovered herself almost immediately.

"Oh, yes, it was." She leaned forward, taking an argumentative stance. "It was reported stolen. The Sullivans—"

"Your mother knew them?"

"Sure. She was the insurance investigator. When they reported their Degas stolen, she was asked to look into it. Make sure this wasn't a case of fraud. That they weren't simply looking to collect on the work."

"She worked for Morgana Insurance—Hugh Norton's company?"

"Yes. Is that a crime?"

"Of course not," Blake replied smoothly. "Sounds like it was a job that paid off."

He allowed his eyes to travel around the living room again. "Was it a better job than the one she had at Dodd Life Insurance?"

Mary's eyes flashed. "I suppose it was."

"Did she keep in touch with Henry Dodd?" He had to know given how close the two lived.

"No, why would she?" Mary seemed genuinely puzzled.

"Because he lived not more than half a mile away." Blake pointed in the direction of Scott Street. "He's dead," he added. "Passed away just this morning."

"Oh." Mary shrugged. It was a noncommittal gesture. She truly had no idea who Dodd was. "I'm sorry to hear that."

"You're saying she didn't keep in touch with Dodd. Did she resent him?"

"No, of course not. She's never spoken of him. I'm sorry he's passed away. But I really don't see what that has to do with me or my mom."

"How did your mother find out about the Degas?" Blake pressed her. "It wasn't from Henry Dodd?"

"No, it was not. She saw it in the Van Hoyt catalog. Look, I can show you." Mary got out of her chair and went around to the coffee table in the living room. She brought the catalog back, opening it to the page that pictured Dodd's pastel.

The Van Hoyt had informed its readers that the pastel—a rare Degas work —had been donated by a collector, but hadn't gone so far as to name him. Was it possible Maureen hadn't known that Dodd was the current owner?

"This was stolen in 1998," Blake said. "A long time ago. I'm surprised your mother recalled the facts of the case and recognized the work after all these years?"

"What can I say, Special Agent Markham? She has a good eye. She's always been very interested in the Impressionists."

"From what I hear"—Blake raised his head—"she isn't quite as knowledgeable about the Impressionists as she's led people to believe. Apparently she acquired a Manet that an art expert roundly dismissed as a fake—worth nothing."

It was a shot in the dark, but it paid off. Mary's face flushed.

"Okay, so she was duped. She had no reason to believe she was being cheated. So I guess she didn't look too closely at it."

"Is it here? May I look around?" Blake rose.

"No, it's not." Mary stood up as well. "And, no, you may not. Not without a search warrant. I think you'd better leave."

He hadn't played his cards well, Blake thought ruefully. Mary's apprehension about being arrested had dissipated. And, truth to tell, building a case for her arrest was more trouble than it was worth.

At the door, he turned around.

"What did your mother know about the Gardner heist?"

Mary froze again. "I have no idea what you're talking about."

"She called a newspaper—shortly after she called us—hinting at a connection between the Gardner theft and the Degas pastel stolen from the Sullivans. Any idea what that was about?"

"Nope, you'll have to ask her yourself. Oh, wait," Mary continued sarcastically. "She's in the hospital dying of cancer, so you're plumb out of luck. What makes you think it was her in any case? Wasn't the call anonymous?"

"How'd you know it was anonymous?" Blake stepped out onto the porch. A big mistake because Mary, instead of answering his question, resolutely shut the door in his face. Still, he'd gotten more than he'd anticipated.

A reason to keep pursuing Norton. Dodd was officially off the hook.

Based on what Celine had sensed, Maureen Rita Flynn had been looking to get someone in trouble.

But that someone clearly hadn't been Dodd.

Chapter Sixty

Nervously gripping the menu the waiter had handed her, Ella studied the dishes on offer. She wasn't sure what she'd expected when, on an impulse, she'd dialed Harrison Sullivan Jr.'s number and requested a meeting to update him on the case.

He'd agreed readily enough, but she'd been startled by his choice of venue —Stefano's, an upscale restaurant on 40 Charles Street. Located in Beacon Hill, it was a little over four miles from the FBI office in Chelsea. Sullivan Jr. had offered to pick her up, but Ella had opted to call a cab instead.

"I dine there regularly, and I already have a reservation," he'd explained. "I'd hate to cancel it."

Now, sitting across from him, Ella felt as nervous as a Victorian bride alone for the first time with her husband. With its beautiful oil paintings, white tablecloth-covered tables featuring a single red rose as a centerpiece, and the courtly, old-fashioned manners of the waiters, Stefano's had a distinctly romantic vibe to it.

"Care for a glass of wine?" Harrison Sullivan Jr. looked up from his menu and smiled warmly at Ella. "Or are you still on duty?"

He was easy on the eye. Six feet tall with a rangy, athletic build. His hair was dark, threaded through with a few strands of white; his eyes a vivid blue, oozing warmth behind their glasses.

"I guess a glass of white wine couldn't hurt," Ella replied, tucking a thick lock of her dark hair behind her ear. "Viognier, please." The citrusy notes of the wine would pair well with the honey lemon chicken with asparagus she planned to order.

Sullivan caught a waiter's eye, summoning him with a graceful wave of his long fingers. Then, having placed their orders, he took off his glasses—"My reading glasses," he'd told her ruefully before perching them atop his nose. "The doubtful blessings of old age"—and steepled his fingers.

"So tell me, Ella—may I call you Ella?"—she nodded, and he continued— "what's new with the case?"

He couldn't possibly be more than forty, Ella reflected inconsequentially. He'd been eighteen at the time of the theft. Tugging the ends of her bob cut, she marshaled her thoughts.

"We're very close to establishing that the Degas on display at the Van Hoyt Museum in Connecticut is the work that was stolen from your parents' house," she began.

Sullivan Jr.'s eyebrows rose as he leaned forward. "No sh—sorry. Pardon my language. That isn't what I was expecting to hear."

Ella felt her cheeks flame at the apology. "Don't worry about it. Blake—I mean Special Agent Markham—isn't exactly very careful with his language either. I'm used to it."

Sullivan Jr. grinned. "Is *Blake—I mean Special Agent Markham*—a special friend?"

"No, of course not. Anyway, back to the Degas. Now that we're reasonably certain that the Degas is the one your family reported stolen, there are a few small legalities that need to be taken care of."

"Such as?" Sullivan Jr. frowned. The warmth in his blue eyes had dissipated, replaced by a piercing glare.

"There's a question of ownership, for one thing."

"I don't understand, Ella. As I explained when you first called, my parents transferred ownership of the Degas to the Lowell Museum. I have the paperwork. I'm sure the Lowell still has a copy."

"But your parents were paying the premium on the insurance policy?"

"Yes, mainly because it was on loan to us. We had an agreement to allow it to remain in our possession until my parents passed."

Ella frowned. This was going to be difficult to explain.

"Did your insurance company"—she pretended to consult the tiny notebook by her fork—"Morgana Insurance, right?"

"Yes, that's right."

She glanced up as a waiter arrived with her white wine and the red Sullivan had ordered for himself. Sullivan Jr. took a sip of his drink, his gaze riveted on her features.

"When your folks asked for a payout—"

"It was actually Morgana that offered to make the payment," Sullivan Jr. corrected her. "It had been well over a year. They figured the chances of the work being recovered were slim to none. It made no sense to keep making payments on the insurance policy."

Ella digested this information in silence. Morgana had insisted the Sullivans accept a payout. From what Blake had told her, Dodd had acquired the work well before the Sullivans had received a cent from their insurance company.

"Our understanding, Mr. Sullivan—"

"Harrison, please," he interrupted her. "Call me Harrison."

Ella tamped down her irritation. She wished he wouldn't keep interrupting. It was disrupting her thought process.

"All right, Harrison." She gave him a tight smile. "We understand that Morgana Insurance made it clear that once your family accepted the payout that the Degas, if recovered, would belong to the insurance company."

"That's bullshit!" Harrison brought his wine glass down with a thump. Ella winced.

"The paperwork—" she began.

"Is quite clear," Harrison spoke firmly. "We would never have accepted a payout. We might have canceled the policy, but we were certainly not going to accept a payout if it meant our agreement with the Lowell would be negated. What kind of people do you take us for?"

"Are you sure about this?" Ella peered at him uncertainly. "It was a long time ago. I imagine it must have been a stressful time as well. Could you perhaps have misunderstood?"

Harrison smiled. "Nope. I can still remember the insurance investigator who came to us with the offer. Maureen Rita Flynn."

"Maureen Rita Flynn?" Ella gaped at him. It was the woman in Norwalk, wasn't it?

"Old-fashioned name, I know. But she was anything but old-fashioned. She was gorgeous! I was eighteen at the time, and well. . ." He grinned. "I guess I don't need to tell you, I couldn't keep my eyes off of her. I made sure to attend every meeting she had with my folks.

"She assured us the payout wouldn't affect our agreement with the Lowell. It was a generous amount, too, as I recall. Not that we needed the money."

"And you have the paperwork to prove it?" Ella tried to keep her mind on the matter at hand rather than Harrison's revelation that he'd found Maureen Rita extremely attractive. Why the thought had given rise to a violent twinge of jealousy, she had no idea.

"With her signature," Harrison confirmed. "There's a copy on my desk at home. You can request the original from my bank. I have a digital copy I can send over after we finish up here."

"Yes, that would be good," Ella murmured, her mind preoccupied. Had Maureen Rita Flynn been acting on her own initiative? Had she been the one to sell the work to Dodd?

On the other hand, hadn't Blake told her that Norton wasn't claiming the work either? Norton had insisted that the Sullivans had relinquished all claims to the Degas and had understood that all agreements to transfer ownership to a museum would be negated by their acceptance of a payout.

To hear Norton tell it, Dodd owned the Degas fair and square. But if what Harrison had just told her checked out, then the Lowell was the legal owner of the work. Of course the timing of Dodd's acquisition worked in the Lowell's favor.

But still . . . Why had Norton tried to insinuate insurance fraud on the part of the Sullivans?

Eager to return to the office, she barely tasted her food.

"You won't forget to fax or email your copy of your agreement with Morgana Insurance, will you?" she asked Harrison anxiously as they both stood outside the restaurant.

"I'll do it the minute I get back, Ella," he promised. He rested his hands lightly on her shoulders. "I enjoyed our time together."

To her surprise, he lowered his head to hers and gently touched his lips to her parted mouth. "Maybe we can do this again—when you're not so preoccupied with a case," he suggested before walking off.

Chapter Sixty-One

Blake put his legs up on the ottoman in his hotel room and opened the large pizza box from J.B.'s Deli & Pizza. He'd stopped on the way back to order himself dinner.

The appetizing aromas of meatballs, sausage, pepperoni, and bacon made his mouth water. It had been a long day, and he'd had nothing to eat since breakfast.

Biting off a large piece, he considered his day. Norwalk PD had conducted an initial search of Dodd's home but had unearthed nothing of further interest. No documents that shed light on how Dodd had come by the Degas.

There had to have been a go-between, Blake thought, tearing off another huge chunk of his pizza. Strands of gooey cheese hung from the torn-off edge. He scooped them off with his fingers and stuffed them into his mouth. Boy, was he famished!

Who had brought the Degas to Dodd's attention? Who had brokered the deal?

Dodd had insisted he could prove his purchase was legitimate. But there'd been nothing in his home. Had Dodd's killer—Norton, most likely—made off with the pertinent information?

But there'd been nothing to indicate Dodd's home had been ransacked.

Blake thought back to his meeting with Dodd. Dodd had handed him an envelope with a certificate of authenticity. It had held no interest for him at the time, the authenticity of the Degas not being in question.

But it struck him now that he might be able to glean something useful from it. If the authenticator was any good, the certificate would be accompanied by a detailed report documenting both the physical attributes of the work and its provenance.

Bolting down two additional slices of pizza, he wiped his hands on the stack of paper towels the deli had provided with his order and fished out the envelope from his laptop case.

It was promisingly heavy. Pulling up the brass tabs, he lifted the flap and tilted the envelope. A certificate slid out, followed by a stack of typewritten pages. About ten in all, neatly stapled together.

Impatiently, he cast his eye over the report. The authenticator had meticulously listed the physical condition of the work. The paper was low-quality, machine-made paper consistent with the rough-textured paper Degas tended to use for his pastels. The tint of the paper had faded to a gray.

Having seen the work, Blake could attest to the accuracy of that observation. The millboard on which it was mounted was in fairly good condition but had sustained slight warping.

The technical analysis revealed techniques consistent with the ones Degas used, notably his use of overlapping vertical strokes of pigment. In some areas, the Roche colors Degas had used had been mixed with water and then thickly spread with his fingers. Remarkably, a thumbprint and some fingerprints had been detected—making the work even more valuable than hitherto believed.

X-ray fluorescence revealed the presence of synthetic pigments that had faded. In some key areas, however, the pigment had been expertly re-applied, suggesting the hand of a restorer. Scientific analysis had also revealed the use of a casein-based fixative separating pigment layers in some areas—a feature entirely consistent with Degas's practice.

Blake flipped page after page of the report until he finally came to what he was looking for. The section entitled "Provenance." It was short, listing very little more than he already knew.

What was puzzling, however, was that the Lowell had been listed as the last owner of the work. No mention had been made of the restorer who'd ostensibly acquired the work as payment for his services and was now selling it.

Had the authenticator been unaware of the fact? Or had he simply not considered it significant enough to emphasize? Blake would have to contact the man, assuming he still existed?

He turned to the last page. The report was signed by one Israel Monroe. It was the red stamp under the typed name and signature that caught his eye.

Monroe was an assessor at Morgana Insurance.

Jesus H Christ! Norton's company had provided Dodd with his certificate of authenticity!

Blake's pulse raced. Didn't that establish Norton was aware of the sale to Dodd? Could one go so far as to claim Norton had actively promoted it?

Certainly, he'd taken no action to return the work to the Sullivans or the Lowell Museum.

Blake flipped back to the front page. Too bad, the report hadn't been typed on Morgana stationery. A deliberate move to give Norton plausible deniability?

Blake thought so. Still, this was promising.

Still pensive, he turned back to the last page. A footnote in tiny font caught his gaze. He strained his eyes to read it.

"Report requested by Maureen Rita Flynn on behalf of Henry Dodd"

Jesus Christ! He hadn't been expecting that. Had Maureen Rita brokered the sale? For—whom?—Norton? She could hardly have been acting on her own.

Yet her daughter had been adamant, Maureen Rita was aware the Degas had been stolen. And Maureen's call to the FBI was evidence of that.

He pulled out his phone. He'd missed a call from Ella. Tapping the play button under the voicemail she'd left, he listened intently to the rising pitch of her voice as she urgently conveyed her message.

Maureen Rita Flynn had met with the Sullivans to discuss the implications of their payout. Did Blake know she'd been employed as an insurance investigator at Norton's company?

"Yes, yes, I know," he muttered, hitting the stop button to pause the breathless torrent of Ella's words. There was nothing new there. He'd call his assistant back later to confirm he'd made the same discovery.

He needed to call Israel Monroe. Was the guy still an employee at Morgana Insurance? Blake pulled out his laptop, intending to conduct a preliminary Google search to locate the authenticator. He'd barely typed the name into the search bar when his phone rang.

Dear God, not Ella again. He glanced at his phone and frowned. It wasn't a number he recognized. He was tempted to ignore it, but something made him pick up.

"Special Agent Blake Markham? This is Elizabeth Dodd Surrey, Henry Dodd's daughter."

❧

Celine tossed and turned in the spacious queen-sized hotel bed. Sleep was impossible. What time was it anyway?

She opened one eye, squinting at her phone, plugged into the charger on the base of the LED lamp on her nightstand. Only eleven. They'd decided to retire early. Julia would hunker down in the sitting room, keeping an eye on the surveillance footage coming into her laptop from Clara's room at Hutchinson House.

To conserve battery, the orchid camera Rod had provided them with turned off when it detected no motion. When a door or window opened or when someone moved, sensors within the faux orchid turned the camera on. A small beep sounded on the laptop receiving the video footage, alerting the viewer that recording had resumed.

It wouldn't be a comfortable night for Julia, but at least she'd be able to get some shut-eye. At about one o'clock, Celine would relieve her, moving to the sitting room to monitor the video feed for the rest of the night.

Sighing, Celine closed her eyes, determined to get some rest.

But her brain was on overdrive. Hugh Norton, wealthy art insurer and collector, had a strong motive to strike out at the Gardner. She'd suspected it all along, but with the information Penny had dug up they were on more solid ground now.

It still wasn't enough for an arrest, though. Had Norton been behind Henry Dodd's murder as well?

An overwhelming whiff of cologne suffused the room, suggesting she was on the right track. But had Blake found any concrete evidence?

Probably not. Ella would've shared the news had that been the case.

Dodd had died because of cyanide poisoning. Just like Laurie Robbes. Who had supplied Norton with the cyanide? The tall, burly man with the ice-cold eyes who, with his wife, had been the last person to see Laurie alive?

He'd carried the poison into the museum in an inhaler. Who would've considered a simple red inhaler to be the receptacle for a toxic gas?

Celine's eyes opened again. The sketch lay on her nightstand. She brought it closer, gazing at it?

Did the cyanide that killed Henry Dodd come from you? she silently asked, hoping her guardian angel would hear her and supply an answer.

He's long since killed the goose that laid the poisonous egg, Sister Mary Catherine told her.

What did that mean? That Norton's criminal associate had suffered a falling-out with his cyanide supplier?

A sensation of lightness in her chest—like innumerable Roman candles going off simultaneously—confirmed her impression. So where had the cyanide come from?

She looked again at the sketch. To her surprise, a large apricot sat on the sheet of paper. Where had the fruit come from? Was it artificial, a decorative item the hotel had left on her nightstand, that she'd missed seeing until now?

Confused, she reached out to touch it, but her fingers slipped through the fruit. It was like a hologram. She withdrew her hand, but the apricot remained on her nightstand.

Apricot kernels, she thought. *Bitter apricot kernels.*

Amygda. . . Sister Mary Catherine began, her voice fading out.

What? Celine frowned, straining her ears to hear the word.

The nun repeated herself, but Celine couldn't make out any more of the word than she had the first time.

Tell Blake, her guardian angel advised. *About the apricots. He'll know.*

Celine shook her head. She wasn't about to call Blake. Certainly not at this hour. Nope, she'd call Ella and get her to pass on a message.

Mind made up, she sat up in bed, unplugged her phone from its charger, and proceeded to make her call.

Ella's phone rang several times, eventually going to voicemail. Ella's no-nonsense voice advised her to leave a message and number to receive a call-back.

Celine hung up, unsure what to say. The worst thing you could do with a vague message like the one her guardian angel was conveying to her right now was to deliver it over voicemail. What was she supposed to say? *Look for the apricots. They're significant in this case.*

Besides, where would you get apricots in winter?

Call Blake, Sister Mary Catherine's voice urged her. *Call Blake.*

Determined not to comply, Celine put the phone down, sank back onto her pillows, and closed her eyes. But her guardian angel's voice reverberated in her ear.

Call Blake. Call Blake. Call him now.

Fine, Celine ground out through clenched teeth. Scowling, she sat up in bed again and reached for her phone.

His line was busy. She was about to give up but Sister Mary Catherine's voice prodded at her conscience.

Try again. Don't give up.

Chapter Sixty-Two

Like father, like daughter, Blake thought ruefully, recalling his initial shock at receiving Dodd's call the evening before. But he didn't have long to wonder who'd given Elizabeth Dodd Surrey his number.

"I've been trying to get in touch with Dad all day. He was supposed to visit me. He didn't specify a time, but when he wasn't here by three, I began to worry. I tried calling his cell to no avail. Juana, our housekeeper, is out of reach as well. Then I called his home phone number." Elizabeth paused for breath. "Special Agent, a Norwalk PD detective answered my call and directed me to you. What exactly is going on?"

Blake hesitated. This was the part of the job he hated—having to break the awful news to the victim's family.

"Are you aware . . ." he began delicately.

"Yes," Elizabeth said stiffly. "The detective said you and Juana found Dad. But I don't understand why the FBI is on the case. And where's Juana? I hope you're not insinuating she had anything to do with Dad's"—she choked—"with what happened. She's here legally, if you were wondering. She has her papers."

Jesus, this wasn't going to be easy, was it? Driving his fingers into his hair. Blake got to his feet, cell phone still glued to his ear.

"Your father and I had an arrangement to meet this morning," he said succinctly. "He was supposed to call. When he didn't, I was on edge. I can't explain why—call it a gut feeling."

Stillness followed his words, Elizabeth's breath barely audible over the line.

"Was this about the Degas he'd loaned the Van Hoyt?" she asked eventually.

"He mentioned it to you?" Bake countered. How much did she know?

"Only the gist of it—that there was some issue with its authenticity, but he had it under control. I found the article in the *Massachusetts Post* after I heard what happened. I thought what you'd told him had caused him a heart attack. But you're saying . . ." Her voice quavered.

"We're trying to find out who sold him the Degas? Would you happen to know, Mrs. Surrey? The work was never reported stolen—not to the Art Loss Registry, that's to say. Your father bought it in good faith. Under the circumstances, he wasn't at fault. But given what I know of him, he wouldn't have hesitated to do the right thing"

"Damn right, he wouldn't, Special Agent. I've no idea how he discovered it was on the market. I'm guessing it was through one of his fellow board members on the Gardner. He stayed in touch long after he'd stepped down. It might've been a person called Rafferty. In fact, I'm almost positive it was."

Rafferty. Blake pondered the name. The man who'd returned to the Gardner Museum the night before the theft. The only man with the opportunity to take the *Chez Tortoni,* undetected.

The person who'd acted as Norton's go-between in his interactions with Jonah Hibbert.

Elizabeth's voice intruded upon his musings.

"They both had a partiality for the Impressionists, wishing Mrs. Gardner had collected more of their works."

"This would be Rafferty and your father?" Blake had been so lost in his speculations, he'd missed some of what she'd said.

"That's right," Elizabeth said. "They weren't all that close, but they did see eye-to-eye on some things The conditions at the Gardner, museum security, that kind of thing."

"And Hugh Norton?" Blake was at the window now. He stared out into the darkness. "Was your father close to him?"

His phone buzzed, signaling an incoming call. Blake ignored it. It was most likely Ella. He strained his ears to hear Elizabeth's response.

"They were in the same line of business," she was saying. "Insurance. They had similar interests. They weren't thick as thieves or anything like that. But they were chummy. Dad is—was, I mean—a sociable person. Easy to get to know, with quite a wide circle of friends. I recall there was an FBI agent he was reasonably friendly with—"

"I'm guessing it was Bill McCormick," Blake interjected. Who else would it be?

"Yes, I believe that was his name. You know him?"

"Intimately," was Blake's dry response. "I take it he shared your father's interest in art and the Impressionists."

His phone buzzed insistently. Ella's persistence chafed him, but he forced himself to keep a lid on his temper.

"Oh, absolutely!" Elizabeth's voice had lightened, as though she were smiling at the memory. "That's why I'm so surprised at your saying Dad's Degas was stolen. Bill would've set him straight had that been the case."

Not if Bill happened to be on Norton's payroll. But Blake kept that thought to himself.

"And Israel Monroe—"

"Dad's authenticator," Elizabeth said immediately. "A long-time acquaintance. Dad was his first client, did you know? Israel was still working at Morgana Insurance—I think that was the company—when Dad asked him to authenticate a work he was considering. Israel always says it was Dad who jumpstarted his career in authentication."

He got the number from her and was about to end the call when a thought struck him.

"You say you were expecting your father this morning. Was that a visit he'd planned some days ago?"

"No, actually, he called out of the blue late last night. We usually meet on Sundays, so I was pleasantly surprised."

"What did he want to talk about?"

Whatever it was, could it shed light on the evidence Dodd planned to provide him?

"Well, that's what's so odd. He asked me if I still had a photo album from several years ago. He wanted to look at all our old photos." Elizabeth's voice sobered. "I wonder if he had some inkling it would be his last. . ." Her voice broke as she stifled a sob.

Made uncomfortable by her quiet sobbing, Blake paced the floor of his compact hotel room. He would've given anything to get off the line, but he waited until Elizabeth had composed herself sufficiently to end the call.

If only Dodd had sought to confide in his daughter. But he should've guessed it was too much to hope for. No investigator ever got that lucky!

Chapter Sixty-Three

Celine stared at her phone, then jabbed her finger on the red call button for the third time.

The ringing phone set her nerves on edge. Listening to it, she vowed to call it a night if Blake didn't pick up. Nervous and agitated, she almost hoped he wouldn't.

The trilling ceased.

"Hey!" Blake greeted her.

"Hi." She returned his greeting, adding unnecessarily, "It's Celine." She cleared her throat before continuing. The image of the apricot was still visible on her nightstand. "Ehhmm, I've been thinking about Dodd."

"Me too. I just finished talking with his daughter. She was expecting a visit from him."

"And he never made it," Celine said softly. "How awful."

Unlike Celine when she'd lost her parents, Dodd's daughter was an adult, married and with a life of her own. But the shock of losing a parent would be no less devastating for the poor woman than it had been for Celine all those years ago.

She swallowed the rising lump in her throat. She'd been no more than twelve, an only child eager to see her parents again after their brief trip out of town.

Resolutely, she pushed the memory aside.

"Listen, I'm almost positive Norton did his own dirty work this time. Have you found any evidence of his involvement?"

"Not yet." Blake sounded grim. "But we're getting closer."

She listened intently as he told her about the certificate of authenticity Dodd had received for the Degas pastel.

"You were right about Maureen Rita Flynn," he ended. "She was our anonymous tipster, and she was a Morgana Insurance employee. Norton's mistress, from the look of things. She's the one who requested the certificate of authenticity on Dodd's behalf."

"And she was investigating the Sullivans' insurance claim, right?" Celine asked.

"Yup. That's how she knew it was stolen. I met with her daughter who also happens to be the intern who—"

"I know," she broke in. The incident was a sore point with Blake. He blamed himself for what had nearly happened on her first visit to Boston.

It wasn't the way she remembered it, though, and she reminded him of the fact.

"You insisted Julia and I accompany you to the Gardner." There'd been another car waiting at the airport for them—sent by the General, although they hadn't known it at the time. "We'd have lost the finial if it hadn't been for you. We certainly wouldn't have succeeded in restoring it to the Gardner."

"Mary should never have been hired." Blake's voice was steely. "On the other hand, with the way things are shaping up, we might be able to lean into her and get her to implicate Norton. She's devoted to her mother. Maureen has cancer, and they're drowning in hospital bills."

"It looks like Norton set Maureen up to be his fall guy, doesn't it?" Celine commented, ignoring Sister Mary Catherine's sharply uttered, *You're killing time, Celine.* "I mean if all the paperwork has her name on it . . ."

"She's not going to be too happy about it when she realizes." Blake seemed to be grinning. "Neither is her daughter. It's the ultimate betrayal."

Get to it, Celine.

Celine cleared her throat.

"Do you recall my telling you about the couple who came to see Laurie at the Montague Museum all those years ago?"

"Yup. You sensed that the man might have been her killer."

"I'm almost positive he was. It occurred to me that if he was doing Norton's dirty work at the time, he might still be involved. Specifically, he might be Norton's cyanide supplier."

Blake emitted a low whistle.

"Anything more concrete you can give me."

Celine sighed. *Okay, here goes nothing.*

"I'm seeing apricots."

"Apricots?" He sounded incredulous.

See, I knew this wouldn't work, she griped.

You're omitting details, Celine, Sister Mary Catherine admonished her. *Give him everything.*

She clenched her fists, forcing herself to continue speaking.

"Apricot kernels. Bitter apricot kernels. And I'm hearing the word Amyg—"

"Amygdalin?" Blake exclaimed. "Is that what you're hearing?"

"I guess."

"You could be on to something, Celine." Excitement mingled with something like awe tinged Blake's voice. Celine could see him sitting forward.

"I was thinking more along the lines of potassium cyanide," Blake went on. "It's the most obvious source of cyanide poisoning. But apricot kernels contain amygdalin, which reacts with water converting to cyanide. That's what makes them so toxic."

"So if one were to consume apricot kernels . . ." Celine's sleep-fatigued brain struggled to process Blake's words.

"The amygdalin would react in the water in your blood and saliva, making for a pretty potent combination."

"So he . . . what? . . . ground the kernels into powder and mixed them with the wine?"

"Could be. Or you can boil the kernels in ethanol and then evaporate the solution to get white amygdalin crystals. Either way, you'd have a pretty toxic substance on your hands."

"And you know this how?" Celine wondered.

"High school chemistry." Blake chuckled. "I knew it would come in handy someday. Anyway, I'll have Norwalk PD investigators test the wine—what little we have of it—for amygdalin as well."

"Sounds good." Celine glanced at the clock on her nightstand. It was late. It would soon be time to relieve Julia.

But before she ended the call, there was something she needed to say.

"Listen, back in Paso Robles, I'm sorry about—"

"It's cool," Blake interrupted. "I figure you're not into me."

"I realize I may not be," Celine conceded. "And going ahead would've been a mistake. Although I didn't think so at the time. If Sister Mary Catherine hadn't startled me by bellowing in my ear—"

"You mean that's the only reason I didn't score? Because of your guardian angel? Well, f—" To her amusement. Blake swiftly stifled the expletive.

A moment later, he continued: "So, just to clarify, if it hadn't been for her, you'd have been fine with—"

It was her turn to interject. "Yes, but Sister Mary Catherine was right. We'd have been using each other. Well, I'd have been using you."

❧

Blake stared at the phone, dazed. Celine had ended the call but her voice still rang in his ears. She hadn't rejected him. Hadn't meant to, at any event.

He took in a deep breath, aware of a sensation of lightness in his chest. It felt as though the millstone crushing his lungs these past few days had been lifted off his being.

He took another deep breath. He was feeling lightheaded as well.

If she hadn't been about to reject him—his gaze was riveted on the phone resting in his palm—she must have been somewhat into him. Even if she thought she wasn't. And she cared enough about him not to lead him on.

He could work with that. He could—

His phone buzzed, the vibrations like a pulse of electricity blazing through his palm.

Jolted to awareness, he stared at the number. Detective Hudson from Norwalk PD. There was news on the case, he guessed. Reluctantly tearing his mind away from the pleasantly distracting thoughts of Celine clouding his brain, he answered the call.

"Markham here."

"Special Agent Markham, it's Brad Hudson . . ."

Blake listened carefully as Hudson proceeded to update him on the case.

A half-empty wine bottle had been discarded by the wayside not far from Dodd's residence.

"Looks like the same type of wine as was left in those wine glasses," Hudson said. "But we'll have to test it. There's a nice clear set of fingerprints left on the bottle. Seems like a match for the smudged print we found on the stem and lower portion of the wine glasses."

"Could be our killer," Blake commented.

"Sure could. We ac—"

"And the phone records?" Blake interrupted. "Anything there that could be of interest?"

"I was getting to that," Hudson said. "Dodd did call the number you alerted us to. But it was very brief. Lasted about thirty to forty seconds. But just seconds later, he received another call. This one from a burner number. We were able to track the location of that phone. That's how we discovered the wine bottle. Both had been discarded not too far from Dodd's house."

Blake's lips stretched into a thin smile. Norton was getting careless.

"So it's reasonable to assume the caller using the burner number was the same guy whose number I gave you," he surmised.

"Sure is. We can look into it. Dodd got a call from the burner earlier that day. Looks like the burner had only been active a couple of days prior. It's a local number. Dude probably bought the phone and the SIM from a store in the area. I have my people looking into that."

Blake considered the significance of the news. It was hard to concentrate. He wished Celine hadn't hung up on him so abruptly. But now was not the time to think of her.

Concentrate, Markham, he scolded himself. *Concentrate.*

". . . if the store that sold the burner happens to have video camera footage," Hudson was saying, "we'll be able to put a face to our perp."

Yup. Blake nodded. But that would take time.

"Listen, can you look into the number I gave you?" he asked. "See if you can get some location data off the phone?" He wanted to find out if Norton had been in Norwalk in the days prior to Dodd's murder. It was likely he had.

"Ehhm . . ." Hudson hesitated. But Blake pressed on.

"With that thirty-second call you have on record, I'd say there's sufficient probable cause, wouldn't you? It's more than likely the guy called Dodd back on his burner phone."

"I guess you could say that," Hudson reluctantly conceded.

"And it's data shared with a cell phone carrier. No different than if a witness saw him outside Dodd's house last night."

They both knew that under the federal Stored Communications Act, location data transmitted from Norton's phone to cell phone towers in the vicinity weren't subject to the same Fourth Amendment privacy protections. The act was a Godsend as far as Blake was concerned.

"Yup, I guess there's that. A court order should be easy enough to get. Want to do things as much by the book as possible. You know what defense lawyers are like these days."

Blake knew. He'd witnessed defense teams concoct stories out of whole cloth, feeding them to their guilty clients, who then presented them under oath as eyewitness statements—effectively implicating someone else to get themselves off.

It was reprehensible.

"And the wine—?" he began.

"We'll have to test the stuff in the bottle. There wasn't enough left in the wine glasses."

"I'd test for the presence of amygdalin as well as potassium cyanide," Blake said.

"Amygdalin?" Hudson sounded puzzled. "Any particular reason for that recommendation?"

"Nope. Just a pertinent fact from high school chemistry. Amygdalin is also a source of cyanide poisoning. Often overlooked in criminal cases. But from a criminal's point of view easier to obtain."

He repeated the explanation he'd provided to Celine earlier. Damned if he was going to reveal the true source of his information.

But he was confident the net was closing in on Norton. Finally.

Chapter Sixty-Four

Celine rested the receiver on her shoulder, cradling it between her jaw and collarbone. She was so weak the black plastic felt like a millstone weighing her down. She glanced down at her bony right wrist resting on the voluminous hospital gown hanging loose upon her emaciated frame.

What a pathetic creature she'd become!

"They've come looking for me," she rasped. Growing panic and a bitter fury lent a sharp edge to her voice.

"They're just fishing, Maureen," he tried to soothe her. "They have nothing, remember?"

"I can't stay silent any longer," she warned. She'd done too much for him already. And what had she gained from the deal? "I won't. I need—"

"You're not getting any more money out of me, you conniving bitch." His voice, cold and hard as steel, cut through her threats. "You're up to your neck in this as much as I am."

"Don't forget I know where the bodies are buried. If I talk . . ." Her throat felt sore, but she forced herself to grate out the threat.

"Go right ahead, sweetheart." His cruel chortle of derision stung her. "There's nothing to connect me . . ." His words faded out or perhaps it was just the ringing in Celine's ears that drowned them out. "It has your name written all over it."

Her signature, she recalled in dismay. *On all the papers. Her face. Her signature. Dear God, he'd played her.*

She broke into a cold sweat. Her fingers, wrapped around the receiver, feeling cold and clammy.

A sliver of a memory returned, easing the stiffness in her shoulders. She smiled. Like it or not, he still needed her.

She wasn't going to go down so easily. No, sir, she was not. She still had an ace to play.

❧

An insistent beeping pelted her brain, penetrating the thick fog of sleep.

Celine's eyes opened. For a single disorienting moment she wondered where she was.

She'd barely remembered when the beeping caught her attention again, drawing her gaze toward the laptop perched upon the coffee table in the sitting room of their hotel suite. She squinted at the screen.

Was that someone in Clara's apartment?

The realization propelled her to an upright position. Dear God!

Celine peered anxiously at the screen. Two figures hovered in front of the supply closet that bookended the kitchenette, separating it from the front door.

A female figure in nurse's scrubs stood on the stepladder they'd acquired from Rod, her arms stretched up high as she foraged around on the shelves above her.

It's up high. Celine heard Clara's voice in her brain. *Jonah put it up high.*

The camera picked up a scraping sound as the nurse—Celine was positive it was Beth Hogan—dragged something off the top shelf. Was it Clara's music box?

The hinged lid, Celine knew, was loose. As Beth lowered it, the lid fell open, causing the silvery sound of Tchaikovsky's Swan Lake to pervade the room.

Ron's camera was sensitive enough to capture the barely stifled expletive Beth's male companion, standing at the foot of the stepladder, let out.

Then a bloodcurdling scream rent the air. Clara had woken up.

"For f—'s sake," the orderly growled. "Keep the bitch quiet."

He swung around, his face an ugly mask of pent-up rage.

Celine gasped, eyes wide, watching helplessly as he charged relentlessly toward Clara like a grizzly that had sighted prey.

"Shut up, shut up!" he snarled, approaching her. "Shut the f— up!"

His arms swung out. His sleeve must have brushed against the orchid camera because the next instant there was a crash as something clattered to the floor. Then a muffled scream and more oaths.

But all that was visible was the wood flooring of the apartment.

Don't just sit there, Celine. Do something.

Her guardian angel's sharply snapped order galvanized her into motion.

"Julia!" she screamed, pounding on the former fed's door. "Julia open up!"

Chapter Sixty-Five

Ella stared sightlessly at her tightly clasped hands. She was in a small waiting room at the Brigham & Women's Hospital Emergency Room on 75 Francis Street. How long had she been here? An hour, maybe more—waiting for some word on how Harrison Jr. was doing.

If anything happened to him . . .

She'd hold herself responsible, Ella told herself firmly. That was all. She didn't know Harrison Jr. well enough to care any more than that.

But the thought of Harrison Jr. succumbing to his wounds filled Ella with a desolate ache that was hard to deny.

She'd arrived just in time to see him being wheeled into the facility.

She'd rushed to his side, looking anxiously down at his white features. His glazed eyes had met hers, flickering in recognition.

"You came," he'd said, weakly grasping her fingers. His eyes had closed, a faint trace of a smile on his lips. "Frank," he'd murmured. "Frank," as the men in scrubs wheeling him to an operating room hustled Ella out of the way.

Ella glanced at the clock. They'd put her in a small private waiting room off the lobby. Soothing watercolor paintings of flowers and gently flowing rivers hung on the pale yellow walls. The gray metal chairs were covered in a floral fabric.

The décor failed to calm her overwrought nerves or settle her uneven, jumpy pulse.

Had Harrison Jr. wanted her to call Frank? Or had he meant that Frank —whoever the man was—had shot him?

What was she supposed to do with the information?

She twisted her hands. Would Harrison Jr. survive the attack? It wasn't a fatal wound. The responding officer—the man who'd taken her call when she'd dialed Harrison's home phone number—had assured her of that.

It seemed eons ago that she'd had dinner with Harrison Jr. She'd refused his offer of a ride back to the Chelsea office, preferring to take a cab.

Back at work, she'd eagerly awaited his email with the evidence he'd promised her. When it hadn't come, she'd become increasingly uneasy.

It was a gut feeling alerting her to danger, Ella realized. Although at the time, she'd been aware of a deflating sense of disappointment as well. Had Harrison played her? The suspicion had made her reluctant to call.

But telling herself she was following up because of the case, Ella had forced herself to dial his number. Unable to reach Harrison on his cell phone, she'd dialed his home phone.

The man who'd answered her call had identified himself as a police officer. Harrison Jr. had apparently entered his apartment in the middle of a burglary. His apartment had been ransacked, although it didn't look like anything had been taken.

"Either someone was staging a burglary," the police officer had told Ella. "Or they didn't find what they were looking for. From the little he could tell us when we got here, there were two men. One or both had a gun."

They'd fired at him as they left, the bullet entering just below Harrison's ribcage and barely missing his heart and lungs.

"He's bleeding like a stuck pig, but he'll be fine."

Shocked by the news, Ella had rushed over to Brigham & Women's as soon as she got off the phone. They must have been looking for the paper Maureen Rita had signed, assuring the Sullivans their agreement with the Lowell was intact.

A hot torrent of guilt swept into Ella's being. Had Blake's confrontation with Maureen's daughter earlier that evening led to the assault on Harrison? Could Maureen—or more likely her daughter—have alerted Norton to the fact that the FBI was closing in on them?

We're expecting civilians like Harrison Jr. to help, Ella told herself miserably, *but there's nothing we can do to protect them.*

She pulled her phone out of her black leather tote. She'd felt it buzz a few times but had been too preoccupied to answer it. There were missed calls from Blake and Celine.

Ella tucked the ends of her bob-cut hair back behind her ears and glanced at the time. It was too late to return either call. Blake, no doubt, was acknowledging the message she'd left him. And Celine . . . well, Celine must've been trying to pass on a message to Blake.

It wouldn't do Celine any harm to call Blake herself. It hadn't escaped Ella's notice that Celine and Julia had been routing their messages to him through her. And Blake had been doing the same.

She was about to drop her phone back into the pocket in her tote bag when it buzzed again. It was an unfamiliar number, but she answered it nonetheless.

"Hello, Ella? Ella Rawlins? This is Frank Mancini."

Chapter Sixty-Six

Heart thudding within her ribcage, Celine gripped the steering wheel and punched the gas pedal to the floor. The rental careened out of the hotel parking lot, racing toward Hutchinson House.

Dear God, let Julia get help, she prayed silently. *Let Julia get help.*

She peered into the thick darkness. The glow from her headlights illuminated a narrow path ahead of her. Would she be able to get to Clara in time? And even if she did, what then? She had no weapons.

Heart pounding within her, she floored the gas pedal.

A treacherous surface of ice had formed on the roads, and her tires skidded dangerously, threatening to spin her car out of control.

Careful, Celine, Sister Mary Catherine barked. *You're no good to anyone injured or stranded somewhere on the road.*

Breathing heavily, Celine straightened the wheel and eased her foot off the gas. Her guardian angel was right. She needed to get to Clara in one piece.

Oh, God, let Julia get help.

But even as she uttered the words, she knew it wasn't going to happen. Julia was making no headway with the 911 operator. The conversation played in her mind.

"911, what's your emergency?"

"Listen, this is Julia Hood, a former FBI agent—"

"Ma'am, I don't need your designation. Just your emergency. Where are you calling from?"

"From the Hilton Garden Inn, but my location isn't the issue. The emergency is at Hutchinson House."

In her mind's eye, Celine could see Julia anxiously hunched over the phone as she tried to get across her message to the operator. Clara was in trouble, being violently shaken and abused by a nurse and an orderly.

"Did she call you for help?"

"She's in no position to call for help. We saw this on our camera—"

"Did you have permission to install a camera, ma'am? If not, it's an invasion of her privacy and that of the facility in question."

"For heaven's sake!"

They weren't going to send anyone, were they?

Try Ella, Julia, Celine thought the words with as much intensity as she could muster. *Tell her to try Ella, Sister Mary Catherine. Tell her to call Ella.*

Would Julia get her message? Would Sister Mary Catherine be able to get through to the former fed?

Exactly four minutes later, she was zooming into the curving driveway of Hutchinson House. Pulling into a parking spot near the entrance, she switched off the ignition and jumped out of her car.

The glass doors were locked, but she caught a glimpse of Sandy walking past the reception desk.

What's she doing here so late? The question streamed through Celine's mind at the same time as a wave of gratitude filled her. *Thank heavens, she's here.*

Celine banged her fists against the thick glass, hoping to cause enough of a ruckus to attract the receptionist's attention.

Sandy turned, her wide eyes testimony to her utter astonishment at seeing Celine.

She hurried to open the door.

"What brings you here?"

"It's Clara," Celine gasped, pushing past Sandy. "She's in danger."

"But—" Sandy protested.

Celine grasped her wrist, ignoring Sandy's grimace of pain. "Just take me up, okay?"

She headed toward the bank of elevators.

"There are two people rifling through her apartment. The noise woke her up. They'll do whatever they need to in order to squelch her screams."

She gazed squarely into Sandy's eyes.

"Even if it means snuffing out her life."

Sandy scurried behind her, barely making it into the elevator. As the doors closed, she turned to Celine.

"How exactly do you know this? Did you see all of it? I mean in a vision or something?"

"Something like that." Celine looked impatiently up at the digital display indicating the floor they were on. There was no time to explain about the camera. Let Sandy think Celine's psychic nerves were screaming at her that something was wrong.

"Have you called 911?" Celine felt Sandy's gaze searching her features.

"Yes, but they may not be here in time. We might need to follow up."

The door to Clara's room was ajar. Had they already left?

Celine tiptoed down the hall floor, careful not to make the slightest rustle. The apartment was a few doors down. Thick carpet muffled their footsteps.

It was eerily quiet. Gently, Celine pushed on the door. The entire apartment was in darkness. Her fingers urgently probed the wall for the switch that turned on the foyer light.

She found it, depressing the switch. A pool of pale yellow light spilled out onto the hallway and into the apartment. The door to the supply closet was open.

On her way to the bed, she threw a quick glance in its direction. Had they taken the music box? The bed itself was in disarray, the quilt in an untidy mound on it, while a long section trailed on the floor.

"Clara?" Celine whispered. She stopped, holding out a hand to keep Sandy from approaching any farther. Were Beth Hogan and the orderly still in the apartment?

"Stay back," she hissed as she walked toward the bed. Fortunately, Sandy didn't protest.

"Clara?" Celine called, a little louder this time. But she got no response.

At the bed, she stretched out her hand, gently touching the pillow and feeling around within the bed.

It was . . . *empty?*

Celine turned around. "She's not here. Clara's not here. Where could she be?"

"Maybe she wandered off," Sandy suggested. She came closer. "It's happened before, hasn't it? Your friend—Julia, is it?—told Ms. Cooke about receiving a phone call from Ms. Hibbert."

It took Celine a moment to remember what Sandy was referring to. It was the pretext Julia had used to get the woman to check on Clara. The former fed had been lying, but Celine couldn't tell Sandy that.

"We should—" she began.

"Call 911," Sandy interjected. "I'll do it right away."

Before Celine could say a word, she was gone. Fumbling for her phone, Celine tried to call Julia, but the former fed's phone was busy.

She left a message and then turned on the lights. The entire apartment had been ransacked. The upper cabinets in the kitchen and in the bathroom were open. Towels, medical supplies, and canned items had been pulled out and littered the countertops.

Only the stepladder had been put away. She pulled it out, setting it up by the supply closet. Climbing up, she peered into the depths of the topmost shelves.

The music box was missing.

"It's gone," she said numbly as Sandy walked in.

"What's gone?" Sandy seemed oddly calm under the circumstances. A patient was missing—under her watch so to speak. But she was remarkably unflustered and unperturbed.

"Clara's music box." Celine clambered down from the ladder. "I knew we should've taken it," she mumbled to herself.

"Was it important?" Sandy studied her features intently.

"The music box?" she repeated when Celine stared back at her. "Was it important?"

"I don't know." Celine dismissed the question. "Did you call 911? Tell them a patient has gone missing?"

"Someone must have already called. They're right outside. They want to speak with you."

Outside? So soon? Had Julia managed to get through to them after all? Careful, Celine.

It was a warning Celine didn't understand. She stepped outside the room. Two uniformed men approached her. They looked strangely familiar.

Her eyes widened.

"Sandy—" Her head twisted around to alert the receptionist.

The next instant, she heard the bone-shattering sound of a fist crashing into her jaw. It was accompanied by a tsunami of intense pain that flooded her senses.

Then night closed in on her, enveloping her entire being.

Chapter Sixty-Seven

The Chase Bank was just past the T-Mobile store on Palmer Street. Instructing her cab driver to pull up to the curb, Ella hurriedly paid the guy and sprang out of the car. Her meeting with Frank Mancini, Harrison Sullivan Jr.'s attorney, was at 9:15 a.m., and she'd made it with barely a minute to spare.

"There's a document Harrison wants me to put in your hands, Ms. Rawlins," Mancini had said when he'd called her that morning. Harrison had contacted his attorney on his way home from dinner the night before.

Fortunately for Harrison, the two men had arranged to meet that night. It was Mancini who'd discovered Harrison sprawled in the living room, bleeding heavily, barely conscious. It was Mancini who'd called 911.

Apparently Mancini had also seen what looked like a Boston PD patrol car pulling away from Harrison's premises minutes before he entered the house. Although by the time he'd spoken with Ella, Mancini had begun to second-guess himself.

Even so, Ella had carefully filed away that troubling little detail.

Harrison Jr.'s attackers had disguised themselves as police officers to gain access to his home. They'd used the same M.O. as the men who'd broken into the Gardner three decades ago and were likely the same men who'd threatened Celine. Sent by the same individual, probably.

It was a frightening thought and it reverberated in the back of Ella's mind.

Reassured that Harrison Jr. would survive the ordeal—the bullet had been successfully removed from his ribcage—Ella had made it home in time to get a few hours of sleep before her meeting with Mancini.

She'd missed a call from Julia sometime during the early hours of the morning as well. But whatever it was, it would simply have to wait. There were more pressing matters to attend to right now.

Frazzled, bleary-eyed, and exhausted, Ella barreled through the double glass doors into the blessedly warm lobby of the bank. A tall, gray-haired individual in a gray suit was awaiting her.

"Frank Mancini?" Ella held out her hand. "I'm Ella Rawlins."

"Pleased to meet you, Ella." Frank warmly shook her hand. "Why don't we sit down? You've endured a harrowing experience."

"I'm not the person who got shot," she said gruffly, although she allowed him to lead her to the overstuffed blue armchairs near the wall.

He didn't respond to that, contenting himself with giving her a sympathetic glance. Settling himself into one of the armchairs, he took a white envelope out of his briefcase and handed it to her.

"I don't think Harrison Sr. really trusted Maureen Rita. She was, in his opinion, at best inept. At worst, corrupt. Although the Sullivans never really expected the Degas to surface, Harrison Sr. kept the document Maureen had him sign—just in case. And when he passed, Harrison Jr. continued to keep it in the family safety deposit box."

"This is the original?" Ella fingered the envelope.

Was it this flimsy sheet of paper that had nearly cost Harrison Jr. his life?

"It is," Mancini confirmed. "Harrison Jr. has a digital copy, as do I. But that"—he tipped his chin at the envelope on Ella's lap—"is the original. You don't want to lose that."

"Trust me, I won't."

She'd use it to get that search warrant Blake had requested for Maureen's Norwalk residence. And if Maureen owned or rented any property here in Boston, Ella would obtain a search warrant for it as well.

"And you'll see to it that your superiors at the FBI ensure the Degas is restored to the Lowell?" Mancini held her gaze with his gray eyes.

"I'll do my best." Ella met his gaze squarely. If Walsh couldn't be persuaded to do the right thing, a little arm-twisting by the media might well be in order. She'd make sure enough of the details were leaked to the *Arts Gazette* to force his and Norton's hand.

Mancini smiled, rising to signal the meeting was over.

"I'm glad Harrison Jr. is seeing a good woman. It's time he settled down, did something to carry on the family name."

"I'm not his girlfriend," Ella found herself compelled to clarify.

"No." Mancini's smile widened. "I guess he must have jumped the gun then when he implied that you were. Harrison Jr. usually does."

He took her hand and gently squeezed it between his own.

"Don't hold it against him, Ella. He's a good man."

Chapter Sixty-Eight

"She managed to get the police out after all! Good girl."

Julia craned her neck, straining against her seat belt, to stare at the patrol car parked on Lakeville Road—a few feet beyond the Hutchinson House gates.

The driver's side window was down. An odd detail, but Julia didn't let it bother her.

She felt the tension easing out of her. Celine was all right.

"She's probably busy talking with the officers."

Scooting back into her seat, Julia smiled at Special Agent Ted Ridgeway.

"That must be why she hasn't responded to my calls."

"Must be," Ridgeway agreed. He turned the wheel, smoothly maneuvering his black Suburban through the gates and onto the winding driveway into Clara's nursing home.

When Celine had raced out of their hotel room hours earlier, Julia had desperately tried to convince the 911 dispatcher to send first responders to Hutchinson House. The dispatcher she'd been talking with had hung up on her.

Undeterred, Julia had called again—only to get the same dispatcher. God, what were the odds of that happening?

She'd given up after the third time, resorting to dialing Sheila Cooke's number instead. But the Resident Care Director's phone had chirped repeatedly, the sound fading out and repeating in a never-ending cycle until a recorded voice informed Julia that the person she was trying to call was unavailable.

No shit, Julia had cursed. Sifting through her phone contacts, she'd found Ella's cell number and called it—only to be redirected to voicemail. Her frustration growing, Julia had tried Celine's number. No response there either.

She'd sunk back onto the couch in the sitting room, helplessly gazing at the laptop screen. It showed a dark image of Clara's bedroom floor. For the first time since she'd retired, Julia felt like a civilian: wretched, alone, and at her wit's end. How was she going to get help?

She didn't have a car. Celine had taken the rental. It was too early to call for another rental. She was damned if she was going to trust herself to an *Uber* driver.

She'd stared at her phone. Was there any point calling Blake?

Telling herself she didn't have a choice, Julia had punched call. He'd picked up immediately and put her in touch with Ted Ridgeway, the lanky special agent who'd helped out with the Reynolds case the previous summer.

Ridgeway, good man, had taken the initiative to call a couple of Boston PD detectives he knew. "They'll meet us there in about a half hour, forty-five minutes tops," he'd assured her when he picked her up.

The memory of the agonizing moments she'd endured reeled through her mind as Ridgeway circled around to the entrance of the nursing home.

It was too early for visitors. Only a few cars were scattered around the parking lot.

"I don't see Celine's car." Julia unbuckled herself as she scanned the lot.

Frowning, she thrust open the door and clambered out of the SUV. Ridgeway joined her as they did a quick tour of the parking lot.

Their rental, a black sedan, was nowhere to be seen.

"Are you sure?" Ridgeway looked down at Julia.

He was well over six feet. In her younger days, Julia might've found his height intimidating. But she was in her sixties now and retired. Ridgeway was—what?—about thirty, if that.

"Sure, I'm sure," she curtly informed him.

"Could she have left?" he tried again, his alert gray eyes searching the parking lot.

"Without informing me?" Julia snapped. It was a ridiculous question. Where was the damned rental?

"Let's go in." Without waiting for a response, she strode toward the entrance.

A distracted young woman with thin, long blonde hair was at the reception desk.

"We're not open for visitors," she intoned, her voice a high-pitched whine.

"We're not visitors." Julia whipped out her FBI badge. She'd kept it although she was retired. Fortunately, Ted took his out as well, handing it to the woman—Tillie, according to her name tag.

"We're responding to a report about an incident," Ted informed the woman. "Regarding one of the residents."

The woman looked as though she was about to dissolve into tears.

"Oh, did Ms. Cooke call you after all? Thank heavens! Yes. Yes, there has been an incident. It's terrible!" The words bubbled out of Tillie's mouth.

She seemed relieved to get it off her chest. "One of our residents has—well, disappeared."

"What do you mean disappeared?" Julia demanded.

"She wasn't in her room. And that's not all, the night shift nurse for her floor, Beth Hogan, was nowhere to be seen either. Kari, our morning shift nurse, came in to find the place in disarray. No Beth. There's an orderly missing as well. Then she noticed the door to Ms. Hibbert's room was ajar. And when she went in, there was no sign of Ms. Hibbert."

"Any sign of Celine Skye?" Julia asked. "She's acting as Clara Hibbert's next of kin."

Tillie shook her head. "Fortunately not. I don't know how we'd explain this to her. Ms. Cooke, that's the Resident Care Director, instructed me to make up some kind of spiel when she heard the news. But I can't for the life of me think what to say."

"You're saying you haven't seen Ms. Skye?" Julia glared at the young woman who cowered back against the wall.

When she shook her head, Julia continued. "What about Sandy? Where is she?"

"I don't know. She should be here. She'd know what to do. It's not like her to be this late. And she hasn't called either, can you believe it?"

Tillie seemed indignant at having to take over Sandy's duties. But Julia wasn't interested in her problems. She rapped out the next question.

"Are the police with Sheila Cooke?"

When Tillie gaped at her, dazed, Julia impatiently jabbed a finger in the direction of the door.

"There's a Boston PD patrol car parked on Lakeville. Celine Skye must have called 911 to report the incident. Where are the police officers?"

Tillie shook her head, confused.

"I've not seen anyone. Ms. Cooke didn't say to call anyone. She specifically said not to—although I guess she changed her mind about that since you're here. But we weren't supposed to be talking about this. Bad publicity, she said. Although I really don't see how you keep something like this under wraps—"

Julia shook her head, disgusted. There was no getting any sense out of Tillie. She was clearly rambling. Irritated, Julia spun away from the desk and strode down the hallway to the bank of elevators.

"We're wasting time here. I think we need to go up and see what's going on," she called over her shoulder to Ridgeway.

She was almost at the elevator bay when another detail from the police car jumped out at her. She came to an abrupt stop as she scoured her memory.

The driver's side window had been down. But stranger than that: both the windshield and the rear window had looked like they needed defrosting.

She spun around.

"That patrol car, Ted. There's something fishy about it. We need to check it out."

❧

"Whoa!" Ted emitted a low whistle as he looked in through the open driver's side window. The key was still in the ignition, but the car engine had been turned off.

A painful grunt came from the rear seat. Ted poked his lean frame in and looked over the front seat.

"Whoa!" he said again.

"What do you see?" Julia tried to peer in, but Ted's frame blocked her view. Before she could express the hope that it was Celine, Ted dashed that expectation to pieces.

"There're two guys, hog-tied, in the back of the car."

He pulled away from the car, unlocked the doors, and then opened the back doors.

"I'm guessing they're the patrol officers on duty."

The men—both stripped down to boxers and short-sleeved white vests with a flannel jacket thrown over them—had bandanas gagging them. One had a large lump on his forehead, and both had gashes in their heads where blood had coagulated.

They were losing time, Julia thought impatiently. Losing time. But she had to concede the officers might have something important to contribute.

Tamping down her irritation, Julia forced herself to help Ted drag the men out of the car. Once their hands and legs had been untied, she and Ted vigorously massaged the blood back into their veins.

While he dragged them in one at a time into the warmth of Hutchinson House, Julia used the radio in their car to call for backup. The detectives Ted had called were on their way as well.

By the time the men had recovered sufficiently to tell their story, Ted's detective friends had arrived. Eager to hear what the two officers had to say, Julia acknowledged the detectives' greetings with the tersest of responses. She wasn't in the mood to socialize.

"Okay, spill," she said when they'd all sat down. "What exactly happened?"

The officers had sighted two men carrying out an unwieldy roll of carpet to a waiting van. "It was a white Chevy Express. Perfectly nondescript."

Neither man could recall the license plate.

"Any sign of a black sedan?" Julia described the rental Celine had been driving.

The police officers shook their heads, then grimaced, undoubtedly feeling the sharp stabs of pain from their injuries.

"Nope. The carpet roll looked too much like a body to ignore. And it was such a godforsaken hour. It didn't seem like they were up to any good."

"Most likely they weren't," Julia agreed. Had it been Clara's body they'd been carrying out?

The men had seemed cooperative enough, stopping when the police officers hailed them. They'd responded politely to the officers' questions, gesturing toward the nursing home gates where a uniformed woman stood.

Staring into the woman's cold, hard, pebble-like gaze was the last thing the cops remembered until Ted rousted them.

Had Celine spied the men and decided to follow them? A foolhardy move, but Julia wouldn't put it past her. Celine never hesitated to put herself in danger.

But why hadn't she called her friend? Why hadn't she thought to let Julia know where she was?

Anxiety wracked Julia's mind and her gut. Nervous and edgy, she turned to Ted.

"Let's go upstairs," she said.

Chapter Sixty-Nine

The light falling on her eyelids was the first thing Celine was aware of. Her eyelids stirred, responding to the weak morning light.

Her eye muscles strained against her closed eyelids but couldn't prevail. Giving up the effort, she shifted her awareness. There was a dull pain in her jaw. It intensified, making her grimace.

She tried to move her body but felt restricted. Something was chafing her wrists. They seemed to be fastened to cold, clammy metal. She unclenched her fists, feeling the rope scratching the tender skin of her wrists.

Had she been restrained? Where was she?

The explosive force of the questions jerked her eyelids open. She was in a dank, dingy room with a musty odor. Her ankles were firmly tied together. Her hands had been forced behind her back.

She twisted, turning her head just enough to see the metal pole—flakes of white paint peeling off it—pressing uncomfortably into her backbone. Her wrists had been tied around it.

Who had done this?

In the pale light that came in through the window above her, she made out the gardening tools, wheelbarrows, bags of soil and fertilizer, and the green lawn mower that kept her company. Near her was a thick roll of carpet.

"You're awake! Finally."

The voice took her by surprise. She glanced up.

"Clara! What are you doing here? I thought—"

She struggled to recall the events of the past few hours. How had she got here? How had Clara, for that matter?

"What brought you here, Clara?" Celine surveyed the room. It was a tool shed or a room in a service building. Were they somewhere on the premises of Hutchinson House?

She turned to see Clara, leaning forward—she was sitting on her haunches; an undignified position. Uncomfortable, too. Clara gazed expectantly at her like a teacher waiting for an otherwise bright pupil to come up with the correct answer to the conundrum she'd posed.

Celine's eyes swiveled, inspecting her surroundings.

"Is this where Jonah hid"—she shrugged, unsure how to describe the evidence Jonah might have uncovered—"whatever it is he wants us to find."

She turned back to Clara. "Did you come here to retrieve it?"

It still didn't explain who had tied her? Or why?

Clara looked sadly at her. *You'll need to keep your wits about you. I can't help you anymore.*

Celine looked closely. Clara's lips weren't moving. How odd! She'd spoken but her lips had remained pressed together. Her gaze fell on the rolled-up carpet near her.

It had a weird shape now that she thought about it. As though a body were—*Oh!*

Her head jerked up.

"You're dead?"

Yes, dear. But it doesn't matter. It's safe. They didn't find it.

Whatever Jonah had hidden.

"But where is it?" she asked. They'd searched everywhere. "The music box. . .?"

Her memory was returning. Hadn't it been stolen?

Clara shook her head.

Jonah told me to scream every time someone came near it. She grinned. *To throw them off the scent.*

"So it's not in the music box. Then where is it?"

Up high. Safe, above my bed. Will you remember that? Clara regarded her anxiously. *Will you remember?*

Yes, but . . . Celine couldn't even begin to understand what the older woman was referring to.

Stay brave.

Clara disappeared.

Forcing herself to slide up against the thick metal pipe she was fastened to, Celine rose high enough to look out the window.

Rounded stone tablets peered above the blanket of snow that covered the ground outside.

Headstones. They'd brought her to a cemetery. Why?

Panic shot through her. A thin, jagged edge of dark brown earth interrupted the white landscape, its rectangular shape indicating where a grave had been dug.

They were going to bury Clara. But what were their plans for her?

Don't think of that, Celine, Sister Mary Catherine advised.

But it was easier said than done. Her labored breathing revealed the entire story to her.

They were going to bury her alive. Oh, dear God, they were going to bury her alive!

Voices filtered through the muffled stillness that enveloped the room. They were here.

❧

"She's missing." Julia's voice was flat, the note of fear underlying the words so well-contained as to be nearly undetectable.

His former colleague had gotten right to the point when he'd answered her call, but Blake didn't have to ask who she was talking about.

"Are you sure?"

"She's gone, Blake. There's no sign of her."

He listened intently as she filled him in. The patrol officers left hog-tied in their police car; Clara gone as well, most likely carried out in a rolled-up carpet the two men who'd attacked the police officers had been carrying.

"One of them was in scrubs," Julia said.

"The orderly, I'm guessing."

Blake took a sip of his coffee. It was strong, black, and unsweetened, not the way he preferred it. But after the night he'd had, he needed the bitter strength the caffeine provided.

"The guy Celine witnessed on camera attacking Clara."

Who knew whether the video evidence would hold up in court? Although now was not the time to think of that.

"It's a safe bet," Julia replied. "The other guy could've passed for a cop apparently."

"Like the men who conned their way into the parking garage?" Blake tapped his foot impatiently on the carpeted cab floor. Traffic was bad despite the early hour. There was a bottleneck up ahead he didn't really like the look of. *Damn!*

"That's not all." Julia sounded grim.

Blake sat up, bracing himself for more bad news.

"The cops Ridgeway contacted said their department had responded to another call earlier in the night with a similar M.O. It was a break-in—somewhere in Beacon Hill. The perps were dressed like cops. Care to take a guess who the victim was?"

"Harrison Sullivan Jr." It didn't take much intelligence to know who it could've been. What Blake didn't understand was why?

Maureen Rita Flynn had a motive, sure—he'd listened to the rest of Ella's message—but at this point wasn't it just Sullivan's word against hers? He was guessing Ella hadn't received the document she was expecting.

She hadn't updated him, and he'd hesitated to call her in the wee hours of the morning just to get him a flight out of Norwalk. Just this once he'd do it his own damn self.

Besides, was Maureen in any condition to orchestrate something like this? Had her daughter alerted Norton?

"Norton's behind this, I'm certain."

"They shot Sullivan Jr., Blake."

"*Jesus!*" They were getting closer, but could they hang in long enough to get the evidence they needed? Or would Norton kill every potential witness before they got what they needed to put him away for good?

"Listen, back to Celine." It took every ounce of effort to stay calm. "Could she have followed the van?"

It was a foolhardy move, but Blake was hoping against hope she'd made it.

"I'd consider it a possibility," Julia responded evenly, "if I hadn't found her phone, badly cracked, in Clara's trash can."

"Oh!" She'd been taken. There was no denying it.

Despair threatened to overwhelm him. How were they going to find her?

"Is there anything else you've found?" he demanded harshly. "Anything useful?"

Julia exhaled heavily.

"Not really. Looks like there's a receptionist missing as well. She hasn't turned up for work. Ridgeway's gone to her home to track her down. I'm not holding out much hope of her being there. Either she was taken. Or she's involved. She was a new hire, just like the other two."

"Oh?" Blake frowned. "Is that the only connection between them?"

It was such a tenuous link.

"Their recruitment was tied to a grant Hutchinson House received. The Resident Care Director was cagey about revealing the name of their benefactor. But I managed to get it out of her today that it was Dean Rafferty. Jonah's handler from the church."

"I'll bet the money came from Norton. Do you have a picture of Rafferty? Have her confirm his identity. I'll be there in a few."

He tilted his head to the side, looking over his cabbie's shoulder. Traffic seemed to be clearing up.

"You're here?" Julia's voice rose, astounded. "In Boston?"

"Booked myself on an early-morning flight after you called."

He should've been in Norwalk, he knew. He wasn't through with the Dodd-Degas case.

But something had urged Blake to head back to Boston. The last couple of times Celine had gotten herself kidnapped, Julia had been instrumental in finding her. But this time—

This time, Blake felt it was up to him. Julia was a capable agent, but the panic in her voice when she'd initially called him had been palpable. And although she seemed to have recovered her equanimity, he sensed his former colleague was still frazzled and on edge.

Chapter Seventy

Celine turned her head, straining to locate the source of the loudly murmuring voices—rising and falling like the hum of angry bees.

The wall opposite was devoid of openings. But at the corner, she glimpsed a thick metal door, open just a sliver.

A thumping sound—like someone banging an object against a hard surface—was followed by the loud clatter of wood crashing on the floor and the tinkle of thin metal and fragile glass.

The music box. They're breaking it.

"Goddammit!" a rough male voice swore. "There's nothing here."

"This was a f—in' waste of time!" another male voice growled. "A f—in' waste. We killed the old biddy for nothin'. Annoying piece of s—t!"

She heard a kick and another crash.

Celine braced herself. If they hadn't found what they were looking for, they'd seek out someone to vent their fury on. It was only a matter of time.

"Stop that!" The voice was cold, female.

Beth! So the nurse had been involved all along.

"We have more urgent issues to deal with. What do we do about the bodies?"

"Get rid of them," the first male voice growled. "You retarded or what? Why'd you think we brought them here?"

There'd be a funeral later that afternoon, Celine gathered. Clara would be dumped into the empty grave and covered with sod well before the coffins were lowered in.

"It's a double funeral." The first guy chortled. "We'll put the other one— the psychic— in as well."

"No!" Beth's voice was sharp. "We're not doing that. I'm not doing it. I don't want any more blood on my hands."

"You don't wanna kill her, fine. But we're not letting her go," the second voice grated. "She knows who we are; she knows what we're up to. We throw her in after the old biddy."

Celine shuddered as the image of their cruel plans filled her mind. Who was Beth working with? One of them was probably the orderly from Hutchinson House. Who was the other guy?

❧

Ridgeway's black SUV cruised through the gates of Hutchinson House just as Blake's cab pulled up to the nursing home.

"Follow the Suburban," Blake instructed his cab driver.

Inside the premises, he hailed Ridgeway as his cab came to a halt. Climbing out, he hurriedly paid the driver, pulled his laptop case and luggage out of the back seat, and carried both to Ridgeway's parked vehicle.

"You're back?" Ridgeway unlocked and lowered the tailgate, allowing Blake to stow his belongings in the cargo area. "Was that a last-minute decision? Or are you d—"

"Yup." Blake didn't see the need to elaborate any further. He hefted the sole piece of travel luggage he had on him into the back of the SUV and then perched the laptop case atop it. "What's going on? Any news of the receptionist—what's her name again?"

"Sandy." Ridgeway still looked bewildered at seeing his superior back but fortunately didn't ask any questions.

The double doors of the nursing home opened and Julia emerged. Blake had never seen her look more haggard. Silver strands of hair escaped from her untidy ponytail. Her orange hooded sweatshirt clashed wildly with the pink shirt she had on underneath it.

"I'm glad you're both here." She hurried up to them. "Any word on Sandy?"

"She never made it home," Ridgeway reported. "She gets off at six. Roommates say she's usually home by seven."

"Is that like her?" Blake wanted to know. He lifted the tailgate, closing it with a firm snap.

Ridgeway shrugged. "She's spent the night elsewhere on occasion. But she usually brings her laptop home before heading out. And she's back the next morning to pick it up before leaving for work."

Julia frowned. "So she didn't make it home. Her laptop and phone are . . . on her, maybe? Did anyone try to call her?"

"Yup." Ridgeway nodded. "I had her roommates call a couple of times. I called as well. We got no response. The fact that she's missed work has the girls worried. It's not like her."

Blake processed the information. "So either she was kidnapped or—"

"Most likely she's involved," Julia concluded grimly.

"How do you figure that?" Ridgeway wasn't buying it. Blake didn't blame him. They'd uncovered nothing to indicate that Sandy wasn't also a victim.

"Think about it." Julia regarded them both fiercely. A sudden gust of wind whipped the strands of hair away from her face. Blake recoiled against the cold wrapping itself around his neck, wishing they could carry on their conference inside.

But Julia, worked up and indignant, was oblivious to the elements.

"Sandy gets off at six every evening," she recited the facts. "She's out of Beth Hogan's hair, who can then search Clara's room along with her pal, the orderly. His name's Diego, by the way. Those two never make their move until later at night—after midnight based on the video footage we've got. Why would they go to all the trouble of kidnapping Sandy? It's one more person to take care of. Of course, she's involved."

"Goddamned rat! Pretending to be on our side. She had me fooled, that's for sure!"

Blake nodded. It made sense. "Can we use her phone to track her?"

"If she's as intelligent as I suspect she might be," Julia said bitterly, "she's ditched her phone. They had the sense to leave Celine's phone behind." She held out the cracked phone. "It was in the trash can."

"But not Sandy's phone?"

Julia shook her head. "Of course, I haven't searched the reception area or the room behind it."

"We'll need to get on that," Blake decided. "But first, let's get a hold of that Resident Care Director. See if we can get phone numbers for Beth and Diego and start tracking those numbers."

"I wonder how they even knew Celine was going to show up here?" Julia wondered.

The same question had presented itself to Blake. Had they managed to attach a second bug on Celine's rental? Without either Julia or Celine being aware of it? If Sandy, Beth, and the orderly were working together, they'd had three times the opportunity to tag the rental again.

He scanned the parking lot. "They've obviously taken the rental you guys were driving."

"Makes it seem more likely Celine drove off by herself without bothering to inform anyone," Ridgeway agreed.

Julia jutted her chin out. "Well, their plan didn't exactly work. Not seeing her car was the first hint something was horribly wrong as far as I was concerned. Celine would never leave without telling me where she was going. And if she'd managed to get the cops out, there'd be even less reason to just up and leave."

"Wonder where they could've gone to." Ridgeway surveyed the parking lot as well as though expecting it to offer up an answer.

"They have a dead body to bury," Blake mused. Assuming Clara was dead, of course. That did seem to be the case, unfortunately.

"So a cemetery?" Ridgeway ventured. His gray eyes met Blake's, tense with anxiety.

Blake shared his colleague's dismay. There were several cemeteries in the Boston area. It would take hours to locate the one the kidnappers had selected.

And by that time—he suppressed a shudder at the thought—it might be too late for Celine.

"We need more—"

"Ms. Hood?" A loud, shrill voice interrupted Julia's words.

The door opened wider. A burly, grizzled man in navy pants and a flannel work shirt emerged. Celine gaped. *Mike.* The man who'd toured her winery. The guy who'd impersonated a cop and driven into the parking garage of their hotel. He'd tried to run her down.

The second guy—the orderly she'd seen in Hutchinson House–was taller, lean, and mean-looking. He wore a blue button-down shirt over navy pants. She'd mistaken them both for policemen, she recalled.

They approached her, staring down at her speculatively.

"You didn't predict any of this, did you?" the orderly asked. "Guess you're not much of a psychic."

Celine shrugged. "Guess not."

"Shut the f— up!" The orderly snarled. He bent down, tugging hard on her arm. The force made Celine slide up against the metal pipe. "Get the f — up, bitch!"

His eyes never left her face.

"Get her legs free!" he called over his shoulder. "We need her to walk to her grave in a few. Loosen the rope around her hands as well."

Mike pulled out a knife, slicing through the cords that bound her hands and feet.

"Okay!" The orderly shoved her toward the door. "Let's go."

They were heading out to the cemetery, Celine realized. *It's now or never,* she told herself.

"You didn't find anything in the music box, did you?" she asked as she stumbled forward.

"No." It was a woman's voice. Not Beth. "But you knew that, didn't you?"

Heels smartly tapped their way toward them.

"We're wasting time," the orderly groused.

"Give it a rest, Diego," the newcomer said. "She might know something."

The footsteps came to a halt. Celine struggled against the orderly's tight grip on her wrists, wrenching herself sufficiently free to face the woman, whoever she was.

"Sandy!"

❀

Blake glanced toward the nursing home's entrance to see a magnificently large woman bursting out of it.

She headed toward them, irritation writ large on her face.

"Ms. Hood!" The woman halted before his colleague. "How long do you propose to keep the nursing home closed to visitors? I've had to field several calls this morning. This is simply untenable. Besides, may I remind you that as a civilian you don't have the authority—"

Blake had heard enough. Whipping out his badge, he flashed it at the woman.

"This is a crime scene, Ms—Whoever you are?" He didn't care what her name was. "You've had a kidnapping and potentially a murder. It'll stay Goddamned closed as long as we say it needs to be closed. Get it?"

The woman's pupils enlarged. She hadn't appreciated his tone or his words, he could tell, but she remained silent, stepping back a little.

"Meet Sheila Cooke, Resident Care Director of the place," Julia said dryly.

"Blake Markham." Blake glared at the large woman. She was nearly as tall as he was and twice as wide, but he wasn't intimidated.

"These missing employees of yours," he continued, never taking his gaze off her. "They're all three of them new hires."

"Yes." Cooke's lips were pursed and she returned his stare.

"Recommended by Dean Rafferty?" He snapped out the question.

"Yes, as I've already told your colleague." Cooke threw Julia a contemptuous glance.

"But she didn't recognize Rafferty's picture." Julia held out a newsletter—it looked like a parish news bulletin from what Blake could see. "He's aged a lot. Cancer."

"That was not the man I met," Cooke insisted.

"Was it this guy?" Blake withdrew a picture from his jacket pocket. His new pals at Norwalk PD had obligingly provided him with a copy of Norton's driver's license. Blake had both a digital copy and a print-out.

He folded the paper so Norton's name and information weren't visible and held it up before him.

Cooke regarded the picture, then lifted her gaze toward him.

"Yes, that's the man. That's Dean Rafferty."

"And he paid his donation in cash?"

"Yes." Cooke seemed impatient by his line of questioning. She'd gone over the same information umpteen times, her attitude suggested, and she was heartily sick of it.

"And the fact that he gave you a bundle of cash—which came with strings attached in the form of people you had to hire—didn't send up any red flags for you?"

Cooke turned a deep shade of beetroot at the question and her eyes flashed dangerously.

"Hutchinson House needed the money. To provide the best care for our patients. What did you expect us to do? Turn down an extremely generous donation for the sake of a few scruples?"

"I'd say doing a background check on your employees might go farther toward providing quality care to your patients than a dubious donation," Blake told her. He moved in closer as he continued to speak.

"Your lack of oversight has caused a patient's death and the kidnapping of an individual associated with her. You really think your patients' families won't sue when they hear about this? Trust me they will if you do anything —anything at all—to obstruct our investigation."

Chapter Seventy-One

Sandy smiled. It wasn't the bright, friendly smile Celine remembered. Her heart sank. Sandy was cold, emotionless, and she was enjoying this.

"Nice to see you remember my name, Ms. Skye. So many don't." Sandy sashayed forward, bringing her face close to Celine's.

"Now, about this incriminating evidence that your friend Jonah is supposed to have had on Mr. Norton—"

"Jeez, Sandy!" Mike snapped. "You weren't supposed to mention the big guy by name."

"Does it matter?" Sandy was dismissive. "She won't live long enough to tell any tales. But before we get rid of her, we need to find out what she knows." She turned back to Celine. "Where is it?"

"I take it, it wasn't in the music box," Celine stalled for time.

She saw the white flash of Sandy's palm and then felt the sting of the backhanded slap that resounded against her lips. A trickle of salty blood ran down the side of her mouth. Celine jerked her shoulder up, wiping the trickle off as best she could.

"Where is it?" Sandy demanded.

"It's up high. Remember the stepladder."

"Where?" Sandy demanded again.

"High above Clara's bed." Wasn't that what Clara had said?

Another stinging slap. "There's nothing above her bed, you twit!" Sandy screamed. "Are you really going to play games with us? Do you understand your life's on the line?"

"So is yours," Celine shot back, "if you don't give Mr. Norton what he wants. He's spent too much money on you already—"

Her head was yanked back, the hair straining against its roots. The pain was so intense, Celine felt herself tearing up.

"I wouldn't tell you even if I did know," she managed to mumble.

Endure, Celine. Endure with all your might. It was Sister Mary Catherine's voice.

But Celine didn't know if she could do it. Dear God, how long would she be able to hold out?

It was high above Clara's bed. Safely above her bed. An image floated into her mind—a vivid shade of blue . . . *Oh!*

The realization startled her. But the next second, darkness enveloped her.

∾

"I don't know." Tillie looked doubtfully over her bony shoulder at the closed door. "I've never been back there."

Blake had asked the nurse to allow them into the office behind the reception desk. According to Julia, Sandy had taken her and Celine in there when they'd first arrived.

Tillie turned around, an apologetic smile on her thin face. Blake sensed rather than saw Julia's rising fury. She was about to blow a gasket. Tillie seemed to wilt under the force of it as well.

Quickly placing his palm over Julia's closed fist to restrain an outburst, Blake prepared to reason with Tillie.

"You do realize Sandy may have been kidnapped." He watched as Tillie's mouth fell open. "She never made it back to her apartment according to her roommates." He indicated the door behind Tillie. "Her cell phone and her laptop—if they're in there—could help us locate her and figure out what the heck is going on."

"Oh!" Tillie gasped. "Of course."

She hurriedly backed away from the desk, lifting up the counter to let them in.

"There's no need to follow us in there," Julia snapped at her as she preceded Blake to the door.

"Okay." Tillie hesitated, wringing her hands. "I guess I'll attend to any visitors we get."

"No!" Julia barked, making Tillie recoil. Blake almost felt sorry for the girl.

"You're going to be closed to visitors today," Blake informed her. "With three employees and a patient missing, it's not a good idea to have a stream of people coming in. Not until we've had time to search the premises."

He'd sent Ridgeway on that task, accompanied by Sheila Cooke.

"Oh, okay." Tillie bobbed her head. "Then . . ." She surveyed the lobby, then turned toward them. "May I go back to my nursing duties?"

"No." Julia spun around. "You stay right there, making sure no visitor gets so much as an inch past that front door." Her finger wagged emphatically as she spoke.

Defeated, Tillie bowed her head and retreated behind the reception desk.

The office was tiny. Blake immediately saw the laptop sitting on the small desk. The phone was next to it.

"Looks like Sandy's phone," Julia said.

Blake nodded. It wasn't exactly proof, one way or the other, of Sandy's involvement. He retrieved a couple of pairs of nitrile gloves from his pocket, tossed one to Julia, and tugged the other pair on.

Approaching the table, he picked up the phone. The red warning light indicated it was on low charge. He saw the charger plugged into an outlet in the wall and plugged the phone in.

"Missed calls from her roommates and Ridgeway." He read the notifications on the phone.

"What's the call log look like?" Julia peered over his wrist at the device.

He accessed it. A single call had been made in the early hours of the morning.

"That would've been about the time Celine got here," Julia said grimly. "I'd say she called the kidnappers."

Blake swiped the screen, scrolling down the list of incoming and outgoing calls. Sandy had received a call between six and seven in the evening. The number looked familiar.

Feeling around in his back pocket, he pulled a notebook out, flipped open the pages, and consulted it.

"That's Maureen Rita Flynn's Norwalk home phone number."

Julia frowned. "What was she doing calling Sandy?"

"I'm guessing it was her daughter who called." He succinctly filled her in. "Looks like she called shortly after I left her home."

Was it because of the incriminating document Maureen had left all those years ago with the Sullivans? Had Ella managed to get a hold of it? He'd have to remember to find out.

Blake scanned the screen. Sandy had dialed a number immediately after Maureen's call. He scrolled back up to the last call she'd made.

"It's the same number," he observed.

"Which tells us what exactly?"

"Damned if I know," Blake admitted. But there was a connection. "Could be Sandy passed on Mary's instructions to these bozos, then had them take out Celine and Clara later that evening."

A twinge of guilt assailed him. Had his spur-of-the-moment visit to Maureen's home triggered Clara's death? But what incriminating facts could Clara have on Maureen? As Dodd's employees, the women had been one-time colleagues, but other than that . . .

"Most likely, they were planning a hit on Sullivan Jr.," Julia surmised when Blake confided his misgivings. "Especially if he still has the document she signed, assuring them that the Degas, if it was ever retrieved, would go to the Lowell."

"You're right." Blake nodded slowly. "There's definite proof of Maureen's involvement there. And, like it or not, it doesn't implicate Norton." Although it was unlikely she'd done anything without Norton's knowledge.

He returned his attention to Sandy's phone. She'd made calls at regular intervals to a particular number. Frequently, her calls had been prompted by a two-second call made by the number itself.

Blake tapped the screen with his forefinger.

"I'm betting that's Norton. Wanna find out?"

"Sure." Julia eyed him. "What do you have in mind?"

He jerked his chin toward the door.

"We'll need your pal Tillie there to play ball."

Julia regarded the section of the lobby visible through the slender opening in the doorway.

"Fine. I'll bring her in. You brief her."

❧

Five minutes later, with Tillie seated at the table between himself and Julia, Blake tapped the number Sandy had regularly called. He leaned forward, tensely listening to the persistent ringing on the other end of the line.

Would he get a response? He held the phone away from him, making sure to put the phone on speaker. He'd barely done so when the ringing stopped.

"Hello." The voice, curt and masculine, didn't identify itself.

Blake abruptly stopped on an inhale. It was Norton. Blake recognized his voice.

He scribbled a few words on the notepad in front of him and pushed it toward Tillie. She leaned over to read it, nodded, and then lowered her head toward the phone.

Covering her mouth with Julia's bandana to disguise her voice, she spoke into the phone.

"Just calling to report current status. We are on target."

"The patient's been discharged?"

Tillie looked at Blake. He pulled the pad to himself and scribbled a response. Tillie nodded and spoke into the phone.

"Yes sir."

"Her family's been taken care of?"

When Tillie looked at him, Blake circled the "yes" in his previous response.

"Yes." She kept her eyes on Blake as she spoke, her eyes wide, seeking positive reinforcement.

He gave her an encouraging thumbs-up. "You're doing great," he mouthed.

"The paperwork? Has it been found?"

What paperwork, Blake wondered as Tillie's gaze encountered his questioningly. He wrote his response.

"No." Tillie's brow furrowed a little as she read the response.

"Goddammit!" Norton cursed. "Don't call me until you've found it. It's valuable, you hear me. Worth far more than you'll earn in a single year."

There was a loud click as Norton hung up.

Blake released the breath he'd been holding. That had gone better than planned. Norton hadn't suspected a thing.

He smiled reassuringly at Tillie. "Thanks. You were great!"

She rose to her feet, a worried frown on her face. "Who was that?"

"It could be the person holding Sandy hostage," he replied.

"And you can find him—and Sandy—based on that call?" Her eyes lit up. "I kept him talking a good long while, didn't I?"

"Oh, absolutely." Julia ushered her toward the door. "Make sure not to mention this to anyone. It could jeopardize the operation."

Closing the door, Julia returned to the table.

"It doesn't tell us where Celine is," she reminded him softly.

"I know." The jubilation drained out of him. They were running out of time.

But Blake refused to dwell on the thought. He'd find her. He'd find Celine.

Chapter Seventy-Two

Blake pulled the laptop toward himself.

"Let's see if this has anything to tell us."

The screen came to life as soon as he lifted it, revealing an open tab on Chrome. Sandy had been looking up an address on Google Maps.

"Looks like a residence," Blake said, switching to street view. Was Celine being held here?

"And the directions to it are from Hutchinson House." Julia pointed to the address field.

Blake took his cursor up to the three vertically stacked dots on the right side of the screen. A menu came up with a list of options. Selecting history, he clicked the cursor.

"That search was made after 3 a.m."

"Then that's where they were going." Julia stood up. "Let's go."

But Blake found himself unable to move. He stared at the screen. Would Sandy have been dumb enough to leave behind such an obvious clue to their whereabouts? On the other hand, what else did they have?

He scanned the rest of the search history. Around about 7 p.m., Sandy had looked up directions to an address on Beacon Hill. Squinting at it, he consulted his notebook. It was Sullivan Jr.'s address.

"There's nothing else to find, Blake. Let's go." Julia's harsh voice broke into his musings.

He nodded, about to lower the screen when a soft ping startled them both.

"What was that?" Julia reached out to grab the laptop screen.

A pulsing green icon at the bottom of the screen caught his attention. He moved the cursor to it and clicked.

A window opened up.

"Tracking software!" He whistled. "For a vehicle."

The make and model of the car were on the report as well as the VIN.

"You mean they've got a GPS tracker on our rental?" Julia's voice rose. "Another one?"

Blake nodded.

"How the f—?" Blake smiled as Julia bit her lip to prevent the expletive bursting out of her mouth. It was a testimony to her agitated state of mind that she was so close to swearing.

"Must've been when we returned to Hutchinson House yesterday," she muttered. "It was such a short visit. Dammit!"

Blake read the report. The car engine had been turned off at about four in the morning. A report on its current location had come in every hour after that. He exhaled heavily.

"Turns out you're right. It's the same address Sandy called up on Google Maps at 3 a.m." What were the odds?

"That's where they're holding Celine. Tell Ridgeway to call for backup. We're going there. Pronto." Julia strode out of the room.

Blake shook his head. It still felt like a decoy. They had a dead body with them. It made no sense to drive to a residential area.

Cold snow thudded onto her face. Celine flinched, jerking her face away. Icy rivulets of snow trickled down her face, stinging the bruises on her cheeks and chin.

"Where are the documents?" Sandy pushed her thumb into Celine's eyelids, forcing them open. "Where the hell are they?" Her voice vibrated, thick with fury.

Celine gazed blearily up at the young woman. Burly Mike leaned over Sandy's shoulder, staring down at her with undisguised disgust. He'd been driving the car that had nearly run her over in front of the church.

In her mind's eye, she saw the sedan again. It swerved dangerously, heading relentlessly for her. Shaken, she flinched again. The image faded out of view.

"You ran me down," she murmured. "How did you know where to find me?"

Mike's lips stretched into a cold smile.

"Diego here"—he indicated the dark-haired man beside him—"put a GPS tracker on your car. Did you really think ditching the other one was going to be the end of the story?"

Sandy flung another handful of snow at her.

"She's playing for time," she told the men. "Don't you see that? Where are the Goddamned documents?"

"For heaven's sake, Sandy, she doesn't know." It was Beth's voice. Where was she? She sounded nervous. "We're wasting time. Crack her over the head and let's bury the other one and get outta here."

"We need the documents. We don't get f—in' paid until we get the f—in' documents." Rage caused Sandy's voice to spiral higher and higher until she was shrieking. "Do you understand?"

Beth is the weak link in the chain, Celine, her guardian angel whispered. *Remember that.*

Celine smiled. "Did you remember to take the tracker off my car?"

"Of course, she did!" Mike blurted out. "What kind of dumbass do you take her for?"

"Actually . . ." Beth's face, white as a sheet, floated into view. Her companions turned to face her.

Indignation replaced the panic in Beth's features. "If you'd just left the damned car where it was, it wouldn't have been a problem."

"If you could find me," Celine mumbled, "so can they."

Her eyes closed and she drifted closer to unconsciousness. Julia and Blake would find the tracking software. They'd figure out she was being held at a cemetery.

Wait a minute, Blake was in Norwalk, wasn't he? Then why had she thought—?

The stinging slap aroused her.

"I wouldn't be too sure of that," Sandy assured her grimly. "No one's going to be able to track you down here." Her lips curled into a cruel smile. "Not before it's too late for you, in any case."

Chapter Seventy-Three

Revere Street was less than a mile away from Hutchinson House. Blake maneuvered Ridgeway's Suburban onto Lakeville Road, driving past the patrol car.

"You'd think they'd have towed it." Julia's gaze shifted from Sandy's laptop, perched upon her knees, to the road outside.

Her tone was light, the incessant beating of her fingertips on the laptop the only sign of the nervous tension building within her.

An Emergency vehicle had picked up the patrol officers she and Ridgeway had rescued, taking them to the Brigham & Women's Faulkner Hospital Emergency Room on Centre Street. But the patrol car remained.

"You'd think," Blake agreed, striving to match her tone. It took an effort. He kept his gaze riveted on the road. In six minutes—give or take a few—they'd find Celine's rental.

And hopefully—the knot in his stomach tightened—Celine as well.

He followed the curve on the narrow road, turning right on Centre Street. A long line of cars preceded him.

He tapped the steering wheel. This could take forever.

"We're turning right on Seaverns," Julia reminded him. She enlarged the image on the laptop and squinted at it. "There's a burrito bar at the corner."

"Yup," Blake acknowledged the information.

It seemed to take an eternity, but he caught sight of the restaurant's gray building eventually, its name proclaimed in purple letters on the front and side. Wheels squealing, he took the turn, wincing at the too-colorful, spooky mural on the building.

The street was, if possible, even narrower than Centre, widening only at the section where Seaverns forked off onto Alveston, their next turn.

"Left on Revere," Julia recited, sounding like an automaton. "Then keep going until we get to Elm. The house is on the corner of Revere and Elm."

Number 3 Revere Street boasted a vast Colonial mansion, set back within a white picket fence that blocked in a well-manicured front lawn. Gray siding, white window and door frames, and a black asphalt roof made for an elegant structure.

Blake let out a whistle as he pulled up to the curb.

"Wonder who this belongs to." He hunched his frame over the steering wheel, looking past Julia through the passenger-side window. "It's gotta be at least two-million-dollars. I mean look at the size of that lot."

He stared at the place. There was an eerie, unsettling stillness about the house. The blinds at every visible window were pulled shut.

Did Norton own it? Had Celine's kidnappers actually brought her to his home? Blake's misgivings were growing.

Celine's sedan was nowhere in sight. There were no other cars parked in front of the house. The paved front yard was car-free as well. The white door of the detached garage was closed.

"Are we sure. . .?" he began.

"It's here." Julia tapped the laptop screen. The tracking software on Sandy's laptop had pinged again. "It's definitely here."

She flung open the door and hopped out. Pulling the key out of the ignition, Blake followed suit. He patted the holster at his side, feeling for his gun. The place looked deserted. But was it?

He strode through the gate, crossed the paved ground in front of the garage, and headed for the porch. Taking the steps in a single leap, he approached the door and hammered on it.

Then he waited on one side of the door, his hand on his holster, while Julia positioned herself on the other side. Any armed intruder lurking inside would have to choose between shooting Julia or him. Tackling them both simultaneously would be impossible.

A minute later, Julia eyed him. "All clear."

"Looks like it."

But he waited another minute, just in case. He jiggled the door handle. It was locked but could be easily forced.

"Let's make sure the car's in the garage," he said. "If it is, we'll enter the house."

The earpiece he was wearing crackled. It was Ridgeway. Backup was on the way.

Acknowledging the message, Blake walked warily to the garage. It had a pull-up door. He waited until Julia was on the other side. Then together they bent low to the ground, tugging on the narrow bottom ledge.

It lifted half an inch.

"It's open," Julia hissed unnecessarily.

Did that mean someone was in there? Carefully, Blake eased the door up a little more and waited, bracing himself for the shots that would surely follow.

Nothing.

"Okay." He tipped his head at Julia, a signal to heave the door all the way up.

A dark-colored sedan had been pulled in askew, parked in the middle of a vast empty garage lined with cabinets. Uppers and lowers, all painted in blue, Blake noted.

"There it is!" Relief rang loud in Julia's voice. She hurried toward the vehicle, cupping her hands on the front and back windows in turn to peer in.

"There's nobody here." She straightened up, features registering her disappointment. "Where could she be?"

"Inside the house?" Blake ventured although it seemed unlikely. They'd taken Celine to a cemetery, he was almost positive. They had a dead body to bury. What better way to dispose of another inconvenient intruder?

This was a waste of time, but the house had to be checked out.

They walked out to find two Boston PD units—the backup Ridgeway had arranged for—waiting outside.

"I doubt she's here, but we've gotta search the house," Blake told the waiting men.

"Wise move." Anderson, the lead detective—a lanky guy in a bullet-proof vest over a long-sleeved white shirt—nodded. He indicated the vests his men were wearing.

"We better take the lead."

"Sure. No problem."

Reaching out to take Julia's hand, Blake fell back.

Anderson directed two of his men to the back of the house, while he and Roscoe, his partner, took the front, storming the door with two solid kicks.

The interior of the house was in darkness. "Looks unoccupied," Anderson said, while Roscoe spoke into his walkie-talkie, instructing the two guys at the back to enter the house.

It was a spacious, four-bedroom home, well-appointed, and—with its faux orchids, paintings, and knick-knacks—remarkably feminine.

"Beth's home, maybe?" Julia asked as they inspected the living room, the kitchen, and the dining room—flicking on lights everywhere. Finding nothing, she headed down a hallway on the left toward a bedroom at the rear of the house.

"On a nurse's salary?" Blake followed close behind her. "I don't think so."

Whoever lived here had a taste for Impressionist works. Among some lesser works by American artists and the odd print or two, he'd noticed a few carefully curated pieces. Two small Monets, a Van Gogh, and a Cezanne.

He'd paused in front of them, puzzled.

"Excellent copies? Or the genuine article?" he'd wondered out loud.

They didn't look like prints. On the other hand, how had the occupant of this house been able to afford these works? Once again, he wondered, if this was another one of Norton's properties.

His gaze moved over the works hanging on either side of him. Could they have been stolen?

Blake's pulse quickened at the thought.

Julia had moved ahead of him and was walking into the bedroom when she abruptly stopped short.

"Is that what I think it is?" she called, her voice echoing down the hallway toward him.

Blake quickened his pace, about to join her, when Anderson and his men appeared.

"House appears to be empty," they reported. "There's no one here."

"You guys need to take a look at this," Julia called again. "You'll never believe it."

Blake marched into the room only to pull up short. *Jesus Christ!*

He stared at the wall facing him.

Was that the *Chez Tortoni?* The piece Rafferty had taken all those years ago from the Blue Room?

Chapter Seventy-Four

Back in the Suburban, Blake gripped the steering wheel hard. They'd left Anderson and his men to gather up the paintings—including the Manet.

"Judging by that one piece, they're all stolen," he'd informed Anderson. He was still holding out hope it was the genuine article, not an excellent forgery.

"Drive, Blake! You don't have to wait for me." Julia shifted impatiently, fumbling with her seat belt. "We need to find Celine. We're running out of time."

"I know," he softly replied. But where was he supposed to drive to? Were there any cemeteries near Revere Street? The kidnappers would likely drive to the closest one.

He was about to instruct Julia to google the nearest cemetery on Sandy's laptop when his phone rang.

"Blake!" His personal assistant sounded excited. "I managed to get that search warrant you wanted for Maureen's Norwalk address. Given her involvement in the theft of the Sullivans' Degas, I also included her Boston address. It's on—"

"Three Revere Street," Blake dully concluded.

"Yes!" Ella's voice sounded far chirpier than he felt "How did you know?"

"That's where I am. With Julia." He heard Ella's sharp intake of breath and continued before she could berate him for abandoning his case in Norwalk. "Celine's been kidnapped."

"Oh!" The cheeriness in Ella's voice subsided. She continued more softly: "So that's why Julia was calling."

Blake bemusedly wondered how his usually efficient personal assistant had managed to miss that call. If it were anyone else, he'd have surmised they were on a date. But Ella—

"Have you . . . ?" Her tentative voice broke into his thoughts.

"No. We've found her car. And the Manet"—Blake thought he heard her repeat the name, a cry of utter astonishment that he ignored—"but not her. We figure she's being held at a cemetery."

He explained his thinking to her.

"Oh! So what led you to Maureen's address?"

"Tracking software on Sandy's laptop. Yep, believe it or not, she's up to her neck in this thing," he said, responding to Ella's disapproving tsking. "The bozos put a GPS tracker on Celine's rental."

The news elicited a yelped, "What!" from Ella.

Blake nodded grimly. "Yep, a second one. Fortunately, they forgot to take it off. Not that it helps her much."

There was a pause, then Ella continued:

"Any idea which cemetery?"

"Nope."

"I don't know if this helps, but the guy who tried to run her down –Mike —works at one. Want me to look up the address?"

"Sure." Blake reached across the center console, tugging on the laptop on Julia's lap.

"And when you have a minute, call Harrison Sullivan Jr., will you?"

Pin-drop silence greeted the instruction.

"Why?" Ella asked, her tone guarded.

"Looks like Sandy—at Maureen's request—might be planning a hit on Sullivan's home." He navigated away from the tab displaying Sandy's route to 3 Revere Street to the one with directions to Sullivan's home.

"He was attacked," Ella said. "Late last night." She exhaled heavily.

Her relief, he noted, seemed far greater than the situation warranted.

"He's okay. He's going to make it. Looks like the intruders were looking for that document implicating Maureen. Fortunately, he kept it in a bank safe, so they weren't able to touch it. But he's received a gunshot wound for his troubles."

Blake could've sworn Ella sounded bitter. But why?

Because Harrison was a civilian, inadvertently drawn into a dangerous situation? Or for a more personal reason?

"So you're saying Maureen's responsible for Harrison's situation?" Ella's voice was ominously quiet.

"Or Norton," Blake said. You couldn't really rule the guy out. His eyes scanned the map that expanded to fill the entire laptop screen. Any cemeteries nearby?

As he studied the laptop screen, he sorted through the information Ella had given him. Mike, the guy who'd attempted a hit-and-run on Celine, worked at a cemetery. Was it anywhere near Revere Street? He was about to ask Ella when his eyes shifted to the boxes located outside the map.

Sandy had typed in Harrison Sullivan Jr.'s address as the destination. But he hadn't until just this moment noticed the departure point.

"Woah!" Blake pulled back, unable to believe his luck. He stared at the screen incredulously. It wasn't possible. It just wasn't possible.

"I think I know where Celine's being held, you two." He could barely contain his excitement. He studied the map on the screen avidly, looking for the best route to take.

Then he turned the key in the ignition. The engine roared to life.

"We'd better go, Ella. Talk to you soon."

Chapter Seventy-Five

"Forest Hills Cemetery?" Julia paled. "They've taken her to a cemetery?"

The implications of the kidnappers' choice of destination weren't lost on her, Blake noted grimly.

"They have a body to dispose of, remember? Clara," he clarified, in case his colleague thought he was referring to Celine.

Julia merely grunted. Out of the corner of his eyes, he saw her spread apart her fingers on the laptop's mouse pad to enlarge the map that filled the screen.

There was a stop sign on Newbern. Muttering a curse, he eased on the gas. The narrow streets and the stop signs were slowing them down. But the Suburban was a private vehicle; FBI agent or not, he couldn't afford to go tearing down Boston streets in it.

"I'm willing to bet that's where Mike, the guy who tried to run you over, works."

Making his turn onto Bishop, Blake glanced at his phone on the center console. Ella had promised to get back to them with the name and address of the cemetery where Mike worked. He drummed an impatient beat on the steering wheel, hoping it would be sooner rather than later.

As if on cue, his phone began ringing.

"Take that, will you?" he said. "It's Ella."

Julia reached out to grab the ringing phone, hit answer, and then put Ella on speaker.

"It's Forest Hills Cemetery, you guys." Ella's voice sounded hollow over the speakerphone. "Looks like Mike's part of the maintenance crew."

"Makes sense." Julia threw him a quick glance. "Whoever planned the attack on Harrison Sullivan was driving from Forest Hills Cemetery." She shared what they'd discovered on Sandy's laptop.

"Plus the attackers were in a patrol car, disguised as police officers from what Harrison was able to tell responding officers," Ella told them before ending the call.

Mike had used the same means to gain entry into the Hilton Garden Inn parking garage, Blake recalled, rolling into the garage in what appeared to be a police squad car.

"Bozo needs to get himself a new costume." It was a vain attempt to lighten the mood.

But Julia's voice was deathly sober when she responded: "He's clearly dangerous." Her head was bent over the laptop, fingers moving the cursor over the website she'd opened up.

"The place is closed on Sunday. That's to say, the office is closed," she amended.

The cemetery office was by the main gate on Forest Hills Avenue.

"You think they're holding Celine there?" Julia asked anxiously after informing him of the fact.

Blake considered her question, then shook his head. He was on Everett Street now.

"Nope. Too risky. Besides, if he's a janitor or gardener, he may not have access to the office."

Although the kidnappers could still have used the main gate.

He saw Julia scroll up to the menu. "There's a ground plan here." She hovered her cursor over it and clicked.

Seconds later, she'd opened a PDF file of a map of the cemetery grounds.

"There are a couple of service buildings. Not far from the office. A path from the pedestrian gate on Tower Street curves down to them, past the Field of Ephron, the oldest part of the cemetery."

"Then that's where we need to be." He cruised past Williams Street, looking, as Julia had instructed him, for Call Street. He needed to get to Washington.

Once there, he punched the gas, eager to get to Tower Street, which dead-ended by way of the pedestrian gate into the cemetery. His pulse was thudding by the time they arrived.

The Suburban screeched to a halt, tires squealing. Blake sprang out of the car, feet thundering on the ground as he headed toward the wrought-iron pedestrian gate.

Was that a padlock on the damn thing?

"We might need to jump the fence. You up for it?" he called over his shoulder as he sprinted toward the gate. Could the lock be picked? He skidded to a halt, bending low to inspect the padlock.

The shackle wasn't engaged! The toe was dangling over the tumbler. He gripped the fence, thanking his lucky stars.

Julia's lighter footsteps sounded behind him, her breath coming in heavy gasps as she stopped.

"They must've come in through here," she panted.

"Looks like it."

He pulled the shackle out of the hasp.

"Guess they weren't expecting company."

Shallow steps led up to a narrow path curving through a thickly wooded area. He could only hope they hadn't arrived too late.

⁂

The acrid smell of smoke hit Celine's nostrils. For a brief moment she thought her kidnappers had decided to burn her alive. Saddled with a dead body they needed to get rid of, they'd left her alone for a while. She'd been drifting in and out of consciousness since then.

But she was alert now, aware of the cold, hard floor beneath her bruised body. Aware of her palms, like blocks of ice, too frozen and numb to detect anything other than the cold.

Were they going to burn her alive? It would be preferable to freezing.

A steady muffled thudding penetrated her awareness. Someone was pacing the floor. The acrid smell intensified, but the heat from whatever was burning wasn't enough to dispel the cold.

The footsteps stopped, and a heel ground itself into the cement floor.

"Do you have to smoke?" Sandy hissed.

"I'm not at work." Beth's voice was low and defiant. Celine heard an audible puff as she drew on her cigarette.

"Maybe you should be." The pacing resumed. "We need to find a way back into Hutchinson House."

Why? Because she'd figured out where Jonah had concealed his evidence? Celine cracked an eye open in time to see Beth stub her cigarette out on the floor.

"I can go back," the nurse offered.

"And tell them what?" Sandy's heels ground into the floor again as she spun around. Her voice grew shrill. "How do you explain leaving without so much as a warning? How do you explain Clara *Frickin'* Hibbert missing from her apartment?"

Sandy came into view.

"The place must be a crime scene by now. You'll be lucky if you're not arrested."

"We can say we were kidnapped along with that one." Beth jerked her head to indicate Celine. "Found ourselves beyond that small brick wall on

Arborway when we came to. She was nowhere to be seen. So we made our way back."

Sandy frowned, pondering the suggestion.

"It might work," she conceded. "But first, we need to get rid of that one." She directed a look of utter disgust at Celine.

Hastily, Celine closed her eyes. She heard approaching footsteps, felt a pair of arms roughly grasping her under the armpits and tugging.

"Help me!" Sandy hissed urgently.

Hands took hold of Celine's ankles. She was awkwardly lifted a few inches off the ground and then half-dragged, half-carried to the doorway. Her jacket lifted up as she was dragged onto the stoop, its hard brick scratching her skin.

This is it, she thought. *They're going to bury me alive.*

No, Celine, you'll be fine. Sister Mary Catherine's voice was comforting. But Celine didn't see how anyone could save her now.

Chapter Seventy-Six

What could Jonah Hibbert possibly have uncovered about the Gardner theft that had put his mother in danger? The question hummed in the back of Ella's mind as she sat in a padded office chair before the bank manager of Rockland Trust Bank.

Clara had been murdered; Celine kidnapped. It was unbelievable.

Rufus Broderick—a dark-haired man in a tweed jacket and large rectangular-framed glasses—perused the subpoena she'd just served him. His lips were pursed and a puzzled frown gathered on his forehead.

Ella watched him nervously. It was an administrative subpoena. Technically, the bank manager could refuse to comply. He could deliberately delay the investigation, biding his time or—worse still—alerting Dean Rafferty or his son to the fact that the FBI had subpoenaed their financial records.

Ella had all the evidence she needed to back the subpoena with a warrant. But the whole process would take time. Hands clasped nervously on her lap, she allowed her glance to stray from Broderick's features toward the tastefully-done landscapes displayed on the wall behind him.

Broderick read through the document, then turned back to the first page and began to scan it a second time.

"I don't understand." He raised puzzled eyes toward her.

Ella braced herself to respond to his objections. But what the bank manager said next made no sense.

"These documents"—he dropped the papers onto his desk and tapped them with his forefinger—"have already been turned over to the FBI."

Turned over to the FBI? Already? Ella stared. It was the last thing she'd expected to hear.

"To Special Agent Blake Markham?" she asked, knowing full well it wasn't Blake.

Broderick shook his head, taking his glasses off to wipe them with a small yellow square of microfiber cloth by his laptop.

"No." He perched his glasses back on the bridge of his nose. "To Special Agent Hibbert."

"Special Agent Hibbert?" Ella struggled to keep her voice neutral.

There was no Special Agent Hibbert in the Chelsea bureau that she knew of. The only Hibbert Ella knew was Jonah. But it could hardly be Jonah, could it? The guy'd had chutzpah, she'd give him that. But could he have been capable of impersonating an FBI agent?

"It was last summer," Broderick added helpfully.

"What did he look like?"

"Skinny. With a mop of curly hair." Broderick smiled. "He looked nothing like an FBI agent. But I expect he was working undercover."

Ella forced herself to stay calm. It sure sounded like Jonah. She was wondering how to confirm the fact when she recalled the passport-sized photo he'd emailed her when SAC Walsh had first given him permission to follow Blake on the Gardner investigation. She'd had a visitor ID prepared for him, but the photo was still in her email.

She pulled her phone out of her leather tote and did a quick search on her email until she found it.

"Is this him?" She turned the phone around so the picture of Jonah in his big round glasses faced Broderick.

"Yes, that's him," the bank manager eagerly confirmed.

Ella withdrew the phone, returning it to her tote.

"I'm afraid Hibbert was killed in the course of an investigation." Broderick's eyes widened; Ella ignored the reaction. "The agency is still trying to figure out what he was working on. Not all his papers have been located."

Technically, nothing she'd said was a lie.

"Wow!" Broderick still looked shell-shocked. He spread his hands wide. "Well, he said something about a money-laundering scheme, possibly involving Mr. Rafferty. There'd been some large deposits into his account."

The bank had reported them, Broderick continued, but had thought nothing of them since the deposits had originated from an American rather than a Swiss or other offshore account.

"Clever of him to figure it out," Ella commented dryly as she rose. She had to hand it to Hibbert. He'd had the makings of an exquisite conman.

Chapter Seventy-Seven

Blake waited as Julia peered through the tree trunks at the clearing beyond. They'd entered through the pedestrian gate, circling around the path until they'd reached this point.

Headstones were scattered around the ground. Two men were busy shoveling snow into an open grave. On the other side of the clearing, concealed behind a thick growth of trees, stood a brick building with weather-beaten wooden doors.

"Must be the service building," Julia said in a low voice.

"Think they're holding her there?"

Or was that her body those men were shoveling snow over?

Blake's heart nearly stopped at the thought. His fingers closed over his Glock. The urge to rush upon the two men was immense, but Julia had restrained him.

"We need to know where she is before we make our move."

"Let me know when you want to take those two down?" he whispered, his eyes trained on the two men. Julia had recognized one of them as Mike.

He edged forward, but his colleague stretched out a warning palm behind her.

"Wait." Then, pointing: "Look."

He narrowed his eyes, following her pointing forefinger.

The wooden doors were flung open. A jacket-clad woman emerged, dragging a slender form.

Blake's breath caught in his throat. It was Celine. Was she alive?

"That's Sandy in the front," Julia said. "The woman at the back is Beth."

Hand clenched, nails digging into his palm, he watched as the women dragged Celine—her body bumping heavily against the ground—toward the open grave.

He waited until the woman in front—Sandy was it?—was getting ready to drop Celine's arms.

"Now!" he ordered. Holding his gun up, he fired a shot into the air.

The sound—louder than a clap of thunder—reverberated, startling the four assailants. Before they could recover, Blake charged forward, Julia behind him.

"FBI! Put your hands in the air!" he yelled. "Get down on your knees. Down! Now!"

Too stunned to react, the men dropped to the ground. He quickly handcuffed both men while Julia tackled the women. Beth had caved, collapsing into an exhausted heap on the ground.

But out of the corner of his eye, he saw Sandy turn, ready to sprint past him. Time slowed down as she advanced toward him. She was a fraction of an inch away when he suddenly kicked his leg out, sending her sprawling to the ground. She scrabbled at the ground, trying to claw her way back to a standing position.

"Oh, no, you don't," he growled, wrenching her arms behind her. He brought his foot up to her back, holding her down.

"Thanks!" Julia grunted, approaching them with her handcuffs held out. While she cuffed the woman, Blake turned his attention to Celine.

Her eyes—vividly green in a face as white as a sheet—stared at him. Was she—? Fear threatened to grip him until he saw her mouth open.

"I can't believe you got here in time," she croaked. "I thought . . ." She swallowed, shuddering as her gaze turned toward the gaping hole behind them. "I thought—"

"Of course, we did." Kneeling down beside her, he pulled her into his arms.

"Thank heavens, you're safe!" he murmured, lips pressed against her hair. "Thank heavens."

❧

Ella was buckling her seat belt when the phone rang. She plucked the device out of her tote, hoping it was Harrison from the hospital. His attorney had called to say he was on the mend.

"He might even be able to receive visitors by this evening. Tomorrow at the latest," he'd reported.

A pang of disappointment pricked her as she glanced at the screen. It wasn't the hospital or Harrison. It was Blake.

"You're not at the office," he said. It was a statement rather than a question. Before she could respond, he continued.

"We've got her. We have Celine. She's safe."

"Hey, that's great!" Ella smiled as she inserted her car keys into the ignition.

"We're off to Clara's apartment to retrieve the documents Jonah concealed —"

"I think I know something about that," she interrupted Blake. Briefly, she summarized what Broderick had told her.

Blake emitted a low whistle.

"I'll bet the bank account traces back to Norton," Ella said, a note of satisfaction arising within her. They had him. They had Norton, at last.

To her surprise, Blake didn't seem quite so sanguine.

"It might," he said cautiously. "But Norton could easily explain those transfers away. Payment for paintings Rafferty had sold him or some such. They don't actually point to any involvement in the Gardner theft. Not directly. So why go to such lengths to keep the information hidden?"

"Because Jonah was a journalist, of course." To Ella the explanation was patently obvious. "With that security footage of Rafferty outside the Gardner and then these money transfers, someone like Jonah could easily concoct a story that could be very damaging to both Norton and Rafferty."

But Blake wasn't buying it.

"I don't know. There has to be something more. There'd better be something more, or it really doesn't make much sense."

She sighed, starting the car. "Well, I'm headed back. Keep me posted."

Chapter Seventy-Eight

Remorse and guilt stabbed Celine in equal degrees as Blake carefully wheeled her into Clara's apartment. She'd sensed the older woman would be murdered but hadn't been able to save her.

She's happier now, Celine, Sister Mary Catherine said. *She's with Jonah.*

Celine pressed her lips together, willing herself not to cry. The apartment was in a shambles. All traces of Clara gone. Evidence placards littered the room. It was a crime scene, just like the rest of Hutchinson House. But as a law enforcement agent, Blake had been allowed to wheel her up.

The thought reminded her of why they were there. Neither Blake nor Julia had said a word to urge her on with the task. But Celine knew she needed to pull herself together.

"It's up there." She pointed to the window behind Clara's bed. A cornice enclosed the upper portion. Drapes in a blue floral pattern fell gracefully from it onto the floor. "You'll need a stepladder, though. There should be one in the supply closet."

Blake squeezed her shoulder in response. Then engaging the brakes on her wheelchair, he moved quietly to the supply closet.

"On top of the cornice?" Julia sounded bemused. "So that's what Jonah was trying to tell me when I was searching Clara's room the first time we were here. I couldn't figure out why the drapes kept fluttering."

They watched as Blake set up the stepladder near the nightstand. Climbing up, he reached out, gloved hand probing the top of the wooden fabric-covered box.

"I'll be damned." He whistled. "There is something here." He threw Celine an apologetic smile. "Not that I didn't believe you. It's just—"

"Incredible?" Celine smiled back. The gesture hurt her bruised cheekbones, but she ignored the pain. "I know. It wouldn't have occurred to me to look up there if Clara hadn't shown it to me."

Blake pulled down a thick, battered manila envelope. Holding it in both hands, he stared at it. Then, coming down from the stepladder, he approached Celine's wheelchair and placed the packet gently on her lap.

"Want to do the honors?"

Celine waited until he'd returned the stepladder to the supply closet, then tore off the clear tape sealing the packet. Reaching inside, she pulled out a thick white envelope. It had the red logo of the Rockland Trust Bank in the left corner.

"These must be the bank records Ella was telling us about." She handed the envelope to Blake.

She reached inside again, this time bringing out a small black notebook. A color photograph stuck out of its pages. She opened the notebook to the page where the photo had been inserted.

"That's Dean Rafferty." She gazed at the photo. It had been taken when the deacon—a trim man in tan slacks and a yellow polo shirt—was in better health. He looked fitter than he had in the church bulletin.

She set the picture aside, looking at the notes scribbled in Jonah's familiar handwriting.

A dark arrow pointed to the picture. Jonah must've gripped his pen hard when he'd drawn it because there were signs his nib had dug into the thick notepad paper.

"Is this Celine's insider?" he'd written.

Jonah had recorded Rafferty's great appreciation for the Impressionists, in particular for Degas. "Gardner board member," he'd noted and "in possession of stolen property." All of this was "strong evidence" in favor of his conclusion. But—the word had been written in all caps—the bank records had given Jonah pause.

"Bank deposits," he'd scrawled a few lines later, adding a huge question mark after the phrase.

"So he'd noticed the deposits," Julia said, looking over Blake's shoulder at Rafferty's bank statements.

"Looks like it," Blake replied. "The large amounts would suggest Rafferty was working for someone, and therefore not our insider."

"Rafferty was working with Norton—and for him," Celine said. She gripped the packet in her hands. There was something else inside it. "I don't think it was greed that motivated Rafferty. But he's a "means-justify-the-end" type of guy. I don't think he realized what Norton and Jonah were up to. He thought Norton was an anonymous donor for research Jonah was conducting on Alzheimer's."

"And Jonah thought Rafferty was the mastermind behind the theft?" Julia asked.

"Something like that."

Behind her, Blake snorted. "Trust a reporter to put two and two together to come up with five. What's the compelling evidence against Rafferty that he's talking about?"

"I think it's this." Celine gently withdrew the last envelope out of the packet and handed it to him. "I'll let you guys handle that. You might want to get it to Penny ASAP."

"What do you mean?" Blake was already opening up the envelope. He drew out three sheets of paper.

"Ho-o-ly Cow!"

"Wow!" Julia breathed reverently. "I've only ever seen photographs of these. Never thought we'd ever be able to recover them."

"No wonder Norton set his sights on Clara."

Blake lowered the papers for Celine to look at.

She stared at the twelve-by-nine black-ink sketch of a jockey struggling to control a horse. Belle had purchased all five Degas sketches in France in 1919. At 2800 francs, this one had been the most expensive. The second work was postcard-sized, showing a procession in sepia wash. The third one, the same size as the first, was done in black chalk.

The upper left corner depicted a ballet dancer holding hands with a man in a suit—both headless. A singer—also headless—stood on the right, one hand clutching her breast, the other holding what was most likely a score. Below the singer, sat a man in a wig and hat. A violin bow angled up from the lower left corner, coming to rest on his hat. Next to him was a harp and in the lower left corner, smoke stacks with clouds of smoke billowing from them and squiggles representing ship masts.

All three drawings had Degas's name stamped on them in red ink. The signature had been stamped by his estate after the artist's death, helping to authenticate the works.

"You think Rafferty sold the other two?" Julia's question interrupted Celine's reverie.

She shook her head. "No, you'll find them in Maureen's house. Norton gave these to Rafferty for safekeeping. I guess he thought no one would think to look for them in a church."

But Jonah had opened up Rafferty's mailbox—Celine could see it in her mind's eye—and combed through its contents. He'd pilfered the envelope, hoping to use it in his exclusive scoop.

"We've looked in Maureen's house, sweetheart," Blake said as he gently squeezed her shoulder. "And other than the Manet, there was nothing there relating to the Gardner theft."

Sweetheart? She heard him but pushed away both the word and the thoughts accompanying it. She'd deal with all that later.

"Her Norwalk house," Celine explained. "I'd go back there as soon as possible. Before Norton gets wind of recent events and takes steps to secure the remaining sketches. You have a search warrant, don't you?"

"Yup."

She felt Blake's hand stroking her hair. It felt good.

She reached up to press her palm over his.

"Make sure no word of today's arrest and our find here gets out before you've searched her house," she said.

Take your time, Celine, her guardian angel advised. *You have an entire lifetime to get to know him. And don't forget the gu.*

"Shoot!" She gripped Blake's hand hard, dismay filling her being.

"What?" Blake and Julia exclaimed together.

"We forgot all about Sofia." Celine twisted her head to regard her friends. "We were supposed to meet her today, remember?"

"It'll have to wait, kiddo," Julia replied. "We're taking you to the ER first to get checked out. After that, Blake's going to get those sketches in to Penny."

"And then I'm heading back to Norwalk," Blake said.

He lowered his head and dropped a kiss on Celine's head.

"Try to stay out of trouble while I'm gone, okay?"

The End

I hope you enjoyed *Bearer of Secrets.* **Look out for Celine's next adventure** on NTUSTIN.COM/BOOKS. Or read the series prequel, VISIONS OF MURDER.

Want more art theft mysteries? Join undercover art sleuth Sophie in a SOPHIE'S ADVENTURE mystery. In the mood for a historical series? Try the JOSEPH HAYDN mysteries.

Grab your next book at NTUSTIN.COM/SHOP

Nupur

ABOUT THE AUTHOR

A former journalist, Nupur Tustin misuses a Ph.D. in Communication and an M.A. in English to paint intrigue. She also orchestrates mayhem in composer Joseph Haydn's Europe.

In addition to writing, she enjoys composing music and painting. She lives in Southern California with her husband and three rambunctious children.

For more details on the Joseph Haydn Mysteries and the Celine Skye Psychic Mysteries, visit: NTUSTIN.COM.

Get Two FREE Mysteries at NTUSTIN.COM

Subscribe to the Mystery Blog at ntustin.com/blog

www.ingramcontent.com/pod-product-compliance
Lightning Source LLC
Chambersburg PA
CBHW071453140726
47997CB00005B/1710